The Sultan's Emu

a tale

R. J. Wilton

'At this critical moment came word of a belated circus at one of the coast towns. It must naturally have been a very poor circus ever to have found itself at that dreary little port, but its advent was welcomed as enthusiastically as if it had been Barnum's entire show.'

– Walter Burton Harris, *Morocco That Was*

Published in 2024 by Elbow Publishing

© Robert Wilton 2024

Robert Wilton has asserted his rights under the Copyright,
Design and Patents Act, 1988, to be identified as the author of
this work.

Cover design by Su Jones & Paddy McEntaggart
(front: Sultan Abd-al-Aziz)

A catalogue record for this book is available from the British
Library.

ISBN 978-1-9163661-9-0

for the tellers of tales

Ali the teller of tales, the capturer of hearts, the conjurer of the most terrifying monsters and the most beautiful slave girls, whose tongue is a moist lithe serpent touched by the Lord, from whose lips all truths are woven into enchanting lies and all lies serve the cause of truth, rubs his hands together and holds them against the fire, and re-adjusts his crossed legs on the mat on the cobbles, and gazes around his audience, and lets that tongue touch once those lips, and begins.

☾

PETERS MOGADOR FROM SOMERLEIGH WITH HM SULTAN MARRAKECH ESSENTIAL RPT ESSENTIAL IN NATIONAL INTEREST YOU COMMANDEER CIRCUS REPORTED LANDED MOGADOR AND SEND THIS LOCATION INSTANTER UNDER BRITISH FLAG STOP ANIMALS AS WELL AS ACROBATS STOP DIPLOMATIC TRIUMPH STOP

'Hamid, is it particularly hot around Marrakech? This time of the year, I mean.'

'Not at night, Sidi. The desert is always cold at night in Morocco. You know this.'

'I mean to say, dear old Somerleigh's sent the most peculiar message. Wonder if the sun's got to him. Wants us to send him a circus, he says.'

Hamid looked at the paper for a long time.

The message refused to give up its secret.

After five minutes, Peters said: 'Could it be crocus, do you think?'

The message was placed in the middle of his desk.

After another five minutes, a smile crept up one side of Peters's face. The eye above it narrowed shrewdly.

'Hamid, is there a Commander Circus? Listed among the tribal chiefs, I mean to say. Not circus circus, obviously, but something like circus. He'll have misheard it somehow. Tricky with these foreign names. Local names, I mean. Your names. Tricky.'

There was an intermittent and one-sided conversation about what exactly a Circassian might be, and how it might relate to Caucasians, caucuses, and censuses.

Eventually Hamid was dispatched to the docks, to investigate any recent arrivals of i) crocuses or other exotic plants, or ii) important tribal chiefs or other titled persons of military significance. Since he was going, he was to keep his eyes open for Circassians too. Also, he might keep half an ear open for anything about circuses, however outlandish that might seem.

Hamid was gone for a day and a half.

At last he returned from the docks, looking rather glum. He told his tale, and with each word Peters's face grew more disappointed.

SOMERLEIGH WITH HM SULTAN VIA MARRAKECH FROM PETERS MOGADOR TREACHERY AND SCANDAL CIRCUS PROCEEDING YOUR LOCATION GERMAN RPT GERMAN FLAG STOP HAVE WIRED TANGIER LONDON AND BERLIN TO RAISE OFFICIAL PROTEST STOP COULD SEND YOU TROUPE ALGERIAN DANCERS OR ARRANGE RELEASE PRISON OF AUSTRIAN MAGICIAN WHO THEN PERSUADABLE TRAVEL TO YOU GRATITUDE STOP ANY GOOD QUESTION QUESTION

⟨⟩

In the café on the corner, where the maze of alleys that make up Marrakech market empties onto the great square, the corner with the fig-seller, morning is at its busiest and hottest. The square is one continuous eruption of noise, as when you remove the lid from a hive of bees, a thousand, a million trinket-peddlers and fruiterers and water-sellers and snake-charmers and story-tellers all coming to life at once with a shout. The latest guest must squeeze apologetically between the bodies, push his way up the stairs, clamber over legs, to reach his customary table. His acquaintances are waiting. He bows to them, hand on heart, and sits. A finger and thumb at his left knee, a finger and thumb at his right knee, he pulls painfully at the crease of his European-style trousers and sits again. He removes a handkerchief from the pocket of his European-style suit and presses it against the sweat on his forehead, as is the manner of men who are careful and who worry about appearances.

After the first bustle of morning and as the heat begins to thicken, the rhythms of the royal palace slow. It is his habit, in this lull, to walk out into the city and to drink a tea with his acquaintances. They appreciate him. They admire him, even. There is always a place for him. He re-folds the handkerchief and replaces it in its pocket.

Not to be indiscreet, but there is excitement in the palace today. His Majesty, who hears of everything that happens in his kingdom, has heard of the arrival of a circus troupe on the coast. His Majesty, who knows the hearts and cares of every one of his subjects, from the mightiest of the tribal chiefs to the boy who walks behind the camel, has declared that this entertainment should first be exhibited for the consideration of his courtiers and foreign guests, and has accordingly summoned the troupe to Marrakech. The circus is known to be the finest in all Europe, its impresario a man of the most illustrious reputation. It includes brilliant acrobats and tumblers from diverse countries of the east, beautiful dancers. There is said to be a woman of grotesque and amusing deformity. There are lions, of course. Or possibly tigers. A giraffe. It is an extravaganza never before seen, an experience beyond imagination.

Or perhaps this particular conversation takes place on the street corner where the herbalists wait for the foreigners getting down from the carriages.

☽

JOURNAL OF THOMAS SOMERLEIGH

I think Youssef might be stealing from me. Hard to be sure, and I don't want to be seen to be checking everything too closely, and I certainly don't want to confront him of course. Little things seem to disappear; this morning, one of the cuff-links from Mama. So easy to be taken advantage of, in these circumstances. One wants to trust, and one puts oneself in a position of dependence, in a foreign culture. Very vulnerable accordingly. Youssef knows I couldn't be confident of replacing him with a better servant. He could probably feed his parents for a month on the proceeds. A fortnight, anyway. In that sense, worth more to him than to me. Still, sentimental value. Guess he can't afford sentiment, poor beggar.

No news from Spain. The great men have gathered there; let the conference games begin for 1906. Here in Marrakech we find ourselves a sea and a mountain range and a desert (and a bit of poetic licence) away from where our fate is being decided. The discussions and *Deus vult* the decisions shall transpire on the other side of the Mediterranean, and shall be transmitted across the straits to the Embassies in Tangier, who may pass the news to our

Moroccan hosts in Fes. All well and good, but Fes is empty, His Majesty having vacated his capital for the south. Because H.M. cannot be left unchivvied by diplomats, and because senior diplomats do not care to leave Tangier, *ergo* the Second XI accompanies. A jolly excursion for self, and a good chance to earn my spurs, except that I still await any guidance, via Mogador, from Sir G. back in Tangier.

Must admit I'm rather chuffed by my circus wheeze. Hope old Peters is awake and can do the necessary. Just the sort of thing that H.M. would love, and I very much doubt anyone else will have thought of it.

☾

The sun comes late to Morocco, like an afterthought. So the world is still blue gloom when Eva walks out of the camp into the desert to relieve herself. Nothing with any depth to it, the bushes flat against the distant mountains, the shadows in the ground unknowable.

Because it's late, the few animals of the circus are awake already, hungry and restless. A lion for a cockerel. Only the horses are silent. She walks until the shuffling and growling has fallen away, the world empty of noise. She finds a bush, squats behind it, listens to the hiss of her water hitting the hard sand and meandering away between her feet. She thinks about snakes.

She walks on to the river-bed, stamping footsteps because apparently that's how you scare the snakes away. There's a wandering stream, temporary gift of spring. She kicks off her sandals and steps into the water and gasps at the chill. She hitches up the hem of her frock, crouches and washes herself. She unbuttons the top half and pulls it down to her waist, and splashes water on her face and rubs it under her arms. The effect is sharp and silver. The urgent flush of warmth inside says her body is fighting to deal with the shock, and she wishes she'd had more stew at supper.

She stands ankle-deep in water for an unnecessary additional moment, bare-breasted and pretending wildness, wondering at the animals that come to the river to drink. Then she accepts the cold and splashes to the shore with hissed breaths and careful poise among the pebbles. Sandals on and buttoning up.

She scrambles up out of the river channel to the endless flat of the desert. The desert is terrifying. There is life there: she has been told this, she supposes she believes it. Creatures, people even. But the idea seems so unlikely, in the cold dawn. Where in this wilderness could there be warmth? How would an animal survive without that hope?

Eva walks quickly back to the circus camp.

◊

JOURNAL OF THOMAS SOMERLEIGH

Blocked again, damnit. Message from Peters finally reaches me. Bloody Germans bloody nabbed my bloody circus first. Somerleigh's lessons in diplomacy, number umpteen. I wanted it to be a surprise for the Royal Court, so I was waiting to announce it until I was sure all was arranged. So now I have nothing and no credit. Now wretched Klug will get to make the announcement, and I'd look a prize ass trying to say 'oh yes I thought of that too'. The result is nothing and the gesture is all: I should have declared my idea immediately and got the credit. Even if the Hun had then Shanghaied the circus I'd still have had some credit. Damnit. In a bit of a funk tonight and no mistake.

Youssef wisely keeping his head down. He can certainly tell when I'm in a bate, and perhaps he even knows why; can't see how on earth he could, but given that the bazaars know everything before it happens they probably know it before it's even thought. Would it make him sneer at me? Embarrassed to be associated? No doubt there's a club for diplomats' servants where they gather for a smoke and a chinwag and compare notes: Klug's man will be very pleased with himself – hitched his wagon to the big train – and Youssef will be feeling he's stuck working for a real lemon.

Still nothing from Sir G. in Tangier.

☥

Circus gossip is always performance. This is because circus everything is performance; every member of the circus, Bulgarian acrobat or Dutch horsewoman or indeed Ethiopian lion, must believe themselves distinctive and best because otherwise where is the spectacle? Also, no two people in the circus speak the same language fluently, so every conversation depends on pantomime and guesswork.

Which is to say: Eva has – we all have – set off into the desert on the basis of imagination, not fact.

The circus wasn't supposed to be in Mogador.

She still does not believe she has the name right. Mogador should be a mythical beast, half-lizard half-dog; or an Indian magician who's really from Birmingham. But they were assured that Mogador was the whitewashed city rising out of the sea, and one elegant square of sunshine and cafés and a warren of winding dark alleys that became tunnels that became dead ends, alleys and tunnels and dead ends hung with leather and every possible item you could make from raffia and herbal remedies and sardines grilled in ovens cut into the walls, and all they knew was that they were not supposed to be there.

But there they were, and the Maestro was tearing his hair out because he knows what every night of lodging and every day of animal fodder and every moment of wear and tear and every item of unnecessary indulgence costs, and costs are eternal and unavoidable, *even when you're not dancing you're still bloody eating ain't it?*, while the income is *chancy, very chancy*. And there they would have stayed, and starved to death because the endless cats were quicker to strip the last bits of flesh from the discarded sardine skeletons in the gutters, except that suddenly there was news.

An invitation to cross the desert and perform. A rich patron obviously: a foreign nobleman, an oriental potentate, a grand vizier, the Sultan himself, because when you're washed up in a mysterious desert kingdom who else would you be summoned to meet? There'd been money, anyway. That bit was certain, because suddenly the Maestro was smiling and bustling and selling dreams with every sentence, *just think of it, the palaces, the princes, the performances we shall give!* When times are bad he deals only in truth. Still it had been rumour, except that the next morning they were packing up again, and instead of getting back onto a boat they were setting off into the desert.

Eva wonders about the circus animals. They're mostly African, aren't they? Circus means exotic means African. The two lions, Otelle the zebra, the giraffe that is emblematic of the Maestro's circus but is now long dead if it ever indeed existed. They all came out of deserts like this, to ports like Mogador, and were shipped off to America and Europe. What are they feeling, as the caravan trudges away from the cooler air of the sea into this brown wilderness? Do they think they're coming home? Can they smell it yet?

As is its way, the circus has acquired another curiosity en route. A little man on a horse, a pith helmet on his head – old-fashioned but practical – and a bow-tie at his throat – old-fashioned and definitely not. In the hours after they passed through Mogador's Marrakech Gate he was noticed now and then, but not really considered. The circus brings a crowd of street boys for its first hundred yards. The circus brings flies for its first morning. A little man on a horse is not so special.

At first he was riding backwards and forwards with great bustle. Eventually he has settled to a steady plod. He has often been seen in intent discussion with the Maestro. He has been heard giving orders to the porters and muleteers who have been employed for the journey. Once or twice he seemed to be trying to chivvy some of the circus people, and not to notice that he was being ignored.

This, it seemed, was the Maestro's new business partner. And let's face it, the outfit's been crying out for a bit of business discipline since forever, and the Maestro talks a good deal but he can barely count. An investor for this trip, at least: bear the costs of the trek across the desert and the stay in Marrakech, fifty percent of the ticket sales once there. The circus attracts romantics like it attracts flies. But then again, there are stories of bandits on the long desert routes, who strike up a friendship with ignorant travellers and then cut their throats. And the Sultan himself is rumoured to travel his kingdom in disguise, the better to know the life of his people. Sultans are always rumoured to travel their kingdoms in disguise; it must be true sometime, surely.

'He's the German representative in Mogador', says Olga.

It's dull enough to be true, and too dull to be accepted as true. Especially at the start of a long journey.

'What does that mean?' Olga does not know what it means.

'He does not look very German', says Magda. She doesn't know what that means; but it's important to contradict her sister.

Shevzod the strongman shrugs. 'Pffff. You all thin and dead-colour.' Eva once tried to explain the difference between Belgium and France and Germany to Shevzod.

But he wasn't having it, and the more she tried the less sure she became herself.

'What should a German look like?'

'Bigger.'

'Yellower.'

'Angrier.'

The averagely-proportioned, rather pale, irritable-yet-otherwise-placid stranger stays with them. He is still there when the circus stops at noon in the shade of some trees, and the animals drink and the humans eat dates and flat bread. He sits apart with the Maestro. His face is always anxious. He is always saying something to the Maestro, and the Maestro is nodding slowly.

Eva has seen European wildernesses: forests, mountains, the grey ravaged coal-country of her birth. In the months in Mexico they once visited the edge of what they were told was the jungle. Morocco is her first desert. Someone was saying that this isn't actually the Sahara, though it's where the Sahara's supposed to be. It certainly doesn't look like the Sahara is supposed to look. Deserts are yellow; this is more brown. Deserts have sand dunes; Eva remembers bigger sand dunes at Nieuwpoort – this is dust and rock.

It stretches out through the afternoon, and it will stretch out through the next days. Somewhere ahead, a city is promised. It seems unlikely. The Maestro is better at making his palaces and princes credible: he offers tantalizing details, he shares his enthusiasm with you. The desert offers no hints of its promised inhabitants; there is no energy urging you on. It is as if at a certain point – a little after they passed through Mogador's Bab Marrakech, with its satisfying detail of carved stone, its beggar squatting and staring out of frosted eyes – the world has run out of creative enthusiasm. Eva's mule will plod on through the brown, and eventually they will simply drop off the edge.

10

By evening, more persuasive details have been added to the story of the German representative of Mogador. The image of him hasn't gone away; he continues to hover around the edge of the caravan, seen out of the corner of an eye, remembered in a glimpse of someone else. Things have been heard. The Maestro has said something to Olga, because talking is virility. The Maestro has said something to Mama Zana, because talking is a boy's search for reassurance. The Maestro has said something to various of the men, because talking is an assertion of authority. There is German money – and that's the best kind of money, *stands to reason, ain't it?* Germans want the circus in Marrakech, and if Germans, with their German money, want the circus in Marrakech then in Marrakech the circus shall be, *no matter how we must all sweat and suffer, my dears, because circus-lovers are the best of souls.*

By now the little man seems to be showing a proprietorial attitude to the circus. Occasionally he wheels his horse to a stop and gives an instruction, in the approximate direction of whoever is nearest him – in German, is that? He has taken to inspecting individual animals: slapping the flanks of the horses; tutting at the state of the lions' fur; asking, a little uneasily, about the giraffe.

'You're just disappointed he's not the Sultan in disguise.' Eva says to Olga.

'Who says he's not?'

Then, in the evening, he makes a speech. A fire has been lit, and its flames have spent themselves and the blackened logs glow with devilry. Everyone has passed in front of Mama Zana to receive a bowl of stew; to each she repeats their name – an accounting, a blessing. The circus is groups of two and three clumped around the fire, some seeking its warmth, some just near enough to be seen in its light. Beyond them, shadows and subdued sounds, the animals.

Eva doesn't listen to what he says. Men say things. She watches him. First she watches the Maestro with him. Standing slightly in front, then stepping aside to reveal him: performance; validation; ownership. Standing close and attentive: deference; partnership. Standing slightly behind: support; supervision; the expression of a parallel or alternative truth.

The little man – off his horse, and whom for the sake of argument we're now accepting as the German representative in Mogador, despite our diverse doubts about his fittedness for whatever that is – has found a kind of strength. It surprises Eva. He's out of place here: the desert is no more his environment than theirs, and they know each other intimately and he is a stranger. He must know they've been scrutinizing him, wondering at him, laughing at him, lying about him. Still he stands up before them to say things. Eva sees him trying possibilities. The neck-tie: is it there? is it right? is it more important to have a straight tie or to seem relaxed? The hands: folded in front? folded behind? one in a pocket? He has a pair of gloves, which he's taken off while he eats, but now he's holding them again: formality? protection? He glances around them: how to address a full circle of people? His feet shuffle in the brown sand: together, on parade? the pose balanced or casually aslant? He is exploring himself; he is wondering who he's about to be.

She has the strong sense he finds it hard to speak in public. She knows now what he is like in official meetings with other men; what he was like as a schoolboy. For once, she's concentrating on him. A thousand times she has stood poised before an audience. The dancer's colon: the moment of calculation, of precision, of absolute control of body and breath before the dam breaks and you start to flood out. For once she knows what's in his head.

In the end he stands with feet apart – a little too wide apart; an over-ambitious assertion of territory, an over-rigid fixing of the legs that will hamper the transition to the next pose – one hand on hip, the other clutching the gloves. He stares out through them into the night. He speaks.

Soon he has finished speaking. Eva hasn't heard. She thinks he spoke German, and then English. To speak your own language to others is to claim that your own language should be understood. To speak English is to claim that you want to be understood. As always, the rules are different if you're English – the English having no talent for languages, along with loving and dancing. The English speak English to others either in arrogance or in desperate hope. Because they can't speak anything else: it has the same social value as a cow mooing.

After his speech, he had turned away – though he didn't really have anywhere to turn away to. Everyone went back to what they'd been doing. Chat. Cards. Tales.

Then a shadow over Eva's clump. The Maestro and the little man off the horse – *well here we all are, my dears! some of my exotic creatures a-taking their ease after the day's exertions, ain't it?* – standing over them. Warily, they'd stood.

A stiff nod from the German; a formal good evening. They'd each murmured something.

Eva sees him looking at each of them in turn. At her first: because her skin is fairer, and he seeks similarity. Her face, down to her breasts, up to her face again. Then Shevzod, because other male because large. As quickly as possible to Olga, because God and Olga have between them put quite a bit of effort into making people look at her.

Then a step forwards, the Maestro beside him, to stand in front of Shevzod, to stare boldly up into the face. The Maestro slaps one meaty bicep, and the little man grips the other, and for a moment they are considering Shevzod's chest and discussing it. Apparently satisfied, the little man takes a second look at the face, and produces a bold smile. 'Good!' he says. 'Very good.'

'I am Shevzod', says Shevzod.

But at the same moment the Maestro is slapping the bicep again: 'Gen–ghis Khaaan!' he says, voice swelling automatically into the greater resonance of performance. 'Migh-ty terror of the East!'

And the little man looks between them, suddenly uneasy. He turns away with the Maestro, whispering urgently 'The giant is not called Genghis?'

'Genghis was not called Genghis either', Shevzod murmurs in the direction of their backs.

Eva is remembering all this as she walks back into the camp after their first night in the desert. And there, natural creation of her thoughts, is the German. He is walking back just as she is, no doubt from the same errand. He sees her now, and their paths converge as they pass the shuffling horses tethered to a tree, and he nods and smiles. Familiar purpose; familiar skin.

She knows that his daily rhythms are very regular. She knows that he cleans his hands carefully. He must be anxious, in the desert.

'Good morning, Fräulein', he says as he comes closer. Eyes down and up over her body again. For a moment she wonders if he will slap her bicep. But no. He should slap her hips instead. 'Today it is fine weather we shall be having.' Smile. 'It is my pleasure again to meet you.'

'Freut mich', she might say to him. 'Gut geschlafen?' But she does not. She doesn't feel like being part of the German-speaking world yet this morning. She nods politely, and walks away.

◌

In the café on the corner, where the maze of alleys that make up Marrakech market empties onto the great square, the corner with the orange-squeezer, morning is at its busiest and hottest. The square is a sea: just as the Atlantic deposits its flotsam and jetsam on the shores of Morocco, so the tides of the square leave bewildered tourists, temporarily-successful traders, fugitive pickpockets and startled cats seeking shelter on its shores. One such refugee stands fat and scowling behind the foreigner unknowingly blocking his way in, barges through the shoulders towards the big table on the right, then stands waiting until his acquaintances have all seen and acknowledged him. Then at last, legs splayed and hands on thighs, he sits.

After the first bustle of morning and as the heat begins to thicken, the rhythms of the royal palace slow. It is his habit, in this lull, to walk out into the city and to drink a tea with his acquaintances. They appreciate him. They admire him, obviously. There is always a place for him. With a fingernail he picks a bit of gristle from his teeth and spits it onto the floor. He smiles at the company.

Not to be indiscreet, but there's a hell of a fuss in the palace today. His Majesty, who is my lord and my light and whom I shall forever serve loyally, and his brother Abd al-Hafid, a most excellent man who knows he can always rely on me and is particularly partial to my *chebakia*, have of course been squabbling since before His Majesty even arrived. First it was who's going to head the ceremonial procession of arrival: does His Majesty feel more important leading, or if everything builds up to him, like the main course of a feast? Then it was bed chambers: is the chamber of Abd al-Hafid, who lives here all the time, more splendid and comfortable than the royal guest chamber which is kept for when His Majesty visits? And His Majesty had heard rumours that Abd al-Hafid had taken to sleeping in the royal chamber when His Majesty wasn't visiting. And now you come to mention it, is anyone really sure any more which chamber was which on the original plans? On the first day, Abd al-Hafid, as host and as Caliph of Marrakech, declared that it would be his honour to speak first and introduce His Majesty. His Majesty is no fool – seriously, my brothers, don't smirk and don't believe everything you hear, His Majesty has ears to hear and eyes to see and knows what's what – and anyway he decreed that obviously he would speak first. His brother accordingly spoke last. On the second day, Abd al-Hafid declared that he would naturally be pleased to continue to obey his brother's command, and so would speak last again. His Majesty wasn't going to let him get away with re-interpreting and concluding everything to his own advantage again, and so graciously decreed that his brother would speak first. So it was. And then what do you reckon happened yesterday? Abd al-Hafid, brother to His Majesty, Caliph of Marrakech, shrewd and silver-tongued guardian of this region, spoke... not a word. Just sat there! Just bowed to His Majesty whenever His Majesty turned to him. They say you never saw anything so dignified. His Majesty is livid.

The Roumi? Sure, they're up to something. Those bleached faces make it hard for them to hide in the shadows.

Or perhaps this particular conversation takes place in the shadow of the Bab Ahmar, where the sentry and the one-legged beggar pass the day in congenial mutual contempt.

☦

JOURNAL OF THOMAS SOMERLEIGH

Bravura performance from France today. French may or may not be the language of diplomacy, but it's certainly the mentality. All of us have been itching to get a conversation with H.M., and after a couple of days' to and fro and useless loitering – Somerleigh's lessons in diplomacy: comfortable shoes and an endless supply of cigarettes top of the kit list, and ideally a good book – at last there was the official summons. All accredited foreign diplomats doing His Majesty the honour to have travelled hither with him etc. etc., 2 p.m. sharp in the Grand Meshwar, shoes polished and homework ready for inspection. Self accordingly there a quarter hour before, couple of good lines ready about Britain's commitment to the health and peace of the Kingdom of Morocco and looking forwards to more detailed discussions on the tea trade. Usual welcome from little Abdelilah, robes even smarter than normal, fussing over us diplomats like an elementary school teacher taking the register.

Klug arrives about the same time, bit anxious. The wretched business of wondering how soon one should sit, risk of the wrong person then sitting next to you and you can't escape; or another ghastly humiliation when the protocol wallahs have to move you on because they've got a secret seating plan and you ain't part of it. Politely ask Klug what news of the circus – generous compliment and keep a finger in that pie, handily done Somerleigh – and he looks at me like I've made a dirty joke about the Kaiser. He has no news, he says; the circus good progress across the desert it makes. By which inconsistency I assume he means it's lost. Poor chap's obviously staked a handful on the circus, and if the lions starve to death in the desert or maul the Sultan he'll have a hell of a time explaining himself back in Berlin. And he, like the rest of us, trying to do the right thing re his national position on the conference in Spain, despite being at several removes from the action, and too junior to do anything more than drop the umbrellas at an inopportune moment and muck it all up. Gradually the others filter in: Ray's there, and even McKenna puts in an appearance. Klug's even more alert: just one chair empty. Sure enough Prudhomme is missing. Bit of a surprise, and good news for Germany. Only at the very last minute – beyond the last minute, H.M. absolutely walking in already – does Prudhomme slip in; v. bad form. Not a glance at the rest of us: snooty as ever, bit embarrassed no doubt. Klug irritated that France avoided diplomatic humiliation by a whisker – they'll make him Chancellor if he gets one over Prudhomme – but for once feeling more comfortable than his rival.

The grand audience is a bit of a bust. H.M. distracted, few *pro forma* courtesies, couple of grumpy references to the Spanish conference, why is no one taking the local security situation more seriously? Then, just as we're expecting to move to the real discussion, he thanks us for our presence and wishes us a nice day and delegates the rest of the meeting to his brother the esteemed Caliph. And out he goes. *Corps Diplomatique* sitting there with mouths agape: my prepared lines weren't the biggest thing ever in international relations, but I'll get no credit in Tangier for not saying a single damn word to the big cheese. Another day of what Sir G. is pleased to call this 'gallivant', another total wash-out. Klug stunned: unless he can report back every evening with a kindly royal word and a couple of trade deals, Berlin will just leave him here in the desert. Prudhomme looks stuffed and sniffy.

Caliph-brother Abd al-Hafid probably feels H.M. has let the side down a bit, but maintains his usual *sang-froid*. The rest of the crew are catching their breath so I jump in for Britain with message as prepared. The Caliph v. gracious: grateful for wise British engagement in the country, interested re tea and hope Mr Somerleigh will discuss with his officials. Not sure if that really counts, but it's something positive to put in the telegram. Klug, poor chap, looking rather sorry for himself, goes through his lines: German support for Moroccan identity, personal sentiments of affection from Kaiser for H.M., hoping to use Algeciras conference to stand side-by-side and build stronger more independent Morocco. His heart's not in it, and he sits down again rather forlorn. We're all waiting for Prudhomme, and eventually he gives that little cough of his and stands up. French respects for H.M. and of course for the esteemed Caliph, and never forget France's continued close interest in Morocco. How could we? says Caliph, ironic surely, and damn me if he doesn't produce a little smile. Rare – and a bit of a slap in the face for Prudhomme. That had been the end of his rather empty statement. Klug chirpier: Prudhomme well below par.

Concluding pleasantries and out goes the Caliph and out go we. I'm still trying to make my name with Prudhomme, so slip in a word: saw him arriving late and hope all is well. He gazes at me, and then that thin smile of his. Loud enough to be heard by others, he thanks me and confirms all very well: much pre-occupied by the case of a French businessman working the Algerian border who's been getting threats, and he arrived late only because he'd had a prior private audience with His Majesty to raise this. Prim little nod and off he goes.

Checkmate France. Klug turns purple and storms out. The rest of us got half a minute of nothing from H.M. today: set of empty reports going back to Tangier. But because of one Froggie fig-peddler – and I wouldn't be surprised if he's a total fiction – Prudhomme's claimed a one-to-one Royal audience.

Somerleigh's lessons in diplomacy, number umpteen: see the whole board. I wanted to to get the meeting right, I concentrated on the meeting, but today wasn't about the meeting at all.

That sort of sneaky business'll do you no favours in the long run, surely. Getting up the noses of all your colleagues. But then Prudhomme will hardly care what the Marrakech exiles community thinks of him, when he's a *chef de file* in Paris and getting his first Ambassadorship.

Hell. Somerleigh's lessons in diplomacy, number umpteen-and-a-bit: play the man, not the ball. Prudhomme didn't just get a head start on the rest of us; he grabbed the trophy and had the race called off. Almost certainly H.M.

was off-hand with the rest of us precisely because he'd had France nagging him about security for a full hour beforehand. The French are wrapped round this King and this Kingdom like a well-tailored suit. And Prudhomme and his Ambassador are the bow-tie and button-hole. I'm just not playing in the same league. Buck up Somerleigh.

Prudhomme did make a little pleasantry to me. For once he stepped out of French and into English, just to murmur: 'a pretty little line from you there, Somerleigh; from the inoffensive generality to the efficacious specificity – a most elegant *glissando*'.

Should I feel chuffed at the compliment, or irked by the patronizing? Sure he didn't mean it. He's the best part of a generation older, I suppose, so it must grate being stuck out here with the likes of me, essentially on the same level.

Word from Tangier at last. Though, thanks to Sir G's idiosyncratic use of the diplomatic cipher, it contains instructions on how I may ensure my conformity to British engagement with the current international herring in Zanzibar. London apparently taking the conference pretty big. Confess I'm not even sure where Algeciras is, but all of Europe watching one Spanish seaside town. Close personal attention from the Foreign Secretary himself. Strong British support for the principle of the international concert and therefore the conference – meaning: we didn't want it but now the Germans have forced everyone's hand we'll smile and pretend we like it. Foreign Secretary clear that British priority is to protect the Entente with France and Rutland (I'll risk assuming Russia), and not to allow Germany to outmanoeuvre France (fat chance). Pressure on France only if serious threat of war. All members of crew – meaning Somerleigh gallivanting in Marrakech – to ensure rowing in same direction. No mention of Morocco.

On reflection, I don't know if Tangier would have quite approved of the circus. I'm still sure H.M. would have loved the idea. But tricky trying to explain all that to Sir G. Not least its conformity to the international herring.

⟊

Dance is the relationship between movement and time. It is beautiful in so far as the speed and evenness of the movement accord with the cultured viewer's independent perception of time. Eva is trying to remember the name of the little professor who tried to explain this. A funny name; was it? No reason why she should remember. But the track ahead is so empty, and she has nothing else to fill it.

A winter. A grey resort town on the French coast. Winter and grey and the French coast are impossible now, trudging into the desert. Madame had started drinking more, and as usual grown tipsy with enthusiasms. Hence the little professor with the funny name, whom Madame had chivvied into an afternoon improving her girls. It had not been a success – the girls first bewildered and then bored and then boisterous – and the only thing anyone remembered afterwards was the professor's face when he'd interrupted them while they were changing.

Classical dance insists that natural movement conform to time. Modern dance strives to alter the perception of time to conform to natural movement.

All Eva is aware of are her thighs rubbing against the mule. She's trying to pretend the vibration is good for muscle tone. Not just another pain stored up.

And what if there is no such thing as time? They have been promised another miraculous city, rising out of the infinite, after a journey of unknown duration. This is not to be depended on; this cannot be measured. You cannot conform to the tempo of this mule-ride, stopping and starting at random, stomping forever across a landscape unregulated by milestones, landmarks or even a destination. The sickly brown blanket of sand stretches away from her, the same in all directions so directions no longer exist. There can be no beauty if life has no rhythm to set it against. There is no one to count the measure; there is no one to watch.

The cold woke them early, to another lightless dawn. They sat wrapped in jackets and blankets and darkness, arguing about what time it was. It was obvious to most of them – the cold, the pitch black, the awful silence – that it was three or four in the morning. Salomon explained that his lions knew it was later – six, or even seven. This was implausible, though the restive growling sounded like morning.

'They're more frightening in the darkness', Eva had said. 'Just growling. I can't tell how big they are, or how close.'

'Do not fear, little Eva. Lion know you.'

'How do they know what time it is', said Olga, 'when it's too dark for them to see their clocks?'

'Lion know time better than human. Only: they wake up, they must agree who they are, where they are.'

'You don't know what they're saying, old fool', said Magda. 'Save your stories for the tourists.'

'Maybe they discuss which one of you to eat first.'

'Maybe they're arguing about what time it is.'

Eventually someone said that the German man had said it was eight o'clock. No one believed this. But he has a very modern watch. Pfff, watches… Darkness and day bled into one another, and neither related to time anymore. The German man was fidgeting to start. The Maestro had told them not to light fires. They lit fires and ate a furtive breakfast, wrapped like fugitives cast onto the sand by the stormy tides of night, and scowling at each other.

The mule stumbles. Shies, recovers, plods on. Eva leans forward and places her hand against its neck, holds it there. She reassures. She pleads with it, her last companion in this world, not to abandon her; to keep its hooves thumping rhythmically over the desert floor.

She can't remember anything of the last hour or so. The mule between her legs, the sand all around, her sluggish thoughts: everything seems brown.

Olga is close by again, eyes half closed. It's impossible for Olga's body – almost entirely sinew, with occasional curve or tinsel added to catch the eye – to be anything other than poised. But her face looks slumped, and when they catch each other's eye and there's no reaction Eva knows her face looks the same.

The game – as children – the tree which was home or victory or something – lots of squealing and racing around and you could run back to the tree to be safe. *Cache-cache*? *Cours-cours*? For Olga, other women are her tree.

Like some sun-baked worm, out there in the desert, her mind has flickered briefly and now it slows and settles into the sand again. Blood is thickening and soon it will solidify. The world might just stop. Around her, in the brown haze, shapes shimmer and blur.

If there is no time anymore – no distinguishable anymore anymore – around me nothing changes – I have no way of measuring change in myself... have I stopped living?

Her hearing is muffled now. Faint hoof-thumps. Somewhere a tinkling rattle of metal. *If I don't speak to anyone else, have I stopped living?*

When they finally stop for lunch, where a huddle of derelict buildings offers shade for the humans and an unlikely pool offers water for the animals, Eva takes herself off into the desert. She doesn't think anybody notices her go. She wonders if the German might: might wonder at her rhythms as she wondered at his. Normally she wouldn't be so private. In the circus everyone knows everything; even the men know most of what there is to know about the women. The details of circus life – accommodation, performance, costume, fitness – are necessarily too intimate for it to be otherwise.

Still Eva takes herself off into the desert. When she is sure she is alone, when the circus and the rest of the world have disappeared behind some variation in the ground, she stretches a cloth on the sand, and lays out on it.

It is impossible to dance now: no blood, no gaze, no life. But Eva closes her eyes, and begins to make an accounting of her body. She flexes the big toe on her left foot. Then, as independently as possible, each of the other toes on the left foot. The ball of her left foot: she explores its contraction and expansion.

The dancer's reconnaissance: she reacquaints herself with each smallest part of her body, and then rediscovers their relationship one with another. By this she comes to know her left foot again, stalwart friend. Her left leg, an oft-travelled path. And so on. By degrees she progresses to a set of exercises, for strength and for suppleness. And at last she knows her own body again, comprehending its glories and fond of its flaws like an old lover.

Loose-limbed, slow-breathing, she walks back. No one has noticed anything.

◍

In the café on the corner, where the maze of alleys that make up Marrakech market empties onto the great square, the corner where the preachers sing their prayers and promises, with one eye on paradise and the other on the police, morning is at its busiest and hottest. The square is life: every kind of person, every manner of entertainment, every possible product, every version of the truth may be found here; you stride into it looking for something in particular, or hoping to enjoy yourself, and in the end you're just happy to survive it. One particular traveller emerges having expected a knife in his back at every step.

A wall of people blocks the entrance, but he slips in anyway by cracks and breezes because he cannot risk standing still and being noticed. He crosses the café behind others' bodies, in the shadows of those who want to be seen, in the moments after people have stopped looking, and – a breath; is it death or another day behind this curtain? – slips into the back room.

After the first bustle of morning and as the heat begins to thicken, the rhythms of the royal palace slow. It is his habit, in this lull, to walk out into the city and to drink a tea with his acquaintances. They appreciate him. They admire him. Or probably they despise him. He wishes they might, in some way, admire him. There is always a place for him. He squeezes himself into the corner, like a book that does not really fit on this shelf.

Not to be indiscreet, but – that is to say, trusting you to guard and reward my indiscretions, for when I put them into your hands I put my life there with them – I have a story to tell you that will flow into your ears like the spring river through the desert. It concerns a certain man, and a certain feast. Of the feast no one knows but I; of the man everyone knows including your good selves, for here he is the greatest of men. No, obviously not him; honestly, how could his feasts ever be secret? No, nor him. He is great here, certainly, but he is not from here. Now perhaps you know. I mean, of course, the eagle of these mountains; the great oasis of this desert; he whose family have been great since before the Roumi knew of Morocco and will be great when you have all gone again. Seriously? How is it even possible you don't know? If I must say the name you must pay me double. Please do think about it. I mean Madani the cannon, of course: the great Glaoui, the falcon of Telouet, the sun in the sky of southern Morocco. And now I think you understand why it is so significant that he feasts with the Caliph of Marrakech, the king's very brother. And no one knows of this feast but those two men and I, who heard it from a blind man who heard it from a deaf man who heard it from a dead man, who was cook and servant and sacrifice. But already its ripples are felt in the waters of the court, and in every village from Agadir to Zagora. Of course it is not unusual that these two men meet. Of course it is not unusual that they eat together. But that they meet together and eat together and do not want you or anyone else to know, this is a story worth my life and your generosity. Surely?

Or perhaps this particular conversation takes place in the alley behind the tannery, where the stink of treachery and pigeon excrement deter those not over-familiar with them.

◑

JOURNAL OF THOMAS SOMERLEIGH

Klug detonated his mine at last; hope the blast was satisfying enough. I'll bet the cafés are buzzing.

For me: bitterness that it was him not me; respect for his doggedness, and for his determination not to be overawed by France.

We all got a short-notice summons this morning – messenger hammering on the door while I was finishing the breakfast cigarette – H.M. fancied a ceremonial stroll and would be glad if the diplomats would accompany. Half dozen of us duly at the Ukkaz Gate at the appointed hour, dressed of course for a formal dinner rather than any kind of a walk. Sober nod for each of us from anxious little Abdelilah, more mother hen than ever. His chiefs have made it his responsibility to keep us foreigners happy, except he knows his real responsibility is to keep us properly corralled for the Sultan; so, no fooling around in the playground, no coming back late from lunch-break, and no one letting the side down with a scruffy necktie or dirty nails.

H.M. doesn't get diplomacy or protocol at all. Suppose he's the one chap who doesn't need to. An outing like this should be the perfect opportunity for a bit of business: chance for an individual conversation with each of us, pretend he's glad we're here, pretend to care about whatever point we raise, just a little something to keep us each sweet, something to write home about. But he barely notices we're there. Just strolls off through the Agdal gardens, eyes only for the fruit trees.

We've done half a circuit, and we're reaching the lake, and we're all sweating into our formal collars and rather wondering why we're here. Then H.M. sees the little rowing boats: wouldn't it be splendid if we all went for a row?

Diplomats of course wondering i) if we'd bought the wrong trousers, and ii) which of us would get to go in H.M.'s boat. Prudhomme started to say something about us having no desire to distract H.M. from his duties, and Klug absolutely jumped into the moment, interrupting Pr. Entirely agree with dear French colleague, no desire to trouble H.M., on the contrary – here an elegant *glissando* of his own – we wish to support H.M. and bring something positive to the Kingdom. Accordingly v. pleased to announce, having noted H.M.'s enthusiastic interest in the report of the circus at Mogador, Germany has immediately hired same and is bringing it across the desert to Marrakech to perform for H.M., Germany to pick up all the costs, have a nice day. It was well done: positive but not lacking the appropriate reserve; diplomatic but also human. He'd been rushed into his speech, and he'd been most het up – actually stuttered a couple of times – but the effect was fine.

I thought about adding some immediate encouragement – best jump onto the bandwagon before it's moving too fast, remind H.M. that Britain always engaged – but then remembered Sir G.'s instructions from last night. Foreign Secretary putting the Entente above all. So I kept my mouth shut and waited to see how Prudhomme would react.

Rather frostily, was the answer. He's a prim fellow at the best of times, stiff collar and pince-nez, and I very much doubt that circuses are his cup of tea. So being interrupted, and diverted, by a German, talking about a circus, was the beverage least like his cup of tea imaginable. He forced a tiny smile onto his lips, and I could see all the muscles of his face straining to keep it there.

Made me glad I'd held back; well done Somerleigh. Irrelevant anyway, because there was no stopping H.M. the Sultan of Morocco. He was delighted, Father Christmas brought a big bag of sweets-type delighted. He can look pretty downtrodden a lot of the time, a bit hang-dog, uneasy lies the head that wears the crown and so on, and it probably can't be much fun spending half the day refereeing arguments over lost sheep and the other half listening to the diplomatic B-team prosing on. Now the boyish face was ecstatic. He pretty much skipped over to Klug, didn't actually kiss him but was only holding back with difficulty, clasped him in both hands and called him brother, promised to mention as much next time he was talking to the Kaiser. Klug held himself together well, no kissing from him either, don't mention it your Maj., anything for such a close friend of Germany.

Another stab of Somerleigh's Bitter Regret that it could have been me getting that reaction. But one could only feel some happiness for Klug. He's so very earnest about everything, and he'd been so very worked up about his big idea. He was fighting to keep his face controlled, the big eyes wide under the dome of a forehead, but you could tell he was chuffed. Hope his Ambassador is enough of a sport to keep Klug's name attached when passing the glad tidings to Berlin.

H.M. got called away to something else at this point. I swallowed my pride and did the decent thing re Klug: sincere compliments for idea and management of same. At first he looked wary, like he thought I was needling him somehow. 'Thank you, Thomas', he said after a moment. 'Yes, most satisfactory. Thank you Thomas.' And then he was striding off, head thrust forwards and jaw set, man with his own circus to manage can't dawdle. I wondered whether he'd had permission from Tangier to be offering to pay all the costs.

As ever, Prudhomme the model of old-fashioned diplomatic smartness. As ever, a touch out of place in a Moroccan street. Rather a coup for our German friend, he said. Well yes, I said, and for some reason I added that I'd half thought of getting the circus myself. Prudhomme raised an eyebrow at this, but then murmured: 'I suspect you would have announced it with more grace and less stuttering'. The little smile, and he turned away. Then: would I do him the honour of joining the Prudhommes for supper one evening this week? Well well well.

Not sure how to score today for Britain. The big noise wasn't mine. But I fancy I deserve some credit for keeping in with everyone.

There is darkness. Then – after hours of huddled murmured fretful hoping – there is light.

Eva is still riding her mule.

'There are no roads in Morocco.'

It is a simple truth. Because it is so exactly consistent with her own understanding at that moment, she registers it at first as just another thought, a mirage crystallizing in her head and then flickering away again. Then she is aware of movement. The little German is there beside her, on his horse. He has spoken to her.

Strange to start a conversation by saying what is not.

'So… how does anyone go anywhere?'

'The people go where they want to. Mostly they go nowhere.'

She glances at him. Still the pith helmet – slightly askew – and still the bow-tie. She wants to find him ridiculous, but admiration keeps nagging at her instead. If his determination cannot deliver impossible cities out of the desert, he is determined at least to be himself.

Neither of them mentions that what he has just said makes what they are doing mad.

But she does say, five minutes later: 'How do you know where we're going?'

He looks at her as if she's tricked him; looks even younger. He gestures vaguely towards the nearest of the muleteers. 'There are… tracks', he says. 'Signs. They know. For a thousand years this has been a route of trade, out of the heart of Africa.'

It is a powerful idea. It doesn't change the fact that it doesn't look like much of a route of trade. It doesn't address the issue of why one would choose to go into a place that people have been coming out of for a thousand years.

Eva looks at the nearest muleteer. He looks asleep.

And then, imperceptibly swelling, a city rises out of the desert. First the empty horizon begins to tremble, the line refusing to stay flat after each jolt of mule hoof. Then the horizon is broken, fragments of debris littering its centre. The effect is horrifying: Eva gazes at it, wondering if this flickering on the edge of the world is where it all ends. There is a crack in the mirror and the image is no longer true; there is a tear in the curtain. The mule will carry her right through the edge of this illusion and out… Into a backstage of canvas and rope and coughing stagehands; into the Oude Markt in Leuven; into the void.

Still the city grows, inevitable. Eva knows that if she could turn her mule and send it trudging in the opposite direction, still the city would be growing in front of her. A city that cannot exist anywhere could exist everywhere.

Brown shapes. Brown blocks. By piling the desert in this way, they assert that it is now buildings; believe what you will. By making two parallel lines of buildings, they have pretended that there is a road in Morocco; that it is possible to go somewhere. Out into the desert again, to nowhere.

'This style is I believe typical of the region', says her companion. 'The earth is baked into bricks. Also I believe they merely press the earth' – his sudden emphasis makes her look at him – 'into its necessary shape.' He is grinding one fist into the other palm, face and teeth clenched. To force a construction out of this unlikely, indifferent place requires a ferocious determination.

The buildings are around them now: crude houses drawn by a child – a block, an empty doorway, two empty windows. The flatness of the desert has bent upwards into walls. The bricks are just another illusion of the sand.

There are people in the dream, too. Wrapped in white – why, of all colours? – or cloaked in long brown robes. A shrill clanging: a man, crouched by the road and hammering at something she can't see. He is utterly focused on it. She thinks of her determined companion. Two men stand close in front of each other, talking and waving at the same time; she can't tell if they're angry or entertained. Things are being sold, laid out on cloths in the gutter: vegetables she doesn't recognize; tools; live chickens; dead chickens. A thick brown liquid is being ladled into vats: it has the same colour as the earth, and she wonders at the futility of transferring the ground itself from container to container forever; or the genius of being able to sell it.

The people on the street are mainly men. Women she only glimpses: a flare of light across a window; a figure moving away from a doorway; turning inwards, to things unseen. Too quickly the mule has carried her past a gateway, through which she has glimpsed a huddle of women working at something on the ground between them.

At first the people are indifferent. The circus caravan cannot seem very impressive. A straggle of slouched, dead-eyed lunatics, trudging through the wilderness. Faces see them, look away. Even so early in spring the day is hot, and no one rushes.

Gradually the inhabitants notice that this is more than a regular caravan. Seen from the outside: there are others on mules, within the perimeter of skirmishing muleteers; the others sit differently, they are unused to all this; the clothes are foreign; the skins are very mixed – some have the complexions we know, of north Africa and the heart, but others are pale like Frenchmen and others are just different, with shades from beyond Egypt and shapes from beyond the Sahara. There are two dozen carts – and carts, so clumsy in the desert, always mean special cargo. The carts are lashed unusually tight and secure, covers with different colours and many ropes.

Some of the young men begin to wander closer, to pass the time in watching, to call out a question. Eva sees them looking at her, one or two pointing: to where some of her hair has worked loose and now curls down over her shoulder; to her leg, bare up to the knee as she sits on the mule. Then the traders get interested: foreign skins mean foreign purses. A new set of cries are woven into the noise: insistent, rhythmic, ululating, flirting. A man with one tooth thrusts a chicken up at her, and she and the chicken respond similarly and the man cackles.

Near her, the German is anxious. Fortunately the mules haven't noticed anything, and trudge onwards. Eva tries to tell herself that it is only performance: she is used to being gazed at; she is used to shouts of interest. She hears changes in the tone of the shouting, as when the acrobats vault to a third tier or when Jan the Pierrot loses love, every night this week and twice on Saturdays. She assumes the higher-pitched incoherence is for Olga, and the lower wonder is for Shevzod.

Then the crowd sees Otelle, trudging tethered and skittish, nose-bag awry. Then the crowd sees Ras and Negus in their cage, growling grumpily with each lurch of the cart.

Squeezed into an alley, a group of children: the first she has seen. They're all sitting cross-legged in the dust, looking at something or someone she can't see. She wonders at their games. She wonders if they must hide from the strangers. Then she supposes it's the school. She doubts the intense focus will survive the arrival of the lions in a few moments' time.

She thinks: I must have been that age, when I did school. Except I sat at at a desk. Except, really, the image of a schoolgirl sitting at a desk, with a meringue of pinafore and a big toothy smile and a wide-eyed ecstasy at the revelation that A is for Arbre, she's remembering that from a biscuit tin, where – not her mother, surely – must have been one of the endless aunts – kept the housekeeping money. Maybe I did sit in an alley. Seems more likely. The tree; the tree she definitely remembers, but even though A is for Arbre the arbre she thinks she sees is the one from their games.

Then she thinks: but what does it matter? Even if one of those children has parents, and more brain than I did, and some odd instinct to sit still and pay attention to the adult chanting mysteries, what difference will it make? Even if one of them grows up with the brain of a... La-...

La-something, wasn't it? – or a Molière, what will they do with their genius?

The Molière of this town will have nothing to do with his wit but annoy his friends or sell scrawny chickens with unusually elegant repartee.

The young men calling to her just now: she wonders what they were really saying.

For a few minutes, their trudge through the desert along this temporarily imagined road becomes a procession; a parade. At last they have arrived. And because they have arrived – because they are being welcomed as if they have arrived – then they must have arrived somewhere. Fantastical Marrakech, impossible delusion of people bought by little Germans on horses and lost in the desert, is more real now. Eva sees its people living real lives in its gutters and alleys and doorways, and so Marrakech exists.

The German is still trotting nearby, as nervous as his horse, eyes wild and quick to perceive risk. She has new respect for him. He has willed this city out of the desert.

They're not stopping. With persistent back and forth and urgent shouts the German representative keeps the parade moving. None of his charges shall be lured into the lurking shadows, nor savaged by a chicken, nor stop to rest.

And now the dirt-block constructions are falling away again, getting smaller, sparser. The audience has lost interest, the noise has dwindled, and now the city from the desert is disappearing somewhere behind them.

After all, probably this was not Marrakech. That promise is still out there, in the sand without roads or hours, for those who dare to believe.

Soon – perhaps by evening – they will doubt whether this place even existed. So much has lived briefly in these days of tramping, glimpsed in the corners of eyes, in the borderlands of dreams, lost or changed between first glance and second. What did you think of that town? Shevzod and

Salomon will instead argue about other towns they remember, differently. Did you see that camel? Olga will not have seen it, but will be excited to think she might have done, and the unlikely creature with its hump and its luxuriant eyelashes will grow daily more elaborate in memory, and though when you think about it no one's ever actually seen a camel with two humps you can never be sure. Whatever happened to our giraffe? If it survives the day, this town will be rebuilt on rather different lines in conversations at the fireside. Individual people will disappear in a shrug over the stew. What is remembered and what is imagined, both will settle in the mind, begin to put down roots, adapt, expand. What was lost and what was only hoped, both will ache like a once-injured knee.

And in the town that does not exist, the children will tell their children of the pale lady who rode out of the desert with two lions, and they will not be believed.

◑

In the café on the corner, where the maze of alleys that make up Marrakech market empties onto the great square, the corner where the students of religion gather and dispute, morning is at its busiest and hottest. The square is contested ground: every trade believes it theirs, every tourist experiences it differently. We cannot even agree on what the name of the square means. One version of the truth approaches the café with easy confidence. He walks briskly, a man keen to show that he has employment, purpose; he looks at the world around him with sureness, with tolerance, because it is all working to his convenience. The currents of people in the café entrance favour him, and he glides to the table where other men like him are waiting.

After the first bustle of morning and as the heat begins to thicken, the rhythms of the royal palace slow – and that means that the visiting foreign men will be having meetings with other foreign men or busy in their endless writing. It is his habit, in this lull, to walk out into the city and to drink a tea with his acquaintances. They appreciate him. They admire him. Like them, he was quickly snapped up as a trustworthy servant for a visiting diplomat. He sits in the spot they have kept for him. He is satisfied to have a distinguished employment. He is comfortable that there is always a place for him on this bench.

Not to be indiscreet, but the Roumi is edgy. Didn't sleep easy: you can always tell from the sheets. Everything wrong with breakfast. Anxious to leave early. Left late. And lots of writing last night. Yeah, I know they're always writing, don't know where they get all the words from and I can't think anybody's ever going to read any of it, but if you're not eating or praying or fucking in the evening what else are you going to do? No, of course not! Wouldn't understand a word if I did, so what's the point? Even if I did, you really think it'd amount to anything?

Yours too? And you? Figures. They're up to something. No, you're right, they've wound each other up about something. Well, no, of course it's not going to be anything good. Best you can hope for: it's not going to be anything. Good chance it keeps them here, though, and I'm not complaining. Another month of indoor work while it's still cold? Thanks God, your servant knows his duty.

But what could we possibly say to them? Sorry to interrupt the writing, Master, but you've got it all wrong? The real problem is the state of the gutters in the Mellah and the price of bread and my cousin's mother has the skin-blight and the tax-police are simply stealing now and it's months since a trader's come through Tizi'n'Tichka with all his bollocks still attached. Yes, yes they are talking about police. Yes, no, I've got ears to hear same as you. All I'm saying is, I'd like to see a Frenchman trying to police the Ouarzazate trail. They think they want this place, they think it's all like the north, easy girls and easy boys and extra honey on your pastry, just wait till the M'touggi turn up to tea with a severed head or two.

Or perhaps this particular conversation takes place on the doorstep of the house that has been rented by an Englishman, where Youssef sits to smoke and to watch the bedroom window at the end of the alley.

☯

JOURNAL OF THOMAS SOMERLEIGH

Lot of to and fro today. One tries to keep the old *sang froid*; mustn't run because it unsettles the horses, etc. Some of my European colleagues a bit hot under the collar.

Bimbled up to the Ukkaz Gate as usual this a.m. just to see what's doing. Prudhomme positively bursting with intent: stiff collar extra tight and a fat dossier bulging out under his arm. He's absolutely haranguing the vizier who's been deputed to keep an eye on us. Haranguing in the French diplomatic style, that is: back stiff, face stone and ice, finger raised rigid, a voice of slow solemnity and not drawing breath once, and always the dossier threatening in his armpit. Appalling scandal, he was saying in the magisterial French, total breakdown of order, gravest concern in Paris – presumably this was his wretched fig-toter again, or some other convenient chancer – unless able to agree response with H.M. personally, France may have no option but to arrange her own security operations here from next door in Algeria. Strong stuff, and the vizier was looking suitably alarmed and trying to placate, and acknowledged my bow very distracted. Poor Abdelilah distraught in the background, sweating under those neat robes: a foreigner dissatisfied, and a foreigner out of control – the vizier'll throw him to the lions twice for that.

McKenna there for once – though as usual not apparently all there – lounging against a pillar and having a smoke. Greeted each other – he tends to fix on me – common blood, I suppose. He's a highly intelligent chap, and very hard-working when he feels like it – real yankee get-up-and-go – as I believe State Department chaps tend to be. But insecure about his limited French. I explained Prudhomme getting a bit Old Testament about French commercial interests and the security situation – never knew a diplomat who cared so much about the fig trade, says McKenna with a sly smile – threats of this and that but hopefully not too serious. McKenna more thoughtful: did I think real trouble was possible, with Germany's new energy? Everyone more on edge with the conference. I said I hoped not, but he didn't seem reassured.

Then H.M. appeared unexpected, and we all made our humble courtesies. Much bowing and scraping from the vizier: from the gestures and glances I gathered he was passing on some version of Prudhomme's concern; Prudhomme v. stuffed and self-righteous. Eventually H.M. declared that he would as always be willing to discuss any French concerns with his esteemed friend Prudhomme – satisfaction and relaxation on the face of friend Prudhomme; but first he wanted to talk to dear Klug – some ideas he wanted his advice on. He trotted down the steps and took Klug by the arm and they strode off for a circuit of the square.

Prudhomme bowed with the rest of us, but didn't even turn to watch them go; just stared at the step where H.M. had been. McKenna let out a long whistle. Couldn't have put it better myself.

I managed to grab Klug a bit later: not wanting to interfere in German affairs, but had H.M. said anything that might be of interest to the rest of us? Klug looking a little self-important: easy with that big puffy face of his. Nothing to worry about, dear Thomas: Germany not trying to secure anything more than her equal share here. Then please to excuse – he had a delegation of German businessmen he was escorting to meet officials. Note to self: must try to get an idea of what sectors Germany interested in.

Walking back through the market quarter – not exactly a breath of fresh air, but good to see something of the real Marrakech – vaguely familiar face hails me. Still trying to remember the occasions I've met him during our couple of months here. Odd how the mind works and doesn't work. It's Brahim again, anyway, and Brahim invites me to drink a tea with him. And why not? Bit of a change from my usual round, and interesting to have a local acquaintance of my own age. Come to think of it, I suppose I'd say we're of the same class: educated but not moneyed; know what quality is but can't generally afford it.

Brahim is a poet. But that's not really a job, is it? More an adolescent affectation that hasn't yet been replaced by something people will pay you for.

Perhaps that makes him more a gentleman of leisure, i.e. a rung or two higher up the ladder compared to a journeyman diplomat who has to save up for new shoes and can only manage a new suit every couple of years.

Friendly chat, anyway. Very interested to hear how I find Marrakech: do I sleep well? have I good servant? have I had dysentery? was I molested on the way here? Not exactly tea at the vicarage – and at the vicarage there isn't usually a pomegranate-seller coming to blows with a chap with a python right beside you – but all v. pleasant. Right at the end – he absolutely insisted on paying, though I'm sure I can afford it ten times more easily; hospitality such a big thing here – he asked what I expect of the conference in Spain. Rather surprised me. Personally, I suppose I've not been expecting anything from it. It happens, I said, and that's a good thing because it's better than war, isn't it? And hopefully – taking my lines from the Foreign Secretary, as ever – the concert of powers will be preserved. Brahim didn't seem too fussed by the concert of powers: What about Morocco? – and fair enough. I reassured that we stay interested and engaged and supportive. He still didn't look convinced. I may have to refer him to Sir Edward Grey in person next time.

Later: Trying to compose something for Peters in Mogador to forward to Tangier; not sure how much of the human drama to put in for Sir G.'s benefit, and he surely won't want to hear that France is in a snit because H.M. is going to the circus with Germany. Worried that I'm not hitting the trade drum as much as I should; Sir G. very enthusiastic about possibilities for tea here. I was still wondering if I could work in some reference to my comment to H.M. the other day – Somerleigh not asleep at the tiller yet, serious side to the gallivanting – when Youssef came in, very formal. He was bearing an envelope – definitely bearing: two-handed, finger-tips only, obviously something very sacred or very polluted – and handed it to me with a little bow, which is a step up. 'France', he said, the way he might have said 'the King wishes to knight you for services to the tea trade' or 'your first-born is dying of malaria'.

Sure enough, the envelope is a fancy embossed job and it contains an invite from Prudhomme: supper tomorrow as promised, *en famille*. Very encouraging, and I've added a reference to close liaison with the French to my Tangier wire. When I went to look for Youssef a little later, I found him polishing all my shoes. Normally I have to ask three times to get even one shoe done, let alone a pair.

Still wondering about that cuff-link. I've locked up the other one now: it's no use, but I guess I've got it as a memento, no risk of losing it somewhere. Bit of home always with me.

◉

Eva wakes, nowhere. The world has no light. The place has no name. The day has no event.

The ground beneath is hard, but the hardness has no feature or texture or scent; it is a foundational, elemental hardness. For thousands of years, young women have been stretched out on rocks as offerings to unknowable Gods. Here she is: waiting to discover if she is acceptable, and what will be offered in return. A rich harvest; a fair wind; another dawn.

Beyond her clenched blanket is absence: of warmth, of sound, of breeze, of life. Emptiness is relative. An empty street still has so many cobblestones, so much mud, and so many people about to enter it through so many doorways. An empty room supposes a house around it, bare floorboards and greasy wallpaper and the memory of someone sobbing. An empty mind is nonetheless the climax of God's creation, of the idea of God and the history of all animal life. But outside the thin protection of this blanket, there might be absolutely nothing.

She tries to remember details of the little town they passed through yesterday, individual faces that definitely existed, specific moments that surely happened. Already her mind is playing tricks with the memory; she wonders if she's still dreaming.

She could roll off her mat and drop into infinity.

She rolls off her mat.

Faint, in the distance, imagined and hoped like a Moroccan city, a dawn of tepid milk is beginning to trickle into the sky. Eva walks towards the dawn, because this is all we can do.

She hasn't gone far – somewhere behind her there might be noise, a grumpy lion on a nearby star or a circus strongman on the adjacent planet waking from a bad dream – when she knows with a gasp that the dawn is hurrying to meet her. It is the homecoming embrace of an imagined childhood, a biscuit-tin smile. The sky is warming as she gets nearer; it is glowing for her. She feels herself opening to it: shoulders, and then lungs; the clenches of our little anxieties easing; chambers and channels deep in her rediscovered, thawing and flowing.

She walks looser, muscles easy, legs supple, the balls of her feet flowing naturally from firm ground to firmer. And at last in one incalculable moment, the moment when the wave surges stronger and the water over your feet becomes your feet being swept away under the water, the moment when at last she is alone and free and the world is hers, her arms swing high and higher and take flight and do not stop, and she floods forwards and upwards and now around in a swirl that cannot end and her heart is in the sky.

The desert floor, soft-surfaced and firm-based, is a resilient dance floor. Her feet move sure, position after position not planted in the sand but growing out of it, inhabiting emotion after emotion precisely and absolutely, always balanced in her own momentum, between earth and heaven, muscular and graceful and human and enchanted and the sun pours itself out over her.

She stops at once.

A little boy is watching her.

His face is bemusement; wonder. Eva doesn't know children; four years old? six maybe?

He cannot have come from anywhere, because there is nowhere. Probably she has conjured him. How long has he been watching? Probably he imagines he has conjured her.

Eyes wide, mouth open, she releases one long controlled breath, rebalances, feels herself settling back into the sand.

He giggles. She is a captivating toy. For him, the whole world is still new and strange, and unnaturally pale spirits of the air that dance for him in the dawn are not so unusual. A woman's body has yet to ask any questions of his body; he has yet to need to assert a woman's reaction to him, her nature.

A last captivated gaze at her: he is too young even to need to hope that she will be part of his every dawn; perhaps, when she does not appear to him tomorrow, he will not even remember. He turns and scuttles away into the sand.

The male regard: by this we know ourselves alive and meaningful. The dance exists because it is seen.

Who knows? *In this desert, perhaps I will appear to him tomorrow.*

Back at the circus encampment, no one knows of her flirtation in the dawn. Breakfast is being rushed; packing up to set off is irritable. Salomon is telling everyone of his fears for the health of Negus's chest and the state of Ras's paw, and no one is listening to him. Olga is demanding to be allowed to unpack her trunk to check her costumes, and the Maestro is ignoring her, *my fucking bowels, if I don't get a hot bath and a decent meal soon I will simply turn my toes up you can feed me to the fucking camels, ain't it?* There is a feud between the muleteers and the cart-drivers. The sacred relationship between Shevzod and the muleteers seems to have soured: at first his vastness and his impossibly distant oriental origin inspired their awe and reverence; after he contrived to pull a coin from someone's ear, it was unfeigned worship. But divinity is tough to maintain: after a particularly bad night's sleep, and less and less meat in the stew, and a couple of cases of pest in the mules and one having to be killed, there was an unspoken sense that heaven wasn't being as bountiful to the muleteers as it could be; and maybe Shevzod – always a martyr to his sinuses, especially in a place as dusty as this – was looking a little less godlike. And now the wide-eyed delegations asking for another miracle of the ear have stopped, and they glower and mumble and avoid him, and Shevzod seems lonely, and smaller.

Eva sees the German, tip-toeing through the camp and forever just about to try to say something helpful and never quite daring. He's grown thinner over the last few days, she sees that now. She stops repacking her bundle, and watches him. There's one last moment, when he stands near the centre of his scattered little empire and tries to recapture the poise of that first fireside speech: the posture, the charisma, the confidence. But at the last minute his faith fails him. She sees his shoulders fall, and he turns away.

In the end, he simply mounts his horse and begins to trot into the desert, towards the memory of his hope. Gradually, the disparate elements of the circus notice him, and hurriedly tie bags and clutch clumsily at mules and begin to follow.

☉

JOURNAL OF THOMAS SOMERLEIGH

A tedious day of weeding in the diplomatic undergrowth. I fear I am supposed to enjoy this sort of thing. This morning a colloquium on the security situation, H.M. opening but – reading between the lines – Prudhomme had had to do the hard work to make it happen.

Klug put in an appearance at the start, and intermittently thereafter, but was generally represented by a stand-in, who said not a word and gave the impression he didn't have the adequate English or French to understand what was being said, let alone contribute. I managed to catch Klug just before kick off: good morning and a friendly enquiry about his circus. He looked startled, but then nodded energetically and confirmed how splendid it was all going to be. Wonder if he's bitten off more than he can chew, logistics-wise. Then he asked – rather endearing – did I think H.M. would really appreciate it? Sure of it, I said.

H.M.'s opening remarks started well – he's a good chap, and naturally encouraging to us, and tries to say the right thing – though he wandered off into a bit of a bleat about what this or that tribe is up to. Fascinating for the enthusiasts, no doubt, but footnote stuff. I suppose it served as a symptom of the sort of thing we're dealing with. Then he handed over for general discussion, and we all fiddled with our papers – from somewhere in his trim folds, dear Abdelilah had conjured leather blotters and document dossiers for everyone – and waited for Prudhomme, it obviously being his sort of thing. He did the thing well: clear mind + good prep. = convincing performance. Effective *tour d'horizon* of the challenges, and his awareness of security issues extended to things like sanitation – informal treatment of meat, presence of unmanaged animals in cities and so forth. Doesn't sound like international diplomacy, perhaps, but it's real world business and someone has to take it seriously; my mind wandered to the circus animals.

By coincidence, during the discussion Ray mentioned that Spanish contacts have heard rumours going round the bazaars that the circus caravan has been attacked in the desert en route. Neither H.M. nor Klug in the room for that bit, which was probably a good thing. If true, it would be devastating for poor old Klug. Though he'll still have the credit for the idea; suppose he'll even save a bit on accommodation and feed.

H.M. appeared again at the end to give the *nunc dimittis* and let us escape to find some long-overdue lunch. He listened to Prudhomme's rather skilful summary, and his approximately fair picture of our attitudes, but the conclusions didn't seem to register. I wonder if H.M.'s even sickening for something; seems generally down in the dumps these days. His concluding remarks were spontaneous – which was probably a mistake – and rather missed the point of the proceedings by harking back to his domestic anxieties. Then, very last word, perhaps feeling that he himself needing bucking up, or that he'd lost the audience a bit, he perked up enough to remind us that the circus was due in town any time, thanks to his dear German friends, and he hoped that his diplomatic guests as well as his people would enjoy the positive spirits. And off he popped.

Klug would have been ecstatic, but Klug was not in the room; and his stand-in probably hadn't understood. So that little fillip for German diplomacy seems unlikely ever to be known in Berlin. Prudhomme, meantime, must have been very irked. Spent the day doing a thoroughly professional and painstaking job of herding cats and building a consensus on a serious issue, and just when he's ready to show his homework the headmaster cancels the lesson and announces it's sports day after all.

To my surprise, he seemed pretty jolly, and that's impressive diplomacy: to seem cheerful when you're the opposite. He reminded me about supper loud enough for some of the others to hear, so that was handy too.

Good news is lots of meaty stuff to send back to Tangier. Summary of all the positions, good atmospherics on the mood among the Europeans, and an understated but unmistakeable indication of the British representative playing a central role to keep all in tune. No question but Somerleigh earning his salt.

☉

Having started, the circus caravan has stopped. Then again, given how meaningless the idea of progress has become, stopping and starting have lost their meaning too.

Sometimes, beyond her knees, Eva sees the brown ground blurred. Sometimes it congeals, hardens, stops; individual stones become clear, individual grains. Through the stones, through the grains even, she can see patterns; constellations; faces.

The ground is still now. A unicorn is nuzzling her ankle, and Jan the Pierrot is telling her about something terrible that once happened to him in Russia. Many terrible things happen to Jan the Pierrot in Russia. No one ever asks why he continues to go there.

She becomes aware of other people, voices, nearby. The stop has roused curiosity; a spark in their dead brains.

The track is clearer here, winding round between a rise in the ground and a shallow ravine. Beyond the bend they can see birds in the sky, more in one place than they've seen since they set off however many days ago. The birds promise life, and everyone is a little happier at the idea.

There is sudden movement, and it rouses them all. The German is hurrying back towards them, from the front of their procession, worried, looking for... Looking just behind her. He has found Shevzod, and is beckoning to him. Unsure of what to call the strongman, let alone what language he might understand, he has given up on speech and communicates his urgency only in his emphatic arm movements, his pleading eyes. With uneasy glances at his companions, Shevzod kicks his mule into movement and follows the German forwards.

Now that they're paying attention, at the front of their procession they can make out two figures on horseback. The two figures are... blocking their way. The two figures have rifles.

Eva is looking around herself more consciously. The familiar faces, she notices them. They've seemed distant for the last day or two; perhaps absent. Now they reassure. Then she pays attention to the muleteers: she can see their alertness, their anxiety. The one nearest her keeps looking to the side, into the nothing, and sometimes over his shoulder. Eva's whole existence has been vulnerable, a fragile unlikely thing. She knows to pay attention to peoples' fear.

'Bandits!' says Olga. She says it because it's what she should say. In all the stories of European women venturing into the desert, the unexpected stranger with a rifle is always a bandit; rather than, say, a prudent nut-trader, or another European, or a man selling rifles. She doesn't know what she's talking about.

Except she does know what she's talking about. On her way to join up with a different circus, a different lifetime – in Hungary, was it? Italy? – Olga was noticed by a notorious bandit, a kind of modern highwayman, a Robin Hood reborn, a man of whom stirring folk songs are still sung. He raped her. Eva learned this from her in a murmured conversation – a forgotten boarding house in a forgotten town, a shared bed, a window nailed shut, cabbage-scented nightmares – about fortune-telling. Olga's romantic fantasies about bandits are the dream that they might be different; might have been different.

From muleteer to muleteer, word is passed back along the procession. Here and there – a gesture, an apparently familiar phrase – it crosses to members of the circus, and is passed back among them.

They are agents of the German. One of them is the German's long-lost brother; both, indeed. They are agents of the French. They are emissaries of the local chieftain, who bids them dine with him in his fortress high in the Atlas mountains. A rich traveller wants to buy the circus off the German so that they may perform for him every evening in his life of perpetual travel. They are all to be sold into slavery. There has been a revolt in Marrakech and they must get back to Mogador as fast as possible. It's the Sultan in disguise.

What will turn out to have been true: today they're bandits.

They don't call themselves bandits. They're members of a local tribe who survive on the money they collect from travellers crossing their territory. Depending on your point of view – depending on what thought is most vivid in your head as you decide to pay, and what stories you like hearing – they are customs officers, guides, beggars, ushers, gangsters... or bandits.

Today, they are alone in this quarter of their territory. It's hot, and they can see that the circus is a bit of a handful for two men to intimidate unaided, and by the Prophet the blessings and peace of Allah be upon him look at the size of this lad coming up, and is that a wild animal they can hear? So today they're more like a couple of unruly children given something shiny to stop them pestering the adults. The natural earnestness of the German, and the skill of his interpreter who knows he's talking to save his life, make the financial transaction dignified for everyone.

The circus procession begins to move forwards again. The two tribesmen watch it for a few moments, poised against the sun with commanding height and rifles just long enough to give Olga an appropriately romantic image to believe in, and to give themselves the chance to get a glimpse of the women and wonder if they've made the right decision and what they'll leave out when they report. Then they canter away into the desert.

In different versions of the story, there are fewer travellers and more tribesmen. Sometimes the mood is slightly different.

Just round the bend, it's a different story. The horror floods through the procession as the realization of how others are reacting, the chill flush of blood that something is irrevocably wrong. The people ahead are hesitating, mules straying and colliding, the chatter replaced with wordless moans. The wave is spreading down the column towards Eva, scarves being wrapped more completely around faces, heads turned away from something. And still she is being carried onwards and she knows something is wrong and she's looking around like the fearful muleteer and still she is being carried onwards.

Round the bend they go. All the flies in Africa have swarmed to this few yards of sand: they are a dense black smoke rolling over the ground, shimmering and throbbing and buzzing. The flies veil what they hunger for: the scattered bodies of the previous group of travellers who passed this way, deluding themselves that they were going somewhere. It's impossible to be sure how many there were in the group; the killing has robbed them of individuality too.

The German is urging the circus onwards. Somewhere the Maestro is shouting something. The muleteers have come to life, faces masked and hurrying to and fro and whipping and scolding the animals to keep moving. The circus members push on through a thick curtain of flies. You might as well shoo away a hailstorm. They hiss and pester and probe in ears and eyes, they crawl up sleeves and round collars and under hems, because you too might be a corpse or close enough at least.

As they plod insanely onwards, each face in the procession revolts in turn. Eva sees the ripple of reaction coming nearer to her, and nearer. One hunches and shies, head buried in shoulder. One gapes. One moans. One spasms and lurches and throws up and almost falls. Her turn comes nearer.

They don't really look like bodies. Violence, death, sun, heat, insects, birds and foraging animals in the night: they've a terrible way with the human body. These are scattered bundles of clothing, a bloody tantrum in a pile of rags. These are an explosion of meat. Eva cannot look, cannot bear the idea of seeing a body as a body, cannot stop her eyes sneaking out from under her scarf until they find a detail of massacre lying in the sand. Blood dries brown, in the desert sun. The tearing and scattering of the long robes makes it look as though the bodies themselves have unravelled; a bucket of dirty laundry has been poured down the slope, and its liquid has soaked into the sand and what is left is crusty and reeking. There is a moaning coming from somewhere, someone clinging agonized to life; she realizes it's her. She cannot bear to imagine the terror those eyes last showed. She cannot avoid wondering what it was like, in that moment of shouts and begging, when they knew. And always the flies, fussing all over her body and she has not hands enough to keep them away from her face.

The lions go berserk. Salomon has spent his life – risks his life, over and over again – inducing animals to forget that humans are meat. Every other kind of flesh: go ahead, enjoy yourself, keep your strength up. The scrawny excitable flesh in little hats: nothing to see here, basically under-seasoned vegetables with big ideas, try another squirrel instead. Now the lions have been eating too little for too long, and just through the bars of their makeshift cage there is human-shaped flesh, and it is raw-red and stench-ripe. The lions are bellowing their lust and hurling themselves at the sides of the cage. Improvised to fit on a cart, in the Maestro's haste to get moving before the client changed his mind, the cage now seems terrifyingly fragile: a child's drawing of bars, rough and uneven and spindly and now straining under the assault of the two massive bodies, simply lashed together as much to give the effect of binding. Raffia-work is a big thing in this part of Morocco, of course: the tiny strands of leaf are woven into attractive baskets and charming souvenirs. In their lurching, the lions are likely to topple the cart any moment and then the cage will shatter and they will be free to feast.

Salomon is screaming at the carter to move faster, trying to placate his animals with tiny lumps of whatever food he can grab in time, but they're not his animals any more. All the training and experience and wise understanding and carefully-evolved human strategies to control: the lions have stopped choosing to believe in any of it.

The circus emerges crying and desperate and ravaged from the bend in the track. Eva feels herself adrift in her own fear; naked; lost. She feels her eyes straying towards her companions, just as they slunk towards the savaged bodies. Swearing: uncontrolled mantras of profanity, muttered from white gaping faces. Sobbing: the moan when you hope it's just a nightmare and try to wake yourself. Clutching: I am not alone; do not leave me. Weeping: we are not supposed to know it is all so fragile. They plod, bunched closer now, desperate for air, fighting to hold down clean breaths, staring at each other, ashamed to be seen so abandoned and shamelessly longing for comfort. The mules have saved them, believing what might be ahead to be fractionally better than what's currently unsettling, trudging onwards.

Eva never wants to stop moving again.

The circus creeps into Marrakech in the indifferent darkness of mid-evening. But they no longer believe in cities.

JOURNAL OF THOMAS SOMERLEIGH

p.s. V. pleasant supper *chez* Prudhomme. Always the tricky balance on these occasions: keeping up the pretence of informality, while not letting the mind wander from the diplomatic business. Like having to do a performance of yourself in a game of charades. Prudhomme has done very well for himself, accommodation-wise: I must ask him whether the French Embassy keeps a place or two here in Marrakech on long-term rent. Staff too, perhaps. The smart and skilful pair who waited on us were a world a way from dear old Youssef. Horrible possibility: will I have to reciprocate the invitation, and give my man a primer in table-service, and indeed the wearing of shoes? We get the government we deserve, as the saying goes: I fear I have the accommodation and servant appropriate to a bachelor Englishman of my character and station. Bet Prudhomme never misses a cuff-link or a bit of loose change. *Maison Prudhomme* is discreetly tucked away in a neat back-street not too far from the palace. Not huge, but in beautiful repair, with the little courtyard all exquisite tiles and well-tended palms. Traditional local style, but modern European fittings, as far as I could gather – again, must summon up the courage to suggest to Sir G. a similar arrangement here for the British Embassy – though Madame P. made one reference to *'les pipes'*, in exactly the voice she'd used describing the threat to her daughter from the mountain tribesmen, so all may not be quite perfect.

And so to *les femmes* Prudhomme. Funny business, bringing your wife and daughter all this way. Rough old journey. Though no doubt the French will have managed better transport than the British-bought nags. I wonder whether it's because he worries about them alone in Tangier, or they worry about him alone in Marrakech. Perhaps it's just the done thing, *a la française*; they are rather sweet together. And having Madame is an advantage, not just keeping an eye on the household but also offering appropriate hospitality. Note to self: I really ought to be entertaining here now, and I really daren't unless I can smarten up the bachelor digs a bit. I suppose there's a generational element. For younger men, foreign diplomatic postings mean adventure and even experimentation – the sordid realities of night behind the austere facades of day. Then you find the right wife – a woman who can preside over an appropriate table on the far side of the Moroccan desert – and it's all hearth and home and setting a good example to the younger chaps.

Feels rather a stretch, to think of myself being the wise old mentor to a future generation of young dips.

(The terrifying, lizard-eyed homily from O'Neill, when I showed up in Cairo, the more unsettling for being delivered in his Scottish Presbyterian pulpit voice: 'In the springtime of yer manhood, ye shall from time to time feel within ye the urrrrrge for errrotic release. Number one, never on Brritish government prremises. Number tu, never during working hours nor Chrristian holidays. Number three, any more than once per week is over-indulgent, debilitating to the spirits and likely to provoke anti-Brritish sentiment. For a list of the more hygienic establishments, tell Omar the senior clerk that ye wish to get yer handkerchiefs laundered.' There really had been a list, too. 'And nothing tu exotic, Somerleigh; not while ye're still on prrobation.')

Madame Prudhomme is something else. Unsettling. On the surface v. quiet, meek even, speaking as though nothing she could ever say should ever interrupt her husband. But still waters: the sense one's being watched; measured. Just in case I pinch one of the spoons or make an off-colour remark about Anglo-French military conversations. Prudhomme will make a good Ambassador, because Mme Prudhomme will make an excellent Ambassador's wife. She was probably quite pretty, when she was young, and the young Prudhomme was summoning the courage to invite her for a *crème de menthe*. All seems rather frozen now: the precise black parting, the pale face. A very carefully-pruned warmth, in her polite greeting and supper-table formalities. Makes it even harder to pretend that I'm enjoying a relaxed supper party with friends. The more so because Monsieur, by contrast, is surprisingly genial off-duty. Not exactly rollicking, but certainly a surprise compared to the daytime diplomat *par excellence*. Better to say: he's much better than I at the performance of informality.

He was 'cher Thomas'-ing me as soon as I was through the door, and I was immediately on the back foot because I wasn't more than fifty percent sure his name's Hector. I sort of mumbled it, and he was too polite to correct me, and it was only halfway through main course that I caught Madame – who insists on referring to him as 'my husband' in conversation, or even 'Monsieur Prudhomme' – using the name. Then again, perhaps she was also just being too polite to correct me. Let's see how long they keep this one up. I opened with a polite compliment about the morning's colloquium: 'oh, that!' he said, like it was a vaguely interesting cricket match from last month; 'yes... the things we must do to – you would say "put on a good show"? We don't want dear little Klug breathing all of the oxygen, do we Thomas?' I agreed that we certainly don't. I added, a touch roguish, it must be an awful trial to him, having to worry about all those fig-sellers. He replied, likewise, that they had their uses, and he was now more worried about the case of an accordion-merchant, to which he might have to give more attention for variety's sake at least.

Then he turns to Madame, and says: 'Do you like circuses, my dear?' She doesn't commit, and he's not paying attention anyway. He absolutely dived into the circus, and how are we going to deal with this most amusing initiative? Quite to my surprise, he seems most entertained by the whole business. Asked me, apparently quite serious, whether there was anyone in the British community in Marrakech who could be added to the programme – he was likewise enquiring around the French – so we were seen to be supporting the initiative, and so the Sultan wouldn't forget us altogether. I scored an unqualified triumph – absolutely brought the house down; Madame may actually have smiled – by confirming, *faux*-sombre, that he wasn't seriously suggesting that members of the diplomatic community should participate. Hysteria; wiping his eyes behind the pince-nez. In an even greater triumph –

Somerleigh's lessons in diplomacy, number umpteen: what you don't say can be vastly wiser than what you do – I just managed to stop myself, drawn the breath and words on tip of tongue and only then had heaven-sent second thoughts, from developing the gag into a specific comment about the idea of Prudhomme himself in some sort of circus role. As I looked at him, his performance of mirth, I suddenly knew, absolute certainty, that the slightest suggestion of personal ridicule would have turned the food to ash and made all the palms shrivel and had France and Britain at war before breakfast. Thank God for my last precious vestige of anxiety; the prudence behind the performance.

What to write about Mademoiselle Prudhomme? Perhaps best to say that the *Entente* passed through three phases: indifference, *protocolaire* formality, and then more sincere liaison. Arriving, I hadn't thought about the daughter at all: Prudhomme never makes more than a general passing reference to *la famille*, and I was focused entirely on strengthening my relationship with him. The fact that this was supper with the family was just a diplomatic way of saying there wouldn't be many other dips there. Then I'd arrived, and it was all Cher Thomas and Dear Hector and making sure I was over-courteous to Madame. The daughter was no more than Chère Hortense and a very traditional curtsey and I was bowing but not really paying attention because we'd been talking about old Mokri, and I couldn't have told you whether Hortense was fourteen or forty.

Then we were at table: Prudhomme opposite me led the conversation and I naturally let him while keeping the British end up as regards the balance in Europe and likely developments in the East, and the women of course left us to it. When I wasn't talking opium and Algeciras I was making appropriate compliments to Madame about the hospitality, and if anything I was avoiding paying attention to the daughter because I didn't want her parents to think I couldn't behave. There was only one moment of difficulty, when Madame turned the conversation to life for her and Hortense here in Marrakech and there was silence, and I had to make a polite enquiry about how Miss Hortense passed the day, and Miss Hortense predictably replied reading and music but they only had three discs for the gramophone and there were only so many hours one could play the piano (a piano! Surely they didn't bring that across the desert with them? I'd got dirty looks when I politely enquired about an extra ration of tobacco and a couple of magazines), and Prudhomme got going again and the danger had passed.

I have, I suppose, rather more experience talking to middle-ranking Arab trade clerks than to women; and considerably more to talk about. So when Prudhomme had to go and sort out an unexpected visitor, and Madame was getting the kitchen back on track, and Hortense and I found ourselves unexpectedly alone together, I was a bit at sea. I had to look at her, of course. Realized I hadn't yet done so. Realized that she is, in her way, a jolly pretty little thing. Prudhomme is rather sharp-featured, and in his daughter this is softened and made fine by the delicacy of her mother. And big, dark eyes from somewhere. The French are also a Latin people, aren't they? I didn't have aught to say, anyway, and didn't want to seem crass, but she wasn't going to say anything, and so eventually I said how very pleasant an evening it was, and what a treat it was to be somewhere where it was mild so early in the year, and she agreed very earnestly, and I was wondering when one of the parents would return. They didn't, and so we looked at each other emptily a bit longer, and then she asked did I like poetry? Well, I mean, you have to say yes, don't you? She leaned a little closer, glanced quickly to check that Mummy and Daddy weren't in view, and whispered that Baudelaire was her constant companion, and was I shocked? Now, I confess I couldn't distinguish

Baudelaire from a leg of ham, but one doesn't want to say so. I assumed we were still on poetry, though she spoke of him the way she would a favourite pony. Fortunately I remembered Brahim, my café chum. Never like to pass judgement on a poet, says I, as far likelier to make myself foolish than them. (Not a bad line, though I say so myself.) But very interested in poetry as a way into a nation's character, and only talking just the other day to a chap...

Not sure how much of this diplomatic triumph will make it into the report to Tangier. Sir G., I suspect, only too ready to pass judgement on poets. But v. handy spadework with Prudhomme to maintain the Anglo-French *Entente*, and I shall say as much.

She's only a couple of years younger than me, I suppose. Jolly pretty. Attractive, without forcing it on you. I found, anyway, that it was becoming important to me to interest her. The thought of old O'Neill kept me on the straight and narrow, together with the more immediate regard of Madame, ever-watchful. The walk home: that particular buoyancy one gets when, under the influence of a glass too many of white burgundy, one feels one has been charming in charming company.

◐

The worthy Somerleigh treats his journal as a kind of commonplace book. It contains the occasional drawing: a significant building, an interesting plant; he obviously considered that an amateur facility in sketching was a fitting hobby for the young diplomat. There is poetry, of course: bits of Victorian and Edwardian woolly mammoth, some French aphorisms, and some fragments of Arabic poetry which he found in French translation, and may not have fully understood but apparently liked the sound of. There are hints of abortive projects to produce anthologies of ethnographic material, or significant buildings, or curious recipes, or even to attempt a history.

Amid this miscellany he includes a tale told by the boy Ali, the famous story-teller of Marrakech. Somerleigh may not have heard the story at first hand: it is clear that during his wandering of the city he spent time absorbing the atmosphere of Marrakech's famous main square, the Jamaa el-Fna, and enjoying the spirit of the story-tellers even though he couldn't know what they were saying; he seems to have tried to find Ali, but his journal does not record whether he succeeded.

In a discreet back-street near the Royal Palace of Marrakech – a street we may ourselves have walked every day, but I doubt we notice it, for it lacks excessive noise or unpleasant odour or unnecessary colour – there lived for many years a merchant. He was neither a poor man, nor a rich man. He was successful enough to maintain a pleasant house, a hearty table and a healthy family. His wealth lay in his reputation, for everyone – from the humblest passer-by to the greatest vizier – would trust him and would buy from him. The merchant's greatest love was his wife, a worthy woman who had been the only daughter of his first master. And together their greatest love was their only son, a fine young man named Taleb.

Now, moving right along, for let's face it worthiness has limited dramatic appeal, came the day when Taleb reached his age of maturity, and should decide for himself the course of his life.

'Stay!' said his mother; 'your father's enterprise is your inheritance. Already he respects you as a hard worker as much as he respects you as his only son. You shall continue here, as his student and then as his partner. Our reputation shall nourish your virtues, and your virtues shall enhance our reputation.'

There were tears in Taleb's eyes. 'My beloved mother,' he said, 'I cannot express my gratitude for all you have given and all you offer, but I must refuse. My life shall be earned, and not merely taken.'

'Stay!' said his father; 'in Marrakech our name is your key to any worthy position you choose, and already your promise has earned the respect of respectable men. Your uncle, I know, is ready to give you a position. Our neighbour, I know, is ready to give you a position. A customer in the palace, a man I do not presume to name but am honoured to know, he is ready to give you a position. Just say the word!'

A stab of manly affection pierced Taleb's breast. 'My beloved father,' he said, 'I cannot express my gratitude for all you have given and all you offer, but I must refuse. My life shall be earned, and not merely taken.' And with that he set off, out of the city and into the desert, accepting only food enough for a day and money enough for a week.

Full a month he travelled across the desert, moving steadily from village to village, working at this or that to earn a meal or a bed, and all he met were struck by his steadiness and virtue.

One evening, footsore and hungry and weary, he came to a town; he knocked at the first door he saw, a stout wooden affair which proved to be the house of a rich trader. 'May I beg a night's sleep and a meal', he said, 'in return for any labour you may need of me?'

'Here we do not sell hospitality', replied the trader. 'A virtuous man is welcome.'

Taleb slept in a comfortable bed, with white sheets, and woke rested. The trader's daughter, a dark-haired girl of tender shyness and great beauty, brought him breakfast. He passed the day quizzing the trader about the particular habits of business in the district, and all the time the beautiful daughter waited on him.

He was a stranger to them, but they admired his fine figure and his sober manner and his worthy attitude. At last the trader said: 'Stay! I have neither son nor partner to follow me. I shall make you both, and I shall welcome you to my family.' And at this the dark girl smiled a shy smile.

Their ways were strange to him, and yet Taleb had tried to make himself comfortable among them. 'I cannot express my gratitude for all you have given and all you offer,' he said, 'but I must refuse. My life shall be earned, and not merely taken.'

Full a month he travelled across the desert, moving steadily from village to village, working at this or that to earn a meal or a bed, and all he met were struck by his steadiness and virtue.

One evening, footsore and hungry and weary, he came to a town; he knocked at the first door he saw, a stout wooden affair which proved to be the house of the local pasha. 'May I beg a night's sleep and a meal', he said, 'in return for any labour you may need of me?'

'Here we do not sell hospitality', replied the pasha. 'A virtuous man is welcome.'

Taleb slept in a luxuriant bed, among cushions of softest feather, and woke rested. The pasha's daughter, a fair-haired girl of bold charm and great beauty, brought him breakfast. He passed the day quizzing the pasha about the peculiar conventions of the town, and all the time the beautiful daughter waited on him.

He was a stranger to them, but they admired his fine figure and his sober manner and his worthy attitude. At last the pasha said: 'Stay! Compared to you, all the other men hereabouts are fools and rogues. I shall train you to my responsibility, and I shall welcome you to my family.' And at this the fair girl smiled a bold smile.

Their ways were strange to him, and yet Taleb had tried to make himself comfortable among them. 'I cannot express my gratitude for all you have given and all you offer,' he said, 'but I must refuse. My life shall be earned, and not merely taken.'

Full a month he travelled across the desert, moving steadily from village to village, working at this or that to earn a meal or a bed, and all he met were struck by his steadiness and virtue.

One evening, footsore and hungry and weary, he came to a city. As usual he began to look for a door at which he could knock to beg a meal and a bed. But the first place he came to – the only place near, among the gardens on this side of the city – was a ruin. Its roof had collapsed, its garden looked as if a tempest had rushed through it

Taleb was not too proud to beg of a beggar, and he approached. But as he approached, he heard the sounds of argument and violence. Suddenly two men rushed away from the property, carrying bags and pieces of jewellery and a chicken each, and leapt on their horses. The horses shoved past Taleb as he continued towards the front door. As he reached the door, another man came bustling out of it, clutching a chicken which was squawking in panic. 'I beg you!' cried a voice from the interior, 'Leave me just one thing!'

It was the voice of an old man, and now Taleb saw him, clutching at the man with the chicken. 'You have humiliated me. You have destroyed what is left of my home. You have robbed me of my every possession. You have slaughtered and stolen my flock. Leave me, I beg you, just one thing!'

But the man just gave a scornful laugh, and flung the old arms aside and turned to leave. He had not seen Taleb, however, and now as he turned to escape they bumped violently into each other. Both men went staggering, and the chicken got loose and began to flap and squawk in a circle. The man started to complain and to curse Taleb and looked like he wanted to fight him, but Taleb stood firm, saying nothing but gazing defiant at the robber. The man had a second look at this young strong determined figure, and turned and hurried away on his horse after his comrades.

Taleb picked up the anxious chicken, in two careful hands, and presented it back to the old man. The old man, tears in his eyes, just gazed at the young man. Neither of them said anything. Taleb nodded respectfully, and stepped forwards into the remains of the house. Everything, gentlemen, was chaos. The air was a cloud of dust and chicken feathers, for whoever these bandits were they had come through like a whirlwind.

Another pair of eyes was staring at Taleb: the old man's daughter, a silent flame-haired girl of great beauty. Taleb smiled politely at her, and then he picked up a fallen timber and began to help them tidy their home. All through the evening they worked, until some order was restored in the house and they each had somewhere to sleep. Taleb said good night to the old man, and to the flame-haired daughter, and as he was turning away the young woman stopped him: playfully, shyly, she tucked a chicken feather behind his ear.

The next day they began to do the best they could with the structure of the house, and to tidy the garden, and at the end of the day the flame-haired daughter tucked another feather behind Taleb's ear. The days passed, and soon they had made the place a going concern again. And every evening, of course, Taleb was rewarded with his feather.

We know what happens. The renewed prosperity of the old man attracted the attention of jealous eyes, and came the day when the bandits returned. Alas, it was a day when the old man had been in particularly good spirits, and he had summoned his daughter and Taleb to hear some news, and just at that moment he saw the horsemen crashing through the garden towards them and he cried out in fear and anger.

But this time Taleb was ready, and he made a fight of it. The old man and his daughter threw rocks at the attackers and swung pots and pans at them, and Taleb fought bare-handed. It was a hard fight and he was badly injured, and he knew he could not last much longer. But the men were thieves and thugs wanting easy returns, we all know the sort, and a fight like Taleb was giving them was too much to pay for a few scrawny chickens, and at last they staggered away to nurse their wounds.

Taleb collapsed on his bed, and felt the flame-haired girl mopping his wounds. The old man was delighted, hardly noticing the young man's discomfort. This time the old eyes were filled with tears of joy. 'Again you have saved me', he said. 'And this time those thieves have lost a thousand times more, and you have saved a thousand times more.' Taleb could not understand him. 'I used to be a pasha in this city', went on the old man. 'But I fell from favour, and was banished outside the walls, and had to rely on simple trading and investment. Ill-fortune, and attacks from those who saw my weakness, reduced me to the sorry state you first saw. Today I learned that a ship I sent across the sea and long feared lost has made it home, with a great cargo. And there has been a scandal in the city, and I am summoned back to office as pasha. My wealth is regained, and more importantly my reputation is restored, and most importantly my family is saved.' He looked down at the figure on the bed, and the beautiful figure tending him so thoughtfully. 'And you shall share it all.'

At last Taleb understood. He nodded slowly to the old man. 'This at last', he said, 'I have earned.' And he smiled a smile of contentment. He felt his strength failing him, for his wounds were grave and his exhaustion great. His eyes flickered, misty with delirium and misty with joy at the beautiful face that hovered so attentively over him. Then they closed.

When they opened again, Taleb found his mother gazing down at him. She seemed overjoyed to see him. 'What a time you've been out', she said. And Taleb started to tell her of all the extraordinary things he could remember. She patted his shoulder. 'You're here now,' she said; 'and that's all that matters.' Then she stopped in surprise. 'But what is this, and how on earth did it get here?'

From Taleb's pillow, just beside his ear, she picked up a chicken feather.

⟐

The circus roams the back streets of Marrakech, like a dream. Apparently straight alleys prove to have brought them back on themselves. Unsettling, unnatural figures loom at them out of the doorways, hooded, wheedling, disfigured. Some really are disfigured; others lurch and stretch and distort in the lantern-light. Impossible creatures come to life as they approach: a huge cat, a figure with a snake curling and uncurling around its neck, half-human things that drag and creep and whimper. All the spices of the world waft in the gutters; every one of its pains and excesses is cried from behind shutters.

There has been a mix-up with their arrival. Their little German was expecting to be met before they got into the city. Now he is desperately wandering this unknown state of delusion, looking for an end to the journey. And surely a man who can conjure a city out of the sand could manage a single clerk with directions to a boarding house; but he seems very tired now.

The circus begins to break down. So obvious and so huddled out in the desert, its coherence weakens amid darkness and possibilities. Orange light glowing from a doorway promises good food and warm atmosphere, and the hungry are lost into it. Unseen lips whisper joys; curves swell almost within reach; an anklet jingles and for an instant catches the light.

For a time, Eva finds herself wandering the alleys alone. None of it can be real, this delirium of monstrous labyrinth and glimpsed Aladdin's caves. But unknown, and unknowing, she finds herself unexpectedly free. As long as none of the wheedlers and tempters and hecklers actually attacks her, she is safe to drift through their chatter. The alleys feel warm: sudden knots of people; bursts of light. She doesn't know what time it is, but many of the shops are still open. Another explosion of spices, a bustle of bright yellows and oranges: the collision of scents is overwhelming, and she clutches for individual tastes, but they are gone like fragments of childhood. A glimpsed gloom of pots and jugs, hanging dark and bulbous and filling their cavern; as she moves past, light silvers the curves, and they wink and swell. A carpenter's workshop, naked doors fresh-carved, ankle-deep in shavings, and the heart-stabbing smell of goodness that hides only in wood.

She cannot begin to know where she is, but she knows she is somewhere; she doesn't mind where she's going as long as she stays here.

☪

JOURNAL OF THOMAS SOMERLEIGH

p.p.s.(!) Hardly dropped off when roused by hammering at front door. Vague idea that the good householder doesn't hide under the blanket and leave this sort of thing to the staff, so go and open up in dressing gown and unchristian mood. It's Klug, would you believe? in shirt-sleeves and something like panic. The puffy face is desperate in the light from my lamp. Have you heard the news? he says. Have you heard of the pocket-watch? think I, but sympathy for his distress keeps me silent. The most terrible news, he says: he's been waiting and waiting, and delay and delay, and the circus has vanished; apparently there's been an attack by one of the tribes, not far out of Marrakech. Word is the circus has been slaughtered to the last man and performing monkey.

Horrible thought, of course. The tribes'd just butcher any animals they didn't want to steal, and presumably there were women in the group too. Ruin, he says, face ghastly, absolute ruin. And I have to feel for him: he'd obviously staked big on the circus, and in the foreign service it's the sort of wheeze that gets you credit if it succeeds entirely, but otherwise leaves you looking an imbecile. Don't have the sense that the Germany Foreign Ministry are all that flexible or sporting when a junior bod bets the Embassy budget on a funfair. I felt myself going cold at the idea it could so easily have been me in this grim predicament. Then, shamefully perhaps, part of my mind was calculating the benefit to Britain, if Germany has offered H.M. the Sultan a jolly night out and instead given him a major public order embarrassment.

For want of anything better to say I invited him in: stiff drink and work out if there's anything to do. He backed away, shaking his head, and disappeared into the darkness. Strange evening.

☾

In the café on the corner, someone has seen a lion in the street tonight. Opinions divide: for some it is ridiculous – whoever saw a lion in the streets of Marrakech? for some it is obvious – who hasn't seen a lion in the streets of Marrakech?

In the next café someone has seen a giraffe. In the next a zebra. In the next an emu: no doubt the Sultan's has escaped. In one café someone has seen two lions, but this tale dies quickly: one lion, sure; three lions is neat; or a pride of them if necessary; but what kind of story has two lions?

In many cafés there is a story from someone who has met a fortune teller, a mysterious foreign woman, here in Marrakech, just now. Her hair was black as a raven's wing. Or it gleamed like gold. The shadows didn't exactly help; or perhaps it was the strangely-scented smoke, or the exotic veil. Each has been told – a private guarantee, a blessing, a command – that there is a fortune to be seized in the city this night. Immediately people are slipping away from the backs of the groups of listeners, out into the street – because, well, you wouldn't say no to a bit of that, would you?

The news moves through the alleys of Marrakech like a flood. At every slightest junction in the backstreets it diverges, and part continues more strongly in this direction, and part in that direction. Here and there among the cafés and shops it is held up, and it builds and swells, and then it surges out again.

Unnatural creatures have been seen: multi-headed animals; giants. Something wonderful is happening in the city tonight. Something terrible is loose. The Sultan has gone mad at last and is throwing gold coins from the top of the Bab Agnaou. French spies have been hiding in the Jewish quarter for months and now they are capturing the city. The women of a starving Berber village are offering themselves in return for food. A sorceress who cursed the previous Sultan for his lack of respect is taking her terrible revenge. Fear and enthusiasm fill the streets with people. It's a night of panic and a night of revelry. Some men are dragged away by monsters, some by flame-haired fairy women. If you step out of your house at midnight you'll be blinded, or you'll be burgled.

In the square this evening, the faces surrounding him glowing in enthralment and lamplight, Ali the teller of tales has told a remarkable history. Histories. The foreign prince who came to seek his fortune and his bride, and was turned into a monster for his vanity and prowls the night still greedy for the sustenance denied him. The monster transformed by a worthy bride into a prince and picking up a fortune as well. Vice fulfilled and virtue rewarded.

In the café on the corner, the next morning is slower than usual, heavier. The proprietor stares sourly across the half-empty tables, from eyes hollow and red. He is irritable, quick to kick the boy circulating with nuts, and then missing him. Conversations are mumbled, incoherent. No one tips.

No one mentions last night. Everyone seems to have had strange dreams. Wild dreams. Turbulent, sheet-twisting moaning dreams. Beautiful women still beckon from the doorways of memories, or imaginations, calling confused minds back into the shadows. Sins lurk there too, and humiliations. No one can look square at an acquaintance, or a wife.

'It's the night spirits.'

'It's eating too late; I told you the yoghourt had turned.'

◉

JOURNAL OF THOMAS SOMERLEIGH

Klug's big day. Have to say he carried it off rather well: understated; obviously chuffed, but keeping himself in check. Good lesson. Nothing formal called for today, but as usual the dips gathered at the Ukkaz Gate in the morning. Ray nattering to Prudhomme, Prudhomme giving him no encouragement and fixed on the doorway where the Sultan or his officials might appear, our Spanish friend ignoring the fact he's being ignored. No Klug. McKenna and I nod to each other, and he offers me a cigarette.

'I hear the famous circus got in last night', he drawls through smoke. Oh, says I; I heard it got cut up long before it arrived. He considered this, and added: 'Before now the consensus was there was no circus. Or at least it never left Mogador.' Another puff for reflection. 'How many circuses you think there are round this place? Damn desert must be full of them.' Well, I said, at least you don't have to count the one that doesn't exist. 'You think?' says McKenna; 'Strikes me the circus that doesn't exist might be the most powerful one of all right now.' He nodded towards Prudhomme. 'You could guarantee it would have all the weight of France behind it, and that's something.'

As if he'd heard our chat, Klug appeared. But he appeared from inside the Palace. He was looking very busy, very focused; very stuffed. I glanced instinctively at Prudhomme. He'd seen, and his face was frozen. He then turned a look of terrifying amiability on Ray: if he's pretending to be nice to the Spanish things must be bad.

Then a vizier appeared, usual white-robed dignity, little Abdelilah in tow. H.M.'s compliments, and he'd be delighted if the *Corps Diplomatique* would join him for a promenade in the gardens at four this afternoon. Prudhomme quick off the mark as ever, thanks and accepts on behalf of all of us, and trusts that H.M. is in good health. Tip-top, says the vizier: H.M. in excellent spirits, and particularly bucked by the news he has just received from Monsieur Klug.

He looks at Klug, Abdelilah looks at Klug, and we all look at Klug. Klug contrives to look v. calm and business-like, and part of me is admiring this and part of me is worrying that I'm starting to fall very far off the pace. I'm imagining the reports he's able to write to Tangier and Berlin. I can't think of a single occasion this trip when I've been able to report anything one-tenth as meaty. Pretty hopeless. Klug still v. composed, waits the extra moment with us all watching him, and then gives a little bow to the vizier: 'With your permission, sir', he says, v. nice touch, 'I can report the safe and satisfactory arrival of the circus in

Marrakech.' Now he looks round us. 'It is at the disposal of His Majesty, very naturally, but I am hopeful that you will all be able to share the enjoyment of this occasion.'

I managed to trot after him at the end – he was full steam ahead as usual – and said I was glad everything had worked out all right. Polite thanks, no let up in pace. I added: 'After all the alarms last night, I mean.' Now he stopped, and looked at me. His expression suggested he hadn't the faintest idea what I was talking about: not embarrassed, not hiding anything. I was about to mention his turning up on my doorstep, but it didn't seem quite the thing, and... Well, he was so blank that I started to wonder whether I'd imagined the whole business. I mumbled something about the circus being here now, anyway.

He nodded once, firm and satisfied. According to all aspects of the German Embassy administrative procedures, he said – it would be a brave man who disagreed with Germany Embassy administrative procedures – the circus has arrived this morning.

So, whatever did happen last night, it can't have been anything to do with the circus. Shortly afterwards, he's bustling in again through the Ukkaz Gate. There's an older chap beside him, struggling to keep up: rather short, and very fat, and in a suit that's fifty years out of date and doesn't look like it's fitted since. They're met by an official, and there's much bowing – the little fat man puffing hard and his suit straining even more desperately each time he bobs forwards.

'Perhaps', Prudhomme murmured into my ear, 'this is Klug's acrobat.' I said perhaps this chap had eaten the rest of the circus, but Prudhomme didn't catch it: he was gazing at Klug. Then he grabbed me – if one raised finger and one raised eyebrow count as a grab: Madame Prudhomme very much hoping I will join the family for supper again. Still not sure how to communicate to Tangier what the Germans are up to and how little I'm doing about it, but it's handy to have a bit of good news about relations with France.

Wandered town for a bit. After a while I realized I was unconsciously looking out for a circus tent. Proper big striped business, surely. I didn't find one.

I was back at the palace at four prompt, along with my colleagues. No Sultan. No Klug, either. We waited five minutes; ten. A quarter after four, an official appeared in the doorway: H.M. sends his profound regrets, no promenade today. H.M. has been caught up in a meeting with a German municipal lighting engineer.

☽

Eva wakes late, and lost.

She has slept heavily. She must have tired her body yesterday, but there was no excess of food or drink. The ceiling above her is thin varnished branches, packed tight over beams. The walls are plaster, or perhaps smoothed stone. She's at least half undressed. She's on a mattress of... straw maybe. She's in a proper bed, with chunky crude-carved corner-posts. She's sharing the bed, with... Olga, and... Johanna of the horses. There is light, but only what can push through a feeble bit of cloth covering a square hole cut high in one wall. There's another bed, containing two very dark women she doesn't think she recognizes.

These things all feel like normality: a bed, a shared bed, Olga's unconscious skill in capturing most of the blanket, a shared boarding house room, the never-fully-resolved confusions of life on the road, the day's first dilemma over outhouse or chamberpot, well-slept optimism about the possibility of really fresh water to wash in.

She has had the most peculiar dream. A sea voyage, a forced landfall, a mysterious new country, men with dark beautiful eyes, cats, European politics, uncanny musical instruments, an endless journey across the desert, an impossible city rising out of the sand, delirium.

She finds clothes enough to cover herself, but doesn't properly fasten them. She wonders where her bag might be. The floor is stone under her bare feet, or perhaps hard earth. She finds shoes. She sees Johanna open one eye and blows her a kiss. Steps over Magda, snoring on the floor. The door is like the bed: someone has an instinct for carving, but not the time or the tools for finery. She steps cautiously down a narrow and uneven flight of steps, all still bare stone or plaster.

In a tiny courtyard there's a butt of water. She wonders at it, approaches it, sniffs it, stirs it with a finger. Eventually she takes the risk and splashes handfuls of it over her face and body.

The morning – she feels it's still morning – is warm. The courtyard has another, heavier wooden door. Still fastening up her frock, she steps through it into whatever is outside.

All the stonework is a thick, sickly pink.

She's in an alley. Here the alley is open to the sky, a ribbon of perfect blue stretched far above her. Farther along the alley is covered, disappearing under more of the brutish pink buildings. The alley is lined with empty trading tables and small shuttered shop-fronts. There are a few people around. They all wear long thick gowns that are surely too hot for a morning like this. They're gliding past her along the alley, or murmuring to each other, or beginning to open the shutters of the shops. A one-armed man piles round, inch-thick loaves of bread on a table. A cat sniffs at her ankle, and rubs itself around her shin.

The inhabitants seem to move slowly, silently, unsurely, as if they like her are only discovering the town this morning.

While she's wondering which way to turn, a woman beckons to her from an entrance a couple of yards off. The woman is bulky, swaddled in bright sheets that also cover her head, and the tan skin of her face is blotchy. She beckons again. Eva approaches warily. A single square room set back into the wall, all greasy patterned tiles. The woman points at a stool, gestures her urgently to sit. Eva sits. Immediately there is a metal saucer in front of her, then on the saucer there is a glass, then in the glass there is a fistful of mint, then amid the mint there is a thumb-sized chunk of sugar, each item pulled out of the air with a deftness surprising in the bulky woman. Eva considers the movements, recognizes the sense of performance, double-checks for the pickpocket or whatever else she's being distracted from. For the climax of the trick, the woman swings round with a huge iron kettle, and begins to pour; as she pours she lifts the kettle higher and higher until it is at shoulder-height and still the liquid is arcing down precisely into the glass and then the kettle lowers and just as the liquid reaches the top of the glass the kettle is level beside it again and swings away and disappears.

This is Morocco. A town conjured out of the desert and called Marrakech.

The tea is sharp sweet scented; thrilling.

The woman starts to chatter at her. Eva smiles blankly. She mimes that she likes the tea. The woman gives up. Then she starts up again, chattering as she gets on with her morning preparations, the wiping and arranging and chopping, apparently just glad of an audience, however dumb. She turns and chatters something new, mimes putting something in her mouth; Eva shakes her head and the woman shrugs and returns to her work.

Marrakech continues to wake around her. The gowns drift to and fro, the thin desert-coloured faces, the high cheeks and dark eyes. Everyone notices her – her skin, her uncovered head, her frock – and then looks again.

She has learned to classify places by the different ways the men look at her. Whether they pretend not to look when looking. Whether they look at her face at all. Whether they speak. Whether they speak at her or about her. Whether the sound they make is angry, curious or coarse. Thus urban Morocco: the looking is blatant; her face gets her noticed, but then they're more interested in her hair, her alien dress, her calves emerging under her hem; when there's noise it's directed at her, and it sounds friendly. More than one man tries in basic French to encourage her to visit his shop just around the corner.

A pocket in Eva's frock holds small change from half a dozen countries. She holds out a few coins. The woman considers the options carefully, then picks one she likes the look of. Neither of them knows how much it's worth.

As she's walking back past her lodging and wondering where she might go, a man is standing in the open doorway. He looks at her, of course, and notices her, and makes noise. 'Fräulein!' It's the German representative from Mogador, their escort in the desert. He's beckoning her urgently back inside, her freedom somehow unseemly. 'Please – Please.'

Indifferent, she obeys. On the whole, she thinks, she preferred the Moroccan men: at least they had the promise of a shop.

His reappearance brings: order; some confirmation that a lot of what she thinks she remembers of recent days is probably true; an end to unrestraint, to her sense that she was free to roam, free from too precise an identity.

The circus – meaning its animals and heavy wagons – is camped by a cemetery on the northern edge of the city. The people… well, we're not sure where they've got to, but over the course of the day they'll come drifting back. *Circus folks is rogues and vagabonds, ain't it, till they misses their supper and comes a-running?*

Olga asks where the Maestro is, and the German reassures her that the Maestro was well accommodated for the night. Olga had not doubted this point, and the

German's expression suggests that a disproportionate amount of his last twelve hours of anxiety has been focused on the Maestro's accommodation. The Herr Maestro has already accompanied the senior representative of the German Embassy to a meeting with senior officials of His Majesty the Sultan.

All that accumulated seniority topped off with a touch of fairy-tale doesn't seem to have the impact he hoped. Eva sees it in his eyes. She sees him seeing them: half awake and half dressed; herself wandering in from the street; Olga, whom men require to be exquisite, currently small-eyed and coughing; Magda, determinedly the opposite of her sister and now barely awake; Johanna who is more or less half horse. By instinct and curiosity one of the dark women from the other bed is standing on the edge of their group now, and she's much the most attentive and the German just assumes she's part of the circus. Eva finds herself pitying the little man again: the spectacles so fragile amid the stonework and indifference. He is so very tired now, so very desperate, and with all his anxiety he has carried them through the desert and he so needs them to be what they are supposed to be.

'Everything in order by nightfall', Eva says to him, in German. 'Circus never looks good in daylight.' At first he's as startled as if Otelle the zebra had spoken to him; then he wonders if she's somehow making fun of his concerns. But this is why she has spoken in German: all of the confusion has happened in English and mime; German is the language of his authority, of business, and a statement in German is truth and he just nods.

The circus camp is normality, and another city with its particular tint of stone and its particular accent of lewd remark falls away into the background. Is the ground good or marshy? Are we upwind of the stink of the city, or down? What can the animals eat? Is this road the one used by rich travellers, or jackals and bandits and burial parties?

The circus camp has its own smell, mighty and inescapable and distinctive, and the smell is reassuringly familiar.

This site isn't so bad. No European circus ever knew a warmer dryer spring. There's water nearby, but not too nearby. We're beside one of the Muslim cemeteries, rather than the Jewish one on the other side of town. Someone has heard someone trying to interpret a comment by one of the locals about the old leper quarter, but we're pretending that's a mis-hearing or a joke. Everyone has been among other humans again, and so is feeling human again.

Johanna is in conversation with her horses. Shevzod has a headache and is slumped against a tree. Overnight, Jan the Pierrot has become an expert in Islam and is lecturing anyone he can about mystics and wandering preachers. Olga and Magda are sitting cross-legged and combing each other's hair and scolding each other in the rocky tides of some Slavic language. Salomon has bruised hands and a cut on his cheek and seems very contented. Eva walks through the camp twice, until she has recognized all the faces and all the animals, and then she checks her bag, and then she settles down with the sun on her face and waits.

Sometime during the afternoon the Maestro turns up, with another European. Only the briefest flicker of hope that this might at last be the Sultan in disguise, extinguished by the first sight of the pale and obviously European face and the formal European suit. An important European: it's clear from the Maestro's fussing, and from the German representative hurrying along a step behind.

Eva is too far off to make out much detail of the newcomer. But she is – we are all – reading the Maestro's performance. His presentation of the circus to an Important Visitor – his posture, his gestures, his tone, his words – has subtle variations depending on whether the person is of high social status, rich and thus a potential source of money, or already a source of money. The repeated bobs of the Maestro's head, the glances to check reaction, tell us a person of some status. We can guess some of what's he's saying – but it's more likely 'behold, my dear sir' rather than 'feast your eyes, excellency!' Because the relative restraint of the Maestro's arm movements is telling us that this visitor, while important, is not here for enthusiasm. Even if they hadn't seen the pale face, they'd know this isn't the Sultan. This person is for money. And the fact that the Maestro spends less time bending close to the visitor and more time pointing out details of the circus that may be inaccurate but at least sound authoritative tells us that he's not conjuring dreams for a potential backer – *Only people of imagination and culture such as your good self can truly know how the circus speaks to the he-yuman spirit – Why, all them Roman Emperors, they knew, didn't they? – A byword, ain't it?* – but demonstrating the impressiveness and correctness of what a backer has already paid for. We strongly suspect that the Maestro has said: 'Behold, my dear sir, *your* circus'. Long before the first rumours reach us, and among them perhaps the truth, we know this is the senior German diplomat in Marrakech.

The Maestro and his visitors disappear. The afternoon heat slumps over the circus.

After half an hour, Eva is summoned.

The Maestro and his Visitor are sitting on folding chairs in the shade of a wagon. The German representative from Mogador sits a little behind them. He attempts a reassuring smile at Eva. It is buried behind the presence of the man in front.

There's no chair for Eva.

The Visitor is looking at a paper in his hand, and then glancing at the paper in the Maestro's hand. Eventually he looks up. His face seems to sag: the top is a bony dome, with a very clipped rim of fair hair; all the flesh has fallen into his jowls, which bulge out from behind a moustache. He looks permanently disappointed by the world.

'Dancer', the Maestro says.

'Dancer?' the Visitor says. 'In a circus?'

'Circus is a little empire, my dear sir. I pick up all sorts. It's the har-moany I was speaking of. The artistry of the ring-master is in combining the four elements: he-yumour, beauty, excitement, and wonder – earth, air, fire and water, d'you see? Ancient wisdom. We stand on the shoulders of giants.'

The Visitor has yet to find a firm footing. 'And so this dancing is..?'

'Arabian Nights, ain't it? The Mystic East! And so forth. The dance of the seven veils!'

The attempted reassurance doesn't improve the Visitor's expression. 'Nothing immoral, I trust', he says urgently. He glares darkly at Eva, expecting some spontaneous eruption of immorality at any moment.

'Immoral? The very thought of it! Artistic, ain't it? And all very correct, all very seemly. It's – It's all them veils, ain't it? And classical music, of course; very classical.'

'I must repeat, Professor:' – this at least Eva notices. The Maestro thinks that Europeans prefer a professor; non-Europeans get a baron, and even once a prince – 'this audience is Muslim. The strictest standards of public decency. The slightest misjudgement or mis-step could have... the most serious consequences for public order.'

Nice to have a sense of power, Eva thinks. Aloud she says: 'Is it my breasts you're bothered about?'

The three men stare at her.

It is now.

Eva wanders off. She can hear the Visitor saying: 'We are men of the world.' Yes, she thinks, you surely are. 'We know what happens with actresses, dancers, women of this type. There must be the strictest restrictions...'

Under a tree, some of the men are playing cards. Eva settles next to Olga. The two of them re-adjust until their shoulders blend comfortably.

Olga says: 'The Maestro get a good price for you?'

'Apparently I'm going to start a riot.'

'You could definitely do this.'

Eva shrugs. 'Helen of Troy started a war. Saying anything less is an insult.'

'You dance for Muslims before, Eva?'

She shrugs again. 'I've danced for men.'

Salomon sucks his teeth. 'Funny attitudes, some of these places.'

'Your lions tell the difference between Christians and Muslims?'

Salomon cackles. 'Jews maybe; depending which end they start.'

'You have care, little Eva', Shevzod seems to have recovered from his headache, but he's slumped against a crate with his eyes closed. 'Maybe Sultan will steal you for his harem.' She can feel Olga shifting, interested.

'I've had twenty-seven proposals of marriage,' Eva says, 'and the best was a violin teacher.'

'No,' says Olga, 'the best was the man in Prague with the toy-shop.'

'Either way, I'm saying a Sultan's worth thinking about.'

The thought is lost in a disagreement among the card-players. As usual, confusion about whether the 2 of Clover with the red blob on it is the Ace of Hearts or the Queen of Tiles has led to unhappiness.

Olga settles into her shoulder again. 'You should have married the toy-shop man', she says quietly.

Eva nods at the wagons and crates herded in the dirt, the little cauldron of funny-looking men grumbling and pointing at each other's cards. 'And give up all this? If I was going to marry anyone, I should have married the violin man. Nice hands. Nicer breath.'

'Toy-shop man had nicer manners.' Quieter: 'You should have married one of them, anyway.'

'You think I'm immoral too?' It's an old argument and, as she prepares to go at it again like a battered boxer staggering into the ring for another round, she feels anger and weariness lurching inside her. 'All the ex-dancers I've ever known were miserable creatures.' Madame coughing herself to death in Biarritz. That terrifying painted creature in Berlin, La Précieuse. Dixon, the American whore, rotten and ghastly behind her wall of make up.

Olga runs a finger-nail along her thigh. 'I think one day your wonderful legs get tired. And I think those women are sad because they think of themselves as ex-dancers, instead of something new.'

'I choose not to think about it. I don't have to.'

Olga leaves her hand where it is, and lets her head fall against Eva's.

☽

JOURNAL OF THOMAS SOMERLEIGH

Klug's damned circus getting a few people steamed up. No Sultan or other official presence today, but the dips were gathered as usual and some kind soul took pity and found a spare receiving chamber and served us mint tea. Ray sitting next to Prudhomme, which was unusual in itself: in the past P. has discreetly referred to R. as more African than European – touchy subject given Moorish history in Spain and Spanish history in Morocco – and R. has less discreetly called P. a too-old fish in a too-old collar. Ray opened up with polite enquiry to Klug about how his circus was settling in. Klug giving the impression of having better things to do elsewhere, but managed polite reply. Jolly good, continued Ray, and wished to take the opportunity to express the hope that the *Corps Diplomatique* could soon receive a list detailing the persons, livestock and special equipment that have entered the city under the auspices of the circus, and confirmation of where all would be lodged. A little pernickety, and Klug took it like a punch on the nose; general reply to the effect that he's delighted to discuss the circus anytime, though naturally the administrative details aren't his business and nor presumably any other diplomat's. Jolly good – Ray again – but given the very volatile situation in Marrakech we ought to be careful about the unregulated arrival of unusual elements: potential security issue. Plus of course exotic animals: public health issue.

One doesn't want to make too much fuss about a circus, for goodness' sake, but the point is a valid one. The potential for over-excitement from the circus is high, and all kinds of misunderstanding could arise from the aspect of foreign sponsorship. Prudhomme and I had touched on some of this at supper. I'm not sure how Marrakech's public health could get any worse than it already is, but that point's valid at least in principle too. Klug didn't seem to find them so. Repeated Germany's strong support for equal voice for all in guiding Moroccan affairs, and equal access for all in commercial enterprises, but presumed we weren't going to start producing and sharing inventories of all of our commercial players in Morocco. (Nice point of theology about the status of the circus: is it a purely commercial entity, or has it acquired any kind of diplomatic status from German sponsorship? is it a collection of people of business, or tourists, or livestock, or goods? were a rhinoceros of the circus to run amok and savage a child, who would be liable?)

I could see we were getting into choppy water. Klug obviously nettled to have pulled off his great wheeze and get heckling rather than applause. But his replies, though temperate, were tending – and this may even have been deliberate – to trespass on French sensibilities about her pre-eminence here. I thought it prudent to mediate a little. Recognize and admire Germany's initiative in getting the circus here, I said, G. deserves the credit for it, but would it make things easier if we looked at the oversight and management of it as an essentially Moroccan issue, and drew Moroccan attention to the security and health concerns? Germany quick off the mark: very glad to hear British endorsement of sovereign rights of Morocco, grateful for courteous British acknowledgement of German lead in this visit, and expecting to take no more than reasonable profile in proceedings given German financial and political sponsorship. Typical elaborate but unsubtle eloquence from Ray for Spain: it might seem over-optimistic to expect Morocco to start to take responsibility for the security and health of anything. Then at last Prudhomme weighed in: slight frown to Ray, cold dignity to Klug. Naturally it would be inappropriate to expect diplomats to become accountants and veterinarians of the commercial enterprises entering Morocco under their auspices or sponsorship. But it was precisely this uncertainty, and the impossibility of sharing detailed data, that made it essential to have a collective international oversight of the situation, rather than leaving things to chance or the Moroccans or putting an inappropriate expectation on any one Embassy. I fear he rather missed the emphasis of my remarks, and neither Klug nor Ray looked particularly cheerful, but it brought us in any case to an acceptable position on a principle of equality which changes nothing in practice.

Klug afterwards: the big eyes more anxious. Do I think there's something wrong with the circus? Have the other countries been talking about the German initiative? Is there a concerted effort to stop it? Poor chap quite worked up. I tried to reassure him: no suggestion of organized opposition, nothing at all really, but a few natural tactical concerns – and perhaps a bit of jealousy at his good idea. He's half-reassured: the anxiety eases in the eyes but the muscles are still thick in the neck, straining bullish at the collar. Circus must go ahead, must be a success; Sultan expects it, Berlin expects it.

And there it is. You don't want to shout the odds before you've checked the turf, but you do want to get the credit for a successful punt. He's had to sell the whole package to his Embassy in Tangier, and thus HQ in Berlin. But now the stakes are dramatically higher: if he hadn't mentioned it, and it had stayed as just an interesting idea discussed in far-off Marrakech, and there had subsequently been problems, Berlin wouldn't even have heard of it and no harm done. But he's had to get support, and so he's had to go large: Klug, coming man in German diplomacy, has bet the house on his circus; this is now career-defining stuff.

At the last, all the air goes out of him. The eyes are almost pleading. Hope we can work together on this, Dear Thomas; not looking for any favours, but Germany always relies on Britain to ensure fair play.

Walking away, after our friendly handshake, I wondered: how many careers are depending on this circus?

☉

After that first night of wildness, then a warm afternoon, and then a chilly evening, and the accumulated weariness of the journey through the desert, most of the circus has slept in the camp, huddled and wrapped in the familiar.

Morning has been cold again, and stiff, and surely the point of reaching the city was to escape the discomfort. In the thinner air of dawn, the story has spread more quickly that the Maestro took a wad of money off the Germans – *not so much the people I worries about, circus people is hardy people ain't it? as the diseases if they're with the animals too much* – to cover accommodation. Though himself now a sworn ascetic, one foot in paradise already, Jan the Pierrot leads the delegation of protestors after breakfast. The Maestro concedes quickly, and after brief consultation a fixed sum per person is agreed, *trust me my friends you'd be far better here, don't blame me when you're rat-eaten and rancid with all the plagues of Egypt, it's terrible things they say about the linen here.* Implicit in the deal is no questions being asked about the Maestro's accommodation.

The Maestro will still have taken a cut, and now he's saving on food and a lot of trouble, and if a few of the humans get permanently lost in the back-streets of Marrakech who's counting? As long as the giraffe doesn't go out whoring and end up as dinner, the circus will survive adequately.

The members of the circus wander out into Marrakech again, not sure if they've done the right thing. Miraculously, though, every person they meet is eager to show them a room he has available for rent, and miraculously the price can be haggled down to the same figure wherever they go, and whatever the room looks like: by chance the figure is exactly right for their allowance.

We pride ourselves on having outsmarted the meanest of landlords; we have endured the very worst accommodation in the whole of Europe and beyond. For every tale of fleas there is a tale of mice, of rats, of cats, of packs of feral dogs, even a tale of a wild boar. For every anecdote of penny-pinching there is a counter-anecdote of extortion, of 3 a.m. pillage, of highway robbery, and Olga sitting silently trying to forget bandits and dreaming of harems. So we're cynical about the young men with their lovely eyes and big smiles and insistent interest in where we come from and how welcome we are. We know to refuse the first thing they offer us, and the second, and then to find the critical flaw in the third, and then to tell them what we really want instead.

Because we have all day, because everything has miraculously assumed the same price, and because we are not allowed to see the things that are truly unavailable, we find ourselves able to wish for whatever we want and wait until we find it: the happy condition of a fairy-tale.

Jan the Pierrot disappears into the shadows, dreaming of a holy man and his cell. Johanna finds a wooden kiosk on a rooftop, elegant windows on all sides, so she can feel the wind whichever way it blows. Salomon finds a widowed seamstress and moves in with her, and they come to an arrangement about the money and everything else. At the end of a courtyard in the Jewish quarter is the stoutest bed in all Morocco, each post hewn from a whole tree, assembled where it stands because it was otherwise too big and heavy, and there lies Shevzod in mighty state, murmuring over and over 'no creak – think of it – no creak' and attended by a pair of beautiful awe-struck boys. Olga and Magda move into a set of rooms together, fresh white plaster walls and charming painted woodwork; Olga has a tiny inner room to herself, barely big enough for the bed, and Magda has the larger bedroom which controls access to it. Like servant, says Olga, or guard dog. Like whore-mistress, says Magda.

There has been discussion about Eva sharing with them. But: I don't want to be talking about ex-dancers for a while, she thinks; nice to escape them, just for a moment. When did I last have a place of my own?

The lovely-eyed over-courteous young men of Marrakech are happy to oblige.

Eva ignores them. She quickly stops even hearing them.

Lost in the wandering lanes of the east of the city, she sees a cat sprawled under a tree that grows out of a wall. The cat has found and occupied the last patch of direct sunlight left as the sun starts to move behind the crowd of buildings.

Life freezes in the sunlight. Dust caught in its rays, dust on the dry stones, frosts the scene. It is a still life, a theatrical tableau; a biscuit tin. And Eva finds herself transported into it. Able to look around. To smell: fertile things warmed up; something cooking; a sharp real tang from the tanneries nearby. She knows she must not break the moment. She must not challenge its reality with her own.

As cats will in the sun, the cat pulses and murmurs contentedly, like a heart at rest.

It's a moment before Eva notices that the cat is sitting on the feet of a girl, who squats in the shade against the tree-trunk, slowly chewing something. The girl has a cloth wrapped loose over her head, otherwise a slender bundle of skirts and rags.

Eva takes a step, and the cat is startled. It lifts its head, stares at her, then stands and trots across the cobblestones and pushes through a wooden door. The girl flexes her toes, and goes back to her chewing.

Eva steps cautiously forwards, trying to cling to fragments of the dream. Colour gleams through the cat's doorway, and she is drawn to it. A vivid yellow: a lemon tree. The door opens more fully as she approaches it, and an old woman is looking up at her.

They consider each other's realness a moment: the stumpy ancient raisin of a woman, heavily wrapped, and the pale-skinned fair-haired alien, her head and ankles bare. Then the old woman is beckoning her in.

The courtyard is tiny: she could not lie down in it, however idyllic the shade and scent of the lemon tree. But the door behind it leads to a little room heavy with shadows and fabrics.

Immediately a young man is there with them, genie-like, as always when you rub your purse. Miraculously, the price exactly suits her allowance. Life has made Eva sceptical of genies, and she hesitates, drifts back towards the door out of the courtyard. The old woman growls something; the price naturally includes breakfast, explains the genie. Eva's hand rests on the door frame: her fingertips trace the cracks in the wood, the crackling of ancient paint; her knuckles scrape cool against the stone. The old woman growls something else, and points across the street to the girl squatting under the tree. The price, says the man, also includes a maid.

The girl looks up. For twenty seconds there is a screeching exchange between the old woman and the young man and the girl – who, it becomes clear, doesn't know any of these people and has never been a maid – while Eva tries to hide among the different scents. Then the girl shrugs, and walks across the street and pushes past Eva into the courtyard with a nod of the head and then squats down under the lemon tree. She goes back to chewing what looks like a date. The cat, pleased to have re-summoned her, settles back onto her feet.

☉

In the café on the corner, where the maze of alleys that make up Marrakech market empties onto the great square, the corner where the dried apricots glow, morning is at its busiest and hottest. The square seems to have become a camp for fugitives and refugees. Hungry, they have drifted in from the villages because there must be more bread in a city. Scared, they have fled here because hunger has made the tribes savage and the villages are not safe. Frustrated in every part of their life, they want to be where things happen. Everyone knows that it feels better to be in a crowd. Together we are bigger and stronger and louder. Also, in a world where being noticed gets you a cut throat or an eternity in a cell of darkness and rats and shit, I prefer to do my shouting in a big group; here, maybe, next to this tall fellow. Everyone is trying to escape something; and here comes just one more.

After the first bustle of morning and as the heat begins to thicken, the rhythms of the royal palace slow. It is his habit, in this lull, to walk out into the city and to drink a tea with his acquaintances. Today he feels he must get something off his chest; they will understand him, and advise him. His anxiety signals seriousness and sincerity before he has opened his mouth, and by some instinct of harmony they let a silence swell until he is ready.

Not to be indiscreet, but my brother's daughter: she is... not at home. It has been... some time. She has no reason to be outside. She has... gone.

God is greatest, and in his wisdom he gives no end to the worries of a man. How is your brother's shop?

We've never known the city like this: so hungry, so angry; anything is possible.

The Sultan and the Caliph are both trying to use the tribes for their own ends: bandits wander freely in the streets and think they can't be touched; a man isn't safe from insult.

Women are seen in the streets more freely these days: what can you expect?

Prostitution's out of control now there are so many foreigners here.

How old is she? Fifteen. Ah. Has anyone seen anything, or heard anything? Everyone will have seen something. Has she done anything like this before? This is my family we're talking about. Was she maybe in the habit of meeting someone? My brother has eyes and the door has a lock. Yes but: girls. No but: not her.

It's witchcraft: this is a cursed city now. It's the tribes. The foreigners. The slaves. The Jews.

It's women.

Have you spoken to a judge? Speak of this – to an outsider? But they might investigate. Pffff.

His acquaintances gaze sadly at him. Each of them knows the truth. Better to say: each of them knows a truth. But the endless trials of a man with a wife or a daughter are to be respected. They owe him a silence, for suffering what they hope not to.

He has shared. He has been understood. The proper order is restored. The girls will continue to disappear this spring.

Or perhaps this particular conversation takes place in the tannery, where men with ruined legs trample old flesh in poison for ever.

◎

JOURNAL OF THOMAS SOMERLEIGH

More hours in the diplomatic undergrowth; a bit hole-and-corner, perhaps, though there's always a thrill when things seem to be hotting up. What one's in the game for, I suppose. Nice to feel one fits.

I was sharing a smoke with my Italian and American colleagues, when there was a little cough and a bow beside me: a figure in Moroccan court robes. Took me a moment to recognize him, but that sort of thing always goes down well: one tries not to be the type who thinks all foreigners are the same. The new arrival was a vizier to the Caliph: i.e. technically on the Sultan's brother's team, based permanently in Marrakech rather than just here in H.M.'s retinue.

He drew me aside and pulled a paper out of the folds of his robes. (Probably got a whole filing cabinet's worth in there, and an inkwell.) This turned out to be the day's edition of the Marrakech version of the official gazette: published decisions and so forth, all copied out by hand in the most beautiful and most minuscule Arabic script. Further to previous preliminary conversations I had had about the tea trade, his chief wished the esteemed British Representative to see this latest regulation on the procedures for the monitoring of imported tea, perhaps not the most exciting news in the world but Britain should see this as a sign of good faith preparatory to any final agreement we are able to conclude, and perhaps of interest for the esteemed B. R. to be aware that any such agreement would likewise be published in this way. Here it is, he said, down between the new arrangements for the supervision of the circus and the thing about who can slaughter which animals where, perhaps the esteemed B.R. has already learned enough of our alphabet to see the letters for 'tea'.

A bit of procedural rigour around import is genuinely good news for Britain, and shall be reported as such to Tangier. Genuine credit for Somerleigh there, good nuts-and-bolts stuff. But naturally I was alert to that casual reference to the circus. Jolly exciting business that, I said, offhand-like; out of interest what sort of details does it give about the circus? Really just an administrative detail, says my pal: a generous loan by the German Government has enabled the temporary enhancement of His Majesty the Sultan's household retinue to the tune of one circus.

Well now... It'll only get a passing reference in the wire for Tangier, but of course it played bigger this evening: supper *chez* Prudhomme, Round Two.

The family as before, plus self, plus Ray – Prudhomme noticeably more attentive to Spain, ever since Klug started rocking the boat by dumping a circus in it – plus a French doctor who lives here in Marrakech. Supper itself strictly according to the manual: mainly the doctor talking about health conditions in the city, and a couple of fruity stories about folk traditions in different parts of Africa. Self seated next to Madame: a generous honour, and no doubt Sir G. and Youssef would both approve. Though this meant Ray got to sit next to the excellent Hortense; he's as charming as they come, of course, so probably made the most of it, the brute.

We only got onto business once the ladies had left us to it, and the doctor chappie had pushed off to check on some critical patient. Prudhomme opened with general comment about how we need to make sure that the circus, now apparently such an excitement for H.M., is managed in a way that doesn't rock the status quo as regards international oversight of Morocco. Now, France and Spain have of course been jostling for yonks over what the status quo looks like; but for now we all seem to be tolerating the position that what it is is better than what it might be.

Anyway, this was the moment to uncover my howitzer: Interesting you should say that, says I, for Klug seems to have snuck a measure through the administrative system getting the circus badged as part of H.M.'s household. Much sucking of teeth and ay-ay-ay from Ray, cold glare from Prudhomme. I had to hit the point: much harder for the rest of us to intervene in oversight of the circus now. Ray and I waited for the official French reaction. Prudhomme sat in silence a time, one fingernail tapping incessantly at a tooth. We shall see, he said at last; we shall see.

That was about that. Prudhomme suggested it was perhaps unlikely we'd see the ladies again tonight, but he would be happy to put some Gounod (?) on the gramophone and chat some more. Ray's refusal was almost polite enough – he blurted a collection of words which included references to long days, early starts and dangerous back streets, without actually saying anything coherent – and I felt that if he was going I ought as well. Farewells on the doorstep, then Prudhomme remembered he'd something extra to say to me on the new importation regulation, and Ray left us to it. What Prudhomme really wanted to say, it transpired, was thanks for the active and constructive British voice at the moment: France had been feeling a little alarmed at the direction of events, but if there's good Anglo-French co-ordination and collaboration hopefully most of the others will behave themselves. All grist to my mill, of course, and Tangier shall get a version of the French attitude; I managed a humble acknowledgement that I hope adequately mixed personal courtesy to him and some sense of London's attitude to protecting the *Entente*. And then Madame and Mademoiselle re-appeared, and I was persuaded to stay for a cordial.

And jolly cordial it was. Very much on a whim I'd come with little gifts for the two ladies. Not necessary for what was still essentially a diplomatic invitation, and I've had some chiefs would have considered it actually contrary to protocol; O'Neill viewed personal sentiment towards diplomatic acquaintances much as he viewed fornication. Anyway, I'd found a little carved wooden head business lying around, and that did for Madame – icon of wisdom and tradition in the local culture, that sort of thing – and with rare inspiration I'd thought to find out that my poet acquaintance Brahim had published a little volume of his stuff. I assured Hortense it was just a curiosity, given her interest: unless her Arabic was much better than mine, I said, there couldn't be any question of anything inappropriate in it, and I'd checked and there weren't any pictures.

For a moment I thought I'd overstepped: Prudhomme's expression suggested what he thought about Arabic poetry, and Madame's what she thought about any poetry if given to her daughter, but my reassurances just about did the trick. Sincere appreciation at my having thought to bring gifts, and Hortense clutched the book of verse to her chest and then began picking through it commenting on how pretty the Arabic script was. That had been at the start of the evening and, whatever the parents' initial reaction, it had set the tone for the end. Definitely pleasant, I'd say. A shade more relaxed, more familiar. Hortense, a little pert, asked what the men had been talking about. Prudhomme brushed it off, but then she asked what the Sultan was really like.

'Oh', said Prudhomme, 'he's a ridiculous little monkey!' Rather farther than I'd have gone, but interesting to see the French collar unbuttoned. 'Really, in physiognomy as well as behaviours, a little monkey! Jabbering and tinkering with his absurd collection of European souvenirs. A state of permanent infantilism.' Souvenirs? asked Hortense, and he listed some of the more notorious curiosities in H.M.'s collection: the billiard table, the bagpipes, the elaborate carriage he was pulled around in once and left out in the rain, the animals, the underclothing. I'd never go as far as to call Hector Prudhomme playful, but it was amusing – and I think significant – to be allowed to see him *en famille*. Hortense wide-eyed and most entertained and the more charming for it. She then asked me for my opinion, but I wasn't to be caught out – neither in excess nor in any divergence from her father. As ever, I find it best on these occasions to imagine Sir Edward Grey standing at my shoulder. 'Oh, he's a decent enough fellow', I said. 'Inexperienced, and that's why he must depend on France' – courteous nod to papa – 'and others of us for advice.'

Otherwise we didn't really talk about anything, just this and that and what the desert air does to the sinuses, but: pleasant. At one point Prudhomme started fretting he'd run out of cigarettes in the presentation box and nipped out to find the reserves, and Madame declared she needed to get the servants sorted for the end of the evening and the morning, and that left Hortense and I alone together for a couple of minutes. She was a picture: the delicate features, the smart outfit, sitting there with such poise; it hit her that we'd wound up alone together, and for a moment she just sat there, gazing at the candle, not daring to look at me, tiny smile, breathing rather hard, a sense of such excitement held tight in. Eventually – head half-turned, still not quite looking at me – she said again how grateful she was for the poetry book, and how very rare it was to find someone who paid attention to her interests and was so kind accordingly. To which I said – spur of the moment, rush of blood to the head – that it was so rare to find someone who inspired one to buy books of poetry. Then Papa and Mama were back with fistfuls of cigarettes and renewed concerns about *les pipes*, respectively.

Definite spring in the old step, walking home. She's charming, surely she is; and given how isolated and thrown together we all are out here, I must be in with a shout if I feel like pushing the thing. Bit of a step: with the family around, it would have to get rather formal rather quickly. Definitely charming. Surely.

☪

It looks as though the circus is going to have to rediscover itself each morning. It's not unheard of, this business of having different accommodation spread over a place, but it's not usual. We're used to the circus being more of our life, more of the twenty-four hours. We're comfortably familiar with each other's habits: knowing when the lions tend to be more restive, who picks their teeth during meals, who snores. We've hardened, or deafened, ourselves to the chatter of those who annoy us. As if finding our way round a room in the dark, we recognize our days by the old rituals and remarks and irritations we bump into.

No timetable has been set: the circus must be exact precision during performance, and so tends to extra casualness outside it. Eva drifts into the camp late in the morning. She finds herself accounting it: here are the horses, gently restive on the grassless ground; here – yes – is the purring of the lions, from deep in the earth; here is Jan, his daily discipline of the juggling clubs, his personal form of meditation; here is the chaos of discarded crates and the satisfaction of carefully-coiled ropes; here is the smell of shit; here is the smell of meat.

Normally she doesn't pay attention to the faces. Normally she has seen all that they have seen, has absorbed everything they have felt. Now the reappearance of each face invites a question about its absence. Johanna: has slept well, in her breezes, and is in good humour because she has been with her horses already and they are content. Salomon: his face looks strained beyond his habitual worry, and she suspects some evening of excess has made him late in visiting his lions. Shevzod: hasn't showed up yet. She sees the others seeing her, interrogating her face in the same way. Instinctively she tries to perform innocence; then wonders if she'd rather they suspect her of some little debauchery, back in those alleys.

Mama Zana is sitting on the step of her wagon, looking even heavier than normal and a little gloomy. She's found fresh bread and fresh fruit, but she doesn't know if there's supposed to be lunch and if anyone will come. Eva settles cross-legged in front of her, and Mama Zana slaps a kiss on her forehead as Eva hoped she would.

'What's going round, Mama?' The usual question, the usual shrug of reply lurching up through the big body. 'We play tonight?' Another shrug, then a shake of the head. 'When do we play?'

'Maestro don't know. Maestro not control so much this trip, maybe. Maestro pretend he cross, Maestro do what they say. Then little Eva not hungry.'

From within the folds of her she produces a peach and hands it over. It's warm, and seems to suck at Eva's lips.

Eva finds a square of flat firm ground, secluded enough among the wagons on the far side of the camp. She strips down to the minimum, to feel loose and not too hot. She stretches and tests her body, greeting and reacquaintance. She works through some sequences. Warming down afterwards, she wonders what Marrakech dancing is like. As usual, she wonders how frequently she must dance to call herself a dancer.

☾

JOURNAL OF THOMAS SOMERLEIGH

We shall see, Prudhomme had said. And today we did. *Pro forma* invitation had come round – bureaucratic rather than fancy – from the French office to a chat about security policy for the city in the current period. Not the most festive of prospects, but not something to which one can say no.

I'd expected more grip from Hector Prudhomme; he's never slow to play the first among equals. But today he started rather quiet. No suggestion of formality, no proper chairing of the meeting. The preliminary chat drifted on, and then Prudhomme said to me: 'Dear Thomas, what was it you were saying the other evening, about the security concerns in the city during the presence of His Majesty and the diplomatic corps?' For the life of me I couldn't remember what he was talking about. But that didn't make any difference, as I wouldn't necessarily have repeated it even if I'd remembered it. Lesson: it's not what you said, it's what you say you said. I improvised a quick *tour d'horizon* of the security questions as I see them – marauding tribes, brigandage, public order, petty crime, public health, food supply, etc. Pretty crisp, if I do say so myself, and it will read very crisply in the wire for Tangier. General nods of agreement; sort of thing I do well. This started a bit of general chat around those themes. Then Ray asked whether we thought the Sultan was up to managing any of it. McKenna added a bit about the particular question of H.M.'s authority this far from the capital, with the competing authority of his brother and the local chiefs. And we went round the houses on that for a bit. Then Klug noted that he assumed we were all committed to supporting H.M.'s independence and authority, and we all agreed, and we agreed that we needed actively to be using our influence to that end.

That seemed more or less that, and I surely wasn't the only one wondering if it was time to escape for a quiet cigarette and a bit of lunch, when Prudhomme added that that reminded him – good you prompted it, dear Ernst – how very pleased he was to read the announcement that the administration of the excellent circus initiative had now been formalized within the Sultan's household. Commendable German efficiency and propriety – dear Ernst nodded warily – It meant that, given the diplomatic community's established semi-formal role in overseeing the security of the independent Morocco, we would now be able to exercise a prudent oversight to make sure that the circus had the positive effect that everyone hoped.

Ray then wondered – unusual energy from him – whether we oughtn't to have some sort of semi-formal group to discuss these issues, for as long as the risk is more apparent. Sort of a sub-committee of the informal Ambassadors' group in Tangier, as he put it. He asked if Prudhomme wouldn't mind taking the chair, to mirror the French pre-eminence in Tangier. Well, coming from Spain towards France that was unusually collegial, and it seemed the kind of idea that would go down well with Sir G., being so consistent with the Foreign Secretary's guidance etc etc, and so let the record show that Britain jumped in and seconded the motion.

The stable door had been kicked open and the horse was halfway out of the yard already, but Klug had to try. Red-faced and eyes popping and fighting to control his voice, he just about managed a line to the effect that Germany was totally committed to the cause of security in an independent Morocco, Germany more than most, and colleagues' support always gratefully received, but pretty irregular to start interfering in any bilateral commercial or diplomatic enterprises, very slippery slope.

Prudhomme just welcomed all that, France and Germany as one on the points of principle. Meanwhile, on the technical point of international oversight of potentially disruptive activities by the Sultan's household, France willing to take the chairmanship for the time being. As ever, he who sums up wins. Klug's ruse of getting the circus into the Royal household has backfired on him.

I've decided I must bite the bullet and reciprocate the Prudhomme hospitality. Back in Tangier I'd have half a dozen reliable restaurants to use, but there's nothing like that here as far as I'm aware. The dive in which the Embassy have stowed me hasn't got one tenth the stuff necessary to host an adequate supper. So afternoon tea it shall have to be.

I spent the best part of an hour trying to explain afternoon tea to Youssef. It was not a success. I'm not sure he's familiar with the idea of sitting at table, he's never shown any understanding of cutlery, and for fear of giving myself a seizure I had to abandon trying to establish mutual agreement on the concept of a sandwich. Finally, in exasperation, I went back to first principles and explained that Monsieur the French representative would be here, right here in this chair here, at x time and date, and that with him would be Madame and indeed Mademoiselle, and by the way did anything strike Youssef about the number of chairs currently in the room are they supposed to sit in each other's laps, and what the hell were we going to do about it?

Youssef's eyes went wide, and he grabbed my hand and shook it enthusiastically as if I'd announced I was engaged or we'd won a war. 'Very good!' he exclaimed: his one sure English phrase. Then he added 'Excellency!', and then he turned and rushed out. So apparently I'm back in his good books, but still haven't got anywhere with the one thing he actually needs to do.

☪

Eva has started to notice something new, as she walks the back-streets of Marrakech. She tries to grasp what it is, but everything is so elusive here.

It's not that the streets feel familiar. The endless fading pink stone, the veils of dust and ghostly kidnapped sunbeams, the gowned figures almost appearing and forever disappearing in doorways, the sudden eruptions of chanting out of the sky, the unexpected dogs and cats: all of this will always be alien. Marrakech can never be known: even on a clear-headed purposeful morning like today, the city is a blurred impression over her shoulder, the uncomfortable nostalgia for a fairy-tale, a murmuring out of a dream. It's not that she knows her way, because she has now established quite clearly – her whole life has been a counting of steps, a cultivated awareness of the space around her – that these alleys never lead to the same place two days running. She's always stepping cautiously under spindly wooden scaffolding, around eruptions of unfinished cobblestones; presumably they remake the alleys every night. Doors, heavy wood or fine, intricate carving or fat iron studs, are always opening onto something different, curtains are swept aside and fingers and spices beckon her in because in here is what you want, Mademoiselle. This city, this shadowed doorway, this moment is exactly whatever you want. Finding your way in Marrakech is a work of meditation, not map-reading.

I have a million tales, says Ali the story-teller, eyes glistening in the firelight, arms stretching puny out of his djellaba to embrace the whole world of his audience. I have one tale, he says, with a million paths, and every night it takes a new turn so even if you came here every night

Monsieur you would never hear the same thing twice. Then again, you would never be the same person twice. Now, where was I?

Eva stops. She keeps walking past this spot. This branch, emerging frustrated and ambitious from some unseen tree the other side of this wall. She puts her hand on it, feels its muscles and wrinkles. There is some strong scent coming over the wall, herb or spice. Also, the warm greasy tang of cooking: the kitchen round the corner which seems to serve as breakfast canteen for the men on their way to open up their stalls. Also, animals: their shit; their fur.

This place is hers. No; never. For the time being, she is its. For as long as she has a room here and a bed here, every day whatever she does she will always be heading home.

The first day she returned to her little room in her little courtyard, it reeked of some sharp detergent, over-generously scrubbed everywhere. Quickly the smells of the woodwork, the musty fabrics, the tree from the courtyard, recaptured the space. When she woke after her first night, a mischievous feeling of luxury as much from the sense of possession as the impossibly white sheets, and took the two barefoot steps over the flagstones to open the shutter, she learned that her unexpected maid would be sleeping wrapped in a blanket at the foot of her bed.

℧

JOURNAL OF THOMAS SOMERLEIGH

Tea Day. Prudhomme's a funny stick, one of the funniest. I suppose I fear, given his relative seniority, that any perception of diplomatic underperformance by Somerleigh while gallivanting in Marrakech will find its way back to Sir G. (French Ambassador to Sir G. over the brandy: 'I hear from my worthy Prudhomme that your youngster very kindly gave the most *amusing* tea-party…' Ghastly.) And – be honest – it feels important to seem competent in front of the fair Hortense. Not fussy, not particularly charming, certainly not; just… reliably unruffled.

But my last desperate attempts to explain necessaries to Youssef went nowhere. Utter incomprehension. Utter indifference. Almost sacked the blighter on the spot. Just the same enthusiastic 'Very good, excellency!' and then I had to dash off to a meeting of the wretched committee on the security of the wretched circus.

We were at Ray's temporary residence here: great barn of a place in pretty desperate repair. As ever, interesting to note how the different Embassies support their junior officials when in Marrakech. Ray has a residence theoretically fitting one of the old colonial powers of Morocco – while I have a residence fitting a mediocre shopkeeper – but it's not been renovated or apparently even cleaned since before the Moors crossed into Spain. No wonder he spends all his time in the cafés and the night-spots. Elaborate welcome from him. Then Prudhomme, as chairman, very much playing it down. Manifestation of the concert of Europe playing its proper role to manage the appropriate independence of Morocco, good habit to discuss the circus, given its potential to provoke unrest or – more worryingly – public enthusiasm; perhaps even a force for good, if managed properly. But nothing to discuss today as far as he was aware. Anything dear Ernst wanted to discuss or present? Obviously not. Any other business? Then – afterthought, more an aside from Prudhomme to Ray – if everyone's getting worried about lions running amok and acrobats spreading diseases, do we have an accurate list of the animals and persons involved? Presumably available, now that formally part of the Sultan's household. Ray looks blank, and then at Klug.

Perhaps dear Ernst is the man with the answers? Dear Ernst can't say no.

I hurried off to the market, desperate for inspiration for my blasted tea. No inspiration to be had at any price. After a fraught hour, running late, I hurried back with a paper bag of some rather lurid sweet biscuits, I as well as the biscuits hot and shaken up.

I almost missed my house. I thought I'd got pretty familiar with the street, over the last weeks, but it was different now. Either a new building had sprung up, or a pretty serious restoration: what looked like fresh stonework, gleaming wooden door, and a smart-looking chap standing by it.

'Very good, excellency!' he said, and turned to open my door for me.

My sense of being in the wrong place only grew. What passes for my courtyard is a rather gloomy little cell of grey stone and rotting vegetation where cats come to die. I found myself in a pleasant, even charming little space, light and verdant. Four handsome wooden chairs around an elegant metal table. Still bewildered, I hurried into the house. 'I assume we're having tea at the table inside?' I said over my shoulder, trying to get the message clear without seeming too autocratic. But Youssef didn't understand. And we didn't have tea inside. In the kitchen there was a woman I'd never met before, big and well-wrapped in the traditional style and bustling around. I started trying to find out who on earth she was and to give some instructions, but she didn't apparently have a word of English nor, after a deep but very quick bow in my direction, any inclination to pay any attention to me. I held out the paper bag to her and started to explain, but she just snatched it and turned away to whatever she was doing. I was starting one last effort to impose some order when I heard Youssef calling. I never saw the biscuits again.

Youssef was escorting les Prudhommes into the courtyard, very regal-like, and I greeted them and they settled in the new chairs. Polite observation about the courtyard from Prudhomme – who probably has cupboards larger and in better repair. 'To be honest,' I said, 'it's one of the reasons I'm grateful for the visit. The prospect of Madame Prudhomme being here inspired me to tidy up a bit. Certain standards, you know, even the English, ha-ha.' Demure little nod from Madame, stronger approval from Monsieur. 'And to be more honest, it's mainly the work of my man here. He was desperately pleased when he found we had French visitors, quite made his week.' I felt it deserved saying, though it didn't seem to interest the Prudhommes.

And away we went. Pleasant occasion – the most refreshing mint tea, with a pot of the black stuff I normally drink available but untouched, rather forlorn next to a jug of the milk one can never normally get hold of – and some excellent almond biscuits and pieces of chopped date. Pleasant conversation, though I can't remember a word of it. The wire for Tangier shall report energetic British inter-mediation within the circle of European diplomats, inclining towards a reinforcement of French pre-eminence as mandated by London, underpinned by some dignified social cultivation of the relationship with the French representative and his wife. Have to mention the latter, partly because it will help convince Sir G. that I'm not whooping it up in the back-streets all the time, and also as the start of a no-doubt protracted bureaucratic procedure to bill the Embassy for the expenses of afternoon tea.

Early on I had to ask – I hope without seeming over-forward – about the absence of Hortense. A slight headache, said Madame; the heat, you know. Rather delicate, added Monsieur; asked us to send her regrets.

☬

The most notable resident of Marrakech, says Hector Prudhomme, is as it happens not His Majesty, though of course he remains the greatest and most venerated and I take this opportunity to emphasize France's determination to support and guide him to the fullest. Nor – and here we may imagine a little twinkle through the pince-nez, and a swelling in that tightly-corseted chest – is it a foreign diplomat. This, we infer, is not true – not if notability means civilization, world wisdom, *savoir-faire*. But we're in on the joke and – because Hector is our host and does have rather good wine – we put on a face that shows we dispute his self-deprecation but are going along with the hypothesis for entertainment's sake, and perhaps our own chest swells a little as we wonder if we might be the second-most notable resident of Marrakech. Or is it the third? The wine and the hypothesis and the rather elaborate rhetorical construction of this bit make it hard to be sure now.

No, my dear friend, says Cher Hector, the most notable resident of Marrakech is a filthy street boy who exists only in the gutter of that monstrous square of theirs and tells stories. The story-tellers, as you know, are much admired here, both entertainers and fortune-tellers, and this wretched lad is esteemed the greatest of them. Ali is his name – Ali, of course, was one of the first and one of the youngest of the followers of the Moslem Prophet. Anyway – perhaps here Prudhomme's cheroot has gone out, and we must wait while he relights it, trying to hold the amused anticipation on our face – the boy Ali tells the following most charming story.

Once upon a time there was a Sultan. We do not say his name, because to be too precise about this might offend some people. He was – do you see? – a terrible ruler: stupid, brutal and debauched, the epitome of the excess that unrestraint can lead to. Fortunately the Lord took him soon, for the Lord knows what He's doing. There was the usual kerfuffle about succession, a certain amount of tension, bloodshed, that sort of thing. But at last a successor emerged. This fellow, now, was a very different sort of animal: his virtues and qualities promised considerable improvement for the country.

The problem was that the appalling standards of the previous reign, and the chaos of the succession, had led to anarchy. The population was in a condition of permanent riot. Culture and learning and civility – it's all only skin-deep, of course – had been quite forgotten. Any new ruler who presented himself to govern might just as easily find himself torn apart by the mob. So even the most wise and skilful of men might feel trepidation as he took the throne. But now that the successor had emerged, and everyone knew that he had emerged, the crowds began to gather outside the royal palace, and it was unavoidable that soon the new Sultan must show himself to them – or find himself thrown out before he had even properly stepped in.

On the first day of his reign, the new Sultan summoned the wise men of the city to his presence. Already they were anxious. 'You must present yourself to the representatives of the people, great lord,' they said, 'even at the risk of them finding you unacceptable.'

'Have this announcement made known to them:' replied the Sultan. 'Today the Sultan is consulting his advisors.'

Well, the wise men glanced at each other, uneasy at this and wondering if the Sultan's advisors were likely to get caught up in the inevitable bloodshed; but naturally they did as they were bidden.

On the second day, these advisors grew yet more anxious. 'You must present yourself to the representatives of the people, great lord,' they said, 'even at the risk of them finding you unacceptable.'

'Have this announcement made known to them:' replied the Sultan. 'Today the Sultan is studying the books of learning passed down to us by our ancestors.'

Well, the advisors glanced at each other, uneasy at this; but naturally they did as they were bidden.

On the third day, the advisors grew yet more anxious. 'You must present yourself to the representatives of the people, great lord,' they said, 'even at the risk of them finding you unacceptable.'

'Have this announcement made known to them:' replied the Sultan. 'Today the Sultan is studying the geography and economics of his realm.'

Well, the advisors glanced at each other, uneasy at this; but naturally they did as they were bidden.

On the fourth day, the advisors grew yet more anxious. 'You must present yourself to the representatives of the people, great lord,' they said, 'even at the risk of them finding you unacceptable.'

'Have this announcement made known to them:' replied the Sultan. 'Today the Sultan is meeting with the professors and doctors and judges of our country, and is giving them his instructions.'

Well, the advisors glanced at each other, uneasy at this; but naturally they did as they were bidden.

On the fifth day, the advisors grew yet more anxious. 'You must present yourself to the representatives of the people, great lord,' they said, 'even at the risk of them finding you unacceptable.'

'Have this announcement made known to them:' replied the Sultan. 'Today the Sultan is consulting the emissaries of all of our neighbours, and all the great powers of Europe.'

Well, the advisors glanced at each other, uneasy at this; but naturally they did as they were bidden.

On the sixth day, the advisors grew yet more anxious. 'You must present yourself to the representatives of the people, great lord,' they said, 'even at the risk of them finding you unacceptable.'

'Have this announcement made known to them:' replied the Sultan. 'Today the Sultan is listening to some of our traditional musicians.'

Well, the advisors glanced at each other, uneasy at this; but naturally they did as they were bidden.

On the seventh day, the advisors grew yet more anxious. 'You must present yourself to the representatives of the people, great lord,' they said, 'even at the risk of them finding you unacceptable.'

'Have this announcement made known to them:' replied the Sultan. 'Today the Sultan is spending time with his first-born son.'

Well, the advisors glanced at each other, uneasy at this; but naturally they did as they were bidden.

On the eighth day, the advisors grew yet more anxious. 'You must present yourself to the representatives of the people, great lord,' they said, 'even at the risk of them finding you unacceptable.'

'Have this announcement made known to them:' replied the Sultan. 'Today the Sultan is devoting his attentions to his favourite wife.'

Well, the advisors glanced at each other, uneasy at this; but naturally they did as they were bidden.

On the ninth day, the advisors grew yet more anxious. 'You must present yourself to the representatives of the people, great lord,' they said, 'even at the risk of them finding you unacceptable.'

'Have this announcement made known to them:' replied the Sultan. 'Today the Sultan is taking a bath, so that he is at his cleanest before he meets his people.'

Well, the advisors glanced at each other, uneasy at this; but naturally they did as they were bidden.

On the tenth day, the advisors' anxiety was unrestrained. 'We beseech you, great lord,' they said on their knees, 'you must present yourself to the representatives of the people, even at the risk of them finding you unacceptable.'

'Have this announcement made known to them:' replied the Sultan. 'Today the Sultan is at prayer.'

Well, the advisors glanced at each other, uneasy at this; but naturally they did as they were bidden.

The next day the advisors came to the Sultan with a message: the representatives of the people had knocked at the palace gate, and were seeking permission to present themselves to their Sultan, to see if he would find them acceptable.

☬

The maid has been avoiding her.

Eva has never had a maid; perhaps this is what they're supposed to do. Then again, she's not had the impression that the girl has ever been a maid. They're both pretending.

Eva hasn't been a maid either. She doesn't have many sources of inspiration for how to be a woman with a maid. She realizes that her poses of authority – pretending not to see the person pretending to be invisible, making great shows of gratitude for trivialities while quickly taking for granted the more sordid basics, playing grandly along until some inconvenience switches her to irrational irritation – are borrowed from her sense of what it's like to be a man. All men find servants, one way or another.

It quickly becomes silly.

Eva catches the startled girl by the arm, and sits her down. One sitting on the only chair, one on the only bed, their knees are touching. Eva is suddenly aware of the difference between the thigh of a relatively well-nourished and exceptionally well-exercised European dancer and the thigh of a malnourished Moroccan street girl. There's not much difference in height, but Eva feels like an elephant next to this bundle of sticks wrapped in a sheet.

The girl is still alarmed. This isn't part of anyone's game of woman-and-maid.

'Hallo', Eva says. The girl looks up, wary of being blinded by this European sun. Her eyes are large and very dark. *How has she learned this fear?* What aspect of Eva, who has never considered herself particularly intimidating, inspires such deference? *Given how ridiculously vast I am, she must imagine I'm going to eat her.*

'Name?' says Eva. 'Nom?' She points clumsily to herself. 'Eva.' The girl watches uneasily. More pointing, the incomprehensible word repeated. 'E-v-a.' I-am-going-to-eat-you. She points at the girl.

'Assia'

'Ah. Hallo Assia.' Again pointing to herself: 'Eva.'

A nod. 'Mam'zelle.'

It seems terribly hard work to be a kind man with a servant.

◍

JOURNAL OF THOMAS SOMERLEIGH

Another meeting of the good old circus committee. Hope this isn't going to become too frequent a business. For the first time, I think, little Abdelilah actually sitting among us – instead of fussing endlessly in the background. Once he'd seen all his foreigners properly seated, it turned out there was still an empty chair, and this he took – rearranging his robes carefully as he sat, readjusting some unknowable under-robes, and then from within them drawing out a fine-carved box, which he opened to reveal a fountain pen.

Prudhomme opened. Hoped the meetings aren't going to become too frequent a business. But he emphasized the importance, and it's hard to disagree. Note to self: worth emphasizing to Tangier, too – Marrakech not a side-show, and Somerleigh in the thick of the action; more than deserving of an Embassy-funded afternoon tea or two. The stability and balance of Europe, said Prudhomme, are presently focused on the stability and balance of Morocco, as properly overseen by the Europeans. None of us wishes to do anything to disrupt this present harmony. Hear hear, called Klug. Prudhomme immediately double-checking what he'd said, so surprised was he to get German agreement on anything. Cautiously on: the stability and balance of Morocco now disproportionately dependent on the stable and balanced international management of the circus; the Sultan's circus, he added – nasty smile at Klug. On top of the dangers posed by wild and unsanitary animals wandering a crowded city without proper regulation, there needed to be very careful handling of any public activity by the circus, appearances as well as – very sombre face – performance. One should consider the effect on the public mood, the misunderstandings among a volatile and superstitious populace. One should consider the ways in which management of the circus might be exploited by the Sultan himself, and by those jostling for influence within his court – his brother the Caliph, and the chiefs of the south.

Poor chap just wants to see some acrobats, an unworthy part of me was thinking; but Prudhomme is right.

Given all this – we sat up, hopeful of some meaningful statement at last – he wished to emphasize the importance of avoiding any rash decision involving the circus, any rush to display any part of it.

Except, added Prudhomme, he was thinking to organize an informal diplomatic reception, naturally including some elements of the Sultan's court as usual, and this would include some personnel from the circus.

A small point of clarification, said Klug. Prudhomme immediately on the alert, the little eyes staring cold through the pince-nez. Technically, said Klug, the circus is part of His Majesty's household, not his court. It would be an intrusion on the independent decision-making of His Majesty to specify the members of his household to bring, rather unusually, to a diplomatic event. Even the slightest action brings costs – appropriate dress, and so forth.

Pained smile from Prudhomme. Confident that he would be able to encourage His Majesty to bring an appropriate representation from his household. The glare through those pince-nez could have cracked the Atlas.

Quite right, went on Klug, and Prudhomme turned redder. Klug thumped his Ace down on the table: as has been clearly acknowledged, every action by the circus is being funded by Germany; if the committee would submit a list of the circus members they wish to invite, Klug would hasten to seek authority from Berlin via Tangier to approve the necessary expenditure.

Wire from Tangier via Mogador. Oddly, it seemed to be verging on complimentary. Sir G.'s iffy cypher-work, no doubt. Full support your solid approach. Essential Britain upholds position of neutral and benign vegetables – can only guess Sir G. meant 'actor' or similar – and maintains firm partnership with Fiji – presumably France – while not alienating Germany. Social activities pursuant to diplomacy covered by Annex IV to Diplomatic Staff Regulations (version 1878).

Found myself dwelling, much more than I would have expected, on the absence of the charming Hortense from my surprisingly undisastrous afternoon tea. Playing out how it might have gone, had she been there: compliments I might have made, endearing to her while yet reassuring Madame as to my propriety; *bon mots* I might have produced, playing to Hector Prudhomme's intellect while impressing his daughter; how she might have reacted – the prettily-suppressed excitement, the sense of how daring and how pleasant it was to be so close to Thomas Somerleigh. Fat chance.

☪

In the café on the corner, where the maze of alleys that make up Marrakech market empties onto the great square, the corner where the monkey juggles walnuts, morning is at its busiest and hottest. Out of the great basin of the city, every living thing and every developing tale will eventually swirl into the square and be churned round and round and eventually swallowed. The square is the digesting of everything in Marrakech. The square is inevitable.

After the first bustle of morning and as the heat begins to thicken, the rhythms of the royal palace slow. It is his habit, in this lull, to walk out into the city and to drink a tea with his acquaintances. Today, he finds that he is not the centre of attention he would typically expect to be. He cannot even enter with his usual ease, for the rhythms of the café have somehow been unsettled.

Not to be indiscreet, but what are we supposed to do with a creature like this? Are we even permitted to talk to her? Is she just going to stand there all day?

She's definitely a she, no doubt about it. We're all men here, we've seen a few women in our time, and this is definitely one of them. But... Her hair is the colour of chestnut, or almond paste, or rubies, or fire, or blood. More importantly, her hair is visible. Her skin is pale: sickly; leprous. Her dress is an indoor dress that she has mistakenly worn outdoors. It is the indoor dress of a poor woman; none of our wives would be permitted anything so shabby. Her dress — and we're not looking, and we're not saying we've seen anything, it's just a statement of fact — her dress reveals her ankles. She's staring at us, shamelessly.

A woman in a café is a prostitute. This we know. But this one... well, she certainly isn't a very good prostitute.

We have heard stories about foreigners. In the stories, foreigners are always exotic, barbarian, primitive, clumsy, ridiculous. So that would fit. But that's just stories: they're not like that in real life, surely.

So logically, it's more likely she's a devil siren; Aïcha Kandicha herself probably. And what with the hair, and the ankles we've not seen, and the... the everything else, that would work. You could see how you – how some men – might be bewitched.

Also, thing like this, it's a grey area isn't it? You can never be quite sure how much some other world has drifted into ours, or how much we've drifted into it.

Maybe it's just me. Is anybody else seeing this?

Or perhaps this particular conversation takes place in the Mellah, where a Chinese giant taller than a tree has taken to eating breakfasts on a scale that shall be retold in fable and song for many generations.

☽

Visiting a café turns out to be rather an odd experience.

It's a whim and a practicality. The endless alleys of the market are stifling, things bursting out of every doorway, gowned bodies jostling everywhere and trying to squeeze out of her way, the endless pink stone glowing with warmth, the light piercing the lattice of reeds above and turning the dust to steam. Emerging into the vast square is first an immense relief, a bucketful of daylight splashed over her head, a breath of free air. And then it is staggering, because she has never seen so many humans in one space like this, one monstrous wriggling shouting organism.

The ideas of sanctuary and a glass of water are dominating her mind just as she passes a café. Relief: she steps across the invisible threshold between the square and the stones that have been colonized by tables and chairs.

She's used to men pulling away from her, especially here. She's used to men interrogating their own reactions to her – stiffly, defensively, daringly, abusively – she sees the instincts and principles struggling on their faces. The café just makes it more of a squeeze. Men fall over chairs, step on each other's feet, drop their sleeves in strangers' breakfasts, in the bustle to avoid being touched by her. It's supposed to be a square of performers, isn't it? This one's got their attention, right enough. Eva wonders if the multitude behind her have all stopped to watch her trying to get a drink.

Now she's standing in front of a man who looks like he might be the manager. He looks very alone. He's glancing from side to side for support, reassurance, guidance, but he's not getting any. His expression suggests that everyone is watching his performance, around him and indeed above him, and he is undoubtedly going to fluff his lines.

Eventually she is hustled through a curtain into little space where she cannot be seen, or see. Her escort shepherds her without actually touching.

There she is left: alone, in state, thirsty.

Two broken chairs. A tray of rather lovely glasses, used and apparently left in here by mistake. A vast copper thing of mysterious purpose. The curtain is magnificent, thick and green and two metres high. After several minutes, a woman is shoved through the curtain, and begins to cluck at her. When something truly disturbing lands on the doorstep, who else is going to deal with it?

Though apparently indispensable in any crisis of social convention or hygiene, the woman speaks no language that Eva does. For twenty seconds, birds from different continents placed haphazard next to each other in the zoo, they screech names of drinks at each other incomprehensibly. Eva assumes they're names of drinks.

Always more comfortable in movement than words, she produces a precise delicate mime of a jug pouring liquid into a tall glass, shows how refreshing it is, embellishes it with a lemon squeezed over the top. She stops when she realizes that her mime for squeezing a lemon looks like milking a cow's teat. The woman watches the performance and then roars with laughter. Then she resumes her chanting of mysterious words. It's possible, Eva realizes, that it isn't a menu but an exorcism. Then the woman is gone.

A few more minutes of solitude and thirst. Eventually Eva pulls back the curtain to see what progress is being made with her glass of water, or milk. The whole café is standing in a half circle gazing at the curtain, and as her face appears they all shrink back with a great groan. This was not how the magic trick was supposed to work.

Tough audience.

☽

JOURNAL OF THOMAS SOMERLEIGH

The usual morning rendezvous of dips at the palace gate. In most respects we're just the same as the gaggle of beggars who gather at the Bab Hmar: lurking ever-hopeful and oft-disappointed, in our exotic rags. Keen for a sentence for Tangier – day not a total write-off, continued British engagement – I asked Prudhomme re his idea for a reception to mark the arrival of the circus.

Klug immediately alert. And Prudhomme apparently considering whether my question was inappropriate. Eventually the tight little smile, and he expressed the hope that it would soon be realized, given the widespread interest. That was that, except after further reflection he added that he was consulting the legal bods within the Royal Court and in the French Embassy in Tangier to check the wording of the edict incorporating the circus to the Royal household: were animals and equipment as well as the humans included in the restrictions.

Klug's big eyes went wider. When I next looked he was gone.

Two messages waiting for me back home. I read them in the courtyard – as I now call it. I feel more the proper diplomat there: it's a more distinctive idiom, more clearly different to what one would be doing at home, out in the sunlight on the elegant chairs, the young envoy to foreign climes reading his correspondence; if the blighter's lucky, his servant may even have deigned to produce some fresh mint tea.

Message number one: careful lettering, careful French, from Brahim the poet. Sincerely trust no imposition, but hopes I would have lunch with him. Well, why not? Bit of local colour.

The second rather more significant. A note from Hortense, no less! Courteous regret for the *petite maladie* that kept her from tea, Papa and Mama assured her it was a riot. Hopes this finds me well, weather continues charming. Not much to do of course, but she and Mama have the routine of a carriage ride each afternoon, after five when it is not so hot, in the Menara Gardens.

It wasn't in one of the French Embassy's usual fancy envelopes. And Youssef reckoned it had been dropped off by a local woman. So: strong impression it was sent in secret. And yet if by some chance her parents did see the note, there's nothing exceptionable in it – no inappropriate feeling described, no inappropriate action suggested. How very clever of Hortense!

☿

When Eva steps into her little courtyard, a man is waiting there. It feels like violation.

Immediately he is forward, talking. How is Mademoiselle? How is her health? How does she find the beauty and the climate of Marrakech? By now – it took a moment – she thinks she recognizes him as the intermediary who had appeared from nowhere to negotiate this accommodation for her. How is her accommodation? What more could be provided? This place is so small and dirty and he knows a much larger room just around the corner, approximately a palace, with the most beautiful cushions that only a European princess such as herself would appreciate. A more satisfactory maid? He has a cousin...

Yes, thinks Eva, I'll bet you do. Always a cousin, always a palace just around the corner.

Polite thanks, but no, everything is satisfactory. She finds herself hesitating: if she sounds too happy here, will he expect a tip for this instead?

These conversations are hateful. Walking through a pit of snakes: wherever she may put a foot, whatever she says, it will attract an offer and a price.

A better breakfast then? Each morning, fresh and healthy and typical of the cuisine, so hard to find in the city but he has a cousin.

It is so tiresome. May not this be enough? she thinks. May I not live as I am?

No, she says. Thank you. Humble but firm. How to escape this? If I want more breakfast there is an excellent café on the square. Thank you.

He stands in the middle of the courtyard. He could stretch out and touch any of its walls. Her doorway, sanctuary within sanctuary, is beside him.

To turn one's back is to reveal one's vulnerabilities: the neck to the executioner's blade; the rump to the beast. An attempt at a haughty nod of finality, and then she walks sideways to the door, face towards him but eyes lowered. And through.

To close the door would be too rude. She draws the curtain.

Curious. She did not used to be so prickly. The poor man has to live, and perhaps even a dancer's pitiful tip is riches.

May I not live as I am? May not this be enough? These are unfamiliar feelings. She has travelled Europe – travelled the world – night by night and boarding house by boarding house and audience by audience and she has never resented the restless unsettling ways of others.

Assia the silent furtive maid says: 'If M'zelle visits a café on the square she will give the wrong impression. If M'zelle wishes, there is a more appropriate place to which I can escort her.'

The French is so unexpected, the effect so staggering, that for a moment Eva has not understood and thinks she was jabbering in Arabic. The girl has turned away, shrunken again, alarmed by her own boldness.

'Assia, wait!' The girl freezes. 'You – you speak French?' Slowly she turns. Eva waits until there is a wary eye contact. And then a nod. Eva waits some more, not wanting to tread on the frail daring.

At last: 'Or alternatively English, if M'zelle prefers.'

'But – how?'

Assia shrugs. 'There was a man.'

She says it as she might say that a genie came out of a lamp, or that a terrifying pestilence came out of the desert. It explains everything.

But then she sees that Eva is still unclear – or perhaps has a more nuanced sense of the ways in which there can be men. She continues: 'A Roumi – a foreigner. He wanted...' – another shrug – 'a daughter. Or a wife maybe. Say: there was a man and he wanted a girl. He sent me to the Jewish school in Mogador for a few years.'

'How... remarkable. And then..?'

Shrug. 'And then, maybe I am not the girl he wants any longer. And so no longer is there a man.'

Speaking Eva's language, Assia seems immediately more intelligent and more alive. And there is so much Eva wants to ask and cannot. The brief intimacy has only made the girl more exotic and mysterious.

☪

JOURNAL OF THOMAS SOMERLEIGH

Little bit of subterfuge today, a touch of derring-do, the young foreign service wallah in the back-country par excellence, albeit in a domestic cause! Little Hortense surely meant me to take her explicit description of the afternoon carriage ride as a hint. And that given, not only was I keen to see her myself, but it also followed that she'd think me a bit of a dumb brick if I didn't spot the hint and act on it. Whereas, *per contra*, by taking the hint I look more the sort of enterprising, take charge sort of chap she's hoping for.

She'd only said a carriage ride after five in the Menara Gardens. But easy enough to deduce that they don't start much after five, to avoid getting caught up in the less salubrious entertainments of evening. And however large the Menara, in practice they must invariably drive into it along the one road from the east. One further deduction: at the moment they're redoing the cobbles at the junction there, and any carriage must slow almost to nothing. Typically enterprising, more than a few fruit peddlers and so forth congregate there. I was among them by a quarter to five, and keeping a sharp look-out.

My ruse worked splendidly! At perhaps twenty after five – fruit peddlers a little vexed by apparently the most indecisive customer in Moroccan history lurking around their wares – a carriage rolled towards me. I contrived to turn towards it at just the right moment, as it slowed to a walk, and tally ho! there they were and I raised my hat and called a greeting. Pleasant surprise from Hortense, a word to Mama, and the carriage stopped. Formal greeting to Madame, and I was helping Mademoiselle down to the roadside to investigate the fruit.

Very neat she looked too. And, oh! – the look of excitement on her little face!

A few steps away from the carriage, we stuck to neutral courtesies as we considered the dates. I bought a bag and – brain still working as well as heart – made a point of first offering to Mama. 'You are most attentive, Monsieur Somerleigh.' Such a charming sound English words always have on French lips! It had been nice politics – Somerleigh's intentions honourable, no funny business – but with the fruit bought and given, and me standing by the carriage, the only logical thing was for Hortense to get back in with her mother and pootle off again. The Gods smile on intrepid Englishmen, however: Madame decided that on reflection dear Hector would appreciate a goodly pile of dates at home, and would it be too offensive an imposition to ask me to buy a second bag? She settled back in the carriage, checked that her parasol was covering her face, and closed her eyes and began to fan herself.

No imposition at all, chère Madame, and Hortense and I drifted back to the fruit.

'Please don't think me forward,' I said, 'but I wondered – I secretly hoped – that you wished me to take advantage of your description of your afternoon ride.'

The big dark eyes gazed up into mine. 'Perhaps', she said softly, 'I did.'

The fruit had darkened her lips. The features seemed paler, finer, more delicate.

'And regardless, I wished to take advantage of it. I missed your company at tea, Mademoiselle Hortense. In many moments I find myself missing your company. If you will pardon me mentioning it.'

The tiniest gasp from those darkened lips. 'I am sure I should not.' The eyes wider, shining.

It's the man's part to push the point, of course. 'I am optimistic that we will bump into each other on other afternoons.'

The eyes so eager, the voice so soft. 'I too am... optimistic.'

'I can think of nothing more charming than to share some fruit and some verses with a beautiful woman.'

Her exquisite face absolutely glowing. 'A woman could wish for nothing more.'

◑

Like sheep that have strayed too widely, today the members of the circus are summoned back to camp. No reason is given, or necessary. The rendezvous is unsurprising, the gap less usual than the regathering: usually we'd expect to be together every day, wherever we are, however we're lodged.

As she weaves through the market alleys, by now looking to her most effective path through the bodies rather than the potential attractions of the stalls, and avoiding the big square, Eva feels different about it. She's not returning to the circus from a lodging. She's visiting.

And as quickly – a jar of spice is thrust under her nose and she shies and shakes her head and gives a crisp 'no, thank you'; it's the first phrase she's learned, as always – as quickly follows the certainty that soon there shall be upheaval again. A re-simplifying of belongings, a winnowing-out of non-essentials, a sloughing off of temporary skin; farewells and false promises of return. The courtyard and the lemon tree and the remarkable Assia, these have become hers; but soon she will walk away from them in a cold unscented early morning, bearing just the one bag and the scars of severed attachments.

The Maestro's diverse empire has been further diversified by its residence in Marrakech. New habits are already becoming visible on faces. Lack of activity is becoming visible in waistlines. Agustin the swordsman jumps when Eva greets him, and seems defensive when someone asks him about Marrakech: has there been some embarrassment in those alleys? has he found the way to some new vice?

Shevzod has acquired a servant, a boy forever in his shadow, a hand reaching up with a snack or a handkerchief for his brow. Johanna's hair is different somehow. Jan doesn't appear at all today.

It's not Eva's usual considered circuit, but curiosity. She detours to see Mama Zana, but the big woman is asleep in her cart. Because she has space to move and stretch for the first time in days, and because nothing else is happening, she finds her private area among the wagons again and forces herself through a routine.

The Maestro arrives very late. By carriage, not mule. His instincts of anxiety and thrift towards the circus are bone-deep, however, and so he is automatically prowling among us.

Is that a bit of weight Eva's put on there what is it with dancers and honey, dance of the eight veils is it now or do we just lend her a tent? Meat not bread, Genghis old lad, did someone say they eat camels here, you watch yourself, some of the street dogs don't look too healthy. Dearest Olga child just tell me you're being careful, the dreams of the young lads of Marrakech are my nightmares, do 'em good to hear a no occasionally the dirty little beggars good for the spirit, lucky no concerns about good old Magda on that score.

The worries are automatic, the remarks ritualistic: a liturgy remembered but no longer felt.

Here's a familiar face! The phrase he always uses for someone he doesn't recognize. *Marrakech treating you well and not too well? Every variety of vice vies for your attention ain't it?*

The dark woman doesn't answer him; Eva guesses she doesn't understand him. The Maestro hasn't noticed and has moved on. It's the woman who shared her lodging room that first night in the city, the woman who found herself on the fringes of the German representative's conversation with them. Curiosity and an occasional meal have proved stronger than whatever originally brought her to the city.

Eva is feeling the pull of Marrakech at dusk, cinnamon warmth and shadowy anonymity. As she's drifting away there's an explosion of shouting near her, protest and alarm. A fight, and not the daily shove and scratch of proud professional people living too intensely together: Salomon and someone obscured by dust are fighting for real, and it's brutal and vicious.

Eva moves closer, because sometimes a familiar woman shames rather than inflames. But she finds she doesn't recognize the other man. And when, in a moment snatched for breath, Salomon happens to catch her eye, she finds that she doesn't recognize him either.

☬

In the café on the corner, where the maze of alleys that make up Marrakech market empties onto the great square, the corner where the caged birds chirp their feelings of confinement or safety, morning is at its busiest and hottest. The square is where Morocco digests itself; where it gestates. All Morocco is here to exchange, every shade of skin and every style of pottery, every fruit and every dance from the Rif to the Sahara. Foreign blood flows too; foreign seeds are planted. Dark men from imagined countries beyond the desert have come here as slaves, soldiers and traders. Every culture is encountered through its exiles and its extremes. Pale men from over-defined countries beyond the sea have come here to sell visions, or to find them. Armoured in their certainties of faith and map and skin and steel, they seek the most exotic, the most savage, the most dangerous – usefully delimited, like the defanged cobras that sway drowsily on the charmers' mats. Having confronted it, they believe they have controlled it, just as a child who faces its nightmare learns to pretend that darkness is just a shading of light and not the infinitely vaster world where light sometimes flickers to show a face or two; that night is an excursion from day and not the great mother from which day comes and to which it must return; that dreams are but an exotic embellishment of memory, rather than memory one sketch-mapped anxiously-policed corner of the untamed wildness of dreams.

After the first bustle of morning and as the heat begins to thicken, the rhythms of the royal palace slow. It is his habit, in this lull, to walk out into the city and to drink a tea with his acquaintances. Today, he brings a guest; his acquaintances will certainly admire this further proof of his sophistication.

Not to be indiscreet, but my friend here and his friends are quite the most prominent visitors to the court. He is a member of the so-called circus the foreigners have brought. As we know, the religion of the Roumi is performance and sorcery; they have this group of magicians and jesters to protect them and entertain them.

Dangerous? No. I've spent two whole evenings with him and he is always placid and well-behaved.

Corrupt His Majesty? – bewitch him? Surely not. His Majesty carries the blood of the Prophet himself, blessings be upon Him, and it'd take a bit more than a few magic tricks to make him stray from the path.

Comprehension? It's a bit primitive, but you can try: his French isn't so good, but he'll understand if you speak it slowly. I have to mime and point and shout quite a bit.

Women? Nonsense; even the Roumi aren't so debauched. But everyone likes to believe the most exotic story, don't they?

Or perhaps this particular conversation takes place in the hamam, where all manner of impurity may be washed away or hidden in steam.

☠

Now that Assia has proved to have a voice and a past, Eva feels uncomfortable about seeming to command anything. Naming her is an assertion of control as well as familiarity. She says 'Assia' so quietly that Assia doesn't notice, and only stops her folding when she realizes Eva is standing still in the middle of the room looking at her.

'You said there was some place it would be more appropriate for me to have breakfast.' Assia nods. 'If I wish to be appropriate. Can we visit, on the way to the circus camp?' She knows she won't go to the circus camp.

Assia shrugs. The sense of an excursion makes Eva suddenly playful. She mimics the shrug, shoulders exaggerated up to her ears. 'What is this?' she says. 'Excellent French and excellent English and the only language you use is:' – she performs it again.

Assia, not playful, shrugs instinctively. 'The laws of God are very precise and very strict about how we deal with life. In the end it's just:' – shrug.

The alleys of Marrakech, dusty and sleepy in the morning, their pink more bare. One of the alleys that Eva has walked every day passes through a tunnel, a roof of reeds supporting the buildings above. In the tunnel is a doorway she has never noticed. Now that Assia has beckoned her, she sees light through it, a wall of tiles. Assia pushes the door to behind them, and leads her down a passage. The wall-tiles are richly-decorated, blues and golds a-swirl; the floor-tiles are plain and have just been mopped. At the end of the passage Assia turns a corner and pushes through a curtain.

Eva follows with greater unease. She has not found Moroccans any more intimidating than any other people she's ever visited. But a woman entering a secluded unfamiliar doorway anywhere is in danger.

Her first glimpse of the room through the curtain confirms her instinct. She was not, it seems, the first to be lured in here.

At the moment there are half a dozen women in a room no bigger than her bedroom, basically oblong but interrupted by odd corners and protrusions. The women are sitting on a stone bench seat running along two of the walls. The same tiles to waist height; the rest is whitewashed plaster.

The few women she's ever seen in the streets have always seemed dull, shadowed, wrapped up in an empty black. Here, even in the unnatural glow of the lamp, she sees colours: some dark blues, a sumptuous green, browns; one wrap has come loose and reveals a glimpse of something patterned beneath. The women are eating, and murmuring quietly. The women look up as she and Assia enter, and then return to eating and murmuring. A few give her a second glance. One shifts her heavy backside along the bench a little to make space for the two additional backsides.

Eva is keeping her head down, trying not to look around too obviously.

Someone laughs, and instinctively she looks. But the laughter was not about her.

It's a good laugh, hoarse and unrestrained. The face it comes from is puffy, worn, blotched; the laugh is in the eyes too.

The irregular shape of the room confirms that it was never designed for anything: this is a space left over, an accidental vacancy squeezed between and under deliberate and more important buildings.

It takes a moment for Eva to realize that what's unusual is the thing that seemed to her most usual.

She can see all this, she can read the atmosphere, because she can see all of the faces. Confident that there are no men in this place to be cruelly provoked to uncontrollable lust by the mere sight of them – and presumably because it makes eating easier – the women have pulled the shawls and veils away from their faces. Apparently we're just putting up with the risk of another woman being provoked to lust by the sight of us.

Some of the heads are wholly unwrapped. Eva sees glorious long dark hair, plaited and coiled, bunched and pinned, or for once hanging free. One of the women looks like she could be a hundred: a tiny shrivelled walnut face, body bony through rags that hold her together. There's a younger woman who's gorgeous, a dark glory of eyes and toned smooth skin and rich lips. She's deferring to an older woman next to her – a sister; a mother even – but just for a moment as she happens to be looking towards Eva the timidity is replaced with a flounce of poise, of confidence, of beauty enjoyed.

The woman running this canteen of fugitives is handsome too: bulky, weary-enduring, but good eyes, good bones. Watching her swinging to and fro with bowls empty and bowls full, imagining the early mornings hefting vats and late evenings mopping, Eva the dancer wonders at the strains on her posture. She seems maternal – but then the worst tyrant in the world seems maternal if they're ladling out warm soup.

Perhaps she's just imagining it, but the women seem to be moving more freely too. Normally, in the street, their narrow gowns and intricate wrapping force stuttering steps and minimal arm movements; hands are rarely seen and feet never. As she looks along the table, she sees the wrappings looser, arms stretching more naturally. If women are seen in the street, they are untouchable. In here their shoulders squeeze close. Sleeves rub against each other. A naked wrist moves over another naked wrist to reach for something.

There has been no discussion of choices. After thirty seconds a tin bowl is put in front of Eva. She sees the woman's forearm, close-up and bare to the elbow: hard-toned like servers everywhere; repeatedly scarred and scalded. She sees the fingers, calloused and chapped by too much fire and too much water, as the woman turns the bowl and uses the hem of her apron to wipe a slick of soup from the rim. Then one of the ubiquitous loaves of bread, round and flat, is on the table beside her bowl. The woman squawks something, and Assia squawks something, and immediately there are glasses of mint tea in front of them.

She glances to Assia on one side and to the woman eating on the other, to try to check that she's not about to get it wrong. No prayer or ritual or knack. The woman beside her sees this, and Eva worries she now seems intrusive in this most private and protected place. The woman snatches up Eva's bread, and breaks off a lump, and picks up her spoon, and mimes dipping both in the soup to eat. Eva nods and smiles and tries the word for thanks. Her neighbour finds this hilarious, nods vigorously, chatters something at her, and then just for a moment rests her hand on Eva's wrist. Complicity. Guidance. Approval. Soothing. Blessing. The touch of the fingers is so soft, so unusual. Eva notices her own wrist: its frailty; its sinews; the unseen fair hairs straining up to feel the stroke of a finger.

For centuries Europeans have thrilled at the vision of the harem, most sacred and most forbidden sanctuary of power and sex, of subjection and wild abandon, confinement and liberation, slavery and fairy-tale. Now she has been led behind the curtain to discover the secret in the holy of holies: a woman giving a bowl of soup to another woman.

The soup is not as thick as it looks, but the beans and the warmth make it filling, and some spice or other gives it taste and a lurid yellow complexion. Tiny strands of what might be meat have at some point found their way into the bowl or the beans or the cooking pot. No two spoons are the same.

Someone else comes in. As one, the diversely-wrapped and shaded backsides squeeze further along the bench to make room.

Intimacies: a touch, an implication of appetite, a whispered bit of gossip, a quiet admission, my food-moistened lips visible to a stranger. Satisfactions: warmth in the throat, a shut-eyed sigh after a last mouthful, a nose bent eager over a fresh bowl, a body slumped against a cool wall, laughter, a relaxation of my endless brittle pose. Identities: faces, habits, instincts, opinions. The younger woman runs one finger round her bowl and sucks it, and then crumples mischievously at the tut from her companion, another's voice is suddenly stronger and insistent as she articulates an argument about something, and Eva feels that she is in the most abandoned debauched transgressive boudoir imaginable. This accidental soup-kitchen, this secret society of natural women in uncolonized space, might in this moment explode the universe of men and men's Gods.

Too soon they must leave. For a moment Eva wonders if she must ever leave. Then a stab of guilt: are these lives merely a tourist curiosity? Or – hollowness despite the puffy bread – how much was romantic fancy? And the spell is broken.

'What is the price?' she hisses.

Assia shrugs, of course. 'Anything you can. It will be more than she is used to.' After a pause: 'She will give it all to her husband, or whichever son she lives with.'

Eva places some coins in the woman's hand, and tries to make eye contact. But this glimpsed world of intimacy is fading now, and the woman is quickly away to her vat of soup.

They're in the tiled passage. Eva says: 'Maybe she decides how much of it she gives.'

'She will give it all,' Assia says over her shoulder, 'or he will beat her.'

'It's still a kind of decision.' Eva pauses a moment, on the smeared cold tiles. 'Isn't it?'

☽

JOURNAL OF THOMAS SOMERLEIGH

Lunch with Brahim the poet. Rather fine. I'd assumed we'd be getting a pie and a pint, Moroccan equivalent thereof, in a café somewhere. But having met up at the café we'd been in before, he walked me into the labyrinth. I've explored this pretty thoroughly now, and even in Marrakech market one picks up landmarks – a particularly bright collection of slippers in a shop on a corner, a particular beggar, a particular bit of carving above a gate. But he was taking me off the beaten track a bit. We were wiggling to and fro, and it got noticeably quieter than the usual bedlam of the market alleys, and a little cooler. Found myself losing my bearings rather; wondered if I was being led astray. Probably not robbery, but there have been cases of westerners kidnapped by bandits. Embarrass the Sultan, secure some local advantage. I wasn't so bothered about the physical risk; but Gods, the embarrassment to Britain – Sir G. would go gunpowder wild at such a disruption of policy, such a loss of dignity. Somerleigh on the slow boat home within the day; or he'd probably slip the bandits ten bob to cut my throat and solve the problem.

Anyway, we wound up – just as I was asking where exactly we were and where we might be going – in what could have been a house or could have been a sort of restaurant. Tiny doorway, stoop to get through it. Poky little place, rather gloomy, but quite a good atmosphere of scents and comforts. Not luxurious, but a cushion where you needed it. Had a corner to ourselves. Except – further surprise – there was a chap sitting there. Oh, says Brahim, what a nice surprise, though of course I wondered. Older chap: simple local robes, and very gaunt and wrinkled. They tend to thinness here, the men, but this one's positively hollowed out. The robes look like they're on a hanger, nothing else beneath.

Brahim – who I've had the impression is a bit of a progressive – makes a very unprogressive greeting to the old man. Actually kisses the chap's hand. I wonder if he's some religious type. As well as mainstream Islam there's a fair bit of mystic whatnot around the edges of Moroccan society. Always leaves me a bit unsure how to proceed: one doesn't want to jump in with the hearty sportsman's handshake and find out he's some sort of local deity, touching him totally haram. So I waited, and stuck to a courteous nod. Fortunately the oldster took the lead: a firm regular handshake, pleasure to meet our English guest; honour Marrakech by visiting, that sort of thing. The voice another surprise: clear cultured French, quiet and firm. I replied likewise, diplomacy for beginners, honour me by your hospitality. It would be of the greatest interest, says he, to hear the mind of an Englishman of distinct perspective, and perhaps it might amuse the Englishman to meet a cultural curiosity like self. Of course, I said, delighted to have you. And having already written off lunch as merely local colour, I was happy enough if it got more colourful.

Must say, it turned into one of the most extraordinary encounters. The old man – couldn't say how old, between fifty and a hundred – is a true original. One of those sages that only the Orient seems to produce. In touch with more than just the surface. Same theory, I suppose, as religion in England, except utterly different. Our religion is more down-to-earth: practical principles for a good life and fretting about the state of the church roof. Doubt this chap's ever sold a raffle ticket in his life.

Lunch came and went over a couple of hours. Breads and bean soups and one of those big couscous affairs, which if one's doing it properly has to be eaten from a common plate; again, not very vicarage tea but jolly convivial. I remember the conversation as best I can: the tricks we were taught for recalling for the write-up only get you so far. Old chap asked me how I found Marrakech, so I gave the usual page one answer about hospitality and pink stone and snake charmers. He gave the page one polite smile in reply, and I felt I'd failed to impress. 'The north's all very well', I said; 'Tangier, Fes, very impressive. But, coming inland like this, perhaps I feel I'm getting closer to the heart of Morocco.'

This he gave more consideration. Somerleigh stronger in the re-sits. 'Such a very laudable motive,' he said, trowelling out a bit more couscous with his fingers, 'to seek to find the heart. And you Europeans always at it with such energy.'

'You think Marrakech is more like the heart of the country?'

Again I felt I'd got him thinking. 'Every generation of change, of fresh blood to the battle, has charged westwards, down out of the mountains towards the sea. When its energy is spent it finds it has come near to the coast, and there in those fine cities it settles and hardens, layer upon layer as the sea shells form.'

'Certainly,' I said, 'Morocco is at its most modern in the great cities of the north.'

A little smile: 'Most recent, yes.'

Brahim jumped in rather passionate. 'The period of its decadence', he said; 'the moment of its obsolescence', and the old man patted his hand.

I was wondering what to make of their relationship. I pushed on: 'So, if one wants to… well, to predict the future of Morocco, one should look inland, towards its heart?'

He actually wiped his fingers at that one. Then he patted my hand. 'That is rather sharp', he said, admiring. 'But you must excuse us: predicting the future is more of a Christian obsession.'

'Especially' – Brahim again – 'predicting other country's futures.'

And again the little glance from the older man: fondness, caution. 'I understand that England is an island', he said. I nodded, and he turned this over in his mind. 'Such a peculiar sensation, I am sure. Not just the comfort you must feel; but the certainty.' I felt it the moment for the standard line on maintaining the concert of Europe, keeping the seas free etc.

He absorbed it. 'We can only wonder what that feels like. To stand on the deck of your battleship and be able to say: We are here, and You are not. We are this, and You are not.'

One has to keep prodding to get these sorts of chaps onto firmer ground. 'So you think – all sorts of reasons no doubt, climate and education, industrial revolution, that sort of thing – the situation of Morocco is different?'

He looked grave. 'Every Sultan in Fes – and every farmer in his mud hut just to the south of the city here – knows that tomorrow a new storm will charge out of the mountains to upturn his world.'

We were really getting somewhere. 'So Europeans wanting to help should be thinking about defending against that threat?'

'Indeed, the European reaction may be to make your defences stronger.' Little smile, and then through a mouthful of couscous: 'The Moroccan reaction is to keep your wealth portable.'

'You don't strike me', I said – touch of diplomacy – 'as worried too much about your wealth.' I saw Brahim nodding; I'd said the right thing.

'Oh, we must all be concerned about our wealth.' Still the playfulness in the melodious voice. 'To know if we can afford a piece of bread and a bed for the night. It is worrying about other people's wealth that causes the difficulties.' His eyes wandered, and the voice lost its lightness. 'Myself,' he said, 'I have dreamed of a life outside these rhythms and habits of chaos. And having dreamed this life, I choose as much as possible to live it.'

'A different kind of Morocco, you mean?' A glance showed me that Brahim certainly thought so.

He was suddenly wary. The authorities are pretty hot against sedition, that sort of thing.

'When you say that,' he said, 'you mean a Morocco that is more European, or at least more convenient for Europe. When dear Brahim here says it, he means the same Morocco but with different people in power.' Brahim glancing at the door uneasily. 'I – I am but one old man. I cannot change the nature of the Sultan, nor the nature of the rude cobbler who is my landlord, nor the nature of the wind that comes hot and dry out of the emptiness. I cannot aspire to a different kind of Morocco. I prefer... a different perception of Morocco. If I change how I perceive the Sultan and the cobbler and the wind, I change my relationship to them. I do not live against the Sultan or the cobbler or the wind, and it would be equally dangerous to live dependent on them; I strive to live regardless of them.'

'Spiritual sort of thing, you mean?' I said.

'Sort of thing, yes.'

Brahim clutched the old man's wrist. 'Venerable Sa'id is truly a great man. Truly humble and thus truly wise and thus truly great. Many of us are determined to live by his words.'

Again Venerable Sa'id patted the hand that held him. 'If only a few of you would try to understand them first.'

'I'm no kind of expert,' I said, 'but I find all this fascinating. Mysticism. The inner man.'

They both nodded, uncertain. Can be a surprise to find one's own context fitting in to a world system – a universal rhythm. Benefit of the good old British educational tradition. *The Golden Bough*, that sort of thing, and the chance to travel. One sees these traditions and instincts cropping up in all societies.

After an uncomfortable pause: 'I hope I do not bewilder you with my prattle, Monsieur... Somerleigh.' I started to reassure him, makes a lot of sense, all jolly good, but he was pushing on. 'You honour us by visiting our country, Monsieur Somerleigh. You honour us ten times more by your sincere desire to... to understand us; to know us. If you will consider the advice of a poor Moroccan man, who has nevertheless the advantage of a few more years than you' – I looked appropriately considerate – 'please do not be in a hurry to declare success, to plant your flag and proclaim that you have attained the heart of Morocco.'

I smiled. 'You mean I'm not yet a spiritual enough person?'

'You are not a Moroccan enough person.'

It was witty enough that we could all take it as a joke, and I didn't want to hurt his feelings. We moved on. Brahim insisted on an over-earnest repetition of the some of the social issues affecting the city, and by then lunch was more than done. As we were shaping to leave, the old man interrupted the younger.

'But dear Brahim, I fear we have disappointed our guest. An Englishman does not like a vague answer. It will not satisfy his God, nor his diplomatic report. So, shall we tell him a little secret?' Brahim momentarily as curious as I. 'Shall we tell him where is the heart of Morocco? Has he found it here in Marrakech – or is it yet a little farther on?'

'Farther on, certainly', said Brahim, in on the joke now. 'And then a bit to the left.'

They were having fun with me, but I didn't mind. 'You think I should push on a bit? Into Africa?'

'Certainly.' The old man.

'And eventually, I'll find..?'

'Eventually, I suspect, you will come out the other side. No doubt there will be a steamboat available to carry you round to England again.'

'Very well, not the heart then. But what one place is most characteristic of Morocco? The essence, I mean; the energy. Some mountain village, you think?'

He shrugged. Standing, next to Brahim and me, his thinness and lack of height were emphasized. 'Perhaps. But is there no place for the sardine fisherman of Agadir or Mogador, or the scholar of Fes, or the whore of Tangier?' He slipped his arm through mine and we walked slowly towards the door, one of us having to keep more of an eye on the roof-beams. 'I think you are an honest boy', he went on, and I hope I get most of this aright. 'And, like all Christians, you think yourself good. So: I will tell you where is the heart of Morocco. It is a place I am sure you have not been to, a place you have not heard of. There is an oasis in this place, but the sand has been jealous of its water and it is not what a European thinks of when he imagines an oasis. We are forever looking at the sky and testing the ground, and our prayers are anxious. Somewhere to the north of where we stand now; or perhaps I mean the south. There are some buildings, but few residents: there are few who call this place home, fewer whose grandparents ever saw it. It is a place of change and exchange. We come, we encounter other men, and after a certain time we go on. We make necessary adaptation, or we take temporary advantage. Life in this place is a hard wonder, because death is very close. A child balances a feather on its finger, and the wind from the desert is fickle. Yesterday perhaps I died of some sickness come with a caravan, today I die of thirst, tomorrow I will die in the Caliph's dungeon or with a bandit's bullet in my back or knocked down by a Frenchman who cannot control his horse, or perhaps this time I will die old in my bed.' He stopped at the door, which we couldn't negotiate together. 'And over the centuries', he said, now looking directly at me, 'also we have the honour to enjoy visits from Europeans, your merchants and your soldiers, encouraging us to use a little oasis water to float a gunboat, or to brew some tea.'

In some ways this is the sort of thing I went into diplomacy for: sort of experience ninety-nine chaps out of a hundred would never have, never dream of. Certainly no Somerleigh's ever had a lunch like that. And then Brahim insisting on an extra mint-tea together, make sure I'd understood everything. Bit too much of a good thing, but it felt pleasant to indulge him. Marvellous local colour. Edging a little closer to the heart of the thing. Speaking of which, much preoccupied with how I can next contrive to meet dear Hortense.

☪

Across the café, a pale European is chatting to a Moroccan lad. The European is a little uncomfortable, of course; sweating a little. He is pretending ease – leaning back in his chair, arms thrown wide; but a dancer can read muscles.

Eva watches incurious: dulled by the heat; muted by her lack of status. Trying now and then to catch a waiter's attention; giving up.

It takes her a moment to notice, not because it is unfamiliar but because it is too familiar: she has seen this exchange in bars and back rows all over Europe. The pale man, all-but trembling in his daring and his shame and the prospect of young ecstasy. The glance aside: anxiety at being seen; a pretence of indifference. Then, to cover the glance, a pose of suavity and command in shoulders and face: a bully's certainty. Playfully vicious, viciously playful, he pinches the boy's cheek. Acceptable public boisterousness; mastery. The boy giggles.

The poor exist for the rich to exercise the sins they cannot among their own class. The poor are the filth that lurks beneath the surface of the rich, in the dungeons of the spirit; to be ignored – or privily indulged in.

The boy is making a kind of choice. A gift. A meal. Attention. Warmth.

I know that choice.

She watches the boy's performance – of coyness; of mischief. Natural emotions, but today he must fabricate them, to cover the unsightly feelings that will not amuse a rich man. Nature overcome by excess of nature and so wearing a mask of nature. The painted smile of the clown.

She cannot look at the boy any longer; she knows him too well. She looks again at the pale man. His certainty that in this place he will always be right; cannot do wrong. His trembling courage as he overcomes his conventions of home; tries to make something stylish out of his ugly instincts.

We know you. We scorn you – we feel at least that superiority to you.

Still you will fuck us as you wish.

In the café on the corner, where the maze of alleys that make up Marrakech market empties onto the great square, the corner where the trays of herbs are lush and thick-scented, morning is at its busiest and hottest. The square is the courtyard of Africa, and everything of the continent is for sale here: every creature from mouse to man, every part of every beast, every product of every plant, every aroma, every colour.

After the first bustle of morning and as the heat begins to thicken, the rhythms of the royal palace slow. It is his habit, in this lull, to walk out into the city and to drink a tea with his acquaintances. Today, he is more alarmed than usual. His acquaintances respect him and understand him: they see his mood, and they fall silent.

They watch his irritation at the chair that does not move easily. As he sits they notice his restless foot, his fists. One of them commands a tea for him with a flicked and pointed finger but no word. He glares around them, seeking fuel for his frustrations. But the eyes are placid, tolerant, soothing, waiting. He lets out a long breath, and it is lost amid the hot sweet fug of mint.

Not to be indiscreet, but I am very worried, my friends. I think we understand each other; I think we are men of sense. Nods. We agree with you; we embrace you. Perhaps a man has a certain loyalty, and perhaps another man has another loyalty. Perhaps a man is content the way things are, and perhaps another man desires change. But no man of sense wants trouble. Nods; we agree with you and therefore we are all men of sense. Not to be indiscreet, but... Reassuring shakes of the head; we know the truth, and so we do not need to tell the truth. A ruler may be a man of gentleness, of restraint, of mercy, and his people will love him for it. But if he has a rival who is less gentle, less restrained, less merciful, then his people must fear for him. And if he depends upon the support of men who are the most greedy and brutal beasts in all creation, then his people must hate him for his gentleness, his restraint and his mercy, for in truth they would be better ruled by a tyrant. Uncomfortable nods. We only exist by continued permission of the imaginations of the Sultan, and his brother the Caliph, and the chief of the Glaoui and the other chiefs. We know all this, and we agree, and one really should not be indiscreet.

The cells are filling with screams and broken bodies. Because there are plots. Because there might be plots. Because there should be plots. Because there is nothing so brutal as a fearful man trying to pretend he is ruthless. No one is safe any more. No word or action can avoid angering one man or another. One cannot stay silent or inactive when there is a command. When there are two different commands, or three, then a man must be pulled apart as with the pincers.

You know who has the best intelligence system in the city? His Majesty, long may he prosper, our beloved Sultan? You know that can't be true; he's as foreign here as he is in China. His brother, may he be praised, our esteemed Caliph? He's smart and he's busy, but he's only got his official structures. You know who.

Every morning, the Glaoui receives a report from his spy of spies, telling him of everything that has happened in the previous twenty-four hours. He knows every tiny treachery, every curse, every ambition. His brain is a map of the alleyways of this city, he breathes this city, and when he sniffs all Marrakech trembles. This morning in the palace, I hear, His Majesty may the Architect of the World sustain him was enjoying a conversation with one of his doctors of religion; a pious, humble, gentle man, a man of no malice nor even of imagination for malice. This doctor referred to the teachings of a holy man of the city, a man of no prominence in the palace but respected by those who know him in the back-streets; this old man preaches the renunciation of worldliness – they've all got their patter haven't they? – and it's always a good line. Handy way of making your poverty sound holy and it goes down well with those who've left you in poverty. His Majesty may the sun ever warm him and the shade ever cool him starts to talk about the charm of the ascetic life – I know, easy if you don't have to live it – but then the Glaoui jumps in. Very soft, very respectful, presumably this will be the old holy man who, as His Majesty will no doubt be aware, holds private conversations with foreign representatives about the politics of Morocco?

Well, of course, His Majesty hasn't a clue, but he can't say that. All he can do is claim he hasn't time for details, and put the doctor of religion on the spot: is the esteemed chief of the Glaoui right? And now the doctor's in trouble, because obviously he hadn't known but obviously he's not going to contradict the man whose heart is fed by the blood of this city, and all he can say is that he takes it for granted the esteemed Glaoui is spot on, never known him otherwise, but himself he's never been one for politics and the old man had always been reputed harmless but then again he supposes it's always the quiet ones. Upshot is, as we speak the doctor of religion is being fed to the flies in the lowest dungeon, partly because His Majesty may my devotion comfort him has to worry that he was being treasonously kept in the dark, and mainly because even if he's not being treasonously kept in the dark he can't afford to look weak about that sort of thing in front of the most powerful of the tribal chiefs. And because he likes to think he wasn't being treasonously kept in the dark by the person he's just condemned for exactly that, and because he has to show that he's not afraid of any of it anyway, he then spends a quarter hour praising the virtues of the unknown holy man.

And that is why I declare my respect and admiration for the Glaoui, in his beneficence and his wisdom. Because tomorrow morning he will know of our conversation here.

A man could escape, try to hide in the crowd, in normality, in obscurity. But the crowd is starving, and angry, and afraid. A brother ruined. A cousin dying of some anonymous sickness. A child crying for hunger. A fight in the street yesterday, with knives, broad daylight, I was lucky to avoid it. A body actually lying on my doorstep this morning. Another girl known to be missing but her family dare not speak of it, they pretend she is still shut in safe at home, and soon all of the girls of Marrakech will live only behind the veil of the imagination.

By the Prophet, blessings be upon Him, I never thought I'd say this, but: it almost makes me glad we have the Roumi taking more interest in our stability.

Or perhaps this particular conversation takes place in the Menara Gardens, where the bitter orange blossom lends spice to the spirit of lovers, and shade to their passion.

☙

Eva sits in her courtyard, under her lemon tree. They were here before her, she acknowledges, and will be here after. Better to say that she is theirs.

Stone under her backside: firm; cool. Tree trunk against her shoulders and spine: old, alive. Still afternoon air: warm.

The dancer's technique: *I imagine myself into the character, the better to embody its emotions and thus its movements.* The dancer's exercise: *I imagine myself first as some inanimate thing, the better to open my senses to a different reality.*

I cannot ever be Moroccan. I cannot ever be Assia. Can I – a step in the right direction, a test – become a Moroccan tree?

Instinctively her shoulders writhe against it, and the bark scrapes her skin through the fabric of her dress. She feels the fibrous firmness of wood in her bones. She knows the sinewy bulges of its trunk in her forearms, her thighs. She notices the tiny cracks and fissures of its surface if she looks closely at her own ageing skin, or if she wrinkles her forehead. The tree thickens and pushes up through stone into this courtyard, as she grows into the world and seeks light. It is no more fantastical to imagine its juices flowing up through her than to feel her own blood moving in her limbs. If a brief Marrakech alley fumble could plant a human child in her, it would be no more a miracle for a lemon to begin to bud and grow in her core, to sag and swell like a glob of honey from her fingertip.

Could I be that Moroccan lemon? She knows her firmness, knows her ripeness. She considers the juice of herself, within the coarse skin. She wonders at her glow.

A burst of dark colour across her lemony vision, her attention plucked unexpectedly from its branch, Assia is in front of her and she jumps.

The landlady is a blur and a chattering in the doorway and then gone. Eva, startled, turns from her to Assia. Assia sees her bewilderment, shrugs, smiles.

'I'm her daughter.' Eva's face shows her alarm at having misunderstood something so spectacularly. 'I mean, she's not my mother, but now she treats me like her daughter. Because I am in her house, and serving her guest – you – then it follows that I must be her daughter. For now.'

The Moroccan sense of household order is more powerful than any contract. Eva wants to believe that being here has brought something positive. 'That's – that's good, isn't it?'

Shrug. 'I have a roof. I have food.'

'And she expects you to do some more work – for her.'

'I have a roof and I have food. We do what we have to do, don't we?'

'And... nice to have someone worrying about you, perhaps?'

Assia smiles, uncomfortable. 'I have lost the habit of it, M'zelle.'

Eva thinks: So have I. And in an instant she feels like an outcast, an animal; and in another instant she feels tears.

Assia can't read her frozen face, and so talks on. 'I think I have given her too much worry too quickly. A mother's whole life of worry in one conversation. One minute she was curious about what my life could be. The next she was anxious about whether I'll ever be acceptable to a husband. By the end she's already afraid that I've had to become a whore.'

Eva hasn't asked. Is determined never to ask. We do what we have to do.

'I was thinking', she says quickly, 'about that place where we had breakfast – the women there. Wondering... I don't know – what sort of women are they?'

'You mean were they whores? Probably not. Normally whores at least get a place to stay and cook their own meals.' Eva wasn't meaning that, but she's caught by the similarity of the phrase to Assia's description of her own situation here. 'Those were just... average women. Unseen women. They do the jobs around the market that no one notices, no one thinks about. What has to be done to an animal before you cook it. What has to be done to cloth before you sew it. What has to be cleaned before you use it. Perhaps they have a home and a family and they just want to escape for an hour. Or perhaps they don't have a real home and family anymore.'

She sees Eva's question.

'If a woman's husband dies, or leaves her, she should go back to her own family; perhaps become a servant to her in-laws. Some women don't want that, or don't have anyone. So they find a way to survive on their own. There are a few places you can get a room, or usually share a room. Outside the walls there are places where people sleep wild like animals.'

'I've not had the chance to see any Moroccan women. Except you and our landlady. It was just... interesting. Only a very small picture, I know. Also, I felt different there myself.'

For a moment Assia is more serious than usual. 'M'zelle has seen more of those women than any Moroccan man will ever see, except possibly husbands and younger sons. M'zelle has heard more of them than even the husbands ever will.'

Eva remembers something the German said, about mysterious Africa – thinking, no doubt, of unknowably dangerous male Africans. She thinks: He literally doesn't know the half of it. How much more mysterious, given that that half of the continent isn't even known by the other half.

◐

JOURNAL OF THOMAS SOMERLEIGH

Observed to McKenna how curious it was that the one thing we'd not discussed was whether there'd ever actually be a performance by the circus. Oh, says McKenna, I'd kind of assumed that was the point. I didn't quite follow this: said surely Klug'd want a performance sooner rather than later? We agreed that he probably doesn't want to push the thing until he's absolutely sure he can get past Prudhomme.

And then McKenna, in that faux-naive manner which Americans can adopt so well, said: 'Say, you ever stop to wonder whether the damn' circus actually exists at all?'

I haven't stop thinking about it since. Wouldn't it be the most extraordinary ruse by the Germans?

I got ahead of the pack today, thanks to a suggestion from Prudhomme. Klug's been a bit slow to hand over the list of personnel and livestock and kit, and in the end the compromise was that someone could be allowed to chat to the manager of the circus troupe. Apparently this bod might be British, so perhaps least fuss if Cher Somerleigh represents the group. After the meeting Klug button-holed me: I thought he was going to try to warn me off, but he was courteous, even humble. 'Perhaps a good thing, dear Thomas, that you visit this man. You too will see the potential in this event. I remember you were at first an enthusiast for the idea.' Of course I said something sensible – best not to rush, put the cart before the dancing horse etc.

The circus blighter proved hard to pin down. I was starting to think McKenna might be right. The chappie has done very well for himself – or got the Germans to do very well for him. As soon as I walked into his apartment I was glad it hadn't been me trying to get my chief in Tangier to stump up for this kind of lodging. One whole floor of a substantial house, with splendid traditional tiles throughout and sumptuous fabrics draped from and over everything. I doubt the Sultan's much better off. If he'd come to Marrakech under the British flag he'd be dossing on my sofa.

I was ushered in by a servant, and found the man reclining on a divan in the imperial manner. He stood to shake hands, but then flopped down again – trouble with his ankles, he said; perils of a lifetime of unremitting strain. The brief glimpse of him upright showed he's rather below average height and rather above average girth; very brown skin, and a moustache from twenty-five years ago, looping up towards his side-whiskers – and waxed, by the looks. He offered tea, good strong black stuff, and he'd even managed to get hold of some milk, which I never can; two sugars.

I couldn't place his accent. At times it was a resonant and elegant English; at times something like Italian, or Spanish. He was wrapped in some elaborate silky or velvet arrangement, and I wasn't sure if it was his own or some local thing he'd picked up.

I opened with formal welcome on behalf of diplomatic community, and then a less formal bit of rapport: understood we're both English.

'Is that so?' he said; 'really now, bless my soul.' But he made it sound as if he doubted one or both of us. He jumped into rather a detailed interrogation of who I am, and my role in the Embassy, and the nature of British authority here, any police presence, and so forth. Rather an old-fashioned sense of social distinction: Jane Austen-style, or how the tribesmen always sniff round each other.

I finally managed a question of my own. 'And – pardon me; afraid F.O. protocol training doesn't cover circuses – you would call yourself... the manager? the impresario? the ringmaster?'

'Yes indeed!' he chortled. 'That's a-right.'

I waited for an actual answer.

'Whatever you find most convenient, my dear sir!'

And how did he find Marrakech?

'Opened the window and there it was, ha-ha! Pardon the levity, my dear sir. Tolerable comfortable.' I wished he knew how much better off he is than most of us. 'Wonderful, these kinds of place. Mystic orient, ain't it? All that sort of thing.'

A servant appeared – a different one, I think – bringing a tray of sweet pastries; the little fried and honeyed things they like here. Having placed them between us, he began to fuss at the cushions on which the circus chap was reclining, clucking and primping until it was deemed adequate.

Once he was gone, the master leaned forwards, suddenly more serious despite the bits of pastry now stuck to the moustache. 'I cannot tell you', he said, 'how demanding it is to manage an enterprise of this scale in a place like this.' I expressed sympathy. 'The heat! The costs! The risks of unrest, shortages, disease. Regular plagues of Egypt, that's what you have to worry about. All the four 'orsemen of the apocalypse and one on a pony, ain't it? Circus man deals with them all.' He leaned further forwards, and almost over-balanced off his divan. 'Forgive me: your relationship to the German gentleman..?'

I explained the diplomatic community here, and described our collective desire to ensure that the circus is a success: entertainment but not too much excitement, as I put it – and, n.b., will do again in discussions and messages to Tangier. It was an apt moment to put in the question about who and what the circus actually comprises, and when exactly we might expect a performance; smoke out Klug's intentions.

'As and when you wish, my dear sir! As you all wish. We are but paid servants, sir, and glad if we do but amuse you one brief hour or two, while we strut and – er, you know. Tell me, d'you think there'd be interest in a performance or two in... in one of those other towns... er, other Moroccan towns?' I gave him a positive but non-committal answer – and really, given the business we've had to get the thing under control in Marrakech, the idea of going again somewhere else is a bit alarming. Suddenly all of the wind seemed to go out of him. 'Oh, it's so terribly hard', he said. 'Such a worry. Just don't know any more. Just don't know.' He shook his head and a few fragments of pastry came free. 'Just as you say, dear sir. Best not to rush it, eh?'

I said that seemed most prudent, and repeated my sympathy for his many burdens. And that was about that. I slipped in – the Prudhomme suggestion – an invitation for the chief and a select few of his personnel to a reception hosted by the French Embassy. 'Anything you wish, my dear sir! Paid servants, sir. Life's but a passing... er, ain't it?' – So we can get them along as personal guests regardless of Klug.

As I was leaving I tried again on where he was from; had gathered he was British, but... 'A city-zen of the world!' he cried. 'The circus knows no borders.'

Never a good thing to say to the Foreign Office. 'Yes', I said, 'but personally where are you from?'

He looked furtively round the room, as if a German representative might be lurking in one of the many potential hiding places. 'Bethnal Green', he said. 'Tell you what, one London man to another, by any chance you know how to get your hands on something for the old tummy? Lovely grub here, but I'm bunged up for days and then all of a sudden I'm on the thunder-box one hour in every three.' I assured him I would try to assist. British subject in distress.

One thing, I suppose: the existence of the Ringmaster chappie suggests that the circus is real. It does sound rather splendid, when you hear the range of performers and creatures. I've never actually seen a giraffe, and it's an incredible achievement to get one through the desert.

Unless he's just a confidence trickster, an actor, put up by Klug. Or gulling Klug for the fees.

But then he's performing being a performer. So it's still a kind of a circus.

◉

In the café on the corner, where the maze of alleys that make up Marrakech market empties onto the great square, the corner where the blind boy sings of a beautiful world he has never seen, and nor will you, morning is at its busiest and hottest. The square is the natural conclusion of the city; it is where everything ends. Invaders parade here. Public passions are expressed here. The most notorious crimes are punished here. The worst wretchedness and poverty slumps here, to scold us, to warn us, and then, in the chill forgetting of night when we have hurried chastened to what passes for our home, unobtrusively to die.

After the first bustle of morning and as the heat begins to thicken, the rhythms of the royal palace slow. It is his habit, in this lull, to walk out into the city and to drink a tea with his acquaintances. Today, however, though they wait politely a few minutes longer before beginning the elaborate pouring of the tea, he does not appear.

Not to be indiscreet, but was anything amiss? Had he perhaps mentioned something? It is unusual for him to be late, unheard of for him to be absent. But then, we are used to the unusual here; here we have heard everything.

Bit by bit, with each new visitor to the café, with the songs and tales, with the flurries of dust from the square, more is heard.

There was an offence. There was a sinning. There was a mistake, just a moment of clumsiness. There was an irregularity, in the backstreets of the palace accounts. A word was spoken: in error, in haste, in heat. A false report of him. A true report of him.

And today he does not appear.

Justice is swift and cruel. The decision of the Sultan, and the blade is immediate.

Justice is merciful; because, honestly, you'd prefer the blade to most of the alternatives. The rope... We can see each other thinking of the alternatives, as the tea cools. The garrotte. The irons. The hooks. The cuts. The torments beyond imagining, we are starting to imagine them and the scent of fresh mint sours around us.

Our acquaintance, he's not yet dead. The underground cells of Marrakech stretch infinite in the imagination, the chains, the shit, the rats, a labyrinth so much more narrow and winding and dark and obscuring than the alleys above ground, reaching far towards the mountains and deep into the earth. Through the surface, the world of light is reflected in the world of night. Beneath the city of the living is the city of the once living: those we knew and those we heard of; those we loved and those we feared; those less timid than us, and those less fortunate; our sins and our possible sins; our past, and our possible future. Tomorrow's fate is ever-present today, right below where we're sitting; just round the corner.

Our former acquaintance, he's as good as dead.

We do not say of our possible acquaintance: never. We would not of course show any surprise were he to appear tomorrow or in ten years, missing an eye or an ear, ghostly-pale and shrivelled. To express surprise is to question the rightness of the The Absolute Author. At the wrong moment, surprise can be imprudent. But as the day grows warmer it begins to muffle our memories. With the dust and smoke from the square, we do not see what we used to.

We have had an acquaintance. We used to have an acquaintance. We might have had an acquaintance. We have begun to question whether we had an acquaintance. Is it likely we had an acquaintance? Is it possible we had an acquaintance? We cannot be sure we had an acquaintance. We would not want to say we had an acquaintance. On balance we should say no, we did not have an acquaintance. We have forgotten if we had an acquaintance. Such is the grammar of prudence.

Our stories will begin to have a different emphasis. Imperceptibly, telling by telling, the man standing near the centre will say less, will drift to the margins of the group, and then begin to flicker, a mirage glimpsed in the desert; and then tomorrow or perhaps the day after, when the tale is repeated he will no longer be noticed in it at all.

A widow is not visible until she remarries.

Our future is written: we do not challenge or complain. Our past? well, it's only common sense to update it, keep it consistent with our present. Is it me or does this tea need refreshing?

Or perhaps this particular conversation takes place in the alley at the back of the El-Badi Palace where, down in the filth at the bottom of the wall, a tiny vent in the stonework marks the highest level of the cells below, the outlet for the stench and the moans, the one point of light.

⟨Ⓤ⟩

One afternoon Assia leads Eva into the warren of Marrakech to look at fabrics. Eva is clear that she's not going to buy anything, and Assia is clear that she's not expected to. Not a very inspiring excursion, then. The things we are required to do.

The alleys twist and drift, noise and movement and endlessness of things, faces and colours and shapes and scents and no straight path. At some point she realizes she has lost her bearings, distracted by a shout, a surge of mint, a swirl of curtain, something brushing against her hip. Assia is still there, just in front of her, head so poised and so fragile under its tight wrap, thinness obvious even under the shapeless gown. She turns her head frequently to chatter about something. They're no longer in the market streets Eva is used to, half a dozen people wide and everywhere a stall and a shop-front and a face beckoning her. This is gloomier. Life is less obvious. On one side a bare stone wall rising out of sight. Then a doorway: a grand stone arch and thick timbers. But it's closed. The shoe rack says it's a mosque; less grand than others she's passed. Still Assia leads her on. Then narrower still. A passageway now, here and there covered by a reed ceiling. Because the alleys and store-booths of Marrakech follow no pattern or shape, Eva has always wondered what's behind what she can see.

If it's just buildings, how do you get into them? Might there be open space? Might there be in this frenzy of humans, incredibly, something green growing? As the dull pink walls close in on her shoulders, the reeds overhead, she knows that she has fallen through the cracks of the city.

The other day a man at the edge of the big square tried to sell her a map. Eva likes maps: their assertion of certainty and exactness. The quality of this map showed an unusual lack of exactness; or perhaps the impossibility of certainty, in this ever-shifting city. Its painstaking curves, looping fragile around the page, were no different to the ornamental calligraphy she's been offered in shop after shop. Between the simple lines of the map, it was impossible to know what was supposed to be solid and what was not.

So when she falls through the cracks, she can't be sure what she's fallen into. But then Assia is smiling and beckoning through a low doorway, the worn remains of green paint, a foot-polished stone step, and another gorgeous grotto of fabrics sucks her in.

Shopping is supposed to be about things, not people; but here is a woman, with ravaged bony fingers touching her face and her hand, dark blinking peering eyes long-accustomed to fine-work in the gloom, and Eva is wondering about her. She really doesn't want to do more than look, but now she is sitting on a raffia stool. She has no intention of staying more than a couple of minutes, but now out of nowhere there is tea, and ten minutes pass, and fifteen. The sensation is not so much visiting a shop, as hiding in a cupboard. Fabrics of every texture and colour are piled over her and squeeze against her and she has wriggled her way in to burrow among them. Now the woman is taking her hand to run her fingers over some thick weave, pressing a swatch of silk against her cheek, draping something over her shoulder and something else over her thigh.

If I were a proper woman, Eva thinks, I would enjoy these properly. I would imagine how I would sew and wear; I would see the curtain and the cushion and the dress; already I'd be enjoying a little glow of domestic contentment, feeling the comfort and the success. Do you like it, dear? What a splendid woman she is!

So she tries to hide from her mind. Instead she relishes the sensual pleasure of it all. Damn the parlour, I'm off to the harem. A clump of golden material glows complacent. A plunge of dark blue damask, a flood of emerald across her lap, invite her into their sisterhood of power and elegance. A scrap of crimson sprawled across the top of a pile is legs-splayed brazen.

Then the sticky sweet rush of the mint tea has gone flat. There is too much here that she is not. An exchange of chatter, her empty pleasantries and whatever Assia is saying in lieu of translation, and the door is closing on this little hidden transgression, and the stink of the alley is sharp and sour.

'I'm sorry I didn't buy anything. I could just give her-'

'It is not expected. I tell her you will come back.'

'I won't come back.'

'I know. Also, really, she knows. Important to say it is possible, even if we know it is not.'

The ridiculous *politesse* of Europe. 'That's nonsense, Assia.'

A shrug, of course. 'We must say it is possible. Otherwise: what is the purpose of living until tomorrow?'

Eva turns, and immediately a man's face is in front of her. To her irritation, she finds herself lowering her eyes, murmuring something meaningless, stepping aside.

Still the man is looking at her. She looks at him. Hollowed face, eyes gloomy and stern as he glares at her. The traditional dull gown with its hood.

Blue eyes. The effect is so startling that it takes her an extra moment to recognize him.

It is Jan the Pierrot.

He's lost weight. He gazes at her a moment longer, and now she's reading new emotions: surprise, defiance. Then he pushes past her, another man close beside him, and hurries on.

'Are you feeling well, M'zelle?'

Eva realizes her surprise in the reaction to it. 'I'm fine. Sorry. That man – I – I know him.' Assia's face shows how unlikely this is. 'He's a man from the circus. Apparently he's... He's being Moroccan now.'

Shrug. 'Some foreign men do this.'

They drift away. Already, Eva does not recognize the alley.

She tries a tone of playfulness, to cover her lingering surprise at Jan's transformation. 'Shall I try to become Moroccan, Assia?'

'But why would you, M'zelle?' Assia stops. Looks at her. 'You think you know us so well now?'

Eva starts them walking again.

'You have good life with circus, yes M'zelle?'

Now she is shrugging. And now she is stopping. Her hand reaches for the stone beside her. Feels its roughness in her palm, its certainty.

'The circus was... escape. Survival. Probably I would not be alive, if I hadn't become a dancer and found a way to use this.' The younger woman is studying her. 'And yes, often it feels like freedom. Often I tell myself this. I enjoy sneering at women who do not have my liberty, my lack of restriction.' She realizes that her gaze is hard now. 'And one day, I will twist my ankle, and I will hurry the recovery and I will break the other ankle, and very soon after that I shall be a crippled, lonely, ex-dancer, hoping that starvation swallows me quickly.'

She waits for Assia's reply. Waits for the folk wisdom, the simpler truth born of a simpler life, the reassurance that may be found when all the layers of civilized anxiety are stripped away.

Assia nods and walks on. Eva snatches her hand away from the cold stone and follows.

☟

JOURNAL OF THOMAS SOMERLEIGH

The reception with the circus people. Prudhomme had pulled off the affair very deftly – with, I shall humbly report to Tangier, some behind-the-scenes help from Britain. First it was a reception being organized by the French Embassy. Then it was being organized in a chamber in the palace, France generously paying for some improvements and tidying. That had secured Prudhomme a private audience with H.M., at which he'd suggested that it would be his pleasure to have members of H.M.'s circus along, just a few and as his personal guests of course so no need to bother with approvals and so forth and wouldn't that be jolly? H.M. had naturally thought it the jolliest thing ever, and now there was no way Klug was going to stop it.

He carried on trying, right up until this morning. I bumped into Prudhomme at the palace first thing, and he was red-faced and pop-eyed. Klug had managed to stir up three different palace officials to run around with three different concerns to alarm the Sultan: the need to double-check with Berlin whether the reception was consistent with the agreement to finance the circus within the royal household; the public health issues surrounding further unregulated movement of unknown immigrants and livestock in the city; and potential disruptions to public order arising from an unusual and unpredictable social occasion.

I started pointing out – trying to sound supportive – that these were precisely the arguments we'd been using to challenge the presence of the circus, so it was a bit rich etc. Prudhomme near bit my head off: 'The issue is no longer the existence of the circus, but the control of the circus!' A final glare and – just as I was starting to ask whether Madame and Mademoiselle would be joining us – he turned and strode into the palace, his spindly legs looking like they couldn't keep up with him.

I was still doubtful about whether it would happen, when I caught up with Prudhomme again a while later. Little Abdelilah was doing a lot of listening. Prudhomme was still wild-eyed, still breathless – but now triumphant. 'I have impressed on everyone in the palace', he was saying, and from the looks of him he might actually have tracked them down one-by-one, 'how much I agree with my esteemed German colleague.' Abdelilah gaped at him, and though I recognized this as basic diplomacy I still wondered where it was going. 'I am accordingly summoning an emergency meeting of the committee on the administration of the circus… to meet at the earliest hour tomorrow morning.' Now he glanced at me, and he couldn't hold in the little smile. I nodded approval. Our Moroccan friend was still bewildered. 'First point on the agenda will be a review of the lessons we might draw from this evening's reception.'

'But Sidi Ambassador,' – at last Abdelilah managed to get a word out – 'some question whether the event is prudent, and still they may logically ask..'

'Nonsense!' Prudhomme brusque but positive. 'We all agree that the meeting must happen, and if the meeting is to review the reception, then logically the reception must happen.'

So happen it did.

The usual uncanny admixture of dull European styles in an exotic setting: grey suits, conventional ties, murmured conversation, and over us the columns of gleaming gorgeous marble and the wooden ceiling as mighty as a cathedral's and intricate like a beehive, and everything touched with gold. Constant feeling one's not doing justice to the setting, as one gossips of sewage arrangements and internal tariffs. Among the dips and the unavoidable regulars of the international community in Marrakech, a few palace and city officials showing us how to fit in.

Circus delegation a bit of a disappointment. Expected more hoop-la. But we'd kept the numbers down, and perhaps out of performance they don't have much in the way of smart clothes. They looked more like the survivors of some disaster. All rather bewildered and on best behaviour. The impresario-ringmaster chappie, of course: squeezed into a frock coat a generation or two out of date, very hot and rather on edge. The strong man, and he is indeed vast; though rather bashful – often the way with the bigger slower fellows, I suppose. A very pretty little thing, apparently some sort of acrobat; the mind boggles. A handful of others, including a grumpy woman who's supposed to be a dancer.

A sharp clap of hands to get attention, usual palace style. The vizier – Prudhomme next to him, magisterial without trying to hog the attention; he'd got what he wanted by making the event happen over German objections – welcomed us on behalf of H.M., thanked the diplomatic community for our generosity, and said how much H.M. was looking forward to seeing everyone. Oh, and particular thanks to Germany for kind donation of a couple of crates of champagne to the festivities. A sudden hardening around Prudhomme's eyes.

Somerleigh's lessons in diplomacy: when you spot which way the wind is blowing, tack smartly in that direction so you're not caught out by a gust. Credit to my German friend: he swallowed his pride and at the last moment jumped elegantly enough.

Ringmaster chap apparently very pleased to see me again, old pals reunited. He looked a little desperate as he shook my hand. I guessed he was finding it hard to position himself between Prudhomme and Klug. I introduced myself to most of the others, few words of welcome. Rather hard to know what to say to a huge Outer Mongolian or a petite Bulgarian. I doubt they're following the cricket, and I can see why internal tariffs wouldn't interest them. McKenna, as ever with Americans, who feel they don't have to bother with diplomatic form, naturally more relaxed and expressing polite curiosity and surprisingly knowledgeable about Central Asia. Ray, of course, all over the new ladies like a dose of mumps. Klug and Prudhomme equally wary of such unconventional specimens, and equally unwilling to let the other seem to be in charge. The best either of them could manage was an occasional intervention with the impresario, checking in proprietorial fashion that his team were enjoying themselves, or that the lions were eating all right, or that the sewage arrangements weren't too much of a trial. He, utterly bewildered by the diplomatic war being fought over him, increasingly red and sweating in his ancient suit, would nod eagerly and blurt 'All for the best in the best of all worlds!' or 'Vive l'Empereur!' or 'Donner und Blitzen!' or similar, with declining accuracy as the champagne took hold.

Then through the scrum I caught a flash of her face: the pale skin, the exquisite little ear. Hortense here! Then she was gone, but: how significant that I had recognized her so quickly. And the effect it had had on me. I drifted round through the crowd to be in the right spot for them to bump into me. Three minutes later and there they were: warm smile of recognition from Madame, and sincere delight – I could see it – I could see it in the bright eyes and the pretty smile – from Hortense. I got a hold of myself enough to greet Madame first: honour to have her here, raising the tone no end. Then Hortense's fingers were in mine, and I found myself bending over her hand. Think I managed to carry it off as ironic gallantry, but I'm sure she understood. 'We had to bully Papa to let us come and see the circus people!' she said, little giggle behind hand. Mama a touch disapproving at the advertisement of any aspect of domestic politics. 'But he'll be keeping a special eye on us to be sure we are behaving ourselves.' And with that she pulled away, and they each nodded to me and were gone. The slightest extra pressure on my hand as she let it go. Suppose I should be pleased to be considered an example of misbehaviour. And her eyes as we parted: so pleading; so fond.

The only caveat to the official aspect of the proceedings was the absence of H.M. the Sultan of Morocco. A few times the whisper went round that he was about to arrive, and ties and flies were checked and we dips all had a quick look round to see who was going to try to cut in before us with the courteous greeting. And then he wasn't arriving after all, and the buzzing of voices began to rise and we'd relax again. After the third false alarm I think we all individually gave it up. Seemed rather to undermine the whole point of the thing, and when I caught Prudhomme alone in the aftermath I mentioned it very cautiously. Wasn't at all sure how miffed he'd be feeling.

Not at all, it turned out. A quick glance around us to check no one in earshot, and then a light hand on my shoulder. 'For the best, I should say', he murmured. 'So unpredictable. The risk that His Majesty might get carried away by the effect of Klug's mediocre champagne, and think this was all a German idea after all. Let us make sure that we have the thing properly under control first, eh?' He leaned even closer, and I could feel the warmth of his breath and the wine on it. 'I confess, dear Thomas, that I spread, via three different officials, a message of concern about the effect on public order and the royal reputation of an appearance by His Majesty. Better this way, I think, no?'

◑

Eva has been curious about the Sultan of Morocco.

Because, after all, it's not every day, is it? And though life has taken her to diverse remarkable places, and with the endless travel you become more interested in the mattress than the scenery, there's always a moment when the memory of Wallonia and the endless grey sludge of wet coal dust under clogs and the endless grey sky reoccupies your mind, and the warm crystal sky and the fairy-tale detail of fabric on the edge of your vision demand that you worship them because if you do not show adequate respect the dream will fade and you will have to start trudging these last twenty years all over again, with sodden stockings and empty belly.

A palace: high thick blank stone walls, concealing impossibly large courtyards and glimpsed soft-lit arcades, fields of polished marble and towers of exquisite aquamarine tiles, the same culture that produced the market maze here reimagined as a place of quietness and formality, and she wonders about the hidden rituals of the market and she wonders what they're selling here.

The babble around her: look at that sword and I hope there's food and I hear the dungeons stretch for miles and the guards' faces are so black and I don't know how to bow properly to a Sultan, curiosity, unease, awe.

Her strange companions: to share a life with people of such diverse forms and qualities, their mysterious vanished homelands, their unique peculiar talents, the different ways they know her, an overshadowing shoulder, a hand in hers, a wary concern, a smile.

A voyage across the sea. A trek through the desert. Hardship and peril. A city imagined, doubted, and realized.

For once, instead of the dream flickering and distorting with each passing moment, today each step brings new detail.

Eva thinks of a biscuit tin child; pretends that she remembers her dreams. She wonders whether, in this story, the beggar maid's visit to the palace is the liberating climax – dance for me; try on this slipper – or the shabby fantasy pointing the way to her inevitable hobbling poverty unless she learns the right lesson.

The Maestro – fatter, slower – had burbled incoherently of what they were doing today and why they had to look their best, *only as good as our last performance ain't it my dears fairy-tale don't pay no bills*, and they had ignored him. Often in a new town some tedious reception to amuse a patron, people of pretended sophistication gawping to see if they had tails, men in suits gazing at cleavage and brushing past backsides because women who do not conform entirely to the norms of our social circle may be assumed to be entirely wanton. But a greeting from the Sultan: they heard that bit.

The reception itself is disappointing and reassuring. A chamber, yes, that literally takes the breath, as her eyes soar farther upwards and her shoulders open and she gasps: the hours – the fingers – that made that infinity of tiles; the torment to conceive and conjure that intricately-carved ceiling. But the same people as always. The suits. The unhealthy faces. The clumsy conversation: the don't-know-what-to-ask questions; the can't-possibly-say-what-I'm-thinking comments. The glances the murmurs the touches.

There is a Spaniard, smooth skin and Mediterranean complexion and waxed moustache, all of them thrusting closer towards her than is conventional, and revealing good teeth in a smile. Don somethingy-somethingy Reyes-de-somethingy-call-me-Ray. Again the smile. He adds 'as in sun' just as she's asking 'as in sting?'

He kisses her hand and Olga's with equal enthusiasm, which is unusual. Credit for that, at least.

Then there is an American. Correctly pleasant; unmemorably witty. Courteous sensible questions. Guidebook insights on the architecture. Americans are supposed somehow to be different to the rest of us; somehow special. Oddly lifeless and unconvincing, as if by mixing together all the different races they've ended up not with the best characteristics, but none of them.

She recognizes the senior German, from his inspection visit to the circus encampment. He is looking even more stuffed and uncomfortable. His previous unease about her breasts doesn't seem to trouble him as much now. But he is very on edge. Whenever she sees him, he is looking over the shoulder of whomever he's with. It's the anxiety of a man who's made too many treks through the desert, and is ever alert to bandit attack. Most often he's looking across the crowded chamber to another diplomat: also rather stuffed, and dressed in even more artificial old-fashioned style. Perhaps this one is the Sultan in disguise.

Occasionally the anxious glanced is reciprocated. The two diplomats circle the room, forever measuring their distance from each other. Like unruly planets; or novice dancers.

There are other foreign residents in Marrakech. The same lightweight suits. The same efforts to achieve distinction and daring in a handkerchief, a neck-tie, or a waistcoat. A French doctor, with the usual assumptions of familiarity. A German businessman: a blunt wide-eyed compliment, a question about circus life, and then hurrying away; his sincerity is rare on this pantomime stage, and refreshing.

There are wives. She knows she is expected to talk with them. She avoids them.

'Are there any Moroccans here?' she asks. It comes out unbidden, and she realizes too late that the faces in front of her were talking about something else.

'Not enough turbans and elephants, eh?' says an English accent. 'Fear we're rather a disappointment. Perhaps you're all so exotic you've scared them away!'

His words are a pleasant occupation of those few seconds, but neither useful nor particularly amusing, and yet again Eva wonders what all the fuss is about the English: what exactly it is that they contribute to the world, besides colonizing oxygen less unpleasantly than some while they undercut your cloth industry.

She offers a polite smile, then feels her irritation simmering as the previous conversation resumes.

A whisper at her shoulder, beneath the attention of the rest of the group: 'I hoped to meet the Sultan.'

It's a young woman, twenty-odd: petite, dark, pretty. Rather similar to Olga, but the body and the movements are laxer, less trained. Eva smiles, nods sincerely, mouths her agreement.

They turn away together. 'I so like to meet Moroccans', says the dark girl, her words emerging uncomfortable in English. 'But my father forbids it. I am Hortense.'

'Eva.' They shake hands; not the walrus-flipper slap of men but the thumb-over-fingers rustling of women. 'Good theatre, perhaps. The suspense is maintained. The excitement builds.' Because of the girl's name she's speaking French. 'Only at the end do we discover: climax, or bathos; dream or disappointment.' Hortense nods; the theatrical metaphor pleases her. 'One sees Moroccans enough in the streets, though; the market.'

Wariness. 'I… I do not go out so much.'

Eva understands; doesn't pry. 'Here's one!'

Standing on his own at the edge of the hall, eyes darting restless between all of the different groups of conversation, is a short slender Moroccan man. His face is

clearly Moroccan – the complexion, the gauntness, are now
familiar – but he's dressed in an oddly mixed costume: the
traditional robes of a Moroccan official, open at the throat
to reveal a European stiff collar and neck-tie.

Hortense tucked in close beside her, Eva walks up to
him. 'Good afternoon, Monsieur.'

She knows her forwardness is unseemly – wonders at
the last minute if this, after all, is the Sultan – and to her
horror finds herself making an instinctive curtsey.

Its effect on him is even worse. He recoils, physically
startled, as if instead of lowering her hem she'd lifted it.

'No – please – Mademoiselle – welcome to Morocco!'
All of this in a rush of French, muffled by a frenzy of
bowing. Eva has been about to offer him her hand, but
understands it would probably give him a heart attack. He
stares at them. Remembers to whisper 'Mademoiselle' to
Hortense too, in lieu of greeting. Can't look at either of
them. Keeps jerking his head towards some point across
the room.

Dear Lord, Eva is thinking, is our femininity really so
obscene? Our foreignness so overwhelming?

No one else is going to say anything, so eventually she
says: 'We are Eva and Hortense.'

The man mouths 'Hortense', and it seems to cause him
yet further discomfort. Another bow: 'Mademoiselle, I have
the great honour to collaborate with your esteemed father'
– the glance across the room is slight but unmistakeable,
and now Eva realizes where it is aimed – 'in the committee
on the security of the circus. A great honour. A truly great
man. Please to excuse me.' And bow and he is gone.

The two women look at each other, amazement and
amusement. 'I realize who he is now', Hortense says. A
whisper: 'Father is very rude about him!' She giggles.

Eva's dreams of a Sultan have been disappointed today.
But if instead she'd compromised and dreamed of a senior

diplomat, Hortense's father would have been very satisfying.

There is no sign of haste, but as they turn to face the rest of the room immediately he is in front of them. A man of average height, but possessed of that curious quality by which his manner and expression make him seem taller. Everything is sharp: collar points, goatee beard, nose, eyes. Everything is sleek: the sweep of the little moustache, the perfect line of well-oiled hair back from the forehead, the old-fashioned suit. Everything is precision: the tie, the pince-nez.

Everything is gazing at Eva. She finds that the Moroccan man's reverence was infectious: she finds herself lowering her eyes, nodding respectfully to the man, and like all the other times she knows that this is how we conform and she feels her stomach turn.

Hortense remembers her duty and presents Eva. Eva offers her hand, it is loosely taken and considered like some indifferent product on a market stall, and they exchange Monsieur and Mademoiselle. 'Mademoiselle Eva is of the circus!', says Hortense, enthusiasm obvious.

'Yes', says her father. Many things are obvious in the word. Enthusiasm is not one of them.

'From Belgium!'

'Indeed.'

She holds his gaze. He is at least looking at her straight.

His profession is to fill uncomfortable gaps, in conversations as well as maps. 'And what is your role in the circus?'

The remotest connection with culture would be intolerable to a Frenchman. 'I juggle', she says. 'Potatoes. Also sometimes kitchen implements.' He nods, indifferent. What else would he have expected of a female Belgian circus artiste? Safer to be ridiculous than proud.

'You met little Abdelilah, I see.' He reciprocates the other man's glance across the room.

'Oh yes', says Hortense. 'He was most complimentary about you, father.'

The thought wrinkles Monsieur Prudhomme's nose like a bad smell, and the pince-nez twist askew. He straightens them. 'Mm. Funny little fellow. Hard working. Good!' It is not clear what is good.

Satisfied that little Abdelilah has not molested his daughter and – with one final glance of unease as he turns – that nor has Eva, he is gone as imperceptibly as he came.

There is so much that Eva knows it would be unfair to ask. Instead she says: 'So, we still haven't met the Sultan.'

'I thought I had seen him once, at a reception when we arrived in Marrakech. But father said I was wrong.'

There is more champagne, on a tray carried by a beautiful adolescent boy – gown of some rich blue fabric and eyes for the altar – who is gone before they can thank him.

'Has your father met him?'

'Oh yes!' Hortense's pride is rather charming. 'Often. While we are away from the capital, it is father's duty to represent France with the Sultan. So he must work very hard to prevent bad influences on him. Always he must seek official meetings, to advise or request. I don't know details.' Hortense leans closer. 'Your circus has made a lot of extra work! I think father has been very worried.'

'I didn't realize we were so dangerous.'

'Oh yes! Father is very worried about the general atmosphere of instability within the city and the wider security environment given the condition of the tribes.' It is recited like a hard-learned exercise in Latin. Eva is trying to combine her impressions of Marrakech with the horror she saw in the desert, and to understand what the circus has to do with either of them.

More champagne. She is trying to remember a father of her own, and to conjure a memory of such a fond and dutiful Eva. As ever, when she goes looking for resources in the past, she finds the cupboard bare.

'So... does your father tell you what the Sultan's like?'

Hortense's eyes are wide over her glass, all the bubbles going up her nose and illuminating her. She checks there is no one near, and leans closer. 'Father says he's... he's... a ridiculous monkey!'

Eva's reaction is close enough to what Hortense expects, and she giggles furtively behind the glass. But Eva doesn't know what to say and now Hortense's awe at her own daring becomes worry. She takes another mouthful of champagne. 'Yes, yes, apparently he has the most ridiculous collection of... of everything, of silly things, of bric-à-brac. His palaces are bursting with it all. Anything European that he sees or hears of he must buy immediately. Bicycles. Umbrellas. Barrel-organs. Wigs.' – a whisper – 'Ladies' undergarments. Jewels. Carriages – the carriage was washed away in a storm. And animals too, apes and cows and kangaroos and parrots and elephants and everyone says he has an emu.'

'An emu?' For some reason, the idea is particularly delightful.

'Yes! Father says it is the wrong climate for it; he calls it a trophy, a ridiculous import out of place. Me, I think it is very romantic; so graceful, so miraculous! And also he has strange artists and musicians and magicians, and, and...'

'...and circuses?'

Hortense's eyes go wide.

Eva smiles, and contrives a little giggle, and Hortense relaxes. 'Gosh, yes, it does all sound... ridiculous.'

They smile at each other. It doesn't feel so warm now.

Conveniently, Monsieur Prudhomme appears and by some unspoken power of will has summoned Hortense. She grips Eva's hand and says anxiously how much she enjoyed meeting her and how much she hopes they will meet again, and Eva is nodding and agreeing and, curiously, she finds she means it.

Monsieur offers her a brief nod and murmured nothing, and a longer glance of wariness. The Prudhommes depart.

Eva has some more champagne. She stands alone at the edge of the sumptuous hall, not really seeing the figures grazing in the centre.

She thinks: I never have time to make female acquaintances. Find accommodation, food, a laundress or at least some warm water, solitude, music, an occasional fuck, and then move on.

She thinks: Was Monsieur more alarmed that his daughter looked excited, or more alarmed that she was with me?

She thinks: If Monsieur did hear what his daughter said, he would be angry at the repetition of his undiplomatic opinion. Then he would relax, because it was only to a Belgian dancing woman.

She thinks: Why would you need elephants and apes and parrots and bric-à-brac and whatever, when you have Frenchmen and Germans and Spaniards and Americans and Englishmen visiting you?

In the faces drifting in front of her, she doesn't see any of the diplomats she was introduced to. Perhaps they have all gone. Perhaps there is a rule. The worried Moroccan man – Abdelilah – has gone. The Maestro has gone. The reception has entered its sour stupid decline, as do all parties.

Somewhere in this palace there is a Sultan, while down below the party continues. Is he alone? Is he admiring a wig, or a parrot, or a bicycle? Is he sad or glad he is not here, with the blurred foreigners carousing regardless in his home?

She shouldn't drink any more champagne. She drinks just a bit more champagne. A tray clatters to the floor. Olga is looking angry but laughing gamely. The figures are moving more clumsily, or she is seeing them less clearly.

〽

In the café on the corner, where the maze of alleys that make up Marrakech market empties onto the great square, the corner of the tassel-weavers, morning is at its busiest and hottest. The square is the distillation of everything that is truly Moroccan about this city – people, passion, food, craft, trade, song, tale, appetite – turned inside out to be displayed for the foreigners, like a fig obscene and succulent, for them to admire and suck and savour, and to drop dry in the gutter by the snake charmer's mat.

After the first bustle of morning and as the heat begins to thicken, the rhythms of the royal palace slow. It is his habit, in this lull, to walk out into the city and to drink a tea with his acquaintances. Today, as he wriggles with fake casualness through the bodies to the usual table, he is looking more carefully at the other people who might be listening.

Not to be indiscreet, but I must tell you everything. Last night in the palace there was such a revelry: an entertainment, a carousing, a debauchery, an orgy. There was a dancing woman, dressed or better to say undressed in a way that in public is merely obscene, and she twisted and capered and cavorted around the room, teasing and tormenting all that she touched, with but the hem of her diaphanous gown or one strand of her serpentine hair. And there was tobacco and there was alcohol and there was everything that is alien and everything that is ungodly. And the smoke and the foreign incantations made of the dancing woman an evil spirit, seductive and destructive to any man who dared even to look at her. Her unnatural undulations –

oh, to think of her unnatural undulations! I must not – turned all of the women around her into nymphs of the night, to dazzle the eyes and to lead men astray. And truly, they were led astray. His Majesty is made the puppet of the foreign magicians. His Majesty in fact has been locked in a cage and his place is taken by a spirit conjured in his image, and he conducts the ungodly revels.

Of course you always knew, but now you really know.

Never before was it true but now it is true.

Circus? I've seen a circus. You get a monkey, you get a clown, you get a juggler maybe. Few jokes, a song, monkey does a dance, some old hag promises you a fortune, all good clean fun. This is no circus. This is unnatural animals and unnatural women. This is magicians and monsters and evil spirits, this is our city turning into a cesspit, this is what happens when you let foreigners in, this is what happens when you live in sin.

You've heard the music in the street. Everyone has. You've seen the faces. Everyone has. That's the point. The spirits are among us now. It's getting like I don't recognize my own city any more, sometimes you see more pale faces than normal ones; big stupid faces, crafty calculating faces.

If we're not careful, we'll end up behaving like them; they drag us down to their level.

They've even said as much. They want us to behave more like them. Dress like us, dance like us, eat and drink like us, say the Shayatin, and you shall be rewarded with these Francs, these women. Hungry mouths are most vulnerable to the devil.

Or perhaps this particular conversation takes place in the gutter by the snake charmer's mat.

ﷺ

We cannot escape our natures. We cannot escape our physical reality. However much we dream, or philosophize, or create, we must inevitably suffer death, disease, and discomfort and daily defecation.

Put it another way: like it or not, we cannot escape our families. However far we may be lucky enough to separate ourselves in geography, we know that we have an unbreakable physical identity. They are part of us, as much as our fallible failing organs; our relentless anus.

Put it another way: like children warned not to play in shit, not to put their fingers in the fire because they will get burned, Magda and Olga are drawn to each other.

Magda and Olga remember a story told by Ali the tale-teller of the big square. Perhaps Olga heard it via Magda; or perhaps Magda heard it via Olga. Perhaps they heard it together, because as often as they drift away individually into the market, inevitably – we don't need to go into all the unsavoury metaphors again, surely – they sometimes find themselves in the market together. One last simile, if you permit: the alleys of the emotions are as tricksy as the alleys of this city.

Anyway, once upon time – whichever of the sisters is not speaking at this point will contrive to look scornful, while breathlessly awaiting an opportunity to jump in – there was a young lord; the last of a long line of noble blood, a family who had always been lords, a young man of great beauty and virtue.

His name was Hassan – Olga savours the name delicately.

That wasn't his name – says Magda.

Anyway, tragically the family had fallen on ill-times. Due to politics and treachery and jealousy, they lost their influence. Their fortune was stolen, their estates confiscated, their name ruined. After his beloved father broke his heart for grief, young Hassan was forced to flee for his life, and to wander the land in disguise, begging and breaking his back just to survive.

This – Olga notes – is the great cycle of existence, the true romance of life; the greatest shall for a time be the lowest, and in the end virtue shall be rewarded.

Shit happens – confirms Magda.

Anyway, after a year and a day of wandering through the desert, Hassan found himself in the lands of the ancient enemies of his people. At nightfall he came to a great fortress under the mountain, and knocked at the door and begged for the humblest shelter. He was brought before the ruler of the district, and this mighty warlord demanded to know his name. Standing there in his rags, Hassan declared his own name proudly, and his father's. 'I am neither more nor less', he said. 'I bear no ill will or claim against your tribe, whatever your name or history; but nor am I ashamed of my own. I will hide from no one, not even myself.'

Well, the lord – He was an old man now – Oldish, anyway – Forbidding and severe – Wise and respected – The lord, anyway, was charmed by the honesty and spirit of the young man. He welcomed Hassan, and ordered that he be made comfortable for as long as he wished. And the old man explained that the tides of political favour meant that Hassan's family was no longer cast out.

And in any case, here across the desert he did not choose to abide by the political currents of tribes who had been his enemies.

And in any case, he had a duty of hospitality to a man who knocked at his door in peace.

Especially a young handsome man of good family.

Anyway, Hassan found that within the mighty mountain walls a man could be made very comfortable indeed. The walls were hung with richest damask, the beds were laid with softest silk, the tables were decorated with the finest gold ornaments, the meals were the rarest delicacies, and every costume was woven with the choicest jewels.

That's to say, it was a place of great culture. There was a magnificent library, and learned men would travel from far lands to debate, and every evening was accompanied by musicians of great skill, and it was a place where God was worshipped with humility, reverence, and thought.

Anyway, what's important is that the lord had three daughters and no son, and this – as he explained – was a great sadness to him. His first wife – and here his eyes filled with tears – had died giving birth to a daughter. He had married again, to a woman who already had two daughters of her own, but despite his best efforts – here perhaps her eyes filled with tears – his second wife could not bear him a son either.

And this sorrow was typical of his gentleness.

And typical of his cynicism.

What's important is that Hassan realized that this mountain fortress offered him more than shelter, and more than comfort, and more than kindness. Here he could restore his fortunes. Here he could find happiness.

The daughters themselves aren't important.

Obviously.

But one needs to know that the youngest – Her name was Aziza – Or something like that – The youngest was his real daughter from his first wife. Her two step-sisters were older than her – Perhaps that seems confusing because they sort of came into the story later, but it's perfectly possible – Anyway, she did not get on with them at all. They were cruel to her, and told lies about her to their mother who was Aziza's step-mother, and poor Aziza let her father believe them because she could see that it was so important to him to be happy with his new wife.

The step-mother was probably some kind of witch; you get a lot of that sort of thing in Africa.

Even real mothers can be terribly cruel. They torment you and bully you and criticize you. They abandon you and ignore you and leave you desperate for love.

Anyway, the step-sisters were different; in a story you can't have sisters without them being different.

As much as Aziza was fair, the sisters were ugly.

Ugly indeed – echoes Magda – women of the worst reputation, women of no morals.

So ugly! – Olga repeats – wrinkly and hairy and smelly and even the street dogs avoided them.

Vain and snobbish – adds Magda – obsessed with pretty things, and everyone laughed at them behind their backs.

After Hassan had been in the fortress a month, the old lord summoned him. 'Dear Hassan', he said, 'my daughters are all my family and my all future. I seek only for a son, and an heir: a man to marry one of them, and care for all of them. I have been watching you closely, and I am impressed by you. Despite our past differences, I respect your family. You are a worthy heir to your father; perhaps you might be a worthy heir to me.'

At this Hassan was amazed.

Well, not entirely, perhaps. Couldn't be much of a surprise, and young Hassan knew what he was about.

'Yet have a care', went on the old man – It was as if he were reading Hassan's thoughts – 'I want no mercenary for an heir. You will spend three more days here. You will, if you wish, spend time with each of my three daughters. Perhaps none of them interests you, in which case you are free to leave, with my blessing and with safe passage for your journey home and with the assurance that in the future I will work to maintain good relations between our peoples. Or perhaps you will wish to offer yourself as husband to one of them. But here is where you must be most cautious. I must know that they are appreciated for who they are, not for my power or my money.'

Because a man who only wants those will be a bad husband.

And also a bad ruler.

Anyway, the old man went on: 'If I see that your heart and your choice are not pure, I shall have you thrown out into to the desert again, poorer and more despised than ever you were, and you shall wander the rest of your days.'

News of this arrangement reached the women as fast as the wind through the battlements – Probably the wife heard it and rushed to tell her two daughters, and Aziza was in the background sweeping; that would be about right – Anyway, they were immediately overwhelmed with excitement, for Hassan was fair and strong, and a most promising man – A handsome prince and a happy ending: what more can you ask? – Gentleness and kindness: can't they exist outside of fairy-tales? – And they knew that whoever he chose would basically become queen, and they had seen what a splendid situation that was. Immediately the two older sisters began demanding hot water for baths, and screaming for their wardrobes, and selecting the best arrangements of jewellery to set off their features and their favoured costumes. In the meantime, their mother summoned Aziza. 'Pay heed, girl', she said with a sneer. 'Your two sisters are older than you, and it is their right to be considered first. Also, if you try to interfere I shall make very clear to your father that you are being inappropriate and disobedient and hurtful to his wife, and you wouldn't like that, would you my dear?'

Aziza knew that her step-sisters' age did given them priority; and she knew that her step-mother was capable of twisting her father's mind against her. So she nodded and curtseyed.

But she could not resist saying: 'And yet, we all know that when my father dies and either of my step-sisters becomes queen, they will have me thrown out to fend for myself in the street. And we all know what that means.'

'Well, what do you expect?' replied the step-mother with another sneer. 'Same old story, isn't it? As you say, we all know it, so you can hardly be surprised. Now, return to your chores: my daughters need water for their baths, and their clothes at their best, and their apartments spotless.'

The first of the three days dawned. Hassan was looking his best. He made a ceremonial visit to the apartments of the women, and there he found the two elder sisters, one dressed in shining white and one in unalloyed black. They showered him with compliments, and spoke at great length of the duties of women in the home, and the young man was left in no doubt that either way he would be appropriately looked after. Aziza was nowhere to be seen; her absence was not noticed.

At dusk, rather weary, Hassan begged leave to be left alone, and he went at sat by the well which was in a small courtyard tucked away in one corner of the fortress. There he sat, and tried to reflect on the day.

As he sat there, he saw a simple servant girl come into the courtyard carrying a bucket. She was dressed in rags, and she was barefoot and dirty, and her face and hair were unadorned and rather wild. Hassan watched her pulling at the well. He saw her deftness, her strength and her efficiency; he wondered at her endurance with such labours, day after day. When she had finished her labours, she gave the young man a respectful greeting and went about her work. He wondered at the slight smile he had glimpsed as she turned away.

On the second day the two elder sisters were dressed one in a rich red and one in a gorgeous green. They sang to Hassan, and demonstrated their skill on musical instruments of fine-polished wood and gleaming pearl, and they tried to speak of scholarly matters and religious truths, and Hassan was left in no doubt that either way he would have an impressive wife.

We shouldn't be too harsh on them, should we? It's their mother's fault they are the way they are, and they think they're doing the right thing, but we know otherwise.

Aziza was nowhere to be seen; her absence was not noticed.

Once again, Hassan sat by the well at dusk, trying to decide if he had learned anything that would help his decision. Once again the servant girl came to the well, and he watched her. She was perhaps the same age as him, he decided. Today he thought he saw weariness. He stood and politely offered to help her pull up the bucket. Politely she thanked him, and they worked together in silence for a few minutes. At the end she thanked him – and said that she hoped that his day had been pleasant. Hassan laughed, and said that his had surely been easier than hers, but perhaps no more satisfactory.

Her reply surprised him. Instead of saying anything about how hard she had to work, she spoke of his challenges in proving himself a fit man, and of the sisters challenges in making themselves acceptable women to him. Hassan wondered at her wit and her consideration.

On the third day the two elder sisters were dressed one in robes of shining silver and one in robes of glowing gold. The robes clung to them tightly, and they were careful to stand and sit so that their bodies were emphasized, and everything they said and did made it very clear how pleasurable the young man's life would be with either of them. Aziza was nowhere to be seen; her absence was not noticed.

Although Hassan did wonder. The old man had mentioned three daughters, hadn't he? that's the usual form, isn't it?

Once again he sat by the well at dusk, and tried to think. Once again the servant girl was there. Today she seemed even wearier, and Hassan insisted that she rest while he worked the well. They didn't not speak, but as he worked his mind was free to watch the girl. He wondered at the subtle strength of those limbs, and the beauty of the face under the dirt; he remembered her little smile, and tried to provoke it as she bade him a respectful good night.

The next morning the lord summoned Hassan, and demanded to hear the results of his three days of visiting. Imagine his disappointment when – with all the women standing there, waiting eagerly – Hassan replied: 'My lord, I regret that I cannot choose easily, and I dare not choose lightly. I would rather take my leave of you and depart alone. Your daughters offer me everything that is appropriate in a woman, and yet still I know not how to prove myself appropriate to them. Nor, among their many excellent qualities, can I discern any that makes one better than the other.'

Hassan pointed past the two elder sisters to a figure standing discreetly in the shadows, his companion at the well. 'Why,' he said, 'I find at least as much virtue in this servant girl.'

'How dare you?' roared the lord. 'That is no servant! That is my daughter, my beloved Aziza!'

Hassan was amazed, but replied quickly: 'I meant no disrespect, my lord. To me it means little whether she is princess or servant. She is a woman, no more and no less, with all of the virtues and qualities I could ask of any.'

'You see, father?' Aziza said softly. 'Surely you can have no doubts of his fitness as a son.'

The step-mother was furious. 'I ordered you not to interfere!' she screeched at Aziza.

'I was following your orders exactly', replied Aziza. 'I was doing my chores to care for my sisters.'

And the lord was overjoyed, and declared Hassan his son and his heir, and blessed the young couple.

Hassan took Aziza in his arms and they made love – not right there and then, obviously – and the mountains shook and the rivers burst their banks so powerful and glorious was their union.

And it was so beautiful – adds Olga – because first he made her speech of such gentleness and humility, and for a long time they just gazed at each other in silence, and felt the scent of the flowers around them, and only after the longest time did they even touch fingers, and his body in hers felt like a sweet song whispering as the evening breeze in her heart.

It was wholly natural – agrees Magda – No performance, no empty poetry, just two humans who needed each other and could make each other happy, and his body in hers felt like strength and certainty and just reward.

And in the end even her sisters saw that Aziza had been right, and they begged her forgiveness. And she forgave them for after all they were her sisters, and the prince promised to ensure that they too were cared for.

That's right – agrees Magda.

And they all lived happily ever after. Probably the palace was big enough for everyone to have a bit of space.

☽

JOURNAL OF THOMAS SOMERLEIGH

Something Brahim said – The story-tellers of Morocco – the lad in the big square everyone's always going on about: they're always tales of corruption, poverty, wretchedness – and capricious fate. I said I'd gathered as much. As if Dickens was all dying urchins and no comedy bits. It is, he suggested, an insane pretence that they have some kind of influence in their own lives: as if by acknowledging how tough things are, they at least claim a kind of superiority over their own lot; perspective is power. When really all they can do is hide in these fairy-tales. Transformation into a prince; unexpected riches; unexpected riches and a beautiful woman.

Aladdin and the magic lamp, I suggested, and he agreed.

Or an enchantress, put in old Sa'id, or a magical bird, or the local chiefs, or a judge, or the Sultan. 'All to us are supernatural forces, capable of transforming our lives in an instant or destroying them.' And he smiled and added that foreign diplomats are just the same. 'You too – pardon me – are our magic lamp. We... rub you, and we hope for wonders.'

Fantasies of salvation: Brahim's phrase.

'Sort of all a metaphor, isn't?' I suggested. I pointed upwards; one doesn't like to mention religion with these fellows.

And Sa'id smiled and said that metaphor – 'the idea that something can be both itself and something else' – was the beginning of language, and persuasion, and story-telling, and poetry, and dreams.

And Brahim scowled and said that metaphor was the beginning of lies and of oppression: 'the promise of paradise and the imposition of slavery'. The old man patted his arm fondly.

Need a bit more of the 'virtue and hard work rewarded' stuff, I suggested. Brahim replied: you may keep your western fairy-tales.

☪

'Our stories,' says Assia, 'are always about girls who fall. To leave your home, to show your face, to have inappropriate ambitions: it is inevitable you become a prostitute. Much better to be fairy-tale princess, waiting at end of story for brave man.'

Eva doesn't know how she's supposed to answer.

Assia shrugs. 'These are the stories we are told. It must be so exciting to be a European woman – go where you want, do what you want, wear what you want.'

'Yes', says Eva. And she does not know whom she is betraying more.

         ☫

Hassan and Aziza were lying on the roof one evening, looking at the stars – Perhaps it was earlier, during one of the three evenings when they were at the well together – It would depend what season the story was set: whether it got dark enough early enough for the stars to be visible.

Anyway. 'Certain infidels', said Hassan, 'believe that the stars depict creatures, and they name them accordingly. They take those loosely-spaced dots and make identities out of them; stories even.'

'And instead they are but accidents of creation?' Aziza replied.

'They are not accidents, because they are created by the design of our Lord. By them He allows us to find our way across the desert.'

'And He shows us that the world may have beauty. They are not to be explained. They show us that some things are unimaginable and impossible.'

'Certain infidels use them to make stories about their own destiny, which of course is also a great error.'

'But wouldn't that be the most terrifying thing of all?' Instinctively Aziza moved closer to Hassan. 'If the heavens simply did not care about us?'

         ☫

Another day dwindles. They used to climax: performance, liberation, applause. They used to be distinct: a different routine, a different city.

Eva remains determined to exercise her body each day. For a while she told herself she was maintaining her fitness and form out of professional commitment to the circus and to the audience. Now it's for health; for identity. She has a rhythm, a ritual. Twice per day. She has adapted so that she does not coincide with Assia's five prostrations to the muezzin. It might seem like mockery. She expected Assia to be more curious: a face at the window, a bright frank question. But the girl is equally concerned not to disrespect ritual.

This evening, a supper. It is carefully veiled in propriety: the invitation is general; the casual suggestion happens to incorporate some men of the circus as well as some women; at least one of the younger foreigners resident in Marrakech will be there with his wife, and the invitation such as it is comes from them both; it is in a hotel restaurant, neutral terrain and public. But – on the threshold, protected by Shevzod's bulk and Magda's scowl, seeing the predominantly male guests, their relative youth and the specific absence of the two older diplomats she'd noticed at the palace, the smiles and the lamps and the wine and the furtive blank-faced waiters – she knows no one's fooling anyone.

If the veil is tight enough, the features are obvious. She accepted the invitation.

On one side of her, a French scholar spending a year in the city researching spirituality. On the other, Reyes the Spaniard. The sleek charm of his face and manners are immediately remembered, and immediately he re-impresses himself on her, lips to hand and eyes locked on hers a moment too long and good teeth shining and hungry. Among the faces opposite, she recognizes the sincere German from the palace reception – a merchant of some kind, was it? And there's a non-face which might be the vaguely irritating Englishman: a kind of empty pleasantry of feature, fit to produce empty pleasant words. Looking pleasant is the summit of English physiological development, and the most any of them would tolerate;

beauty to them is showy, suspect... foreign. The American is not there. She knows he's too careful.

The wine, which one of the men has provided from imported stock, is fresh, a rare treat, sumptuous, provoking. She doesn't know this herself, and has never had a status to be able to discern or care, but this is how the men describe it. As usual, they are discussing wine in the same way they discuss women. With the same ironic suggestion of independent character. Eva is much more interested in the food – the meat is tender, fine-tasting; flavoured with coconut, perhaps – but no one talks about it.

The convivial atmosphere – and even she feels it – warms, and thaws. Faces become brighter, opinions clearer, movements freer. These foreigners are more distinctive in a Moroccan context; against the plain plaster wall.

Diplomats, indeed, have learned to be professionally distinctive. The Frenchman must speak for France and embody some unmistakeable Frenchness. Likewise the Englishman for England and Englishness, and so on.

So the men are foolish according to their diverse national stereotypes: pedantic; dull; clumsy. And they are foolish according to the strange pretence of diplomacy: the obligation to make the smallest simplest comment a complete and irrefutable statement of global truth; the insane habit of expressing a personal opinion in the third person, as the shared belief of millions; the construction of a parallel world of words, entirely removed from what they're talking about. And then they are foolish according to the universal calculus by which a man who drinks a glass of wine becomes clumsier and more obvious in exactly the same proportion as he thinks himself suaver and more subtle.

But compared to the average audience they are worldly, and articulate, and in some cases open-minded. The group is relatively young, averagely handsome and more than averagely cultured and cosmopolitan and witty.

For once she can pretend to be part of it, rather than performing for it. Eva finds herself relaxing, warming, enjoying herself.

'Do you tell men's fortunes, mystical Eva?' asks Reyes the Spaniard, eyes suddenly large next to her.

'Sometimes.' Deliberately she speaks in the most professional tone, and doesn't look directly at him. 'Usually the women take it in turns to be the fortune-teller. Sometimes Shevzod, in places where they might resent a woman having wisdom.'

'Are not all cultures wary of this?' A hint of rare understanding in the lively face, the soft rich voice. By turning towards her and allowing his knee to brush along her leg he undermines his rarity while reinforcing his generalization.

'Lots of cultures make women wise; I suppose it allows men to be irresponsible. But I don't think there are many that give them the power to go with it.'

'Will you tell me my fortune?' Ancient opening.

'Oh, but I did not take you for one of these men of passive character.' A flicker in his eyes. It was a deliberate tease. Don Whatsisname Reyes Whatsisname does not think himself passive; especially not with his knee within striking distance of a woman's thigh. 'Whatever I might say for you tonight, tomorrow you may overturn it by force of will.' Ancient opening, well-used retort.

'Perhaps I may be so impressed by your wisdom that I dare not overturn it.' Better than average riposte. 'Perhaps you, at least, will prove to have power.' Credit for the elegance of the lie.

'Perhaps you will prove too subtle for my wisdom or my power. Some men are impossible to tell for.'

A rich tut. 'Perhaps after all, mystical Eva, you fear to find the limits of your power.'

It's a shrewd provocation, when most men would have capitalized on her humility rather than her defiance; credit for that. He has dropped his voice, moved a fraction closer; the suggestion of private intimacy rather than public scorn, and credit for that. There is a hit of insistence, too; something a fraction harder in the tone. The Spanish gallant really does want his fortune told, and he will resent obstruction and despise delay.

Very well, handsome Spanish man, let's play. Eva turns her upper body towards him; there's been enough movement among the legs for the time being. 'If in truth you are so brave, you are brave enough for the truth.' The usual patter, and she has deepened her voice and ripened her vowels. He hears it, smiles at it, and then composes his face in mock-gravity. The knowing irony of performance is adequate cover for the knowing irony of flirtation. 'Now let us see.' Which is, surely, why humans perform. 'How may I know your soul, stranger?'

He offers her his palm ready for telling, forcing the touch. She ignores it. She does not want anyone else to see her surrendering her hand to him; and she might want to use it herself at some point. She gestures to his half-full glass. 'Drink, stranger.' He's surprised. 'The end of the wine shall show us the end of the night, and so shall it show us the end of life.' By now she's moved her accent eastwards. Always one must judge what the subject will find most exotic. 'Drink life to the last, if you dare.'

Anglo-Saxons find almost any kind of foreigner exotic. Northern Europeans thrill at the fiery Latin enchantress. Mediterraneans are awed by a touch of the icy northern priestess. Which foreign people did you fear as a child? Which did you fight as a diplomat?

A last glance of wary amusement, and Reyes knocks back his wine. Inviting them to drink is a nice hint of recklessness. And if you haven't got a cloud of incense, a slightly foggier head will do instead.

Almost no one, alas, has ever found a Belgian exotic. But Eva can be French to almost anyone except a

Frenchman. She's sometimes Spanish, indeed, the slurred and thicker 's'; not now, obviously. Sometimes she adopts an English hauteur. Or, as tonight, she borrows the sound of Olga's Slavic melancholy.

'Now, stranger, let us see the last of life.'

He offers the glass. She takes it by the base, careful not to touch his fingers. Holding his gaze, she tilts the glass to the side and lets the last trickle of wine drip to the floor.

It's theatre: old, simple and effective. That last trickle is faintly transgressive and abandoned and unavoidably he's looking at her leg again. The glass up between them and this is a shared game and naturally they must catch each other's eyes. She begins to consider the dregs, and of course both faces are leaning in.

He has resisted the temptation to steady her hand with his. Perhaps he really is subtler than she expected.

The fingers of his hand instead rest on her knee. Perhaps not.

'Ah... Now at last I begin to see you.' He grins, nods expectantly. 'I see a man who has never known a border, a man who must forever wander, a stranger to all and a subject to none.' No one cares about the fortune and favour stuff; their Gods take care of that. They ask because they want to see how they are seen. 'And yet a man whose heart is strong, a man who carries his country with him wherever he wanders.' Every priest who ever lived promised rewards to come; but none ever offered a simple compliment. 'This is courage, I think.' She lifts her eyes from the glass to his. 'This is passion.'

She holds his gaze. 'Your fate will continue to swirl in the wine, because you will never cease to fill the glass. You will never stand still and await destiny. You seek adventure and adventure seeks you.' Sometimes indeed, you grip adventure's knee. 'You will know sadness, and you will know glory.' They're both thinking: yes, but what's the balance tonight? 'You may enjoy renown, but not rest. Tell me, stranger, is your heart strong enough for this journey?'

Now his other hand closes around hers. 'When my fate is in the hands of such beauty, my heart grows only stronger.'

'Someone gets an early performance of the circus, I think!' There's something forced in the phrase, and they both turn. It's the German businessman opposite, looking at them, wide-eyed, uncomfortable.

Eva feels cross. 'Not a performance', she says. 'An advertisement merely.'

Reyes's voice is hard, suave, feline. 'When the ring-master is more skilful, my friend, even the proudest of creatures responds more quickly. Morocco was Spanish territory before the rest of Europe had even discovered her.'

Eva holds the eyes of the man opposite, feeling even crosser.

'Where we were?' says Reyes, hand pulling at hers, voice low and appealing.

But Eva has not yet turned back. She's still gazing across the table.

Seeing the worthy German, his stuffed discomfort, she sees herself in his eyes. Abandoned. Unreliable. Unclean.

And she hesitates.

Then she sees herself as he hoped to see her. Correct. Chaste. Restrained.

And she turns back and offers up the glass to Reyes again. 'About to fill the glass and test your heart.'

People are beginning to enjoy themselves just a little too much. Volume and movement become more chaotic. Diplomatic poise begins to slump, along with posture in the straight-backed chairs. Personal opinions begin to slip out too freely, like the hands wandering along the chair backs. We are surprised by a sincere truth and a hand on our knee. Those who notice it's too much begin to leave, including – a hand on a waist, a deft avoidance of a drunken arm, a murmured farewell – the young married couple whose invitation notionally created this gathering. Eva wonders at the rest of their evening; envies the sense of complacent unfussiness with which they will couple.

Defiant, the German businessman stays; a desert tribesman marauding near the edge of an oasis to catch anyone who strays from their flirtation, offering them a proud banality and a pastry.

Eva says to Reyes: 'Tell me about the Sultan.'

'Already your ambition goes higher than a Spanish gentleman? You realize in his harem you would be one queen among many, whereas in mine–'

'You realize some women might find that confinement a kind of escape? No, I mean what's he like? I hear he collects all kinds of... of ridiculous trinkets and trophies and toys.'

Reyes doesn't mind a brief appeal to his wisdom rather than his virility. 'I like him. He is... lively company. And all of the things he collects – the animals, the costumes, the jewels: it is... the primitive, you understand? The African. An African king has the rare advantage of being able to satisfy his primitive appetites.'

'Even an emu?'

'Oh yes. They are savage creatures, do you know? Bigger and stronger than you expect. This neck, it is all muscle!' The Spaniard's forearm and fist become neck and beak, and the beak snaps at her.

'Like some trophy captured by a pirate.' The voice of the German businessman seems to come from another room, another reality. 'A foreign bride he has brought home to his desert.'

Reyes ignores him. 'This Sultan... He sees something he likes – He can have it – So he must have it.'

Soon there is a small bare lobby, just off the dining room. The lobby leads to some stairs, the stairs will lead to an upper corridor, and the corridor will lead to the first vacant bedroom they can find. Eva is half-perched on the banister rail, one leg just managing contact with the floor, Reyes's head buried in her neck, one of his hands grasping at her breasts and the other thrust on an expedition up her dress and exploring far into the interior. The only decoration in the lobby is a mirror, an over-truthful teller of fortune. Looking over Reyes's shoulder, his hair sleek against her cheek and the scent of him filling her, Eva sees herself.

She doesn't look very elegant; she doesn't look at all comfortable. She manages to grapple Reyes into a slightly less contorted stance, and thus frees one of her legs to be able to hold it in a more harmonious attitude, a *cou-de-pied* balanced by the line of her head and the fall of her hair. Let the mirror at least tell a story of poise.

'Oh – sorry! Do beg your pardon.'

It is the Englishman. The pleasant face is shadowed in the doorway. Reyes and Eva turn, stand approximately straight, breathing hard and too far gone to be embarrassed.

The Englishman looks uneasily at Eva. 'Are you... you all right?'

It is such a very stupid question that Eva almost screams at him. Because how dare you assume that I am not all right when I choose to enjoy myself? Because how can any of this mad lifelong performance be all right? He would not understand. Instead she pats the stupid pleasant cheek and says 'bless you' and allows Reyes to pull her up the stairs.

So when, a few minutes later, she does call a halt – head and back crushed against a door-frame and the man's teeth tearing at her throat and one hand thrust right up inside somewhere under her rib-cage and his other struggling to unleash his trousers – it isn't the ridiculousness, because isn't this whole life ridiculous?

When discomfort and a fleeting clarity are for a fragile moment stronger than her blood and her glory and her melting groin, it isn't the fear or affront at how the elegant mask of a face has become distorted and turned this sport into assault, because beggars can't be choosers and often this is how it is. When she manages to bring her hands up and all her energy into pushing him away just enough to slip away from the door-frame, it isn't the image of the uncomfortable German merchant, his alarm at her, his distaste. When she backs away – counting her legs and re-arranging her cleavage, I quite forgot I promised I would visit my friend in trouble oh mercy you're an extraordinary man my poor little heart I don't deserve you and any other nonsense she can think of to soothe his rampant vanity and avoid him punching her, just please not the face, and really she's done the decent thing by leaving him enough time to go and find some other lucky girl on whom to expend all that energy and elegance – it isn't the image of the Englishman, his concern about her, his naive impotent pleasantry.

It's the image of Assia.

◍

JOURNAL OF THOMAS SOMERLEIGH

Klug doesn't give up easily. Hardly a surprise, and I suppose one must admire it.

Today's meeting of the Committee hadn't seemed to threaten much in the way of anything happening. I'm not even sure that Prudhomme had been aiming to have it at all. But when we emerged from a meeting with the Grand Vizier, there in the ante-chamber was little Abdelilah, collar stiff and neck-tie neat – ! – under the robe and leather document folder at the ready. He stepped forwards, and bowed to Prudhomme, who didn't look best pleased and started to ask whether we needed to be troubled today... But then Klug slipped in very neatly that no doubt Herr Abdelilah was there for the emergency meeting of the Committee on the circus, which Herr Prudhomme had so sensibly announced for today, and Germany was naturally enthusiastic to support.

So we had to postpone morning tea and get down to it, no one really interested – except for the worthy Abdelilah, who opened with an exhaustive recapitulation of the previous meeting and of discussions outwith the meeting yet germane to its matter. This took even longer than it might thanks to his habit of stopping at the end of every sentence to nod and smile respectfully to Prudhomme. And each sentence, each nod and each smile sent Prudhomme closer to bursting point. I've been studying him closely, of course – always healthy to look and learn – and although he doesn't do anger, *Dieu nous en garde*, the stiff collar seems to get tighter and the eyes get colder and harder. These signs were increasingly apparent now, and little Abdelilah just could not see them. Indeed, I think that Prudhomme's iciness only made the poor chap more anxious and deferential, and the sentences grew correspondingly more thorough, the nods deeper and the smiles more desperate.

Just when I thought Prudhomme would actually explode, something astonishing. Somerleigh's lessons in diplomacy, take heed: this is the kind of man who will outlast all others in the knottiest negotiation. Something bright flared in the cold eyes – I waited for the bang – and then... Prudhomme smiled. A big, beatific smile, and the eyes closed in a kind of satisfaction. In that apogee of *protocolaire* nonsense and diplomatic fussiness, Hector Prudhomme had attained a state of grace. Some inner strength had enabled him to relish what was sending the rest of us to sleep.

But having attained that *nirvana* of bureaucratic bliss, he was in no mood to give much room to lesser adepts. As soon as Abdelilah had run out of puff, Prudhomme jumped in rather stronger and sharper than usual. 'I must say,' he began, already sticking his neck out more assertively than a diplomat of his experience typically would, 'that the rigour of these proceedings, combined with the absence of any difficulty during the reception yesterday, gives me considerable reassurance of our prudence in handling them in this manner.' He 'would not venture unilaterally to label the reception a success, not without first hearing the views of the committee' but he hoped 'his dear colleagues would excuse a certain satisfaction' as he contemplated 'the reliability and robustness of our oversight mechanism and the stability it has most efficaciously delivered'.

I thought he'd overdone it. His assertion of control must surely provoke a challenge from Klug. I wondered if I ought to jump in with something to smooth or distract – but I couldn't think of anything. Klug cleared his throat and jumped first.

He agreed wholeheartedly with dear Hector.

Even dear Hector, not fully recalled from Elysium, was wary. Klug said he would be the first to endorse the Chairman's proposal – it had not, of course, been a proposal, but it could not now be considered otherwise – to declare the reception a success. He wished likewise to be the first to offer his compliments to Prudhomme.

His geniality was infectious, and the general enthusiasm that France and Germany seemed for once to be agreeing and we might have a chance to escape for some refreshments prompted much nodding and hear-hearing. Little Abdelilah scribbling busily. Prudhomme was back to earth now, watching all this unprecedented agreeing-with-France uneasily yet unable to stop it.

Klug had noted the very pleasant event organized with typical style and efficiency by France. He had noted the Committee's positive verdict on same – another quick glance, another round of nods and burbles. With the removal of all doubts, he would of course work with the Sultan's officials to arrange a performance and was optimistic that he would be able to get Berlin's agreement to fund. Businesslike, pleasant, and instinctively there were more nods before people had been able to see how far he'd carried them off.

Prudhomme sat frozen. Klug had invoked his logic and his success against him.

I'd never seen him so baffled, and it was with a kind of pity that I attempted a rearguard action to slow Klug down. Britain naturally shared the general sense of satisfaction with our collective – I hit the word – management of the circus; compliments to Prudhomme and thanks to Klug for his energy and generosity. Not wishing to spoil the festive atmosphere, I went on, make the champagne so kindly donated by Germany lose its fizz – shame-faced smile to the company, nods of amusement in response, everyone loves an extended metaphor – and myself very much looking forward to seeing the giraffe, but even if we were more comfortable about the public order issues presumably we would remain cautious about the sanitary aspects; questions of hygiene around the imported wild animals etcetera.

There was something unsettling in Klug's smile. He knew I was trying to block him just for the sake of it, and he wasn't going to be blocked. 'Naturally', he said heavily, 'Germany defers to Britain in matters of sanitation and hygiene. I am confident that with the enthusiasm that here has already been expressed, I may proceed with the arrangements at least as far as it concerns the human performers, and if in the end the Sultan and his people are disappointed not to see the giraffe, they will receive an honest and serious explanation from Britain and France.'

Afterwards, everyone else having hurried off for their delayed tea and pastries, Prudhomme was left sitting rigid in his place. Face stiff, eyes cold, the whole world an offensive odour in his nostrils. Apparently without looking round or blinking, he realized that I was still there too. 'This wretched committee', he said, quiet but bitter, still staring straight ahead, 'begins to interfere in the proper management of the circus.'

Then suddenly a fresh thought, and now he turned to me. 'Thank you for trying to help, Cher Thomas. It was a brave effort, and the triviality nicely judged to pique our German colleague – let him know that Britain and France stand together, eh?' He'd misunderstood, of course, but if this was what he thought then it was all to the good. We began to walk out together, and Prudhomme touched my elbow. 'I wonder if I might intrude on your time further, my dear boy. Can I beg you to join me for supper again – tomorrow? I feel we must ensure that we are properly aligned.'

All to the very good. The telegram to Tangier writes itself: intensified German mischief, which will show Sir G. that Marrakech is definitely not a gallivant; France assured of Britain's support and eager to maintain, thanks to the deft work of the British representative on the spot. A final smile from Prudhomme before we went our separate ways through the old city: 'I am certain that my family will be delighted to see you, too.'

This most satisfactory development set the tone for supper, rather a jolly occasion. Invitation by an Italian couple living here – he something in minerals, bit of a sport – and bringing together some of the livelier diplomats and some Europeans of our generation and a few of the characters from the circus who'd been at Prudhomme's reception. All very relaxed, all very bright; nice to find oneself in intelligent attractive company. In other circs I might have ventured a little sport myself. Congenially-abandoned atmosphere, candlelight, rather sumptuous wine, some very charming women – women living a little freer, because abroad or in the twilight society of the circus. But for some reason I didn't feel like lowering myself.

And that reason, I quickly realized, was the thought of little Hortense. Which seemed rather significant, as I sat back and gazed around the room at my companions letting themselves go – by the end of the evening it was all getting a bit backstage-at-the-ballet; the grumpy Belgian woman absolutely throwing herself at poor Reyes – because when a girl starts to make a chap want to behave better rather than worse, it's quite a different thing, isn't it?

⟐

Olga appears on the doorstep in tears. Eva settles her on the bench under the lemon tree, puts an arm around her, an exquisite little fragility; silent Assia brings orange juice, takes off Olga's shoes and begins to massage her feet. At last the words emerge.

Magda is getting married.

Much more than this is hard to be sure of, because Olga is not entirely coherent, gasping with unhappiness and hissing with anger and apparently hazy on the details.

Magda is getting married. The man is a foreigner in Marrakech – or perhaps a Moroccan, some filthy lecherous savage – but actually he's a foreigner, a man of the lowest character who thinks he can just buy a woman because she is stupid and ugly and not from a sophisticated western European country. Magda is so lucky, and how miraculous that the least charming of women should find her prince – before handsome Eva, before poor little Olga. Magda is a pig and a whore and stupid and will suffer and it will serve her right because she is forgetting the circus and for an acrobat losing a partner is like losing a leg.

Magda is getting married.

Eva has seen Olga talk of rape. But this sense of hurt, of betrayal, she has never seen; this loneliness. She is so tiny now, so lost. 'Who will catch me now?' she sobs.

☪

JOURNAL OF THOMAS SOMERLEIGH

Dramas and developments!

Very congenial supper last night chez Prudhomme. Cher Hector by turns energetic and jovial, better company than I'd ever have given him credit for. Very seized by the possibilities of the circus, to the point that I suggested to him, rather hesitantly, that he seemed to be looking at it in a rather different light now.

There was a flash of the old cold Prudhomme: we diplomats are required to change our minds all the time, but must never appear to have done so – this moment's truth has always been and will always be true, until I am obliged to reverse it in a moment's time – and to suggest such a thing is the height of bad manners. I added quickly that I was merely struck by the fresh clarity of his enthusiasm.

He relaxed again and explained: the Sultan's enthusiasm meant that the circus was definitely going to happen; the only question thus became who would guide it. He trusted I would agree this should be France and England, rather than Germany. I took the point, of course, and agreed. This may be a stronger position to sell to Tangier. And rather fun to be guiding a circus!

Jollier still was the family atmosphere. Madame not exactly lively, but warm: imperialism and elegant word-play seem to be short-cuts to her heart, and I played the wicket accordingly. And with her parents having thawed a bit, the fair Hortense was much relaxed – chattering brightly and occasionally leaning and reaching her fingertips towards my arm to emphasize something, and no alarm-bells ringing across the table.

She really is the most delightful creature. So delicately lovely to look at, and such a gently bright spirit: gee me up a bit, which is probably a good thing. And at the end of the evening, when Prudhomme and I had been chatting à deux, and it eventually came time for me to shove off, my host insisted on calling her down: Monsieur Thomas taking his leave and she should be courteous enough to come and say goodnight. Right enough, thinks I, and so we had a moment on the doorstep, the thick perfume of the fruit trees hanging over us, her fingers held too firmly, my lips too long on her hand, her eyes wide and wishing more and her mouth open and I felt charm becoming passion.

Then this morning the Circus Committee. Klug had moved dashed fast in the forty-eight hours since we'd previously met. Yet again I fear he caught Prudhomme on the hop. Stung by the previous meeting, Prudhomme rather more calculated and thorough, leading the group along a more carefully-worked path – some of which we'd talked about at supper – just enough warmth and just enough time to get a chorus of nods and then he was moving on. Noted the general satisfaction with the functioning of the Committee. Noted the commendable efficiency of Germany. Naturally leads us to make the arrangements within the Committee more robust, more appropriate to the practical demands of a potential performance. As we began to focus more seriously on that, we would need more seriously to consider the sanitation aspects – a glance towards Britain – the public order aspects, the morality aspects, and so forth. France as Chairman proposed that we should look to manage these either in focused plenary discussions, or in Sub-Committees devoted to each. Elegant summary and satisfactory consensus.

But he was still fighting the previous conversation, while old Klug had moved on. Delighted as ever by France's efficiency and engagement, naturally Germany supports all of these evolutions in the structure and proceedings of the esteemed Committee. Meanwhile – and he hit the word, and paused, and in that moment Hector Prudhomme knew that everything he'd secured this morning was about to be torpedoed – he was delighted to report that he had made excellent progress on practical arrangements for the first performance. He had the personal approval – 'better I should say enthusiasm, of the Sultan, and we know what a force this is!', and because this was true we all had to smile, but Prudhomme's smile was like a crack in the ice – and he had the approval of Berlin, and while the discussions of the Committee continued he would be sure to inform us as soon as the date – 'this is very soon, no doubt' – was confirmed.

So the moment when the Committee assumed its greatest elaboration was also the moment when it found itself irrelevant. Most of the group were caught in their own unthinking agreeability: it all seemed natural and logical and unobjectionable, and now apparently they had formalized the division between France and Germany. Still, they were thinking, a circus performance might be fun, mightn't it?

Again the Prudhomme frozen fury. Again he'd been snookered, and he knew it. Despite all our optimistic chat last night, just as he was making the circus his own he was losing it.

He'd left himself no room to speak against Germany, not with any vestige of diplomacy. Those frozen lips would not let him. I jumped in, desperate to say anything to grab hold of the circus before it slipped away completely, and the fraction of a second of pleasantry gave time for inspiration: 'What splendid news!' I said, 'I'm sure we're all most grateful to Germany, and excited by this possibility' –

and now I had the chorus of approval on my side again. 'I wonder if I might propose a small enhancement to ensure the maximum benefit from the occasion. Let us have the first performance as a grand première not only with His Majesty, but with all our Ambassadors from Tangier.'

Eager approval: they all want their chiefs to pay more attention to their local success here; no doubt I'm not the only one suspected of gallivanting. I saw Prudhomme's unspoken relief, the eyes shining through the ice. And I saw Klug: face stone. He knew it would take days to get approval, and weeks to get any Ambassadors down through the desert. He knew he in turn had been outmanoeuvred. He knew I had made myself his opponent, his betrayer even; and I felt the hurt and dislike in the bleak dead eyes, and I felt embarrassed.

Then afterwards, the buoyant Prudhomme. His hand at my elbow, his head close to mine: 'A masterly inspiration, cher Somerleigh. I hope you will not think me improper for mentioning it, but my chief in Tangier shall be most reassured to hear of Britain's solid and skilful partnership.'

I was watching Klug as he hurried out, clearly angry. I knew I would never again have that pleasant sense of his courtesy, his respect.

Prudhomme noticed him too. 'The battle is fierce now,' he said quietly, 'and we may expect another onslaught; but your salvo bought us some time.' Then his fingers at my elbow again. 'Listen, my dear boy: it is best to be open about these things – the twentieth century is well advanced.' I looked at him uneasily. 'Madame Prudhomme and I have noticed that our dear Hortense seems to enjoy your company most particularly. My wife is of course very cautious in these matters, especially when we are in such a wild and barbaric place. But I may say that she finds you to be most correct and pleasant. We like to think ourselves' – little chuckle – 'not so prejudiced on the point of nationality. Should you have leisure some afternoon to escort Hortense in the carriage, or perhaps for a promenade in the palace quarter, I am sure that she would find it agreeable and we would find it not unreassuring.'

'!'

Eva decides to allow herself to be courted by the worthy German merchant.

In her mind, she finds herself defending the decision to Olga. Trying to prove his superiority to the violinist or the toy-shop owner. In her heart she's thinking of Assia.

To Assia she would admit that she wants to stain this dignified man. He has thought her base, unclean; and still he will wish to lower himself to her, beneath her. She will see his indignity. She will know his sweat.

And at the same time she will prove that perhaps she is not so abandoned after all.

And after all, why shouldn't she? Olga has been nagging her to look to her life after the circus, so Olga can hardly complain now can she? The circus will end sometime. On present form – the Maestro obese and debauching in a room of silks somewhere, the arrangements vanished in a puff of diplomatic smoke – it seems possible it has already ended.

Each new town, each new night, demands a new performance. This time a performance of dutiful vulnerability, of a light heart too easily buffeted by masculine winds, now seeking its natural rest.

Hurrying back out through the hotel restaurant that night, she was trying not to hurry, buttoned up to the neck, cold: a posture for the benefit of the audience, and for herself. She caught the eye of the German merchant, still marooned at the table, stiff upright and sipping his wine, and with a sober nod she said – this, she acknowledges to herself, had been deception; this had been self-preservation – 'I see that some men, at least, can hold their drink.'

All the way home that night, irritation at what he thought of her was bickering in her head with irritation at having to care what he thought of her.

Then this chance meeting on the edge of the great square. She's walking past a line of cafés, wondering at each if the appeal of a glass of lemonade is worth the ordeal of getting it. And there he is: turning aside from a conversation; a linen suit and a soft hat; a solid face with blue eyes; he sees her.

Beside him, back to her, is the senior German representative; he's talking to... it might be the Englishman and someone else. The merchant is not interested; he has turned for a moment. He is sudden, and surprised, and she is too.

It is probably only at this moment that the idea comes to her. It begins as determination – she thinks she knows the expression he is about to make – not to be written off, not socially and not morally. Then it is an irritated *why bother?* Then it is a curious *why not?*

She may look a harlot compared to the few Moroccan women around, but her frock is high enough and low enough for European decency in this climate. Her surprise will suggest her fragility and his potency. She is alone in the vast square, and that will pass for vulnerability. Too late she realizes that being out alone is itself another sign of her unsuitability.

She manages a deep nod, eyes lowered; turns it into the hint of a curtsey. As she looks up, he is nodding heavily to her. The face – strong features, good lines, good jaw – is cold. *Oh well.* But then – afterthought; instinct – he raises his hat. Not casual finger to brim, but hand to crown and actually raising it a fraction. *Well now...*

Eyes down again. 'Mein Herr, I am glad to see you...' She wishes to thank him for his courtesy and care, she says, that strange night. She was rather out of her depth, she says, adrift with so many different cultures and languages. She was grateful for at least one man of reassurance. She gives him another nod, and she hurries away. She has wondered if she should make up some kind of apology, a weak woman with strong wine; then at the last minute finds she's not so desperate.

By any normal reckoning, her unfinished sport with Reyes would have ruined her in the eyes of other men. Mischievously, the calculation recalls the emotion: his elegance and charm; the way his energy exalted as well as degraded; her heat, her liquidness, her performer's glory whirling to new heights with the stimulation of a worthy audience. She reimposes calculation. *Ruined, no doubt of it.*

But pig-headedness can be a virtue. By a triumph of persistence and the unknowable all-knowing network of this city, a note will arrive from him the next day, in a small envelope addressed to 'Mademoiselle Eva, Marrakech'.

⟨⟩

JOURNAL OF THOMAS SOMERLEIGH

Vive la France. Joy and content in the little empire of Hector Prudhomme. There was nothing doing at the palace this morning, but this, it transpired, was because Prudhomme had already cornered H.M., and the rest of us were left to smoke and chit-chat.

He swanned out of the royal apartments looking like he owned the place – he may technically do so; I wondered how he'd suit one of the local outfits, his trim little beard amid the austere white robes, rather fine – gracious nod to the palace flunkeys as they bowed to him. We dips got our own gracious nod, and he sailed straight up to me and took my arm and would I care to walk home with him, perhaps a little luncheon?

Well, don't mind if I do, and the telegram back to Tangier was already composing itself in my head as we walked. Prudhomme had got a toe in the royal door on some economic business: 'even though we know these games of protocol and procedure for the circus to be ridiculous pretence, we must never suggest to the natives that they are not to be taken seriously, I am sure you will appreciate the point Cher Thomas'. He'd unveiled his big news to the Sultan: France would be arranging the première of His Majesty's circus, a gala performance in the presence of the Ambassadors from Tangier. Pleased to report that the French Ambassador was already smiling on the proposal, and where he led the other Ambassadors would follow. I meanwhile wondering how to present this to Sir G., who needs a heavily-footnoted briefing paper just to get out of his chair, let alone to trek for hundreds of miles through the Moroccan desert. But H.M. apparently ecstatic: a gala anything gets his vote.

Somerleigh momentarily not so ecstatic: a pang of frustration at the thought that I'd had the idea for the circus and Germany had pinched it, and now I'd had the idea for the première and France had pinched it. But: 'I do hope you will forgive me, my dear boy: I told His Majesty that the particular suggestion was a British one. I think he is rather fond of you, and he is always reassured when Britain is supportive.'

This much better, of course. Rather handily, I'll be able to present this to Tangier as the British guiding hand working behind the scenes but not having to spend a shilling. If there's one thing the Foreign Office likes more than influence, it's stinginess. Anyway, France full steam ahead for the circus now, and Prudhomme has already got a Colonel of the French Army tooling down to Marrakech to improve the advice on security issues, along with some kind of cultural aficionado fellow, presumably to check the decor or make sure there's nothing unseemly. The French machine pirouetting into action, and another insight for the telegram.

Then we were at Chateau Prudhomme, and Madame was delighted to see me, and almost playful as she scolded her cher husband for failing to warn her, and while she roused the staff why didn't I go and find Hortense? Why not, indeed? – and off I went. Wandered the house unaccompanied; upstairs indeed; knocking at her very door. Her face – its prettiness, its flush of surprise and I think excitement – a glimpse of her bedroom beyond – the bed itself – and then bowing over her – my lips on her hand, her fingers in mine. Then lunch, all very pleasant, and then why doesn't Hortense take me off and play me something on the piano?

Bit alarmed in case I had to give an opinion on the music or – worse – a recommendation. Probably not the done thing to ask for Gilbert & Sullivan, and I'd the idea that asking for Beethoven, or that other chap, might be too obvious. Fortunately she stuck to what she knows, and we got a little something by Saint-Saëns – checked the spelling over her shoulder! – and a Polish dance. Most charming, and I sat behind her watching the way she perched so poised on the stool, her little feet working the pedals, her slender neck dropping down into her frock.

Nothing said, of course, but I get the strong impression that she's got the impression that things are on a different footing now. Heard her breathing harder, saw her little chest rising and falling like an excited bird, when she invited me to sit beside her to add a couple of notes of accompaniment in the lower register. Saw our hands, our fingers, fluttering close, and fortunately I didn't make too much of a hash of it.

Tea this afternoon with Brahim, my poet. Trying to get him to explain the translation of one or two of his verses, so I can share with Hortense. But he strangely reluctant; perhaps worried they're not so hot after all. Instead very anxious to explain how wretched everything has become for the average Moroccan – I can well believe – and what are the foreign diplomats doing about it? 'Your hand is on every shoulder; your word is in every ear!' Well, I suppose that's true – talking about diplomats in general – and, of course, in some ways rather a smart feeling – if Sir G. could only hear this, thinks I – but I try to explain to the worthy fellow that this doesn't mean we should dictate every little thing. The Moroccans need to do most of it for themselves. 'There will be blood!' he hisses 'and we know that in every shadow there is a foreigner'. And we're going to stay in the shadows, says I; don't think you can tempt us into the light. Morocco's on the right path, I told him, and the foreigners are working to secure her proper place in the international system.

Brahim curious about the circus: what is it? when will it perform? how do the different foreigners perceive it? I reassured: bit of fun, nothing unseemly I'm sure. What is the attitude of H.M. and the Caliph? Presumably enthusiastic, I said: bit of fun, nothing unseemly.

He's very keen to get me together with the old man again – Sa'id. 'If you are committed to this place, dear Mr Thomas, you know you will learn from him.' No doubt. 'And he would so appreciate the ear of a senior diplomat. You and your colleagues are everything in this place; you know this.'

Then a welcome distraction – or not. Suddenly Brahim was half-standing, and bowing to someone over my shoulder, and 'Excellency'-ing very crisply. I turned to find Klug. A surprise to both of us and all rather uncomfortable. I stood, of course, and we shook hands and managed the courtesies. As ever, my name sounds more melancholy in German (certainly compared to French!): 'Zommerlee…' Didn't know what to say. He looked like he wanted to say more, and I was rather hoping he would. I dearly wish we could reconfirm a respectful relationship: I think he's a good and honest chap, Klug, and it's wretched that his obligation to push the circus in this way has caused a frost. It's forced me into a rather regrettable position.

But what could he say, caught suddenly in a café? Perhaps we might have managed something, but he was obliged to greet Brahim, and Brahim and I had to acknowledge Klug's companion – the German merchant again, Giesberts. And if he and Brahim had chatted – Giesberts is always one to throw himself into the cultural stuff – we still might have managed something, and I was actually preparing an 'I do hope…' when Giesberts was distracted, obliging Klug to keep up the pleasantries with Brahim. The moody Belgian dancer woman had popped up out of nowhere, like some wandering angel of melancholy and diplomatic disruption, and my hope, whatever it might have been, went unexpressed.

☽

In the café on the corner, where the maze of alleys that make up Marrakech market empties onto the great square, the corner where the men from the villages tend to gather before setting out to reconquer their spot to sell or beg, morning is at its busiest and hottest. The square is governed by rhythms and customs unchanged over centuries. The square is not the same from one hour to the next.

After the first bustle of morning and as the heat begins to thicken, the rhythms of the royal palace slow. It is his habit, in this lull, to walk out into the city and to drink a tea with his acquaintances. Today, he is urgent, anxious, jostling impatient past elbows of faces he does not have time or confidence to look at, sitting without greeting, nodding hastily, clutching a tea-glass to him.

For just one moment, as his hands clasp the pleasing perfection of its swollen round base and the scent of mint fills him, he finds a breath.

Not to be indiscreet, but it's all up. Civil war, like as not. Slaughter, certainly. Slaughter always.

Take it from me, His Majesty, may he know endless peace except fat chance, and his brother the Caliph of Marrakech, may he also know endless peace except he and peace are clearly not on speaking terms, they're not pretending any more. The Glaoui, he's always beside the Caliph now. And that means the southern tribes will fight for the Caliph. Or if they fight for His Majesty, he'll have to do whatever they want out of fear they'll fight for the Caliph. The southern tribes, united. Except old Tayyib and his Goundafi, they're watching with long suspicious eyes, so it's probably going to be worse. For Marrakech, the one thing more destructive than the southern tribes united is the southern tribes fighting over us.

This morning the Caliph, may the wisdom of The Ever-Wise The Perceiver guide him, came as usual to offer humble respects to the Sultan, may the wisdom of the The Ever-Wise The Perceiver guide him too, and as quickly as possible or we're all in the shit. The esteemed Caliph also had something on his mind. This new holy man that everyone's talking about, says the Caliph, is His Majesty not alarmed about him?

Now, I don't know who's talking about the holy man, I'm certainly not and I don't think His Majesty is, but the one man who definitely has mentioned him is the Glaoui. This must be the same new holy man he talked about before, and now he's prodded the Caliph to make a thing of it. Or maybe it's a different new holy man but it makes no difference because the point is the same.

What can His Majesty do? The one thing he cannot do is admit fear or weakness, not to his brother, not with the Glaoui standing there hawk-eyed and deciding every second which way to jump. So he has to say that he's utterly unalarmed by the new holy man, couldn't be less alarmed, anyway what holy man? Except he can't say that because he's guaranteed to look a fool when there's any trouble, from the holy man or from anyone else. So he just says that he's not worried about anything because he's confident that the plans of The Generous Provider are certain and just, and his beloved brother the Caliph should have faith in that. Which isn't a bad answer in the circumstances, and obviously the sort of thing he's supposed to say. Except he's still going to look foolish one way or another, and because he's had to correct his brother in order not to look weak, he's made the issue into more of a dispute between them. Blood, I tell you. And not theirs: yours and mine.

You know what scares me most? The Caliph has two new men in his close entourage. Normally the entourage are soft, subtle men: flatterers and clerks, pretty boys with reassuring tongues. Not these two. Dark skins, dead eyes, dusty feet. Not a bit of flesh on them: just sinew and hidden knives. These are mountain men. The Glaoui is bringing the tribes into the city, and he will make himself the Caliph's right hand and guarantee. And here, right in the heart of his kingdom, His Majesty is alone.

Of course it is a foreign plot. The Roumi are all-powerful, all-seeing. They would not allow such madness to unfold without some calculation of their own, some devious purpose.

That's a point, that is. With them behind it, no one's going to be able to stop it. And... we shouldn't want to, should we?

Yes, I know. Hide your gold, hide your girls, and don't bother re-decorating. Marrakech will bleed and burn again.

Or perhaps this particular conversation takes place at the southern gate of the city, eyes peering through the sun towards the nearby mountains.

A small envelope addressed to 'Mademoiselle Eva, Marrakech'. The address alone is worth a tumble.

The French title is a thoughtful touch, too.

It arrives in Assia's hand. It's got rather grubby, in its journey around and across the city, but it is treated with reverence. At first Eva doesn't know what's happening: Assia is in her doorway, face bright even as it ducks into the gloom of the room. She's holding something, but she doesn't give it to Eva. Instead she looks around anxiously, lifts a flower in its improvised vase off a plate, wipes the plate on her hip, places the something on it, and at last with this inspiration of formality presents it to Eva.

Only then does Eva see what it is. And then she reads the address.

She and Assia exchange a smile. A curiosity. A treat.

Assia then contrives enough business replacing the plate and dusting the sill and replacing the vase and checking the flower to be able to loiter while Eva opens her envelope. When she looks up from it, Assia is just standing there, eyes expectant.

'Is it… marriage?'

'It looks like a good tea, anyway', Eva says. 'Which is probably more useful.'

Assia realizes that's all she's going to get, and drifts out into the courtyard again.

Eva's pardon is sought for the liberty of writing. The writer – as he refers to himself, either to avoid too blatant an association with his own emotions, or because he wants his identity to be a nice surprise – is only this bold because of his respect for the way in which she introduced herself the other day, her most excellent combination of frankness and discretion, her obvious correctness and her obvious sincerity.

211

Eva replays the conversation, hears herself again, feels the insincerities.

She reviews the compliment. She has rarely been described as 'most excellent', and never for her frankness and discretion. Does he mean rudeness? Quietness?

The writer – at least – does not believe in postures and deceptions, he says. It is a strange life they both lead, essentially solitary among savages. He feels the want of civilized company. He is naturally interested when a European of artistic inclination is in the city. He trusts that she does not find his writing to her to be inappropriate, or in any way disrespectful to her sense of decency and womanhood – Eva wonders what her sense of those is; she knows what it should be. He would find it very agreeable to continue their conversation about cultural subjects, to exchange a sense of civility and good company.

It is a merchant's courtship: defined; transactional.

It is written in English: for most Europeans a neutral language; for no European a language of romance.

Sometimes – when one has time, and candles, and alternatives – one wants a Spaniard. But sometimes one wants a German. Eva wonders how a man so cautious in expressing his feelings would use his fingers.

He invites her to take tea with him. He emphasizes – because any hint of private association might be shameful – that they shall be in the hotel café. He emphasizes – because any hint of public association might be shameful – that he is also inviting another man and woman.

The signature is clear and compact, each letter of 'Luther Giesberts' emphasized with a contained flourish. He is determined to have a style, but not to let it get out of hand.

Eva wonders about a calculated delay in replying, then realizes that the Marrakech messenger system will provide that anyway. As do the two hours it takes her, Assia and the landlady to find a piece of paper. Eventually, in a small wooden chest, the old lady finds a flimsy half-sheet that had once been a certificate of something but has now faded to nothing. It is the perfect size and quality for a notelet. An envelope defeats them, and so Eva reuses his: a little shabby, but she knows he will approve of thrift.

Mademoiselle Eva, she writes – stimulated by the dispassionate perspective of the third person – is most grateful for Herr Giesberts's discretion underlined and courtesy underlined, and has great pleasure in accepting.

She writes in German. It's hardly the language of romance either, but it politely moves to his ground while showing off her competence. Assia slips out into the street with the reused envelope tucked into her chest, incubating an alternative Eva.

☿

JOURNAL OF THOMAS SOMERLEIGH

Klug had been outmanned in the previous meeting of the Committee, and outmanoeuvred, but back he came today like nothing had happened and he was still prince of the city. Somerleigh's lessons in diplomacy: there is no place for emotion, and there is no place for memory. Forget your own feelings; what audience feelings do you seek to cultivate? Forget yesterday; how do you maintain the conversation today?

I don't think we'd expected a formal meeting today. But we found little Abdelilah waiting for us, all done up in his mixed bureaucrat rig with – rather striking – a tiny pair of spectacles. Where there is a Secretary, there is a Committee.

Prudhomme found it convenient to play along. Always good that everyone – sincere nod to Klug, and then hurrying the sentence on – has the chance to be represented to the fullest extent, and that collectively we exercise proper oversight of the circus. No details to report, we wait for clarification of timing of the première, and naturally no wish to offend the Committee with trivia; everyone will be informed whenever there is something new to report. Then the classic diplomatic two-step, welcoming nay encouraging comments and contributions – but if there isn't anything then jolly good and let's call it a day.

Klug: Prudhomme hadn't wanted to give him a chance, but had to look. Had anticipated – had feared – that precisely stubbornly raised finger... and had to see it. One moment. One German.

A collective wariness. We all knew the tensions, and the last thing you want to see when you're eager for your luncheon is a German with a point to make.

Nothing to add, he added. No need to interrupt our departure for refreshment, he interrupted. Merely to endorse whole-heartedly France's approach. Germany shall of course be delighted to agree with His Majesty funding for whatever use he wishes to make of his circus, in support of whatever entertainment the French are arranging.

German control of the purse-strings emphasized. I was near Klug as we were funnelling out of the hall into the sunlight. 'Nicely done', I said quietly.

He stopped, and turned to me. He seemed to be trying to read my expression. From his I could get nothing.

His hand came up and gripped my shoulder. 'I insist only on fair play', he said. 'I hope for friendly play.' We walked out together.

'I suspect you knew in advance of the latest decree from the Sultan?' he said. I suspect he knew I did not. I just waited. 'This French Colonel of our friend Prudhomme. He is appointed as advisor to the palace on security matters. All servants of the state to give him full obedience, etcetera.'

What was I expected to say? 'Well, you know the French. Love a bit of extra protocol. There's probably a special hat you get for being advisor to a Sultan.' Klug didn't smile. I went on, trying to be both cautious and casual: 'Might be a good thing. Make sure there's no difficulties from – or for – the jolly old circus.'

'I see this. But if he has some interest for the circus *per se*, I fear there should be some difficulties with the hierarchy.'

I knew better than to sound dismissive about the hierarchy to a German. 'Sure we'll make it work all right. I'm sure the initiative is well meant.' I was thinking of Prudhomme, his obligation to keep the French engaged; and my obligation to maintain British support. And I was thinking of Hortense: if I'm to be squiring her about, they need to know that I'm trustworthy; and if I'm showing my diplomatic skill – bit of pep about me – that's got to make an impression on her. 'Stuck out here together, we all just want to get through the day without any dramas, don't we?'

'Well meant...' He considered it. 'If you say so, Thomas.'

'Right you are.'

I was feeling a bit of a louse.

'I fear you go too fast!' said a voice from behind us, and we stopped and turned to wait for Prudhomme. 'For those of us', he added, 'with older legs and older fashions.' He ran a finger round his tight collar, and pulled himself straighter. 'I think I may wish to break up this Saxon fraternity a moment.' The exertion of walking and the attempt at joviality had made him rather pink.

'Do you ask for instructions from Paris,' Klug said without humour, 'or this is a local initiative?' Prudhomme chuckled, and stood his ground.

'Oh that's all right', I said. 'Just chit-chat.' Neither of them liked it.

Walking through the noon streets, insisting on a straight line and a steady pace even when they took him through a roar of sunlight, Prudhomme said: 'I think we make good progress, cher Thomas. With the enthusiasm of His Majesty, and proper administration, we may have a fine success with our circus. A man... a man might make his mark with such a thing.' I said nothing; I may have grunted agreement. 'We should avoid too much delay, I think. Too much chance for German mischief. The little provocations from our friend will be daily, and that will become insupportable.' He leaned a little closer. 'We may need to finesse away the idea of the Ambassadors' première, perhaps.'

☿

'Is he very handsome?' Assia asks.

Eva has not thought about it. She tries to recall Luther Giesberts's face. She doesn't remember handsome.

'Very charming, yes? Very romantic.'

No.

A shrewd smile. 'Very rich, I am sure.'

'Richer than us, certainly.' She thinks about it. 'But if he was truly rich, I doubt he'd still be in Morocco.'

Assia looks confused; even hurt. It's almost amusing – and then irritating. Eva can do without being reminded of the limitations of her life. A man willing and able to provide tea and a pose of cultured conversation, that's not to be sniffed at.

She cups Assia's cheek with her palm, and kisses her briefly. 'You'd like to use my story as an exotic romance, an escape. I'm sorry to disappoint.'

☿

In the café on the corner, where the maze of alleys that make up Marrakech market empties onto the great square, the corner where the tattooists sit on their stools and grip their clients, morning is at its busiest and hottest. The square is where we go to see what Marrakech is today, and to show Marrakech what we are today. Fortune-tellers and story-tellers: the square is interpretation and performance.

After the first bustle of morning and as the heat begins to thicken, the rhythms of the royal palace slow. It is his habit, in this lull, to walk out into the city and to drink a tea with his acquaintances. Today he cannot. Two of his acquaintances are still hanging around the entrance, murmuring; the others have already disappeared back into the anonymity of the alleys.

Not to be indiscreet, but he's gone.

A table has been turned on its side, and blocks the entrance. The café is deserted.

We heard something about this. Last night. A riot.

Not a riot. A scuffle, no more.

We heard something about this. A debt. A daughter. A disagreement. And now it is a matter of blood.

Not blood. Well, not a lot of it. A bit of damage, no more.

We heard something about this. He is no longer safe here; he has fled for ever.

Not for ever. A visit to a cousin in Rabat, no more.

We heard something about this. The Roumi are arguing in their conference across the sea, and Morocco must suffer. The Roumi are playing their games in the shadows, their trades and their soldiers and their circuses, and the Sultan and his brothers and the Glaoui and the other tribes must all fight for influence, and we must swing their swords and suffer their wounds.

The curtain that previously separated the public area from the kitchen area has gone – though its rings still cling to their rail; crooked vertebrae. Through the gap: broken glass across the stones; the remains of a chair; a slick of liquid.

Waste. Dust. Emptiness. Absence. Already the former café is a desolate place. Without people the chairs are so much cheap furniture, easily broken, upended, removed. Without boundaries – a torn curtain, a smashed panel, a stolen shrub – this is no longer even a distinct place. No one will be brave enough to claim a disputed property, and so within a day its remaining markers will move or vanish, and this territory will be swallowed by others, and once again the map of the square will change.

We don't know how many people died last night. We don't know how many men of trade have already put their lives on a cart for the journey across the desert. We don't know how many other cafés are smashed and shut.

Or perhaps this particular conversation takes place half a day's journey out of the city, under an argan tree, hiding from the sun.

☾

Rather to Eva's surprise, Luther Giesberts is not unhandsome. Not actually handsome – and not romantic or charming in a way that would satisfy Assia – but… Seeing him afresh, and feeling that she must somehow defend herself to her maid, and looking for the deformities she must learn to overlook, she finds nothing she can really complain about.

He is standing on the hotel steps when she arrives, and she assumes he is waiting to escort her in. But in fact the hotel has shut unexpectedly. The double doors are locked, and already the outside looks shabby and forgotten.

Giesberts calls to a passing boy to stop – sees Eva – holds the boy with a raised finger – bows to Eva and hopes she is well – then turns to the boy again and says a few words to him in Arabic, pointing over his shoulder to the former hotel. The boy replies and, suspecting that he has exhausted the foreigner's Arabic, points at the hotel and finger-mimes someone walking away, far away. Giesberts says something else in Arabic, and waves a coin, and adds a few more words: instruction and warning.

Then the other couple has arrived – Eva hears the thought, and notices that it makes she and Giesberts a couple – and they are away through the sunshine, the boy trotting ahead to show that he is energetic in their service, the men striding after him to prove that they can keep pace with a Moroccan boy, and the women obliged to hurry after them regardless of who they can keep pace with.

Eva remembers Madame Luzzatti. When they met before, she was aloof, guarded, wary of unhygienic circus women. Now she leans naturally towards her companion, easy with confidences about the heat and other Europeans.

This, Eva understands, is the effect of Giesberts. Under his flag, she becomes entitled to courtesy and gossip.

Then they are in another café, and the boy has his coin, and Giesberts is pulling out a chair for her and sliding it under her and checking her comfort.

Eva can perform the receipt of these courtesies well enough. And if he is doing gallantry, then she will reward him with a little extra sway and poise, chin on finger and attentive eyes leaning towards him. Let's face it, no one else for a hundred miles can glide into a chair and hold herself there with the dancer's studied grace.

Also, she understands, he is making no compromises with her unknown background and sordid profession. If she is with him, he will treat her as he would the most worthy *grande dame* of society.

'The hell of a mess last night', Giesberts says to Luzzatti.

Luzzatti, a dapper little man who apparently shares Giesberts's caution about emotion, produces a large shrug and eventually says: 'These are not a mature people.'

'If they would have one system of law and regulation and implement it, all should run with smoothness.'

'I fear it will need decades of proper supervision.'

'Ah, but here is our disagreement.' Giesberts says it as if he's just spotted an old friend. The two men ration a small smile between them.

Eva is curious to see how this develops – curious to see Giesberts excited – but apparently the reference to their disagreement prompts the two prudent merchants to steer away.

'I fear for the reliability of my personnel.'

'I fear for the reliability of my supply route.'

'You always, dear Luther, fear for the reliability of your supply route.'

Giesberts turns to her. 'We speak of the implications of some unfortunate public unrest last night.' She nods and smiles. This sudden narration of his conversation is patronizing as well as ridiculous, but at least it acknowledges her; at least it almost includes her – if not quite. 'I hope you were not troubled.'

Part of her is already wearying of the performance of delicacy; she's looking forwards to a shouting match with Olga or Salomon. She shakes her head and smiles. In truth, last night the rumour of the rioting reached the little courtyard long before the shouting and the smoke, and the landlady barricaded them in and the three women huddled together on Eva's bed drinking endless sweet tea. She had the strong sense that her foreignness had been swallowed by some deeper and more dependable identity.

'Our French friends promise that greater control of public order will guarantee these matters.'

'Our French friends promise many things.'

The men are focused on each other again. These are not things for women to discuss. Mercifully, the arrangement of the chairs does not allow Eva and Madame

Luzzatti to talk separately about children or crafts or plumbing.

'But I think you wish for them to be more active, is it not so?'

'I wish that if they promise something they deliver it. An Embassy that claims to take control of security and still cannot stop a riot is no better than the boastful salesman who delivers shoddy cloth or broken machinery.'

'This', says Giesberts with heavy nod; 'this.'

As usual, the pose of deferential woman allows Eva to examine a man more than he might feel comfortable with.

Luther Giesberts sits well. She suspects it's sheer bulk of muscle rather than deliberate poise – even under the loose linen jacket she has noticed the strength of his chest and shoulders, and his neck rises proud like a tree-trunk – but the effect is good regardless. Most men here seem to be forever thawing in the heat, their bodies slumping and dripping out at the sides. Luther Giesberts looks alert. Ready. Disciplined. She would trust him for a business deal; she would trust him to keep an appointment. His northern skin has reddened rather than tanned – nothing of Reyes's sleek caramel here – but he looks active rather than uncomfortable. The bones are good: clear jaw, straight nose, no signs of flab gathering round either. The blue eyes are open and clear: the benefit of going easy at those dinners. His hair has unexpected life in it – the hint of a natural wave – but it's cut short and some innate control keeps it up and back away from his forehead.

The dancer chooses to suppress her inclination to pleasure, to abandon. Luther Giesberts looks, if not very handsome, certainly healthy.

'And now', Giesberts says ominously, 'there is arrived this circus.' A silent 'ah' of mournful agreement from Luzzatti. 'We must assume there is some clever diplomatic calculation behind it.'

'All of my sources tell me that the court is in uproar. The authority of the Sultan himself' – Luzzatti glances furtively towards the adjacent tables – 'is weakened. It is a most drastic manoeuvre by the diplomats.'

'Imprudent', says Giesberts conclusively, and the faces of the two men show what a terrible indictment this is. 'The effect among the men of business in the city, it is unhelpful. Rivalry. Worry. Inconsistency.' These, suggest the faces, are afflictions as dangerous as cholera.

Eva takes it for granted that Giesberts will skate over her involvement with the circus. This is not an occasion, this is not a café or a conversation, for Belgian dancers who sleep under carts and parade themselves in public.

Giesberts turns to her and says: 'I would be most interested in your opinion, Miss Eva, regarding the impact of your circus on a primitive society such as this, as compared for example to other places in your experience.'

As Eva replies – certain universals of human curiosity, the role of performance in any culture – Giesberts watches her intently, and occasionally his eyes drift. She assumes his concentration is elsewhere: he's thinking of a trading arrangement, no doubt, or wondering at the social impact of the woman he has chosen as his companion today.

But then he interrupts her – starts to speak – begs her pardon – and goes on speaking. He was absorbing and considering, and now he is challenging what she said: he picks out a phrase she used, explains why recent developments in ethnography, certainly as far as north African peoples are concerned, disprove her point.

It is laughably charmless. It is also honest. For all his careful courtesies, Luther Giesberts treats her as an intellect first and a woman second.

And this – though she knows she'll never be able to explain it to Assia – she finds handsome.

☪

JOURNAL OF THOMAS SOMERLEIGH

McKenna points out – he probably has a budget for an interpreter – a minor decree announcing the awarding by the royal administration of a contract for the rehabilitation of Marrakech's sewerage system... to a French engineering consortium. Another good day for Hector Prudhomme. This is the kind of benefit that accrues to a man with a circus. I've no doubt that Klug has seen the announcement, and I suspect he has the same feelings as I. It'll have to get a mention in the next wire for Tangier: Sir G. loves this kind of commercial detail – well, despises it, but knows it adds ballast to his telegram to London and gives the impression he is a modern Ambassador. And if I phrase it shrewdly – just a hint of frustration colouring my diligence – he might get the point that if I had more budget and leeway for this sort of initiative, perhaps we might be in the Moroccan drains rather than the French.

Plucked up the courage to ask Prudhomme if, further to his previous, it might be appropriate for me to walk Mlle Hortense to the Menara this afternoon. Steered clear of sewerage contracts. For a moment I thought he might refuse; he was looking pretty damn' sure of himself. But then bonhomie: charming idea, sure the dear girl would enjoy, do please have a care to keep her out of the sun.

So it was later afternoon when we strolled out, the sun safely removed behind the taller buildings and trees. Must say I felt rather a swell. Youssef had got wind of what I was up to, and had suddenly remembered how to polish shoes and wouldn't let me out without checking my tie. And beside me the loveliest girl: bright and neat as a new pin, gleaming white from toe-tips to parasol, big eyes forever glancing up at me.

We didn't talk much. She's sweetly shy, and I've always been a dead loss at small talk with girls; better the strong silent type rather than make an ass of myself. But as we walked past the Koutoubia mosque I worked up a line to the effect that she amid the dust and strangeness of the scene was like the hibiscus flower in the desert, and she positively blushed. Then she reminded me of our date-buying incident in the Menara, and we had a little chuckle, and that's got to be good.

To the shadier side of the mosque, a small crowd. Thinking it might be a story-teller – she'd heard of the tradition, the lad Ali, and I'd been telling her all about it – we drifted closer. Unsettling business, a crowd – and her hand slipped into mine. I smiled reassurance, and something else. Well, as we got a bit closer, some of the lads on the fringes noticed us, and out of some natural deference they pulled aside so that we could get a bit closer, see what was going on.

With the satisfaction of familiarity, I recognized old Sa'id, Brahim's mystic philosopher chappie I'd had such a fascinating lunch with. He was standing against the mosque, on a box or something that put him a head above his audience, and he was lecturing. I can't describe the style: not a harangue, but he has quite a pair of lungs tucked away; the guarded murmurs of our lunch had been replaced with a voice of real force, a voice that soared and swooped. He was asking and explaining, reassuring and inspiring. That much I could feel from the sound, and the reaction of the crowd. The language of course was lost on me.

There must have been a good hundred people pressing around him – all men, I suppose. But naturally he noticed the movement in the crowd, and our very different costume, and presumably he recognized me. He pointed at us, rather dramatic, and the whole mob swung to look, and Hortense gasped and I, a touch alarmed no doubt, squeezed her hand.

But the old man put on a remarkable smile and, for our benefit, went on in English. We Moroccans may be a simple, unsophisticated people, he said – the days when Marrakech ruled areas of Europe have been overtaken by days of dependence – but we are a courteous people, and our cities have known their own kind of civilization for at least as long as many in Europe. I don't know how many were getting it all, but there was some nodding, murmurs of approval. Again he pointed. The foreigners – he used this word 'Roumi', which they all seem to – may come as our superiors, but they are also our guests. We allow them to enjoy their diplomatic affairs and amusements. We do not seek, he said, to impose our faith or our culture on them; but we must maintain our faith and our culture, indifferent to the foreign games. More murmuring. We must trust, he added, that our beloved rulers show the same wisdom.

Back at HQ, I mentioned to Prudhomme – as much for diplomatic atmos. – that we'd seen a bit of street-life, old Sa'id doing his Hyde Park Corner stuff. Prudhomme looked very stuffed and uncomfortable. I emphasized that I'd whisked Hortense away without tarrying to get the details, but it didn't improve his expression. Guess he's always been wary of letting her see too much Morocco – get those little feet dirty – and I fear that may be it for the cultural excursions: Mademoiselle to be kept in, classroom amusements only.

I must see her again. As we arrived back at their villa – the gate half-open, we half-in – secluded from the street and still obscured from the house – once again her eyes looking up into mine. Then: her chin lifting, her lips trembling, her eyes closing. That vision – that expectation, that surrender – as thrilling as the touch of the lips, the heat of her breath in my mouth.

On reflection, I realize I've no way of knowing if what old the man said in English was remotely similar to what he'd been saying in Arabic.

☪

When Luther Giesberts has had a second glass of wine, he becomes less cautious about showing his enthusiasm for Moroccan culture. He is surprisingly knowledgeable about music and about handcrafts. And he enjoys recounting anecdotes of his experiences around the city and around the country.

One tale he tells – and already he is chuckling, because a German does not buy weak wine and because he anticipates how funny we will find it – he heard of Ali the story-teller. Ideally, says Giesberts, you would hear this story from the lips of the boy Ali himself, but I guess you would not have the language for this. So:

The busiest land-border in all Morocco is to the east. Every day, a multitude of travellers and traders and officials crosses this border. And, because things are somewhat more let us say relaxed in French Algeria – Giesberts smiles at us, and reminds us how the boy Ali plays on these traditional types to reinforce our sense of familiarity and ease – a great many smugglers are among them.

Well, for many years the Captain of the Border Guards in this district was the worthy Mostapha. Mostapha was a man of virtue and diligence, unlike many of these fellows. Not many smugglers got through when he was on duty, and as his reputation spread they would go to great lengths to avoid him, or indeed to move their business to a different district. One man, however, defied him. This was Omar, king of the smugglers, and legend. All knew him for what he was, his bravado was the talk of the cafés, and yet never was he caught in the act. Once every month he would come across the border, a small plump man with his mule, and the border guards would search him and the mule thoroughly – clothes, saddle, bags, everywhere – and never did they find any contraband. Once every month he would return alone, his legitimate goods all sold, and again he would be searched and again nothing would be found.

For Mostapha, the pursuit of Omar became an obsession, and eventually his sole ambition. He worked longer and longer hours, he turned up on duty at unexpected times, just so as to be on the spot when Omar plodded through the border on his mule. But he never caught Omar out. However intimately Mostapha searched the man, nothing – the most curious expression, and a peculiar noise in Giseberts's throat, when he re-tells Ali's story because Germans are not naturally easy around dirty jokes, and naturally do not wish to seem so – however intimately Mostapha searched the mule, nothing. Omar's nature was a public secret, and his wealth continued to grow – steadily, for he was not a man of excess – and this we might think was part of his secret – and Mostapha never knew how it was done.

At last – for time defeats even the most diligent official and the shrewdest smuggler – both men retired from their respective professions. One morning they found themselves sitting next to each other in the café and, both being men of courtesy, and with a professional respect for each other, having spent so many years in essentially the same business, they fell to talking. At last Mostapha said: 'Grant me one favour, old fellow, would you?' And Omar replied that he would if he possibly could. 'I can tolerate the suspense no longer', Mostapha went on. 'All those years you were smuggling something past me, and all those years I never found it, however closely I searched you or your mule, yes?' Omar waited a moment, and then nodded cautiously. 'Now you have put all that behind you and will never need to smuggle again. And now it is all behind me too, and I will never be able to punish you. So tell me, old fellow: what were you smuggling?'

Omar looked carefully around the café, and then leaned close to Mostapha and, without any drama or bravado, he said quietly: 'I was smuggling mules'.

☽

In the café on the corner, where the maze of alleys that make up Marrakech market empties onto the great square, the corner where the knife-grinder treadles and squeals, morning is at its busiest and hottest. The square is a place of hope, of faith, of surrender. When a man steps out into its bustling vastness, he can see nothing of his future. He cannot know what he will feel ten paces later: a dip's hand in his purse, a boy's hand on his arse, a rival's knife in his back, a grumpy snake's fang in his ankle, or the satisfaction of having struck a good bargain for a sack of pomegranates. The dust on the other side of the square may come from the crowd around the booksellers' stalls, or a charging horde of mountain tribesmen. Deep breath. Brief prayer. Enjoy the moment.

After the first bustle of morning and as the heat begins to thicken, the rhythms of the royal palace slow. It is his habit, in this lull, to walk out into the city and to drink a tea with his acquaintances. The simple routine is more fraught now. The proprietor doesn't bounce genially between his clients any more, fake smile and fake recognition and have another tea my brother; he stands glaring at each new arrival, or prowls the margins of the café waiting for trouble. A pair of hefty cousins have been stationed at the entrance, fat hand on chest blocking too hasty an entry, rummaging in pockets for knives, sour sniff at a darker face or a village gown. This checkpoint passed, he steps forwards towards his acquaintances. But shouts explode in front of him, table-top flung up, fists clutching at chests and throats and the café is a dusty whirl of anger and noise and the two gate-men have barged past him and grabbed whatever they can and a man is being dragged out and again barging and on the threshold they're kicking the man and punch in the face and punch in the face and surely enough punch in the face and whoever he is he is still. Eventually, innocent or guilty, he will drag himself whimpering away.

Not to be indiscreet, but what is a man supposed to believe any more?

We know the answer to this. Don't we? Absolutely whatever he's told.

Well of course, but the old imam disappeared into the cells beneath the palace, so he ain't going to be telling me anything for a while.

Of course the new imam, but they say the new imam is the Caliph's choice, not His Majesty's.

Of course he's the real power in the city, but what if in the end he isn't? Look pretty stupid then, won't I?

Or what if they're wrong, and he isn't the Caliph's choice? Even more stupid, yes, thank you.

And anyway, the man who really is the Caliph's choice today may not be the Caliph's choice tomorrow. A man tries to be loyal, but it's harder when what we're supposed to be loyal to keeps changing. Nice if there was some sort of daily update. Today I'm supposed to believe... Like that.

What the imam says? That's the point. What His Majesty says? Don't be daft. What the Caliph says? The Glaoui? The Roumi? Ali the story-teller?

Right: easier if there weren't all these different voices. You think the leathermens' souk is violent, you want to see the way the men of religion are arguing now.

For instance? For instance, that man you were with once. The foreigner, very pale, very thin. No, I'm not saying you believed it, wouldn't dream of it, another man's soul is none of my business, I'm just saying you and he were at the same table once. All right, my mistake, you've never heard of him, you've never been to Marrakech, may He Who Knows All Sins strike me down if I assume too much. But him, anyway. Very pale. Very thin. Tough, though. Remember you saying – though you've never met him of course, so let's call this an amazingly good guess, shall we? – that he once punched out someone who was arguing with him. All about starving yourself and disappearing into your dreams, wasn't it? Avoid the sins of the physical and exist closer to the infinite, that your final escape to paradise may be the easier.

Yes, as you say: there's always the opposite, isn't there? The Glaoui's always got a few paid preachers doing the rounds, whispering that it's all the Roumi's fault and we should rise up and throw them out. Nice job that, until he decides to cut a few throats to prove to the Roumi how effective and reliable he is.

And who's this old preacher everyone's talking about? Everywhere, apparently. Friend of a friend heard him outside the booksellers' mosque. All of us heard of him, yes? Tells you something. Wonder if he really wants all that publicity.

He's a prophet. Except obviously we don't use that word.

He's a troublemaker. Except he does seem sincerely to be preaching the avoidance of trouble.

Yeah; I know. He's the root of half the unhappy souls in the city, half the fights.

He's the fruit, not the root. He's what happens when the city gets like this. Troubled times breed troubled minds, not the other way round. And every troubled mind has its different idea, and chances are that one of them will come up with something interesting. Troubled minds produce new answers.

Troubled minds produce new troubles. He's the guarantee of unhappiness and dissent, fights in the market, discord between man and wife, His Majesty unable to sleep easy.

He's the solution. He's the one man who's found a way to survive this troubled world.

No one survives it. If you're lucky, you get to choose how you don't survive it.

Makes you wonder who he's working for.

And now the Roumi have brought their own magicians, of course; this so-called circus of theirs.

They're provoking the unrest; that's what their magicians are for.

They want to calm it all down, make us obedient; that's what the magicians are for.

They provoke the unrest in order to be able to have their magicians calm it down.

Everyone still wants to see this circus, don't they? All these conferences and circuses, this is our future. We want to find out what these magicians are offering. See what our options are.

Not everyone, obviously. Not men like us. Not interested.

Dancers, though.

See what I mean? All these voices, all these truths, all these promises. Who am I supposed to listen to? What's a man supposed to believe?

Of course my one care is to attain paradise, but my other care, sort of secondary, call it a preference, is not to get my throat cut before breakfast.

If we listen with a pure heart, we will hear the word of The One regardless.

Great, but we're having to listen really hard right now. And sometimes, amid the shouts and the screams and the roof falling in, we hear... not a thing.

Or perhaps this particular conversation takes place on the edge of a great hall in the palace, two sentries at attention, unable to move, scarce able to move their lips, offering murmurs in the hope of fellowship, there at the side in the shadows.

☪

Giesberts invites her to supper at his house.

For a moment Eva has the same visions as Assia, standing bright-eyed waiting for a hint of the message she has just delivered. A dinner à *deux*, candlelight through twilight, evening breeze through veil curtains, the scent of fruits and blossoms, a naked shoulder, finger-tips, strength and softness and flight. Then – as the one of them who has actually met the man in question – she knows that this is impossible. His reputation; her reputation. Her frown sends Assia away.

There are four others at supper. The senior German diplomat in Marrakech, a dapper box-shaped man named Klug with big worried eyes. A Moroccan called Bin Musa who's something significant in one of the foreign banks, with his wife; Eva is hungry to talk to her but, because she is his wife, or she is his wife because, she is silent. And an older woman, the widow of a French missionary, dutifully sustaining her late husband's dreams, reputedly shut up in a crumbling villa somewhere on the edge of the city.

Giesberts is genuinely pleased to see her – the eyes, his hands gripping hers – and she allows herself to believe this is her charming company as well as the fact that she balances his table. She is scrutinizing his home with, she realizes, calculating eyes. It is substantial but not huge: no lost corners of romance or mystery. It is in good repair: the plaster fresh and clean, the lighting modern and effective; even to a European the bathroom is a kind of miracle.

'Personally I supervised the reinforcement of this wall and the anchoring of the banister', he says: pride. 'The cold storage room – there is there a prototype of a German mechanism' – he and Klug the diplomat nod understanding to each other – 'is adequate that for one month I may remain here without re-supply', he says: secure. 'Only a few dull materials in my study', he says, and 'The piping is an arrangement of my own design': jealousy, of secrets not for profane eyes.

Fate and the European economy have dictated that Luther Giesberts is to spend part of his manhood in this outpost in the desert. Besieged by dirt, disease, noise, rioting, heathenism and foreignness, he has made himself a fortress of purity, a place sacred as well as comfortable.

There is time for only one drink before they eat, and no alcohol is offered. She wonders who is to be impressed by this: hard-working temperate Giesberts himself; the austere diplomatic guest; the banker; or the Muslims outside the walls? Not Eva, anyway, who finds herself oddly tight-wound and gasping for a cocktail. Despite an appealing set of chairs and sofas – leather, cushions in local materials – they stand. There's not much talking, and Giesberts and Klug are doing all of it; she understands that they are more relaxed with each other than they would be with any other human in the city, and still they are cautious, deferential, subdued. Occasionally a specific point is referred to the Moroccan for agreement: tight-wrapped little Monsieur Bin Musa shuts his eyes, digests the idea and eventually nods.

Then they go in to eat.

Eva is understanding more of the peculiar chess of this society of theirs, the mad delicate calculations of strategy, the subtleties of defence and benefit. It is desirable for Giesberts to host the senior diplomat of his country. It is desirable for the diplomat to be hosted by a successful merchant of his country. Eva wonders who of them was allowed to host whom first. It is also desirable for Giesberts to host a significant Moroccan man of business. It is desirable for both the diplomat and the Moroccan to meet each other; and Eva realizes that Giesberts's invitation to each was more attractive because of the presence of the other. Yet diplomat and Moroccan could not easily meet without Giesberts bridging their worlds.

At least there's wine with dinner.

It might be unseemly for the diplomat to meet a local man of money, but the presence of ladies has made this a social occasion. Having the same number of women as men confirms that the women are merely tokens. The wife denotes that the evening is asexual: the relations between none of the participants will change this evening. The older woman confirms that the women are inert, significant only as non-men who do not complicate relationships and conversations.

She doesn't know if the wine is any good, but it's cool enough and calming.

Eva sees that, for Giesberts, she has unlocked this possibility of inviting women. And in return, the presence of the wife and the older woman validates her presence, otherwise dangerously free and sexual.

She's the only person drinking the wine. The older Frenchwoman is too austere, and more importantly the Moroccan and his wife will not touch it, and so the two German men make a point of refusing it. In years to come they will wear their occasional abstinence – 'among the Arabs, naturally, never does one touch alcohol. But this courtesy, it is why Germany is respected among them' – as a badge of suffering, of professionalism.

Eva wonders if Giesberts ever enjoys himself, and how.

Eva wonders why, given the guests, Giesberts bothered to have wine available.

The food is plentiful. Germans are good eaters, and she's gathered enough of Arab culture to know that putting on an impressive front is important – a performer understands this – and generosity is a sign of respect to a guest. Giesberts's silent competent servants – young men, Moroccan, vaguely formal vaguely European tunics over local wraps, lowered eyes and graceful gliding movements, not to be seen – have produced an elegant combination of Morocco's diverse tastes, because we are pretending to adapt to our surroundings and to respect the culture of our guest, around one obvious main dish, because one does not invite a German diplomat to dinner without giving him a lamb chop. The mysterious genius of the cold store provides chilled desserts.

The wine is there precisely to not be drunk. Visible but untouchable, it defines taste and tone for the man and the occasion.

The same, Eva realizes, is true of her.

'Ah, but these diplomats!' says the German diplomat. The merchant and the banker nod sympathy. 'The French – their mentality – it is not nineteenth century, it is seventeenth century. Here, out of respect for the worries of our hosts about stability' – nod to the banker, who nods back; no one's expecting him to speak – 'we must allow them to feel pre-eminent. Really Germany could, if we wished, deliver a success tomorrow. I have the resources, I have the authority.' Everyone shows they recognize and appreciate this. 'Instead, these games, these delays, these endless changes, these illogical compensations. Such an inefficiency.'

'The effect on business,' says Giesberts, 'it is most tiresome. To make allowances for the culture of our hosts' – nod to the Moroccan, nod, silence – 'of course we adapt. But the health of this economy depends on stability – predictability – momentum.' His finger taps the table with each word. The others nod.

'In the conference in Spain, and every day in Marrakech,' Klug says, looking directly at the banker for once, 'Germany is committed to a Morocco that is independent, steady and advancing.' He holds the glance an unnecessary moment longer, and Eva wonders if that sentence was the point of the whole evening; she wishes she'd paid more attention to it.

'The Frenchman', says Klug, 'naturally is proud because he can be Emperor in his committee, so of course we indulge this. He sees the advantages of the circus, and wants to benefit. As good colleagues, Germany accepts this. Today, then, I offer him a new partnership. A performance here in Marrakech, exactly according to his preferences, and on a fixed date; and to match this another confirmed performance in Tangier. Germany seeks only a fair portion of the credit for this success, and France may have an equal glory, or even more.'

'Highly reasonable', Giesberts murmurs.

'This is only good diplomacy. But immediately our Frenchman panics. His eyes are cold and uncomfortable. He is afraid to make a commitment. Culturally,' – Klug hits the word, and gazes round the table – 'he is afraid of clarity.'

'The mind of the poet, the philosopher, the dreamer; not the merchant or the ruler.'

'So! And then the English…' Everyone nods gravely. It's not clear what we're supposed to think, but the English always demand the gravest consideration. 'They control everything of course; we assume everything works according to their design. But externally, they show no grip; no clarity!' Everyone shakes their head, gravely.

The talk is becoming interesting, and Eva is about to interject something about cultural types in foreign contexts, when she realizes with irritation that a Belgian dancing girl intervening in a German male conversation about diplomacy and commerce might easily bring on the apocalypse. And that wearying sense of decorum reminds her of something she once saw in a play: at a certain point in a dinner, after the food has been cleared, the hostess invites the other women to leave the men. To leave them to… the mind boggles. They surely couldn't become any more dull and intense. And it's hard to imagine the steady merchant, the cold diplomat and the little paunchy banker indulging in a riot of homoerotic debauchery, however wildly the unexercised female mind wanders.

The desserts have been cleared, vanishing as imperceptibly as the genies had conjured them.

At this table, in this performance, she has only one line. A bit-player with a dream of stardom should tremble at the opportunity.

Anxiously, she watches the men's faces, waiting for the moment.

'Perhaps,' she says too loudly, and everyone stares at her, 'we ladies, we shall allow the men some freedom.'

Hell, what if she has misunderstood the rules? What if Giesberts disagrees?

Rather satisfyingly, the other two women immediately stand. And Giesberts, Giesberts of the strong jaw and the clear eye, bestows on her a look of such gratitude and – and pride, is it? affection, even? – that for an instant her loins melt.

Having won her freedom and saved her comrades too, she pulls herself together. Unaware of any alternative, she leads the fugitives back to the sitting room, and wonders what's supposed to happen next. She waits for the obvious question: so, you're playing hostess then; what are the terms and conditions of that performance, exactly?

A servant appears, conjured by faith or hope. But how does a hostess speak to a servant? This wasn't covered in the play: the audience had been shown the men's table conversation instead.

This is Giesberts's house. In Giesberts's house, everything is calm and assured. 'Thank you,' she says to the silent young man. 'We shall have drinks.' To the ladies: 'Whatever you wish.' She has no idea if Giesberts's store can back that up, and fortunately neither of the other two takes it seriously enough even to ask: just as at the table, hospitality is grand in the offering and humble in the acceptance. Regardless, each of them is given a tall glass of soda water with fresh mint, and a little glass of sherry: with a protestant host or just discreet servants, religious observance is a matter of individual choice.

Decades of colonial intervention have happily given Madame Bin Musa adequate French, and the three natter freely of the city a decade ago, of children, of traditional music. Eva exploits her newness to ask naive questions about dancing, about female performance; the others are informed, insightful, at ease.

She recalls someone telling her that emus are supposed to represent wisdom. Madame Bin Musa observes that such an animal can only be considered decoration; inanimate. Madame Loubet finds the emu tragic, shut up in a cage in a palace.

Eva has created another soup-kitchen for herself, in another leftover space, unintended and unconsidered and free.

First Bin Musa and his re-silenced wife leave. Then Madame Loubet, escorted by one of the servants. Giesberts and Klug are still smoking their cigars.

'If I may, mein Herr', Giesberts is saying. 'The Embassy could do great service for honest commerce by ensuring there is regulation and proper respect of the protegay system.' It's the third or fourth time Eva has heard the word this evening, and only now does she deduce the French *protégé*.

She is spare on the edge of the room, without ally or status.

'These other Europeans, of course we see the greatest abuses of the system. But it is essential in permitting the honest merchant to fulfil his obligations.'

Is there something she should be doing as hostess, or could be? *Damned if I'm going to make a servant of myself in the hope of squeeze.* She has earned her occupation of the public rooms, planted her flag, and here she will stay.

How much do I wish to stay? How long? And how, exactly?

She has known plenty of men who'd buy her a biscuit and expect a fuck. She has known fewer men who truly preferred a gentler wooing, of companionship and anticipation. One whose chaste and soulful letters followed her around northern Italy for months. She cannot yet read Giesberts's expectations.

And she understands that she cannot be seen to stay: not after Herr Klug; not now the other women have gone. The diplomat would notice. Giesberts would know it was noticed.

Yet as she offers her hand in farewell, she sees that Giesberts's mind is following the same questions, and coming to the same conclusion. And in those fine eyes, and in the press of his fingers, is that the same tentative stirring of regret?

He doesn't know exactly what he wants to say; can't say it. Instead, rushed and impromptu: 'I thank you most deeply, Fräulein Eva; you brought to my table the greatest efficiency as well as the greatest charm.'

It is the highest compliment possible, short of actually conferring a German passport on her, and it earns from the waiting Klug a deep nod of agreement. Eva walks home, one of Giesberts's servants trying to keep up, with the buoyant sense of a satisfactory transaction.

۝

JOURNAL OF THOMAS SOMERLEIGH

Grim business last night, I gather. Riots in more than one quarter of the city. Bloodshed: can't get any clear sense of the number killed, but it is certain that some were. Youssef wide-eyed and skulking this morning: I doubt he was out causing trouble himself, but the situation made him jumpy. He told me the most alarming story, too: apparently some sort of monster is prowling the city preying on young women. And damage to property, especially in the Jewish quarter. Drafted the main lines of an urgent telegram to Tangier, ready for sending as soon as I had the context from the palace.

Some of the shops hadn't opened up by the time I stepped out. And every face watchful, and furtive: I understood where Youssef was getting it from. As if the whole city was feeling guilty.

No sign of any trouble in the diplomatic quarter.

H.M. the Sultan put in an appearance this morning. I assumed he'd be complaining as usual about lack of foreign engagement, or excess of foreign engagement; demanding more autonomy, or more artillery, or money to rebuild. Instead he just sat there: his expression little different from Youssef or anyone in the street, as if he his royal self had been in the streets last night, smashing up shops and knocking merchants on the head.

Each of the dips had heard something (how?). Funnily enough, Prudhomme – who has far and away the best information network here, with his expatriate community and security advisors and so on – was inclined to play it down: usual hysterical stories from an unsophisticated people. But among the rest of us many gloomy looks, and overheard numbers, and tales of violence, and more gloomy looks. Joking aside, this is why we are here: why Morocco needs us, and why we individually have come with the court to Marrakech. As H.M. slouched in and slumped in his throne, we gathered around him, like doctors at a mortal bedside.

Klug launched in the most thunderous, funereal terms, and at first I thought he was over-cooking it rather. 'Your Majesty: taking advantage of your generosity in receiving us, I must express in the strongest terms Germany's great concern at the collapse in public order last night. The very possibility of civilized administration in Morocco seems to wait upon the verdict of the ruffians in the streets.' Strong stuff. 'As I trust Your Majesty knows, Germany is the most devoted friend and supporter of your independence, your prosperity, and Your Majesty's divinely-ordained rule. But there must be a stable environment for honest commerce. Germany's generous investments in this country – I mention for example our sponsorship of the circus in Your Majesty's household – it is expected that these are applied prudently and properly. The health of this economy depends on stability – predictability – momentum. Yet this whole society, we find it is in peril.'

I happened to be watching Prudhomme, and within the habitual austere poise I got a hint of scorn. France has been dealing with public order in North Africa for decades – France has been order, indeed – more familiar with the desert peoples – and no doubt more able to take the long view. Happy enough to have Germany distracted, no doubt.

Klug: 'I regret to report a most disgraceful outrage last night, inflicted on one of the most respected of foreign citizens in Marrakech.' Now we all woke up. Except the Sultan, who slumped even lower. 'Many of my colleagues will know of Madame Loubet: widow of a most worthy French resident here, a most charitable and Christian personality; an older lady both vulnerable and respectable, loved by all local people, who have benefited from her kindness. Last night she was being escorted home, neither late nor away from the safer streets, when she was caught up in the rioting and most disgracefully harassed. The servant escorting her was wounded or killed, and the lady has suffered the greatest shock and indignity, and we cannot yet know in what condition she will survive. As your dearest friend, Majesty, Germany must advise you that this cannot be tolerated.'

Prudhomme adapted fast. An attack on a foreigner was grim enough. An attack on a woman outrageous. And a Frenchwoman... The austere frame became somehow taller, colder, sharper.

'For generations, Your Majesty, France has been friend and companion to Morocco. We have walked beside you; supported you when you stumbled. Twenty-five years ago, in Madrid, we and your other friends sought to regularize our support to you in Treaty form. It has fallen to France to offer the lion's share of this assistance.' I saw Klug and Reyes flinch, but only because I looked for it. 'France asks for nothing in return. It is the duty and the obligation of a more advanced people to carry a more substantial burden, and we accept our duty humbly and execute it faithfully. What now do we find? We find our assistance spurned, and our citizens outraged. France naturally echoes the grave concern so eloquently expressed by Germany' – I saw Klug's further alarm at the compliment – 'and is obliged to give all possible assistance to resolve the situation. The security experts of the French Government, now present in Marrakech to wait on Your Majesty, will prepare a programme of measures to aid Your Majesty in stabilizing the situation. France would be most surprised if any of these proposals are found to be other than immediately implementable.'

Klug on the spot and thinking fast, face hard as he forced his argument on the meeting. 'As always, the words of France carry the greatest weight of international respect and rhetorical power.' Prudhomme looked as if the German had tweaked his nose. 'Germany remains committed to supporting Morocco's independence, through the equal engagement of the major European powers.' McKenna the Yankee looking faintly bored, and the other European dips each trying to work out if they count as major. 'Germany has given finance for part of Your Majesty's household, and if necessary I am confident that more would be possible.

There is now a proper mechanism for managing these assets: our international committee on the circus and related matters, which of course has a Moroccan representative. Having funded these assets, Germany expects them to be used prudently and only in the interests of Morocco's stability. Germany has made a clear proposal for partnership, a demonstration by the circus here in Marrakech, and then in Tangier. The outrage last night only reinforces the importance of such a measured and carefully co-ordinated management of the sensitive resources of Your Majesty. In your best interests, Your Majesty, Germany will insist on this.'

I was trying to work out the Sultan's expression. He was so slumped, I wondered if he might actually have dropped off.

Prudhomme, meanwhile, was looking rather redder than normal, as if Klug had now slapped his cheek. 'Germany is absolutely right, of course.' Klug looked like he'd been punched in the nose. 'Morocco has the assets at its disposal, with generous international funding and proper international oversight. It is more than time that these assets are used, with the careful and good effect that my German colleague rightly describes. By Your Majesty's leave, I shall immediately instruct the French experts to finalize the security plan, including a proper use of the circus.' Deep bow and he was gone.

H.M. silent. Not, I fear, the most impressive performance. A pity, too, for my wire to Tangier, not having the Moroccan side contributing anything.

☫

Her discreet management of dining-table and door-step has brought a subtle change in Eva's relationship with Luther Giesberts. Today she does not meet him at his house, but in the centre of the city, and this is a further liberation. Amid the chatter and colour of the streets, another pale-faced white-clothed stroller, she is less defined by the household roles; less constrained.

And now the city itself is behind them, the great crude pink stone gateway coughing the two of them out into the desert, the walls falling away like a cloak. A man and a woman in the wilderness: what might they become? what might they once have been?

Luther suggested a walk together, and Eva felt she owed the circus a visit.

Away from his house, Luther seems a more natural man. He walks more easily: the strong chest breathes full and hungry, his stamina in the heat is striking, his leg-muscles are firm and poised as he pulls her up onto a wall to admire the view. He talks more easily, too.

He is charmingly earnest on the subject of trade patterns between Central Europe and North Africa. Eva understands little and cares less, but a man is more honest in his passions and more likeable in his weaknesses. His obsession with fairness and efficiency seems both worthy and rather naive. Eva can imagine herself becoming fond of them; affectionate, even.

As well as seeming worthier in the eyes of his world, she would become worthier by adapting to it. She would respect him, she would be proud to speak of him, and she would be fierce in wanting to protect him from less noble spirits. Each of these instincts could serve as love, couldn't they?

He is genuinely interesting on Moroccan culture and society. As a merchant rather than a diplomat, he has had to engage with this society more fully: to adapt himself to it rather than imposing himself on it. He talks with equal conviction about construction methods, education in the villages, the nature of Islamic belief, fabrics and sanitation.

A lull. 'I keep hearing about this... protegay system', she says.

He shrugs, and grabs her arm to steer her around some camel dung. 'A necessary technicality of colonial affairs, which here takes on more political significance.' She can see his mind working, composing a version of the truth to suit her uncommercial womanly mind. 'Like any foreign man of business, I can only have a success here if I can rely on certain principles of trade, yes? Of law. Morocco is not Germany, this I think we can agree' – she likes it when he smiles – 'and it is not Germany in one hundred different ways. Some of these ways perhaps we think are rather enjoyable: even a dull German man who cares too much about mercantile theory and his cold store, perhaps even he enjoys the colours and the light and the food and the chaotic enthusiasms.' It's the first time she's heard him talk about himself like that; it's engaging. 'But still I need to know that a contract will be respected, or at least protected in law. That a price agreed is a price paid. Also, I need to know that my business will not suffer from the chaos. At the national level, Morocco agrees to function according to good European systems of law and commerce. But at the local level...' He puffs out his cheeks, too many exasperations. 'My contract, or my shipment of pottery, or my local representative trying to maintain a good relationship with a supplier, they cannot be the victims of some local corruption or incompetence or feud. So:' – he clicks his fingers in the air, invoking his God of logic and efficiency – 'there is an agreement whereby designated Moroccan servants and representatives of foreign enterprises and foreign embassies enjoy the same legal protections and exemptions as their foreign chiefs. My agent in the mountain village: he speaks for me and acts for me, and so legally he must be protected like me. These are the protegay; the protected people.'

'So why does anyone complain about it?'

Puffed cheeks and shrug. 'Here it is easy to find reasons to complain, yes? Some people do not like the idea of any exemption from local law. As if I or any other foreign representative could be subject to Moroccan law! As if such a thing even exists. Then, among these people, of course there is much envy. A man sees that his cousin or his neighbour enjoys a different status because he has won a good position with a foreigner, and he grows resentful. And then, unfortunately, there are of course certain individual cases where the local representatives abuse their special protections; these oriental corruptions, yes? Certain European cultures are not so rigorous with the discipline of their personnel.'

She's trying to find ways to admire him again. 'I hadn't realized I was walking with such a personage! Why, it makes you a kind of super-man. You are... well, capable of anything; guided only by your own morality and your own will.'

She'd meant it to sound like a tease.

'But this is a responsibility, do you see?' He's not denying anything. 'Not only the diplomats like Herr Klug, but also the men of commerce like myself, we have a mission here; we have a duty. We are trying to do what these people cannot themselves do; we are setting an example. Naturally this demands certain protections, certain status.'

Eva is uncomfortable, because instinctively she sees herself in the position of victim under such a system. A few more moments of silence, watching her familiar feet scuffing this unfamiliar dust, and she is uncomfortable because the opposite may be true.

She has wanted Assia to see her as ally, and equal.

'But only we are talking of my boring business affairs', Luther says unexpectedly. 'Too little have we talked about your circus.'

Eva feels a flash of guilt: painful truth. The circus is only considered as a diplomatic notion now. We have forgotten to think of it as people, creatures, an idea, a community.

They are very near it now. Eva is prompted to look up and see the familiar wagons, laid out ahead. She realizes she hasn't been listening for the first sounds of the horses. She wonders how, in Luther's manner, she should begin to talk about the circus.

'Of course,' he says, 'now that the circus is officially funded by Germany within the royal apparatus, I may guess that you and your comrades are protegay also.' God, is this what makes her acceptable to him? Just as a good Muslim may not couple with a woman who is impure or infidel. 'This is natural, yes? For now you are doing important work for the stability of this country. You are a symbol of the Sultan's power – and, of course' – he touches her arm, less lightly than he imagines – 'of German power. Properly deployed, you will show who it is that governs here; who sets the tone here. You will show calm, and healthy diversion, and you will show what is enlightened culture.'

There is little sign of life in the circus encampment. Someone has been feeding the horses; but they are listless, indifferent. Eva has been inattentive, unfaithful, and they seem less welcoming. The lions too: she used to enjoy the usual circus affectation that the lions knew her, and were protecting rather than threatening. Now she keeps her distance: they just look like wild animals, corralled briefly and coincidentally, slumped and scowling in their ramshackle cage, gnawing bored at the wicker.

Even at rest, the circus should be life: people in movement, animals incompletely constrained, rare colours, strange noises, endless obligations and energies. Now it is being absorbed into the desert around it. Dust and dirt have blown onto the wagons. The breeze is the only suggestion of movement, tugging lazily at rope ends and canvas edges and the grasses growing up around wheels and crates.

Sitting under a parasol on the back of a covered wagon is a familiar figure. Eva smiles instinctively, and her stride lengthens as she walks over. The figure is bulky, settled, the hands busy with some chore.

Halfway over, confusion: Eva sees that it's not Mama Zana. But the figure has noticed her and she can't turn away now.

It's the dark woman: who shared her lodging room that first night in Marrakech, who has been drifting into the circus ever since; who many now be the last living soul in it. She's peeling and quartering an apple.

Can it be she who's doing all the feeding of the animals? She couldn't know how, surely. She wouldn't dare. But if anyone else has visited, just as Eva is visiting, they're not here now.

Eva gives a big smile, reassurance that she is not an unwelcome visitor. 'Hallo!' she says, though she assumes she and the woman have no language in common. 'Keeping an eye on things?' An empty smile in return.

Beyond the bulky figure, dim under the canvas, there's someone lying in the wagon. The dark woman offers Eva a mighty arm and pulls her up.

Vast and slumped, Mama Zana is drowsing. Lying down, her body has given up all shape. She is a puddle of flesh and coloured shawls. Eva finds her hand.

'Mama, it's Eva.' A great snort and a grunt, irritation more than curiosity. 'Eva!'

One vast eye falls open, not quite where it was expected. Mama Zana produces a strange hum of interest and warmth, and squeezes her hand. She licks her lips, and eventually murmurs: 'Where did you go to, little Eva?'

A tremor all through the body, and for a moment Eva thinks Mama Zana is sobbing. In fact she is failing to sit up. In the end she compromises, kissing her fingers and waving them wildly towards Eva's head. Eva ducks into what ends up half-stroke half-slap, and accepts the blessing. Mama Zana mumbles something more; subsides into her doze. Eva scrambles back out of the wagon.

The dark woman gives her a piece of apple.

Eva wonders about doing a set of exercises – showing her commitment to the dark woman, if no one else. But Giesberts is waiting; and anyway, she can more easily do exercises at home.

☉

In the café on the corner, where the maze of alleys that make up Marrakech market empties onto the great square, the corner where the sun burns longest, morning is at its busiest and hottest. The square is what Africa offers up to the universe: our ripest produce, our craft, our diversity, our energy, a kaleidoscope of life visible from the infinite, bustling at noon, burning at midnight, take a look, have a rummage. Here we are. This is us.

After the first bustle of morning and as the heat begins to thicken, the rhythms of the royal palace slow. It is his habit, in this lull, to walk out into the city and to drink a tea with his acquaintances. All the cafés are edgier now: guard over the cashbox, glass hidden away, and conversations between the oldest friends become wary exchanges of formality and banality, because each morning we must re-establish memory and loyalty.

Not to be indiscreet, but have you heard?

We are wary of declaring what we might have heard. Showing interest enough to hear something: it does not do.

What might we have heard?

In the palace, there has been – we do not imply anything uncontrolled, let alone anything negative – in the palace there has been... energy. His Majesty the Sultan and his brother our esteemed Caliph, not to mention – best never to mention – the shrewd and ever-present Glaoui, the Lord grant that I find a way to show my fullest and fittest faithfulness to them all: they had... a conversation. A conversation with a lot of energy. A conversation about the riot. A conversation that demonstrated just how much they each care about the good of the people and the word of the Lord. We may safely agree that their conversation, the more energetic the better, is good and wise. By definition it is, yes; goes without saying.

Best say it anyway.

The product of the energy – and we do not call it a decision, because that might imply superiority or responsibility, so let's just say that fate and fact and the will of the Lord as of the present moment – is this: the old man has been arrested.

What old man?

Any old man.

Presumably. If in doubt, arrest anyone. Because the heart of any matter is better avoided at the moment, we spend more time than we might digressing over whether an old man decomposing in the cells somewhere below us is more of a loss, because of all his accumulated wisdom, or less of a loss because he probably wouldn't last long anyway.

The preacher man. We talked about him. Someone talked about him.

We seem to remember someone saying that His Majesty the Sultan was more sympathetic to the old man; but from such a perspective, His Majesty would feel obliged to act decisively against the old man so as not to show weakness before his brother, our esteemed Caliph.

We seem to remember someone saying that our esteemed Caliph benefits from any discomfort to his brother, His Majesty the Sultan; and the Caliph has a wise sensitivity to the mood of the people – their protests and their passions.

I'd never say so myself, but some people seem to think that riot was hardly the worst.

I'd never say so myself, but some people seem to think the old man had nothing whatever to do with the riot.

We each of us wait. We sip our tea. We have a face of absolute openness and neutrality. How fine it is, the sweet tang of fresh mint.

Very well: perhaps we had heard something of this. But that's no crime, is it? Can't help hearing things. What matters is what we think about them; how we react.

None of us is reacting, I trust. None of us is thinking. The Most Merciful, The Source Of Good, grant that we see each other tomorrow.

Or perhaps this particular conversation takes place among the booksellers at the Koutoubia, the flapping of tongues concealed among the whispering pages.

☪

JOURNAL OF THOMAS SOMERLEIGH

Bit of fever in the air. Formal summons to audience with H.M. the Sultan. Had to kick Youssef into polishing my shoes, and only succeeded by pretending it was for a meeting with les Français. Youssef in a surly mood – grumpy or uneasy about something, and with these fellows you can never tell whether it's the death of a parent or a change in humidity. At the palace, H.M. slumped in his throne with the most peculiar expression on his stamp. Almost as grumpy as Youssef, anxiously watchful as we all sat watching him. His brother the Caliph was in attendance too: smaller throne, better posture – not enthusiastic about the foreigners, but respectful.

I wondered what H.M. was going to say, and the answer turned out to be: nothing. One of his officials stood up and did the talking, reading out an English version of a decree. Following the disgraceful breach of the Sultan's peace and the good order of the city, the shameful offence against all the traditions of Moroccan hospitality, the administration had taken severe and decisive action. The principle trouble-maker, a man of notoriously seditious views and divergent religious tendencies, had immediately been arrested and would soon be made an example of; those of his misguided followers who attempted to thwart the administration's just action had been slaughtered. By this prudent and decisive intervention, peace had been restored, and all citizens should see how much their Sultan cared for their security and for good worship.

'Funny business ain't it?' said McKenna. 'Big Chief sitting there, you think he'd welcome the chance to announce the good news himself.' I said that perhaps H.M. feels he's been chivvied by the foreigners into making the arrest, so wants to show himself indifferent. Bit daft, of course, because he gets less of the credit for finally doing something useful. 'Guess we aren't the audience, are we?' says McKenna; 'the audience is the fellow sitting next to him.'

According to the usual protocol for this level of occasion we foreign dips wouldn't speak. But when the official had finished and it became clear that H.M. wasn't going to say anything himself, Prudhomme stood up. I saw the Sultan glancing anxiously at the official and then even at his brother, but they didn't have any protocol for stopping Prudhomme either. He had none of yesterday's anger, and was much more restrained, but still pretty cold. France of course grateful for His Majesty's invitation to share in his counsels, and as always impressed by H.M.'s firm-handed partnership in maintaining public order, for the benefit of the public as well as distinguished foreigners. The French programme of government public activities, agreed with His Majesty's officials, with the circus at its heart and the carefully-designed follow-up actions, must continue immediately.

Then, unavoidably, Klug. Even the Caliph frowned, wondering if he was going to have to listen to all of us. German respects and compliments to His Majesty, a welcome sign of Morocco's autonomous management of its own affairs, in partnership with international friends. Grateful for such a rapid response to the matter first raised by Germany. In these more challenging circumstances, essential that unusual government activities such as the circus are only implemented with the greatest caution and in full co-ordination with all interested parties.

H.M. stood and bowed, so the Caliph had to stand and bow, so we all of us had to stand and bow, and that was it; bad light stopped play.

I got the full story – or at least an alternative story – in more dramatic fashion. I was walking near the square when I heard running feet and felt someone grabbing at my arm. I was pulling away and covering my wallet when I saw it was Brahim, my poet chum, hellish worked up. 'You see? You see?' he was yelling; 'You see what happens?' I said that if it was getting molested in public I didn't want it, and if he wanted to talk we could do so in civilized fashion. He said something very offensive about tea, and was absolutely gripping my lapel and more or less foaming at the mouth, and I only calmed him down by being very clear that I would of course listen, but only if he was capable of comporting himself in a civilized manner. I frankly felt a little safer once I had a stout table between us.

'Professor Sa'id is arrested!' he hissed furious. I wasn't sure what he was talking about. Fortunately I caught the waiter's eye. The ordering of tea usefully calmed things down. Brahim looked fit to burst. 'Holy Sa'id is arrested!'

At last I caught the name: the extraordinary old wizard with whom I'd lunched – and heard speaking by the mosque, when I'd been out with Hortense.

I said I was sorry to hear it – and immediately wondered if that was going too far, politics-wise. 'That dear old chap,' I added. 'It seems rather unlikely...'

'How can you say this? It is what you want!'

'I beg your pardon?'

'Everyone knows that the Sultan is too stupid to perceive any threat from dear Sa'id, and too mild to do anything about it. He has only done this because you foreigners have ordered him to. Because otherwise the foreigners will switch their support to the Caliph and his hard-line advisors.'

I said something general about how much he over-estimated foreign power, and then camped on the safe ground of reminding him that while we respected and supported the divinely-ordained rule of His Majesty the Sultan, we wouldn't of course intervene in domestic differences. I'm not sure he understood: he looked at me as though I were deranged. 'You will see the chaos this leads to!' he said.

'Steady on,' I cautioned. 'Anyway – and I really don't know the details – I got the impression this was a reaction to the rioting; it should calm things down.'

'You know nothing of this rioting! You do not know if two men argued over a fig, or if the whole Mellah burned. You do not care if one Moroccan was insulted or a thousand were slaughtered. Well? Do you know anything about it?'

I was about to say that I knew all too well what had happened to poor old Madame whatsername, who'd been insulted or assaulted or whatever. But I didn't want to imply that we're not equally concerned about Moroccan lives. There's a difference, obviously. But: all human life. Fortunately he didn't give me time. 'I tell you one truth, anyway: venerable Sa'id had nothing to do with it.'

'Well, you say that...'

'I do say that. Do you say the contrary?'

'I don't. I only mean it's hard to know what causes what, you see? Times like these: restless, you know?'

'The times are restless because you foreigners say they are so. The times are restless because you make them so.'

I wanted to placate the poor fellow. 'I really think there's an exaggerated idea that the foreigners just click their fingers and His Majesty jumps.' I had to hurry on over his unhelpful scorn. 'What is true is that we pay close attention to your country's security. We really only want what's best for Morocco, and we're trying to get some systems and structures in place. Get you in good shape for the long term. Now, of course there'll be some bumps along the way…'

'What is the average price of a bump, in Moroccan blood?' This was the sort of mood he was in. 'Ten dead starving protesters? The torture of one good old man?' But such conversations are the everyday detail of diplomatic life. One learns to overlook the emotional stuff.

'Right now, the proper focus of the government is incorporating the circus with the broader package of administrative and security measures. A positive event to demonstrate His Majesty's authority and judgement. A healthy, mutually-supporting partnership with the international community. This is the high road to stability and prosperity. Now, naturally, there will be the odd…'

'Bump?'

'Complication, I was…'

'How many dead Moroccans to the complication, these days?'

'The devil is always in the detail, after all…'

'No, the devil is in the dungeon somewhere beneath us, pulling out my friend's eyes.'

'But we shouldn't let these things be a distraction…'

'No, certainly the people of Marrakech would not wish to be a distraction.'

I include this kind of exchange as a reminder of the realities. I'll remember it was never exactly a gallivant, even if Sir G. never sees it.

'Listen, my friend: of course I'm sorry about dear old Sa'id. I think he's a decent and well-meaning and rather special fellow. I dearly hope he gets out soon. I sincerely want the best, and I sincerely believe in our partnership – our friendship.'

'By the Lord...' he said, slumping back. I'd got him calm at last. 'I believe you truly do.'

Which is about as good an outcome as one can hope for, from this sort of conversation; but it rarely feels particularly satisfying.

Curious, the business of Youssef's attitude, and its effect on me. Or my effect on it. I'm drifting rather. Failing to click. If my servant is lifting my cuff-links and whatever other shiny thing takes his fancy, he must be pretty contemptuous of me: it suggests something pretty bloody average about the figure I'm cutting here.

I simply want to fit. Make my way. Be the sort of fellow who can impress a girl like Hortense, and her father. Even Klug, rampaging like a bull in a china shop with a gunboat patrolling outside, manages to have an impact. Britain needs to have her proper grip here. And that means that Somerleigh needs to make a bit more of a splash.

☖

'My maid thinks there will be unrest', Eva says. It's a rare pleasure to be able to discuss politics. She feels at ease, competent; manly. 'The palace has arrested someone – an old trouble-maker, she says. He had made himself very popular with his preaching, and now there will be terrible riots in protest at his arrest.'

'I believe it', Luther says.

'You believe her story?'

'I believe that a maid, she would tell this story.'

'You don't think there will be unrest?'

'I am certain there will be unrest. Shall the sun rise tomorrow? Shall I kick my servant for his incompetence with the breakfast? Shall there be unrest? Yes and yes and yes.' Not for the first time, she is trying to find his worldliness charming, or at least impressive. 'There will be unrest, and there was unrest. Probably some rioting prompted the Sultan to arrest this person, but your old man did not cause the rioting that happened and nor will he cause the rioting that shall happen. Chaos, it is by definition not a political choice. It is the product of a mentality which has never recognized the operation of cause and effect. Your maid, only she tells such a story to give meaning to a world she cannot control and cannot understand.'

This business of trying to be wooed is proving tiresome. An honest fuck, a moment of uncompromising abandon, is surely not an unreasonable expectation, and usually – she flatters herself – isn't too hard to come by. But she is experimenting with allowing Luther at least semi-formally to annex her, to develop some kind of structured trading arrangement, and so the most basic and essential element of the relationship has taken on a much greater significance and sanctity, whose protocols she is unfamiliar with. Along with the mysteries of the piping and the German machine that runs the cold store, this intimacy will only be made accessible to her at some carefully-calculated yet obscure stage of the proceedings.

There has been heat, there has been intent, there has been swelling and gasping; there may even have been release, though Luther was quick to start talking about the difficulty of finding a decent café and how much he dislikes her wandering the streets alone. The discussion of trans-Mediterranean customs arrangements is a pleasant sign of the respectful seriousness with which he treats her, but what would also be pleasant is the feel of those firm-muscled shoulders naked and wrapped around her, that strong fine jaw between her thighs.

There is, however, no way of knowing the business model Luther is working on for this transaction; the kind of contractural arrangement he will insist on. Eva has begun to fear that her genitals have some distinctive legal status under the protegay system.

'My maid said they will torture the old man. She was... most descriptive.'

A small composed smile from Luther. It means she is about to hear his brain rather than his heart. 'I believe both that she believes it and that such a thing may happen', he says, fingers picking out the precision. 'The elaboration of torture, it is no different to the elaboration of bureaucratic protocol or of tile decoration: an attempt to demonstrate power and creativity in an existence that allows you neither. The wriggling and wailing of a beast in a cage.' This strain of philosophical reflection, this is admirable and attractive, isn't it? She could enjoy the company of such a mind, couldn't she? 'And the popular imagination about torture, it is the same phenomenon. Imagination to fill the void of ignorance. A primitive awe, as at the rising of the sun. A tale that is told to impress or inspire or entertain. The devil finds work for idle hands, but also the devil he finds ideas for idle minds.'

In Eva's conception of this relationship, Luther Giesberts is cosily dull but reliably, even inspirationally, decent. His casual reference to kicking his servant – even though it is no less a piece of story-telling than Assia's imagination of torture – and the casual way he discusses this torture... it is irritatingly at odds with the mundane and practical fairy-tale she has outlined for herself.

'Have you ever met the Sultan, Luther?'

Shrug. 'Some receptions. I do not pretend any acquaintance.'

258

'I hear he has this... mad collection: ridiculous things he buys and will never use – wigs and fireworks and ladies' underclothes.'

Again the little smile of impending wit, and Eva braces herself. 'Of course you hear these stories. And we ask ourselves: how different are these Europeans telling fantastical stories of extravagance and magic, from the Moroccans with their dreams of Paris and London, or your maid with her tortures? This Sultan, he is determined that Morocco shall fit into the European system. Perhaps he is a feeble fellow, and perhaps this is a futile dream. But he knows he must behave in a certain way. Whenever he hears of some new European product, he must make a big show of contracting for it; and thus, his followers see what is trade, and more of them will buy from Europe, and so the commercial relationship is reciprocal and more healthy.'

Eva nods.

It shows that she thinks him wise, and that she may be thought wise. It is a nice, cosy, companionable sort of gesture.

༄

In the café on the corner, where the maze of alleys that make up Marrakech market empties onto the great square, the corner where the stink of new leather prompts visions of lavender and mortality, morning is at its busiest and hottest. The square is a foreign version of our land: foreigners come here and tread intrepid-trepidatious around the snake-mats and beggars; foreigners are catered to here; foreigners see us through the blur of this place.

After the first bustle of morning and as the heat begins to thicken, the rhythms of the royal palace slow. It is his habit, in this lull, to walk out into the city and to drink a tea with his acquaintances. We have watched dear Abdelilah with amusement and with respect these last weeks: his growing self-importance; his growing anxiety. We have remarked with exaggerated awe his little experiments in European clothing, and he has rightly inferred that we are mocking him. Also rightly, he has understood that we are impressed: he is not straying, but running ahead of us.

Not to be indiscreet, but what am I to make of all this?

Respectful silence. The trickle of tea. The burst of sweet fresh mint in the air above our table.

I mean: a man only wants to fit in, to conform, to deliver what is expected, perhaps get a little credit, no more than his due. But I simply cannot follow what is expected any more.

Abdelilah's face creases in some greater discomfort. An embarrassed and conspiratorial glance at us, and he ducks down and unlaces his European leather shoes. We have all admired these ridiculous and marvellously elegant items; we have all admired the worthiness of his suffering them. He lets out a great sigh. He breathes in deep, and the vivid scent of the mint obscures his swollen over-baked feet and if this is all the mercy we are afforded on earth it is enough.

His Majesty, the Lord grant that I live long only to do him more service, has summoned the circus to join his household. Let there be no doubt about his wisdom or inspiration in doing this, nor that it is the will of the Lord.

We murmur our agreement. The will of the Lord is just and infallible. Also, the foreigners know what they're doing.

His Majesty, the Lord protect him according to his worth, is no doubt fully cognisant of the benefit of prudent and efficacious application of the administrative instruments and performative capacity of his retinue. Properly supervised exploitation of the circus, in conformity with the highest aesthetic standards of Europe and the religious and cultural habits and superstitions of the indigenous people, is a most shrewd exercise of the royal prerogative for the good of Morocco, and should have a most beneficent effect on the security climate.

We murmur our agreement. The priest and the palace and the beggar-boy who does the three-cup-trick at supper, they all have this sort of patter; however much we don't understand, it's best just to go along with it.

But my goodness. The Frenchman naturally is a kind of high priest of protocol and diplomacy: he sees into me deeper than any judge, and before him I tremble as I think of the doubt in my heart and the spots in my linen and the error in my punctuation of the draft regulation on giraffe hygiene. The German naturally is a kind of warrior of colonial administration: at any moment his sword might carve me a path to Mecca, or disembowel me for my obstruction of security sector reform. The Englishman? It's hard to say. I'm sure the English approve and everything is managed according to their satisfaction. Such a pleasant man.

At first it seemed to me – and I crave the pardons of all of our foreign advisors if my understanding of their extraordinary wisdom leads me astray – that there was great enthusiasm for His Majesty's adoption of the circus. And then it seemed there was great doubt. There was a strong desire that the circus should be as Moroccan as possible, and there was a strong desire that the circus should be as foreign as possible. Our task on the committee was to slow Germany's intemperate haste to have the circus operational. Then our task was to speed France's enthusiastic energy to have the circus operational. Yesterday Germany changed her mind and offered encouragement and money for the to circus perform in Fes and Tangier, insisting that this should happen as quickly as possible. Today France changed her mind and offered encouragement and money to refurbish a courtyard in the palace for the circus to perform, insisting that this should happen as cautiously as possible.

A Roumi – a Frenchman – with a very peculiar moustache has arrived out of the desert to help us, and promises to teach me about Moroccan architecture and dance.

I wish only to assist my beloved country to play its proper part in their system; but what is the Morocco that they desire? I wish only to conform to their expectations; but who am I to be?

Or perhaps this particular conversation takes place in an empty meeting room of the palace, an anxious figure trying not to be seen and hurrying to tidy the papers of those who have left and murmuring to himself.

☫

JOURNAL OF THOMAS SOMERLEIGH

An increasing need for Britain's moderating and, as needs be, guiding hand. Which means Somerleigh ready to play his proper part.

Klug is still desperate to exercise some control over the circus: he got it here, he's got control of the purse strings, at least in part, at least in theory. He tried driving the thing, then he tried obstructing it, and then he tried a compromise that gave France what it wanted here in Marrakech while formalizing German influence over a performance in the north, and now he's left trying to obstruct again.

Prudhomme is France and France is Morocco, and Prudhomme knows that if he can just judge the business right then the circus will be his triumph, and French dominance here will be reinforced. So he has to keep Klug out of it as much as possible so he doesn't break everything, and he has to work to make sure that the circus is as good as it can be, and he has to delay until the moment is just right to bring the thing off successfully.

In the end, it rather comes down to this: who is in step with the Sultan's level of enthusiasm? Who can jolly the Sultan into a different level of enthusiasm? Who can read the opaque and convoluted palace politics to predict what level of enthusiasm the Sultan will be allowed?

And down in a dungeon somewhere, there's an old man whose life depends on that enthusiasm, or whose death might be a handy compromise for it.

Café with the Prudhommes, all very pleasant. Hector P. very much asking my advice, now that things are bumpy. Really, he gets quite emotional about the circus: such a strong vision for how it's going to look and the effect it's going to have. Started to talk about curtains and the sacred proportions of temples and Greek theatres. Gets red each time he talks about the circus for more than a moment, and the pince-nez gleam with the energy coming out of him. Might do old Klug good to see: he'd understand Hector is not to be thwarted.

A snatched farewell with Hortense in the vestibule: my hands on her shoulders, and then her sides, and the strongest sense of the slender little body between them; and then my lips on hers!

☾

Luther is repairing something in the mechanism that regulates the cold store: coat off, cuffs rolled evenly and precisely to the elbow, hand plunged deep in metal and grease. There is something rather gynaecological in the arrangement, and something saintly in his expression of delicate attention; nothing of manly pose or performance. He is absorbed in something he cares about. Eva loves both his willingness to be absorbed, and his capacity for care.

This is the moment – his fine head poised, the sinews in his forearm pulsing, and above all his willingness to be this particular Giesberts in her presence – when she understands that she is seriously contemplating giving her life over to a man, to this man, and the thought stuns her like a punch in the stomach, a particularly wretched monthly wrenching in her womb.

'Thank you', he says at last, wiping his hands. 'Excuse me for the delay. Still we are interested to visit the new theatre, yes, where the circus will perform?'

He means: where you will perform. But he's hoping he doesn't mean that. That world is distant now, unreal even to Eva. He in linen suit and panama, she in light frock and floppy-brimmed sun-hat, they will visit like any other curious foreign tourists.

The courtyard has been re-discovered on the edge of the palace complex: a space left behind, by previous generations of improvements; a space forgotten, between more charming and more grand and more useful alternatives. None of the pale haze of marble that softens the other spaces they have seen in the palace and the city's ceremonial buildings. None of the electric bright designs of tiles. The high bare walls and the walkway around the edge of the courtyard are the same sandy stone that has always hidden behind the palace surfaces. Eva remembers the earth city from the trek to Marrakech, rising out of the desert and then collapsing back into it.

Now the rough crumbling walls are busy with scaffolding and shouts: a ramshackle wooden lattice, everywhere men clambering up it and tightroping along it. This circus already has its acrobats, and Eva feels familiarity, and jealousy. Close to, just a few feet above her, a man is balanced on a scaffold-beam – she feels the perpetual trembling in his leg-muscles – to repair the facade. She watches the swoop and flick of his arm as he collects a trowelful of fresh render and flings it deftly along the wall, swoop and flick, swoop and flick and always the right amount and none of it falls.

Carpenters, and masons. Hammering and sawing and chipping. Curses and cries and chants. In one corner, apparently more finished, an enormous plunge of green cloth is hanging the full height of the wall; another is being gathered up to run along the wall.

A few steps away from them, a foreigner is lecturing a huddle of visitors in elaborate French. His costume is a wild confection of Champs-Élysées finery and Arabian fairy-tale. He is sounding equally authoritative on the nature of imagery in Islam, habits of political architecture in the princedoms of the Maghreb, and the proper balance of colour and sound and light – 'the right effect, you will observe, is the one that is not noticed' – to operate tastefully on the senses of a representative of the civilized races.

This wild wizard of culture certainly seems more believable than the figure standing precisely in the middle of the courtyard and gazing at the works: a full suit of traditional diplomatic correctness, of the kind Eva has only seen in plays and portraits. But he must be roasting in the long black coat, and the hard polished shoes should be agony...

The figure turns, and says 'Professeur!' just loud enough to carry, and immediately the sumptuously-dressed connoisseur interrupts his performance and the two men move together for some consultation. Eva has recognized the diplomat now: the aloof Frenchman of the drinks reception; the father of little Hortense. The two men murmur to each other, then each returns to his former place. '... A fusion of styles, as I was saying, and yet in truth every ritual and fashion that we term "modern" is but the echo of some ancient habit, still running in our blood.'

The diplomat is stiff again. Isn't he burning under the sun, Eva wonders, as well as cooking? His determination to stand there, fixed and precisely central, has something saintly about it: the early ascetics who roamed the deserts or sat on top of pillars for years, in order to find something or prove something.

Her eyes stray. And then something stirs in her, queasy like guilt: she finds herself considering the courtyard as a performance space, just as she has considered a thousand new stages. Entrances. Distances. Eye-lines. Room to move. Ground surface. Air flow. Every slightest bump or dip or protrusion that might betray a dancer's foot.

The courtyard is a ridiculous space for a performance. The courtyard is a magnificent space for a performance.

Eva finds herself anxious about the propriety of dancing here. Immediately she is shocked by her anxiety. She becomes anxious about the practicality of dancing here, and that feels better.

But perhaps, after all, this performance will not really happen.

Eva and Luther are in good spirits when they begin to walk back through the city. From somewhere – perhaps it is part of the French vision for the performance area – a breeze is softening the heat. Luther is a boy stepping out with a pretty girl, and his technical mind and his cultural mind have been tuned and exercised today; he is competence, and confidence. Eva has had uncertainties, but she has turned them into choices: there are things she could do, and there are things that for once in her life she could choose not to do. This breeze; this back-street; this body beside me: it all offers freedom. The moment feels like a piece of fruit in its instant of absolute rightness, full and unblemished and healthy-sweet and with barely a touch it falls into your hand.

A boy is selling plums, and he is engaging rather than irritating, and Luther banters with him in Arabic and does not wait for change, and Eva is understanding the strange words now and seeing the beauty in the boy's dark eyes and young legs, and then they are walking away together. Eva pulls at Luther's shoulder, and feeds him a bite of plum. She sees his eyes widen as his appetite tries to encompass her energy, and then the plum bursts in his teeth and its wreckage is running down his chin and she is sucking at his lip and tasting the juice, feeling the sweet heat of his breath, his swelling, his hand on her rump. And then they turn away towards home, hand-in-hand, laughing, carnivorousness unfulfilled by fruit.

'Not wishing to be presumptuous...' he begins as they walk. Eva thinks: I adore this courtliness. Eva thinks: wouldn't do you any harm to try. 'But I could imagine a future where I did not have to make up excursions to occupy our time. This would be most pleasant, I think: our togetherness not something unusual we go out to seek, but something habitual I always return to. Something fundamental, and certain.'

These are fine-sounding words, and Eva tries to savour them like the vestige of plum-juice, ignoring the bit of skin stuck in her teeth.

'Each time I see you in my home, it seems more natural to me. My world, it could be yours. It has, I think, everything you could need. You would not have to wander any more.' His voice drops in an aside – the magician's distraction, the trader's final discount – 'There are reports of increasing outrages against foreigners, following the arrest of the old preacher man.' His voice fills again, more formal. 'You would live cool, and safe, and satisfied.'

A cat slipping into a courtyard; a maid making her place at the foot of the bed. Eva is not feeling resistance, but confusion.

Luther leans closer; she can sense his roguish smile. 'I think you would find some benefit, being more clearly under my flag, no?'

I had convinced myself that this was about independence.

Then the gate clangs shut behind them, and they are safely in his courtyard: its coolness, its quiet. The light, the scents, the noise of the street – everything is fainter now.

Eva wonders what new step the conversation will take. Then she wonders where the conversation might have got to had their journey through the streets taken another minute.

A sudden image from earlier: Luther's face as he worked at the cold store machinery. Just for an instant – some resistance to his mighty forearm, some frustration to his logic – his expression had twisted into something animal; something ferocious. Like Ras and Negus when they had scented massacre-flesh. A naturalness of expression greater even than any she has seen during their discreet flurries of passion.

And suppressed even more quickly, as he remembered where he was; the purity of this place. Just for a moment, she had wondered what he kept shut away, when he was within these walls.

Once again, Luther is the high priest in his sanctuary. His energy is eased, his animal bulk is lighter, his glance calmer. His finger-tips lead her finger-tips indoors – priestess, or sacrifice.

☾

In the café on the corner, where the maze of alleys that make up Marrakech market empties onto the great square, the corner where sometimes the wandering preachers stop, sometimes the beggars pray, morning is at its busiest and hottest. The square gives the lie to all your ignorance about our faith. You think us extreme, over-exacting, and you are suspicious that we bring too much sacred into our daily lives and politics. Your wordy philosophers, your lamb-like prophets, your half-human heralds of other worlds, your painted masquerades and your earnest conventions and your pantheons of clumsy archetypes, nothing in all your millennia has been as ferociously human as this square. You did not escape from Africa; you strayed.

After the first bustle of morning and as the heat begins to thicken, the rhythms of the royal palace slow. It is his habit, in this lull, to walk out into the city and to drink a tea with his acquaintances. Thus we re-confirm who we are, for the new day.

Not to be indiscreet, but I have just heard the most extraordinary man, preaching in a dead end in the market. He is... I don't think I have ever heard the like. He is from some far land, and he speaks only fragments of our language. The rest is French, and Turkish, and Latin, and I don't know what. But often he does not speak in words at all: instead he uses the expressions of his face, and his hands, and you know what he's saying. Even when he is speaking he must often pause, and wait in silence for inspiration. But in his silence you yourself feel his path forwards, and sometimes his listeners will offer suggestions for words or ideas, and he will take them, and so the path turns. His name is Jan, or perhaps Yan – named for the pagan God of beginnings, they say. He offers no certain end, but he opens a path to possibility.

Yeah, we've heard of him before, haven't we?

It's Jan, not Yan. Our Arabic word for guilty. He emphasizes that he's guilty – we're all guilty. Only by accepting this, do we have the true humility to purify ourselves and come closer to God; make ourselves more presentable. I know what they say about that sort of line, but these days it makes sense, doesn't it?

I guess I heard the same one. It's Ja'an, by the way. Hungry – because we all are now, aren't we? And neat little metaphor for spiritual hunger as well. The fat men in the palace hanging around His Majesty, they've got too greedy for bread to think of spiritual nourishment. And the rest of us, we're also obsessed with bread, but t'other way round; our bellies are so empty we forget spiritual nourishment. As men it is our nature to be hungry, and it is our nature to seek sustenance.

He's getting popular, isn't he? But it's Jinn, of course. The wandering spirit. The seer. We think we're so smart, in our big city, and everything outside is desert and peasants. But we see nothing; we know nothing. The jinn who presents himself to our eyes, he is only a herald of all that is unseen. Everyone who has disappeared into the earth. The lies and tricks that weave themselves around us. The truths that we continue to ignore.

Actually, I heard Yan; well, A'yin – but it gets garbled, doesn't it? A'yin, the eye. Very similar idea. When I think about it, I'm blind now. All of the things that shape my life – all the emotions, all the restrictions, all the blessings – I don't see them. He encourages us to see through him.

Oh, he's marvellous; yes indeed. Ain, surely. The spring; the source. The truth has been garbled, like you say, and we must go back to the source. He offers us the Lord's original refreshing truth. Cleansing – purifying, yes?

And surely it's time for something new. Not just the endless brawling in the alleys, but the anger, you know? Everywhere is seething; every conversation becomes a disagreement, and every disagreement becomes a stabbing. And the girls are still disappearing – that wouldn't be happening if things were settled. The foreigners are squabbling, and they've lost a little of their mystique, and they're starting to get their throats cut if they stay out too late. The palace is divided, and corrupt.

Well, yes. Except no – not something new. Something original, and pure. It's the foreigners who've divided and corrupted the palace.

Well, yes. Except no – we can't blame the message, because that's like questioning the word of the Lord. What needs to change is our attitude to the message. We must accept our guilt, and be humble.

Well, yes. Except no – the Lord doesn't want us to be slaves. We must see more clearly. We must seek. We must fight.

And so we go round.

Or perhaps this particular conversation takes place among the djellaba-sellers, all the future selves modelled on hangers or lying in piles waiting.

JOURNAL OF THOMAS SOMERLEIGH

Hell. Wretched, wretched day. Utter bish by Somerleigh.

Unspeakable, but I deserve to have to speak it. Repeat what you said, boy, in front of the whole class.

Lessons in diplomacy, number one. Write it out a hundred times, Somerleigh. Diplomacy is not what you think it is. Diplomacy is not saying what others want, it's saying what you must. Diplomacy is not reciting pleasantries; it is reciting necessary unpleasantries, in as pleasant a way as possible. Diplomacy never made anyone happy; but it strives to limit the violence of the unhappiness.

Palace in a proper fever this morning. Everyone on edge. H.M. and his brother coming into the receiving chamber like a pair of duellists: forever watching each other, keeping their distance; the correct bow between them, but never losing sight; each eyeing the throne as if the other were about to make a grab for it.

Prudhomme frantic about some snag with the performance space for the circus. (McKenna explained in the margins: much dudgeon between the French expert and the local suppliers over the decor, and some scaffolding collapsed and a couple of chaps were badly hurt and so the workers all downed tools.) Obviously he doesn't say, but you could see the intensity in his complexion, his eyes, as if the ancient suit were squeezing him tighter than ever.

Klug played it sneakily: clever, but really rather offensive. His speech was in the form of one long apology, to His Majesty. Germany had brought the circus to Marrakech, no expense spared, as a pleasure for H.M. and as yet another reinforcement of his administration. Germany had insisted the circus become part of H.M.'s retinue, not merely as a gift but on a principle of Moroccan autonomy. Alas, Germany had also allowed the importation of some European bureaucracy, and now the circus had been totally captured by its own administrative processes. Berlin was becoming most anxious about the unnecessary expenditure being diverted into some curious fantasy of questionable cultural modernization and unregulated property speculation, and all honest diplomats were embarrassed by the mismanagement of the whole affair. 'Germany expresses her humble regret to Your Majesty, and her commitment to push for a performance under proper administrative arrangements that properly reflects Your Majesty's authority and desires.'

Hector Prudhomme is about as professional a diplomat as I've ever met. The archetype of correctness and restraint. The man you'd trust with the trickiest negotiation, the man you'd rely on never to be distracted by anything, however offensive or underhand. Now I thought he was going to burst. He didn't, but by the hardest. His face filled with blood, and the seams of the suit were straining at every stitch. 'Your Majesty!' For the very first time, in that thin cold voice, I heard emotion. 'Allow me to reassure you that your circus continues to be managed according to the highest standards of security, and to the very best standards of European taste.' That single word from Klug – mismanagement – had stung the Frenchman viciously. 'The première shall be something splendid: an event unprecedented in the history of Morocco!' At the side of the chamber I saw little Abdelilah, looking distraught at the controversy and nodding energetically at the endorsement of his management. 'Your triumph, Your Majesty! We shall advance even more effectively as soon as all of the European powers are properly collaborating in the committee. Alas some... newer states' – he could not restrain the sneer – 'are not so used to the practices of diplomacy.'

Naturally I was horrified by the display of emotion, and anxious to see what H.M. was thinking of it all. The poor chap seemed quite bewildered, as well he might. With a jolt, I realized that we might be getting close to an opportunity for Britain to calm things down a bit. The guiding hand, the feather in the scale, just like we were always being told in London and Tangier.

Prudhomme's stab had hit home, meanwhile. Germans hate to be reminded that their state is a relative new-boy on the European map. 'Germany, Your Majesty, remains most committed to the practices of diplomacy,' thundered Klug, and then got himself under control; '...and also to the practices of sound financial management.' Prudhomme's eyes bulged behind the pince-nez. 'Germany shall be delighted to approve the funding for this activity by your retinue, Majesty, as soon as there is an agreed programme of performances acceptable to all of the European powers.'

'The première shall naturally occur, Your Majesty, as soon as arrangements are complete for an occasion appropriate to Your Majesty's authority. France shall be the guarantor, Sir, of the prudence of the occasion and of the good taste!'

The poor Sultan. He looked smaller and sadder than ever, hunched and lonely up there on his throne. I remembered his first enthusiasm about the circus, weeks ago now: the childish delight at the possibility it might be brought to Marrakech to perform for him. Near him, his brother the Caliph was watching it all: impassive as ever, and calculating, and I started to wonder if there might be some implications for Moroccan stability from this business.

'Germany shall continue to insist on respect for Morocco's independence of action in managing such affairs, and ensure proper control of the related finances.'

'France shall continue to act as the guardian of Morocco's independence of action!'

'Why not' I said, 'have a special performance for His Majesty immediately?'

I saw the Sultan's reaction in that instant, a sudden brightening, and for that instant I really thought I'd triumphed.

Everyone was staring at me. 'Not exactly a rehearsal', I went on. 'Not appropriate for His Majesty, and I guess these circus people know what they're doing. Just a chance for His Majesty to see the thing, and perhaps the experience will help iron out some of the administration issues. Meanwhile we'll all continue to work towards a proper première according to the French vision, and look for an agreement on performances and management acceptable to the German principles.'

And the whole damn world stopped turning and froze and shrivelled up and dropped off the tree.

Hector Prudhomme's face was ghastly: I'd challenged his authority, and interfered with his vision.

Klug was stone again: he assumed I was just trying to get round German influence on the finances, and he'd never expect progress on the German proposal for the future performances.

I couldn't look at them. Instead I turned back to the Sultan, hoping for some indication that I'd got a bit of credit with him, because in the end that might be enough.

But the Sultan looked sadder than ever. His hopes of a performance were dropping as fast as they'd risen. And now his sadness seemed to be on my behalf.

He gazed at me a moment longer, and then – sweetest of mercies – he stood, bowed to everyone, and wandered out. No protracted torture: a quick death. The meeting was officially over.

I was standing alone. Across the chamber, backs were turning and drifting out together.

McKenna said: 'That was... bold.'

I was still replaying the conversation, as it might affect France and Germany. And therefore what they would think of this British statement; what they would report.

I looked at McKenna. His expression was sympathetic; almost... consoling.

'I just...' I didn't know what I was saying any more. 'I just thought he'd enjoy seeing the giraffe.'

✿

Eva often thinks of a particular tale told by Ali the story-teller. She thinks of the boy himself, squatting on his mat on the cobbles. She wonders at the mat: its age, its significance in his family. She wonders at those knees and hips, the suppleness to sit cross-legged for so long, and whether the fifty-year old Ali will be spry or crippled. She wonders at how his back and shoulders sway and roll to emphasize emotion, to pull his audience into his world. A tale well-told is a dance; and vice-versa.

There was once a certain king, and he ruled a certain city a certain way across the desert from Marrakech – the directions are not exactly secret, gentlemen, but a certain extra consideration will be necessary if you wish to learn them – and he had had seven wives and each wife had borne him a son. These seven princes were all, naturally, fine young men. Each had the virtues and values of their royal father, and the distinctive beauty and spirit of their particular mother.

The eldest, says Ali, and the patter is gentle at this stage, easing the audience into his world, knew that one day he would succeed his father as king, and all seven princes were raised and educated and trained to their exalted station. But while their father lived they had a fair bit of time on their hands and it was their habit to ride out into the desert together to explore their realm. Everywhere they went, they went together; their every adventure was shared.

One of their journeys brought them to the eastern mountains, and to a track into the mountains that no one had seemed to notice before. They followed this track as it wound between the peaks, and at last it opened out into a valley. They could tell that this valley had once been verdant, but now it was dust and rock only. Ahead of them they saw some edifice rising out of the valley floor. From a distance it seemed to be rock, but as they came closer it became a mighty building – the kind of stone fortress that you will see to this day in the mountains, gentlemen – and as they came closer still they saw that had once been a very fine palace indeed, but was now fallen to decay. The stonework was worn and crumbling, its adornments of marble and precious metal long vanished.

They came to the doorway of the palace at evening, and they were wondering whether to explore it immediately or whether to make camp and wait for morning, when they heard the faint frail notes of a shepherd's flute. Sheltering as comfortably as he could, in a crook in the rocks, they found an old blind man.

'Tell us, old man:' said the eldest prince, 'what is this place?'

'I shall tell you,' replied the old man – Ali's body seems to hunch and shrink, and his voice changes – 'though my tale be the most macabre; I beg you to heed me well.' The princes gathered around him, as respectful and generous to a story-teller as you are gentlemen, eager to hear.

'Once there was a great lord', begins the old man/Ali, 'and this was his palace. He was a man of the greatest character and virtue, and when at last he took a wife it was only naturally that she should be a goddess: a mountain nymph, an enchantress of the Atlas. You got a lot of that sort of thing in the old days. With his powers and her powers combined, this rough palace became splendid beyond imagining, and this rocky valley became the most fertile spot in all Africa. And with their powers combined, they produced a child: just one child – a most beauteous daughter.

'Well, the years passed, and naturally there came the question of finding a husband to take the beauteous daughter as his wife. For if no husband could be found to take her, where would all this fabulous heritage go? Where would the story be? Now, I'm sure you're thinking: can't have been too hard. And indeed many a worthy suitor came to seek the daughter for his bride. For besides the gorgeous palace and fertile land that were her dowry, she had grown into a young woman of legendary beauty, a true princess of fairy-tale. And if you can't marry a goddess, a half-goddess is surely the next best thing.

'Alas, she insisted on her right to approve her husband; and her parents loved her too much – their hopes and their futures in this world were too invested in her – to deny her this caprice. And now, dear gentlemen, we come to the strangest part of this terrible tale.' His audience are agog now. 'Each suitor was welcomed most courteously, and feasted, by the lord and his lady. Then, when they had readied themselves, they were allowed into a room on their own. In this room there was a window, and through the window they could at last look on the princess they had come to seek. She, meanwhile, would be standing in the modest room on the other side, and she too would look into the glass. But she would not see the man who had come for her, for what to them was a window to her was a mirror, and this mirror showed her something very particular: it showed her herself – as her potential husband truly saw her.'

The narrator of this extraordinary tale could sense the absorption and bewilderment of his distinguished listeners. 'Well, gentlemen, you can see where that sort of thing would lead. The capricious princess was never satisfied with what she saw in the mirror. Suitor after suitor was rejected, and in the instant that he was rejected he was struck dead. Still the suitors came, and tried their luck, for the prize was great and surely worth it; but none was successful, and suitor after suitor vanished through the gateway behind me and was never seen again. And over time the number of suitors dwindled, for word does get about, and more and more the prospective young men were wondering if they might not be better off with more modest ambitions. As hopes for the future crumbled, so too did the palace. Eventually the lord died, and his nymph wife bore his soul away to her mountain home, and the princess was left there alone.'

The seven princes were captivated, as the old man concluded: 'And there she waits, gentlemen – alone in her fortress – wondering if the right suitor will ever appear.'

'Do you mean she is still inside this ruin, old man?' cried the eldest of the seven. 'And still a man may claim her?'

'She is there still, young man. And still she is beautiful. And still the man who wins her will inherit this valley and this palace, as well as her half-heavenly body. But have a care: for still the suitor who fails to win her approval will immediately be struck dead.'

'Seems a bit impractical of her', said one of the others.

'That's fairy-tales for you. Does any of you young men dare risk it?'

The seven princes gazed at each other. Each was dreaming of what this palace and this valley could become;

278

each was dreaming of a fairy-tale princess. The eldest was naturally the first to speak. 'I claim the right to try first', he said firmly, and his brothers all nodded – respectful, though each was jealous. 'We shall spend the night here together, and at dawn I shall enter and look upon her', he said with manly resolution. 'By the following dawn, either I shall have invited you all in to share my wedding feast, or you shall know that I am gone.'

At dawn the next day, the prince made his farewells to his brothers. He walked up to the crumbling palace alone, took a breath, and stepped in. His feet led him through its chaos to a room with a window in it, and through this window he could see a beautiful young woman, and she was looking back towards him.

But in the glass she saw a reflection of a girl cowering, in chains and bruised.

The prince continued to gaze hopefully through the glass, but from the other side of it there came a terrifying scream, and he was struck dead in an instant and his dead body crumbled to dust and the dust was blown to the winds.

At dawn the next day, the remaining brothers knew they could hope no longer. The second brother looked around the others, sadly and then with a smile of resolution. 'I claim the right to try next. By tomorrow's dawn, either I shall have invited you all in to share my wedding feast, or you shall know that I am gone.'

The prince took a breath, and stepped into the crumbling palace. His feet led him through its chaos to a room with a window in it, and through this window he could see a beautiful young woman, and she was looking back towards him. But in the glass she saw a reflection of a statue formed of ice.

The prince continued to gaze hopefully through the glass, but from the other side of it there came a terrifying scream, and he was struck dead in an instant and his dead body crumbled to dust and the dust was blown to the winds.

At dawn the next day, the third brother made the same resolution and went to find the vision of the beautiful young woman. But in the glass she saw a reflection of a tender doe in the forest, alarmed as the hunters gathered. And the prince was struck dead in an instant and his dead body crumbled to dust and the dust was blown to the winds.

The fourth brother made the same resolution and went to find the vision of the beautiful young woman. But in the glass she saw a reflection that flickered and blurred and was forever changing. And the prince was struck dead in an instant and his dead body crumbled to dust and the dust was blown to the winds.

The fifth brother made the same resolution and went to find the vision of the beautiful young woman. But in the glass she saw a reflection of the prince's own mother. And the prince was struck dead in an instant and his dead body crumbled to dust and the dust was blown to the winds.

The sixth brother made the same resolution and went to find the vision of the beautiful young woman. But in the glass she saw a reflection of – well, it's hard to describe and I'd rather not go into too much detail – but basically it was a grotesque mutation, a being composed almost entirely of... well, of certain parts of a woman's body. And the prince was struck dead in an instant and his dead body crumbled to dust and the dust was blown to the winds.

At dawn the next day, the last brother knew that he had just spent only the first of his nights without his brothers. He – like the mysterious woman in the ruined palace in front of him – was the last of his family. He seriously considered getting back on his horse and riding away; but that didn't seem right. He had no brother left to declare his resolution to, so he asked the old man to remember and recount the story of the seven of them. As an after-thought, he also promised him an invitation to the possible wedding feast. He gave a last look at the world around him, took a deep breath, and strode in through the gate.

The boot-prints in the dust showed the path his six older brothers had taken, and he followed. Heart thumping, he walked through the remains of the mighty architecture and the blown sand, until he came to a door. A polite knock, and he entered. The room was small, unremarkable, gloomy. On the other side of it was a window, and through the window he could make out a figure. He took three steps across the room, and gazed through the glass at the beautiful young woman on the other side. And the princess looked into the glass from her side, and she saw the reflection of... a beautiful young woman, individual in every detail, the prince's precise image of perfect femininity.

At this the glass shattered and fell to the floor, and the prince stepped through the debris into the other room, and there in front of him stood the woman of his dreams. He leapt forwards and embraced her, and immediately the palace was transformed and the valley was transformed, and – who knows? – they probably lived happily ever after. Little did the prince know that he was embracing a mannequin, which in the instant of the glass shattering the princess had conjured and stood in her place. The princess herself had turned into an eagle and flown out the window – through the rather polluted air that hung around the palace, thick with the dust of former suitors – far across the mountains, where the air was pure and the world was invisible.

☽

'Marriage is the prize, M'zelle. The end of the journey.'

Eva is lying on her bed, staring at the tight-bunched reed ceiling. She has not asked the question, not exactly.

281

Assia is always fishing for hints about how things are going with Luther. Assia is romantic, and Assia is concerned about future employment.

Eva remembers the journey across the desert. The dream of a city; the delusion of a city.

'You listened to the story-tellers, M'zelle, in the square? The stories aren't about women, and if they're about women it's always a girl who doesn't listen to her parents and doesn't get married and she ends up a prostitute.'

'They can't all be like that.'

'All.' Assia has stopped pretending to tidy.

'What about the princesses and the fairies?'

'They're not real, though, are they? They're just there to trick men into bad things or encourage them into good things. Anyway, what always happens with the princess at the end of the story?'

'She gets married...' Eva says sourly to the ceiling. 'Aren't there any women story-tellers?'

'A woman – in the street – performing?'

'Of course. Just another prostitute. Heaven forbid.' The grille of reeds is dark and close. The cruellest delusion of all: that a woman could dream of writing a story for herself that didn't involve automatic corruption. And by doing so be automatically corrupted.

Assia sits beside her on the bed, and pats her hand in a kind of reassurance. 'When a man writes your story, it will be a story of how you were foolish and thought you could run away from marriage and in the end you become a prostitute and raped and murdered in the gutter.'

'It's a bad reason to get married!'

'It's not about good and bad, M'zelle.' Assia stands, drifts away. 'You don't need a reason to get married; you just need a man.'

'And then everything is all right?'

Assia shrugs. Eva throws a book at her.

JOURNAL OF THOMAS SOMERLEIGH

Later: I think the warnings about growing unrest in the city might be right. Walking home this afternoon, the city seemed much more on edge than I have known it; even when I was new to it. I saw doorways and alleyways I'd not noticed before. For the first time, I wondered if I'm wise to wander around alone so much; I stand out so obviously. And when one looks closely, there's so much hostility in the faces. Or just emptiness.

Hell of a task to rule or guide a place with the proper grip and wisdom, when you simply can't know the people. Marrakech looks like it really is getting out of control, but how can we tell?

Youssef skulking in the doorway when I got back: some scornful witticism about diplomacy, and needling me about the bill for the wooden chairs. I was naturally in a hurry to get out of the heat and the world, and I actually had to shove the brute aside to do so.

All I've ever wanted is to fit. Ma and Pa have given everything just to put me in a position where I might. Principles. Education. Standards. Right down to a proper pen and a smart enough pair of cuff-links. Oh, but their pride in me... And here I am, stuck in the desert, rampaging around smashing stuff up.

I always wondered how the forgotten legends of the Foreign Office came to be so. The unmentionables, the chaps who haven't been seen in London for twenty years, posted to remote hill-stations and malarial swamps and grass huts and starting to wear native clobber and getting religion and going mad. They began, I fear, like this. Enough of the superficials to get in. Lacking the essentials to get on.

So here I sit, spitting at the page. Youssef isn't daring to come near me, wise beggar. I can hear him creeping about, rat-like, always somewhere in the house and never seen. Probably clearing my pockets out ready to do a flit; no point hanging around on board H.M.S. Somerleigh as the water comes over the scuppers.

Just delivered: a note from Hortense. Been thinking a great deal, come to realization that in this feverish climate emotions become too easily over-heated. When among barbarians, her dear father often reminds them – I'll bet he bloody does – there is heightened risk of starting to behave like barbarians. Would be unfortunate were either of us to get wrong impression, or be tempted to fall from our best selves. In the current circumstances – Christ, how did he describe my performance to her? – one feels it better if we do not see each other any more.

Where the bloody hell am I? Who?

☪

The break, when it happens, is as gentle an adjustment as the union promised to be.

They are in the courtyard of Giesberts's house. A place of entrances and exits. A place where interior and exterior, permanent and transient, buyer and seller, power and possibility touch and briefly overlap, encounter one another and withdraw.

'It is lovely in this place', he says. He looks her down and up; she knows he sees her hair loose amid the abundance of leaves and fruit, sees it wilder in his mind. 'You are lovely in this place. It can be yours; yes?'

'It is lovely in this place. And in this place you are generous, and protecting. And charming. And interesting.' When she shakes her head it is discomfort more than negation. 'But I am not ready for this. Everything is so...

unsettled at the moment. The circus; the city. To hide with you – to cling to you – It's not right. It cannot be; no.'

Luther's pride makes him immediately indifferent; dismissive. Brisk smile; nod. She kisses him on the cheek. She turns to go; neither of them wants this prolonged.

But his eyes... He has frozen them Medusa-hard. His emotion is tight-clenched; but his eyes scream it.

☪

JOURNAL OF THOMAS SOMERLEIGH

Still thinking about Hortense. Confess my thoughts were pretty brutal yesterday. Emotions too easily over-heated, as she put it. Risk when among barbarians. But she had seemed so truly, gently happy. And I'm sure my behaviour towards her was appropriate. You didn't have to look too closely between the lines to see her father standing over her as she wrote them.

Prudhomme has decided that I am no longer suitable. And so dear little Hortense has been put back in her cage.

Any idea I might have had of working my way back into their approval, rebuilding a bit of credibility, was crushed by my first encounter with Prudhomme this morning. I was pretty apprehensive about facing the gang – first day of school stuff – and I don't pretend I was any too pleasant with Youssef this morning, and I was in a bit of a funk all the way to the palace. But: deep breath and get on with it.

I'd expected complaint. I'd expected hostility. I was ready: I knew what I'd have to say. I knew the principles I'd have to emphasize; can't be any doubt about British positions. I was ready, in a straightforward fashion, to confront any difficulty and courteously explore possible ways forward. And then: in a loose clump at the palace gate, the usual faces and outfits; in the middle of them,

Prudhomme. And then he had noticed my arrival, and as I walked towards them his face turned to me and I rather steeled myself for something formal.

Instead: behind the pince-nez the eyes narrowed and gleamed; and the thin smile crept up the face; and – still smiling – Prudhomme gave me a long nod and then turned back to Klug.

No hostility, because apparently I am not a problem for him; apparently I am not anything for him. No hostility, just that haughty indifferent smile.

No Sultan today, so it was just the dips in informal conference. 'I wonder,' Prudhomme began, and then turned to Klug: 'but please, my dear Ernst, will you speak first?'

Formal nod from Klug. 'It is not required, dear Hector; after you.'

Nod and thin smile from Prudhomme. 'Klug and I have been talking, and we feel – I beg you to check with him that I do not misrepresent – that the discussion in this group yesterday became too over-heated. Such a risk in this feverish climate, but I think we all feel that we must try to set an example for our Moroccan friends. We feel' – he turned to Klug, and Klug nodded – 'that it would be best were we to agree that the entire conversation did not happen.' A final, formal nod from Klug. 'You will all have your own information about the violence and tension in the city. You will have your own interpretations of the role of the trouble-making preacher. Everything so... unsettled at the moment. We may safely agree, I think, that – today at least – a decision on a circus performance, in any format, would not be prudent. The circus depends on security.'

They turned to each other, an extra mutual nod, and that was that.

It wouldn't have made any difference if I hadn't spoken at all yesterday.

Telegram in from Tangier. URGENT REPEAT URGENT CONFIRM NATURE OF

MISUNDERSTANDING STOP MOROCCAN
OFFICIAL HERE EXPRESSES SURPRISE AT
BRITISH STATEMENT MARRAKECH IMPLYING
SULTAN MORE INTERESTED IN PANTOMIME
THAN PUBLIC ORDER STOP FRANCE GERMANY
REPORTED IN JOINT MANAGEMENT OF
SECURITY STOP URGENT REASSURE EXACT
STATEMENTS OR CONFIRM NEED SEND MORE
EXPERIENCED OFFICIAL STOP.

Not a single mistake in Sir G's coding.

Best go out for a walk now. Bit of fresh air. Lose myself
in the back-streets a while, hopefully get my throat cut.

☫

Eva is obliged to accompany Giesberts to supper with
the German representative, Klug. An arrangement made
before their split; and an evening of political conversation
might be interesting.

Once again, in practice she is there as any woman
rather than a woman. The tone of the occasion demands
that half of the participants offer breasts and no
interruption. Eva is satisfactorily equipped, and trained to
use movement rather than words to communicate. In public
life, it is convenient for a man to have such an asset at his
disposal. It is her first and last sense of marital duty.

Conversation over dinner is dull in the extreme: the
men are too distracted to drive it, and the women are not
allowed to. But Eva overhears enough of the real
discussion, before and after the men cloister themselves in
female company. The man Klug is angry and alarmed. His
movements and his speech are stilted, clumsy: he is not
used to expressing so much emotion.

'This Frenchman!' he is saying, and through the glass
of the half-opened courtyard door Eva sees the feeling
bursting red in his face. 'He is... deranged!' The three

other men nod sympathetically; Frenchmen... 'The fact that originally this circus it is a German initiative with German finance, even let us set that aside for one moment. Germany offers a constructive model of co-operation. But this Frenchman – The mediaeval costume – The mediaeval mentality – He is now monomaniac on the subject! Today a performance of consensus, but of course this is to distract and neutralize Germany only. We pretend to consider the effect of the radical preacher, but who cares for him? Really the Frenchman is desperate to have his show. And of course he must control it absolutely! He makes of himself a Louis XIV – in this Versailles of the desert.'

Metaphor is unusual for him. The diplomat's mind is roaming wilder than it is used to. His companions nod warily.

'Mark my words! The more he pretends calm, the more he is ready to jump. The more arguments he uses about the circus, the cheaper they become. At any moment he will find the justification he needs. The French will, it will be imposed. And about the chaos that follows they will not care.'

After the meal: the women exiled to the parlour to continue their wait for stimulation; the men left in possession of the table, slumped and sated with wine and dominance. The women have implicit permission to speak now; but they listen more attentively for what the men might be saying in their absence. 'It – is – out – of – control!' thumps Klug, and there are male murmurs of agreement and concern. Giesberts, quieter, says something about nothing being relied upon. Then Klug again: 'These people are angry. They lack firm leadership.' More agreement. 'Anything is possible!'

Eva is supposed to be alarmed. Some part of her is excited.

JOURNAL OF THOMAS SOMERLEIGH

The moon. The moon, distant and cold and alone, shining on the sea – except you're not seeing the moon you're seeing the light on the sea – except the waters and they're thick inky and angry they're always shifting and the light keeps breaking into little pieces of light and so you never really see it for what it is – and the moon it feels so feeble. Or a boat on those same waters, cut loose and drifting, that's me, out into the Atlantic, swaying and drifting and forever drifting out into the night, and feeling very sleepy now I should probably get some sleep – They found him the very next morning, slumped dead over his desk – Dead, inspector! And without a mark on him! – but a desk doesn't feel right now I should drift away into the night on a sea of scarlet cushions. Just one point I wanted to jot down while it's fresh.

Free, though. Why not? They obviously don't want me I don't want them. All of our ridiculous clothes and our fussy way of talking it's all just a pantomime isn't it? It only means something because we all pretend it means something. Tripping over beggar chappie in the big square t'other day and staring at each other and you think what a wretch he looks and they're literally rags and must all stink and lice and so forth and it's only when you walk away you think well gosh how did I look to him?

And now the ridiculous costumes in Marrakech despise me and the ridiculous costumes in Tangier despise me and I'm damned if I'm going to beg. The diplomats they are stuffy complacent lifeless cities on the coast – Brahim and the old chap of course, Sa'id – and it always stinks of fish, a fish wearing pince-nez, because there's no fresh wind coming out of the mountains. I could charge down out of the mountains on a white horse, probably a camel, and carry off Hortense in my arms – she'd have to hang on or you'd need at least one hand for the reins or I'm sure she's pretty light. But no... I have turned my back on the cities of the plain. A wandering beggar, staff in hand, just a single cuff-link on a chain around my neck – could I get a lock of her hair? – I turn away from the world with all its hypocrisies and I trudge into the desert. An endless quest. In search... in search of the heart of what-not. You have to cast off the trappings of the world, all the hypocriSirGs, and open your heart. Probably have to brush up my Arabic – wonder if they do puns...

Ah, but it's a wild free city when you open your front door to it. Swim out into the restless inky swirling waters of the night. Quest doesn't have to be in the desert hellish hot and questions about the plumbing obviously – *Sacré bleu, les pipes!* – the night is a desert. Extraordinary business I'm here at my desk now definitely home but no recollection of the front door probably ought to check that's locked or coming through the courtyard. Really it's just the streets, swimming in the streets, the faces around me and it's a lovely warm night and the scents of all the spices and things and what a magical adventure, this is the life.

Anything might happen in those streets and yes that's the point I can make anything happen in those streets. I can be whatever I want to be well something anyway. Everywhere you turn another alley, another door, and when you turn it's a different door in a different alley. The endless alleyways of Marrakech, the infinite doors, and every one a new possibility. A new Somerleigh. Turn to catch a scent to catch an eye and a curtain wafts aside and gosh there you are. Through the door and into a different dream.

But if that could be a dream then this could be a dream. Perhaps I'm not at home sitting at my desk writing up my notes on the day like a good little bureaucrat. Perhaps I'm still out there in the night in the cushions in the tastes in the eyes. So everything written before this sentence could be fantasy. Or everything written after this sentence could be fantasy. Or both. Or maybe everything is true. Upsadaisy. Everything is true in the night.

His Majesty's Foreign Office has no rules for this night: querulous O'Neill is silent. The rules of grammar are suspended. The story may not unfold as we expect, because the story-teller has had a glass too many and is opening doors willy-nilly.

The door is already open as I turn. First scent, rich and sweet, fruit ripe and fruit forbidden. Then movement funny thing about the Arab get-up it covers everything but it emphasizes how the limbs move and a hip turns and a thigh lifts and an arm opens the way in. What a gorgeous secret hearth pulls me in between those timbers, glow of lantern-light and rich dark fabric and the scent of summer dusk and musk and a bare shoulder and a pair of eyes dark and imagine the glory if I could be the kind of man to go through this kind of doorway.

This is where the dream ends, of course, except it doesn't end. I think I feel my footsteps, but it is now a new me, a Somerleigh of scents and unrestraints. The tiles glisten with their exotic trees and the figure leading me is slender and within reach and gliding onwards, no sound but smell and the dark eyes turn over the shoulder to gaze at me and lower quickly and away and onwards.

Anything, anything, the intoxicating realization that the dream might not be a dream and I might be anything. Sa'id, the sneaky old so-and-so: the heart of Morocco was just around the corner and through a scented doorway and a purple curtain and a pair of dark eyes and in the heart of Morocco I found me.

Those eyes. A welcome. An open arm and a gown falling open and I settle like a swirling leaf into scarlet cushions, and the cushions are so right that I seem to swim. A glass, a blessing, a sip, and was that the first kiss? The wine is sweet, and unfamiliar, but I tonight am unfamiliar and so the wine is right. So too the cigarette, so too the herbs burning in the brazier and the genie of a new Somerleigh swirling up through the smoke. A figure swirls beside me, glides down beside me among the scarlet cushions and the gown opens and a glimpse of slender thigh and the bare shoulder reaches to pour me more. Then a head settles on my shoulder, dark-lashed eyes gazing with me into the smoke and my arm pulls us together because I know where we're going, and the dark eyes gaze up into me, pour me more. The lips are dark and sweet and hot fruit and the thigh opens and the boy is beautiful and tonight all doors are open.

In the café on the corner, where the maze of alleys that make up Marrakech market empties onto the great square, the corner with a herd of blacksmith's apprentices looking for a fight, morning is at its busiest and hottest. The square has no clear boundaries: here it becomes a road, or roads; there it merges with the yard around the Koutoubia; set out a few more café tables or a stall with some new weaves just in from Timbuktou, and the square gets smaller; open a door or open your eyes and the square just got larger. The square is not, in truth, a square.

After the first bustle of morning and as the heat begins to thicken, the rhythms of the royal palace slow. It is his habit, in this lull, to walk out into the city and to drink a tea with his acquaintances. Today we can't find the usual café, and some of the acquaintances have gone missing. It's not clear where this conversation can happen, or how. It is hurried: glimpsed between restless bodies. It is elusive: overheard and misheard as we try to avoid trouble.

Not to be indiscreet, but I'm starting to worry that maybe the foreign diplomats haven't got things completely under control.

I know, I know… But listen.

Yesterday the Roumi were all agreed. There wasn't even a discussion: just a polite suggestion that it wasn't the right time to decide on the circus; bit of a shame but probably sensible. And they all agreed, and they all looked like they agreed.

This morning, the German was in the palace early, stamping around the corridors and grabbing anyone he could and insisting on meetings with every possible official. Now, the Germans got the circus here, right? They're paying for it, right? So how come the German diplomat is asking everyone from the Sultan's emu to the beggar at the gate the same question? He asks: When is the circus going to perform? You must warn me, he says, before it happens. Then he goes back to his usual line about how there will be a series of performances, here and here and here, dates, German approvals, all to reinforce the independence of Morocco.

Then, of course, there's the Frenchie. In the palace early this morning, slipping through the corridors and murmuring to anyone he can and insisting on meetings with every possible official. He's everywhere the German isn't. You see the German, you turn around, and in the other direction there's the Frenchie. One going left, the other going right. If the German's concluding a conversation with His Majesty's Surveyor of Estates, the Frenchman's demanding a discussion with the Keeper of the Fabrics. Frenchie's stamping up the ruby staircase, German's jumping out the window into the pear garden.

And what's the Frenchman saying? I've just been in conversation with so-and-so, he says, and I hear that the circus is about to perform. No doubt, he says, it will be such a satisfaction to His Majesty.

Can anyone say who has definitively said that it will perform? Can anyone deny it?

German approval of the performance, says the German, is essential. German approval of the performance, says the Frenchie, is appreciated; such a satisfaction to His Majesty, no doubt.

Can anyone disagree?

The German always looks like he's about to explode. We watch the German like we watch the mountains: waiting for the storm.

The Frenchman surely cannot be about to explode. Such a thing, it is an impossibility in this man. All emotions are constrained, in the perfect diplomat. But what must it be like in there? What would happen to all that emotion if the constraint stopped working?

The English? No... didn't see him this morning.

Right: that must mean that the English really know what's going on; they've got it all under control, right?

Or perhaps this particular conversation takes place in someone's head; someone in the royal palace, watching bewildered and unable to speak their mind.

◉

JOURNAL OF THOMAS SOMERLEIGH

The streets are uncanny this morning. I walk them like old acquaintances, aware of their eccentricities and foibles and threats, warmed by familiarity, uneasy at the growing realization that I may not know them as well as I thought. Doors are memories and possibilities. Solid timber iron studded; handsome blue; five rotting planks hanging off a hinge; panels carved elegant, whorls and wonders and welcome; a curtain that rustles and suggests the light beyond. I had a drink through this one; did I have a meal through that one? I'd like to try whatever's through there.

Faces are individual now, and this is the most unsettling thing of all. Were I putting on a performance of diplomacy today, I should need to describe this city in a word. A gaggle of gargoyles gathers over the ticking telegraph in Tangier, waiting for word from the wanderer: Marrakech is...

...quiet.

Or just possibly unquiet.

And the gargoyles would glance at each other and agree, and then they would wait for word of the atmosphere in Rabat, and Casablanca, and the other cities, and when they had collected the words they would hunch and glower amid smoke and sulphur, and their brilliant minds would winnow and refine and polish material of a vastness and sophistication far above my mortal imagining: a telegram to London, a word.

Morocco is...

I don't even know how this bread-seller is.

Why is he staring at me? I love the smell of bread: cosy afternoons with work all done; musty blankets in the cupboard in a childhood holiday bedroom fond-remembered; instinctively a breath; a hug. I wonder if the bread-seller feels that way. Is he staring at me? Obviously he wants me to buy. He can see I'm foreign. He's grumpy because the price of my old jacket could feed his family for a year. He's grumpy because his wife was insulted by a foreigner last week. He's grumpy because I'm foreign. He's grumpy because he's got tooth-ache. Presumably he'd still prefer me to buy. I think I recognize him, don't I? The peculiar lump on his forehead; mustn't stare, but where else am I supposed to look and he's looking at me isn't he? Ten years his whole existence has been between his home and his oven and this corner, a matter of yards only, just a few dozen images and movements each day and every day, and should he admire or begrudge a foreigner who has been paid to cross a whole continent just to come and look at him and sum him up in a word? Surely buying from him is better than not. Perhaps he's had an argument with his wife; perhaps his wife is sick; perhaps his wife has been injured in the recent unquiet. I do admire the deftness of that gesture, the warm loaf knocked for soundness and brandished for the customer to smell and away into the paper wrap and next! The customer in front of me: shaking hands with the bread-seller, gnarled branch claws clutching, how many years every day the same? The tiny precision of the darn in his gown and how nice to have a woman who cares I bet Hortense would piano similar skill but too snooty a Somerleigh should know an old woman; behind a doorway in Marrakech.

I do recognize the bread-seller. Got a wonky eye; makes it look like he's staring. Hallo, old fellow; yes please – no, you keep the change. Good old Somerleigh. God, imagine having to spend your life grinning gratefully to good old Somerleighs.

Me walking through these alleys – spices peg-leg gorgeous curtains hawkers' cries like Folkestone skies foul meat Aunt Louise angry glare scrawny fish warm bread tears under a shawl – is an immense thawing, the breaking of the spell of night and I have released all this life. Or perhaps it's a circus-show, a morning variety act to entice the tourists. Or – surely that's daft, isn't it? Obviously this isn't for my benefit. My shoes are in better nick and I get fancier social invites than the average bod, but I'm not so special; I can't make that much difference. Perhaps they hardly notice me; better things to worry about. Anyway, among these visions and attitudes and possibilities, I can't be sure how much I'm imagining: perhaps I'm still lying in bed, dreaming of a postcard-exotic Morocco; perhaps I dream all the foolish performance of international diplomacy, lying in scarlet cushions somewhere. Has the fantastical tumult of Marrakech just been conjured in the smoke of a mountain magician's brazier – or around a European conference table? Has that hawk-eyed lad just looked up and imagined me?

I follow a young mother up towards the palace gate. Within the tight wrapping of her gown, her baby is pressed around her chest like an ungainly parcel or a set of bagpipes. Its head hangs over her shoulder: the big eyes bounce and loll with every step, and gaze at me. Doesn't seem any too impressed by the sight of European diplomacy turning up for work.

The palace seems more anxious this morning. Clerks are hurrying to and fro; each face glances warily at me, checking who I am or wondering how to satisfy me or deciding if I matter. I sense Hector Prudhomme before I see him: the eddies of hurrying are becoming more intense, centred on some force just round the corner, and then I hear the voice, and then I see the suit, and the pince-nez flash as he turns. The voice is less measured than normal, the movement less smooth: in the endless austere beauty of these chambers even Prudhomme has started to feel frustrated. 'You may tell this to your master!' The words are all teeth. 'Tell him, howsoever you choose, that this wretched preacher man can no longer be a hindrance to his circus! This absurd situation must be resolved today!'

Two court officials are standing in front of him – three – and they lower their eyes in what they hope could be interpreted as a nod but is really discomfort or fear. Three witches who find they have raised something uncontrollable from their cauldron. They have stopped understanding what he's saying; each judges that one of the others might be responsible.

'Ah, cher Somerleigh!' he yaps as he sees me. Instinctively I find myself shrinking like the officials. 'At last! Come: let us resolve this charade.'

Prudhomme strides into the committee chamber, dust and officials and I swirling in his wake. To his obvious frustration, he cannot continue walking. He all-but bumps into the chair, glares at it, wrenches it aside to sit. 'Security depends on the circus!' The words spit out. 'As we concluded yesterday.' We are all trying to recall what we concluded yesterday; it was something like that, wasn't it? 'Good morning, dear colleagues!' Some instinct of protocol churning deep in his blood delivers the pleasantry. His eyes blaze around the room, his fixed smile. 'We find ourselves at last in a position where our positive action may have a benign effect on the chaos engulfing this excuse for a country.'

Little Abdelilah is perched painfully behind him, as ever, eyes and ears straining to catch nuance and implication. Prudhomme's fever makes the secretary even more uncomfortable, and yet more desperate to conform.

'I have spent the last hours – and I am confident that many of you have done the same – consulting every possible official. A diversity of voices. We may conclude a clear consensus. Marrakech desperately needs its circus performance now.'

What a strange arrangement we are, perched in here like so many hens in someone else's coop. With our argot of courtesy and manoeuvre, reassurance and provocation. Each with our awkward pride, our finicky concerns. Here is Somerleigh, worrying about his lost cuff-link and his lost career. Somerleigh is the average of forty million people, from a Gaelic-speaking Shetland crofter to a Cornish crabber, from a mute brute factory drudge to a Royal Duke; and he is their voice. There is Ray, torn between a dream of Spain's mediaeval glory and his concerns about what he might have caught in a brothel last night. Klug is just one man and relatively junior, required to speak for a nation determined to push itself into the front rank, and who knows what's going on in his head or in his parlour? This fellow is worrying about his promotion, that one about his piles. And by some alchemy of arrogance we declare that with this ad hoc collection of mediocrities all Europe – the world indeed; your pardon, McKenna – is here and that all Europe speaks, and when Europe speaks her word is immaculate. The frustrations of south London, the pretensions of some semi-primitive Spanish province, the echoes of the Battle of Sedan and a Rhineland toothache: these shall determine the fate of Morocco's tribes and cities. Well should little Abdelilah tremble. The doctors peck and cluck and squawk. The doctors jostle to claim their fee.

Among us are greater spirits, of other worlds. In our minds, at our shoulders, confronting us across the table. Here is the Kaiser, yes, and Sir Edward Grey. But here too are Bismarck and Queen Elizabeth I, and the first Saxon tribesman lurking in the forest ready to cut a Roman throat, and the first English merchant who looked at the sea and saw a road not a wall. Louis XVI and Robespierre are both here; the Paris of the highest culture and the Paris of the mob. And Napoleon, of course; always. Napoleon's been muscling into European diplomatic meetings for a whole century. But what's that in the air? Why do these august noses wrinkle so? We are in a more exotic world now, and its currents unsettle and tease. We are ragged adventurers come to woo the Sultan's beautiful daughter, at the same time as we lobby his officials for a contract to put in drains. Morocco's mountains loom over us, heavy with the threat of the Glaoui's intrigues and brutality, and with ruby-mines and nymphs who dance and deliver our dreams. McKenna must shuffle aside: a beautiful boy whispers in my ear, of what might be and what I might be.

And here is Hector Prudhomme in fullest flow. 'The city needs diversion; entertainment; a dash of pleasant normality. And at the very moment when the Sultan's situation is most delicate, he finds that his international friends have equipped him with the instrument he needs. We remember the original inspiration, the stroke of German genius that gave us this possibility.' The empty compliment to a competitor, this is an accepted nicety of rhetoric; oils the wheels, proves we're all still gentlemen. But such a ridiculous hyperbole, used in the moment when we saw that Prudhomme was unstoppable, this was a punch in the face; a declaration of war. Klug's face was frozen in outrage; and behind it all of Germany's gunboats were gathering.

Prudhomme continued to pronounce, through a ghastly smile of pleasantry that paralyzed his cheeks. 'Given the desperate condition of public order in the streets, and given the apparent consensus of his officials, His Majesty's enthusiasm for an immediate performance by the circus is not only understandable but irresistible.'

There it was. Just for the record. Unimpeachable justification plus unverifiable momentum plus unarguable conclusion, in one sentence. Prudhomme's logic was irresistible.

'We may, I suggest, congratulate ourselves as a group for our management of the situation to this point. And if you will excuse me,' – Prudhomme stood – 'His Majesty is expecting a comment from France' – when wasn't he expecting a comment from France? – 'and I shall consider it politic as well as positive to welcome this outcome.'

And then he was gone, little Abdelilah flustering along in his wake. Behind him silence – broken at last by Klug's slow, solitary, hollow clapping.

Diplomacy's like the magic trick at the restaurant table: look too closely, cease taking the elaborate words seriously, and it seems foolish and you feel foolish for having been taken in.

As I walk out of the hall, I realize Sir Edward Grey has stayed behind at the table. I wonder if it gets harder for him to make himself believe the magic, or easier. There's a beautiful Moroccan girl walking just in front of me: the eyes glancing back at me every few steps – leading me, of course, but I think she wants to know I'm there as well. I'm straying, yes, but Somerleigh's the kind of foreigner you like to have around. I think it's a girl; gorgeous eyes. Could be a boy: I try to tell from the hips. And here's Brahim:

wants me to meet his family – fun for them, of course, but also he knows that theirs is the Morocco I seek.

Prudhomme has stopped a few yards ahead. I can see the tension in him, the energy: his body keeps shifting to move, as if the wind is plucking at him and might just whip him up through the window. I wonder what's holding him, and then I realize Abdelilah is hidden behind him.

The little Moroccan's French is as exquisite and anguished as ever. 'Dear excellency, I must express the concern that we find ourselves caught in an inconsistency.' Prudhomme's shoulders are knotted tight like thunder clouds. 'My personal endeavour, it is naturally and always merely to record your deliberations and see them implemented as immediately and effectively as is possible.'

The shoulders surge and clench: 'Well then! Let us get on with it!'

'But dear excellency: the vizier – all of the officials of the administration – they received the conclusions of your deliberations yesterday. That it was not prudent for the circus to perform. In the interests of security.'

'That was yesterday!'

'But I fear... Excellency, they were most impressed by your sagacity. So wise, they said, and so attentive and adapted to the realities of Morocco.'

'Exactly!' The gale is beginning to carry Prudhomme away along the corridor. By the dense energy of his frustration, by the ferocity of his glare, he is trying to pull Abdelilah with him. 'Today the realities of Morocco dictate that the circus shall perform.' But Abdelilah, leaf-light, fears something along the corridor and will not be plucked up.

'Excellency, I told them... That is, if I might advise just a little...'

'You told them?' Prudhomme is untethered from the earth and whirls around Abdelilah. 'You ridiculous little man! What possible weight have you? What possible

301

interest could I have in your advice? How dare you presume to interpret or interrupt French policy?'

And he billows away down the corridor. Little Abdelilah is ripped loose, and flutters and tumbles in his vortex, unbalanced, unable to stop himself, still afraid of what awaits him.

My Moroccan friends and I wander after them.

Fifty yards farther on, a small receiving room where the marble is misty like egg-shell: Prudhomme has come temporarily to rest. He has allowed himself to be turned sideways, so he no longer threatens to charge right through the palace, not so obviously. His poise shows that he has met an obstacle of – if not equal – at least respectable gravity.

On the vizier, the traditional robes are distinguished rather than clumsy; just as Prudhomme makes his old-fashioned coat look dignified. The vizier has held a silent bow, and it forces silence and a bow in return: the elegances and tricks of protocol, these are not European inventions but instincts learned from before there were Europeans, from when the first two beasts circled each other in the wilderness.

The same correctness and the same instinct to take some of the fury out of Prudhomme cause the vizier to notice me. Another bow, which I reciprocate. 'And here is England', he says softly, 'most welcome'. I offer a reply acknowledging his honour and hospitality. 'His Majesty always feels that our deliberations are the surer, when the English are present.'

On this point, Hector Prudhomme does not agree with His Majesty. The pince-nez turn to me, and they blaze and shriek: an eagle about to tear apart some minor mammal. He says nothing; he gazes at me. He is reminding me of what happened the last time I tried to offer an opinion: of humiliations diplomatic and domestic.

'England is at your side and at your service, excellency,' I murmur. Whence this new suavity?

I can see the frustration in Prudhomme, burning in his cheeks and tight in his knuckles. But his courtesy is automatic. He waits for the vizier.

'His Majesty learned of a most prudent consensus among our international friends yesterday. His Majesty learned of a most exciting momentum among our international friends today.' His Majesty learns damn' fast, it appears.

His imposition of calm has revived Prudhomme's eloquence. 'His Majesty has understood most shrewdly', he says. 'A matter directly involving His Majesty's retinue, a matter of such significance to security, is naturally kept under constant review. I am delighted to report that His Majesty's enthusiasm for the circus will be gratified. We have of course only awaited the ideal moment to carry out his will, and there is a general feeling that the security conditions not only permit a circus performance, but would benefit from it.'

The vizier glances to me for comment.

But England is saying nothing. If this initiative, whether French or German, succeeds then England did not oppose it. If it fails then it did not have England's support.

'Naturally', breezes Prudhomme, 'as arrangements proceed for the performance we shall welcome any specific requests from His Majesty regarding the nature of the performance.'

The vizier hesitates: not perhaps a natural authority on circus standards, and no doubt anxious to avoid seeking or endorsing something that subsequently goes wrong. 'As to that', he says eventually, 'perhaps we may rely on English arbitration for any questions over the performance, given that the voices of France and Germany are already so clearly heard.'

Once again Prudhomme's terrifying gaze turns on me. I have no desire to pick a fight with France or Germany on this, and even less knowledge of circus matters than the vizier – chance to put in a word for the giraffe, though – and so again I keep my silence; an ambiguous nod.

The vizier isn't finished. 'Excellency – trusting to your sagacity in these matters, and your respect for our dignity and our needs – are we in truth convinced of the prudence of this performance?'

'Yes.' And Prudhomme smiles, daring the vizier to push the point.

'I ask merely in the context of the so-called preacher. The man arrested to satisfy international concerns about the security situation.'

'Your security situation', Prudhomme puts in. 'France is concerned only for the stability of Morocco; all that we do is to assist you.'

'Let our thanks be as the mightiest river. The preacher remains the focus of much public excitement. He is also, let us say… a temptation, to any more prominent figure who might wish to stir mischief against His Majesty.' The vizier's voice never wavers: measured; pleasant; nuanced but not emotional. A clear breath through a flute. 'There is much discussion of what to do with him. There is pressure from many in the streets that he be released, and this pressure is itself a distraction. And were he to be released, it would stir new public energy and new distraction. These uncertainties and possibilities surrounding the preacher: they incline us to prudence in the matter of the circus, because they are alarming to the public spirit.'

'Then kill him', says Prudhomme. 'Publicly. And let us get on.'

☪

Eva's door is flung open: Assia is first a buzzing of 'M'zelle's and then a shadow against the sunlit courtyard and finally, as Eva adjusts to it all, a face bright with excitement. It is almost a performance of enthusiasm: wide eyes and she may even be clapping her hands.

'M'zelle! The circus: you will perform!'

'What did you say?' Most shocking of all: for a moment Eva is not sure that she wants to perform; not sure that she can. A sick flood of guilt at all that she has forgotten.

'It is everywhere! The Sultan will decree a performance. Tonight. Probably. Not tonight. Tomorrow. Probably.'

Eva knows what her audience wants. 'Well... that's very exciting. At last.'

Now she notices another shadow flickering in the doorway: it's the landlady. She's moaning something in Arabic. Assia takes the prompt. 'Yes! And there is another story going round. Your performance, it will involve killing the old preacher man.' She adds hopefully: 'With the lions?'

The bewilderment is external this time. 'What?'

Eva's obvious alarm makes Assia less sure: she is shrugging and now the landlady is grumbling away again. Eventually Assia attempts a summary of her own excitement and total indifference to fact, Eva's confusion, and whatever the landlady is going on about: 'Who knows? A thousand rumours in the square. Everyone knows the palace have been frightened they lose control of the city, with the old man hidden away. Hard-liners think he is not taken seriously? Big riot. His supporters want to keep using him being in prison as a cause? Big riot. Caliph finds an excuse to cause trouble, or the Glaoui? Huge riot.'

'But what does all that have to do with the circus?'

Shrug. Grumble. 'Who knows? Thousand rumours. People say your circus calms everything down. Also, people say your circus will cause big riot. They say maybe the palace is using the circus' – the landlady surely isn't following this bit, but Assia picks up on something she's mumbled in the background – 'or more likely the Roumi, the foreigners, are using the circus as a distraction. Show they are in charge; show they are relaxed. Solve the problem of old preacher Sa'id.'

Eva snatches at the idea. 'Very well; solve a problem. But – obviously – not actually to kill him?'

Shrug. Grumble. Eventually they all agree it makes much more sense as a metaphor.

☾

BRITEMB TANGIER FROM SOMERLEIGH WITH HM SULTAN MARRAKECH PROGRESS IN EUROPEAN CONSENSUS AND MOROCCAN SECURITY PLANNING UNDER BRITISH OVERSIGHT STOP FORTHCOMING PERFORMANCE BY CIRCUS TROUPE SUMMONED AND FINANCED BY GERMANY NOW DRIVEN BY FRANCE REPRESENTS POSITIVE AND AUTONOMOUS EXERCISE OF ROYAL ADMINISTRATION TO MANAGE SECURITY SITUATION STOP FRANCE AND GERMANY AT ODDS BUT NOT OBSTRUCTIVE EUROPEAN UNITED FRONT TO HOSTS STOP HM ASKED BRITISH REPRESENTATIVE ARBITRATION ANY DIFFERENCES STOP PALACE WITH FRENCH ENCOURAGEMENT AND UNDERSCORE OPTIMISM UNDERSCORE THAT IT CALMS RATHER THAN CAUSES POPULAR FEVER PLANS EXEMPLARY PUNISHMENT OF TROUBLEMAKER STOP SUGGEST APPROPRIATE BRITISH POSTURE TANGIER AS IN MARRAKECH NEUTRAL CLOSE INTEREST STOP

☾

Eva has first stretched out on a rug in her room. But its thick fluffy colours reminded her of how far all this exoticism is from her old life as a dancer. She has caught herself enjoying comfort; forgetting. Irritated, ashamed, she has rolled up the rug and pushed it under her bed. She has stretched out on the stone: she will feel cold; hard; primitive. She is trying to go back through the desert.

A thump, and Assia looms out of the sky. She came in chattering, but now she has stopped. Her face over Eva shines with satisfaction. 'Very good!' she says. 'You will be your best for Morocco.'

Eva was already feeling uncomfortable, and now she feels vulnerable and silly, trying to look up at the upside-down face. She wants to speak, but doesn't have time to decide on protest or reassurance.

'I do not interrupt', continues Assia. 'More news about your performance. Definitely the most important and exciting moment will be the execution of the old man. It is decided that his head will be chopped off. Or some people say he will be hanged. And there is a story, or suggestion, that the crowd will stone him. Or he will be pulled apart by horses – you have horses, yes?' Eva's mind follows a nasty diversion into whether a man could be pulled apart by one elderly zebra. Assia smiles shyly, and adds in polite hope: 'Or lions eat him, perhaps?'

Mercifully, Eva thinks, she doesn't have to worry about the details of how the old man dies. She sits up against the bed, and thinks straighter too. The increasing elaboration of the execution only emphasizes its implausibility. It still makes much more sense as metaphor. And if everyone's as excited as Assia, perhaps the regime is right to try to get a grip.

She is a professional dancer.

Thus: is her performance expected to accompany the execution directly?

Thus: is she to be merely the supporting artiste for this bit of theatre – the conjurer's assistant?

Thus: will her dancing surface still have blood on it – or... other residue?

A sudden obscene flash of ambition: it is she, Eva, who will be the first woman in two millennia to re-perform the dance of Salome with all the true emotions driving her and her audience – and with the right props.

'You should continue your exercises', Assia says rather sternly. Eva feels even more guilty about the hint of strain in her legs. 'Performance will be very important and exciting.'

'Yes.' Eva tries to sound committed and professional. 'Do a good job. Back to how it should be.'

Eva and Assia smile politely at each other, their unspoken optimisms working in rather different directions.

✿

JOURNAL OF THOMAS SOMERLEIGH

Nothing will be done or different in Tangier because nothing can be. My telegram is enough advance notice to demonstrate my appropriate attentiveness, and will allow the Embassy to adopt the appropriate attentiveness, without interfering where we should not or adopting too clear a position for or against.

I have no interest or capacity to mediate on issues about the performance by the wretched circus, but the vizier did ask and that does reflect their respect for my neutral influence and that's what matters. For as long as I'm playing diplomat, I shall try to do it satisfactorily: the telegram emphasizes Britain's disinterested and impartial management of things, because that is what should be emphasized.

It is to be tomorrow. Prudhomme has presented this as a concession to those still worried about the security implications. Allow no time for public uncertainty or emotion to build. Tomorrow, and late: after supper, when much of the city will be at home or in bed. I saw him giving instructions to little Abdelilah earlier, and he'd produced some religious justification too: such entertainments, he said, properly belong to the hours of darkness, and thus there may be no feeling that the performance intrudes on the time or space proper to the practice of religion.

Obviously you can't play host to the whole city – not even after Prudhomme's cultural wizard has worked his magic on the courtyard. The Sultan is both sponsor and guest of honour: he and his retinue, and his brother the Caliph and his retinue, and obviously the Glaoui and his retinue, are audience enough. Then of course the diplomats in Marrakech are to be squeezed in, lucky old us. And prominent figures from the city: the leading judges and merchants, because the whole point of the performance is the palace entertaining and hosting the city. Also among the prominent figures, the palace will invite some of the men of religion: to respect them, to reassure them, and because everyone enjoys the circus.

On the question of invitations, at least, there is no dispute: Prudhomme is glad the performance is happening and does not care who invites as long as we remember who made it happen; Klug must be able to prove to Berlin that German money has served to advance German interests, and that means German backing for the Sultan's retinue and activities; the palace wants to demonstrate its autonomy; and His Majesty just wants to see the giraffe.

Drifting through the palace today, I happened to catch little Abdelilah in his new glory. The dear fellow has made himself the embodiment of the relationship between France and the palace: not only the intermediary in practice, but the image of their intermingling. He behaves like the perfect palace official: bustling, humble, cautious, devout, and he wraps all that in a traditional cloak. He speaks for the ideas of France, and – in admiration, or just to get into the mood – he suffers tight European patent leather shoes and a collar and neck-tie under his cloak, and is perhaps the first native of Marrakech to wear spectacles. I glimpsed him tête-à-tête with the vizier, and behind the vizier a line of clerks: Abdelilah was deferential and attentive, head bowed towards a superior as ever; but the clerks were noting down his every word.

It seems my old preacher man, dear Sa'id, is really going to be executed as part of the proceedings; bit grim.

☫

Eva can't find the circus.

She's set off this morning fairly sure about where it's encamped. But the alleys no longer lead where she expects. She comes out through the fat pink walls onto a road she doesn't recognize. Retreats into the familiar scented fug of the city; tries again.

She's forgotten.

Or perhaps the circus has moved. She tries to remember the profile of the ground from when she last visited; the tree near which she exercised. But ground always looks different before, during and after the circus has been there. Was this ground made barren by the men and animals trampling over it, or by a thirsty god? Were those shrubs stripped of foliage by horses or by wind? Do the leaves on that tree indicate the presence of a non-existent giraffe?

More unsettling than any of this: she, as much as anyone, used to be the circus – to be sought by visitors, to be found. Now she is a visitor, trying to find it; and she's not even sure she wants to.

Somewhere beyond the edge of a different part of the city, she's walking through a vagabond settlement. Desert gypsies have tied their animals under a tree. A flock of sheep waits permission to enter the city and be slaughtered. A hollow brown woman has found shade under a ruined cart to suckle her baby. A flock of children erupts screaming from behind another cart, chasing a football. The football rolls past Eva, and she sees that it is punctured but still holding its shape; a skull of some kind. Two men are slumped against a crate, too lethargic to move their heads; their eyes follow her as far as they can. More animals – horses – and the smell of animals. A find-the-lady sharp is rooking a couple of passers-by; Eva spots his stooge – not just what he's doing, but the same style and cloth of loose trousers he wears. It's life, of a kind, and human community. A dozen yards farther on, a juggler is entertaining some children: a lemon and an orange and a tomato appear in turn over his head, or perhaps one fruit is hanging there and forever changing colour. More long-suffering wagons; crates of unknown cargo.

The tides of sand have washed up these survivors: braver, luckier travellers and what's left of their possessions. They've been worn down almost to nothing, but if they can get into the city life may flourish in them again.

The ground is battered and used up. The people are scrabbling for a foothold, like to be blown away at any moment. It's still life, and where there is life there is entertainment. Under another tree, a circle of listeners have conjured a story-teller.

'Come!' says a big dark face, working hard to produce even a single word of English. 'Magic – horse!'

Even in extremity, there's imagination and the promise of a coin. Eva smiles at it, feels her curiosity glow, nods and follows.

Behind a makeshift screen of canvas, two children are gaping at the magic horse – until the woman chivvies them away. She beams at Eva, mimes a coin in her hand, mimes patting the magic horse.

Eva recognizes Otelle the zebra. Then she recognizes the dark woman – from her first night in the city; from the wagon with Mama Zana.

The circus finds Eva.

Olga has gained a gorgeous long frock in Marrakech, lace layered and sculpted and causing her much anxiety as it trails in the dust. And that's not all: they embrace, first shy and then happy, and Eva has a second look, and knows that the frock is heroically corseting up many weeks of Moroccan pastries. Olga is eventually pressed to admit, bitterly, that Magda is still happily married; there is talk of a return to Europe, the possibility of a family.

Shevzod does not appear. He has doubled in size, we hear. He spends most of his time in the mighty bed, we hear. Eva remembers the two boys, wonder and reverence, trailing around after the vast Asian monster. We hear he has also doubled in strength. Eva knows that, regardless of size or strength, his pride will bring him to the performance.

Someone is moving among the horses. To Eva's different eyes, Johanna looks no different. As ever, life blows through her with the wind and leaves no trace.

Salomon looks a hundred years old, wizened and darkened and now made only of sinew and spite. Today there is more chance of a payout and a fight here; so here he is. The raffia cords holding the lions' cage together have frayed down to their last strands, and Salomon teases at them and grins malicious at anyone who dares to come near. Ras and Negus look as dusty and shabby as their keeper, and even hungrier to perform.

There's no Jan. Eva remembers the face in the market alley: embarrassment; arrogance. She hasn't expected him to return. We hear different things: what he's up to, what he calls himself, what he means. In his effort to reveal to the world its soul, Eva knows he has found an alternative to clowning; another guise for hope and despair than Pierrot.

No one expects the Maestro.

☖

JOURNAL OF THOMAS SOMERLEIGH

Tonight, then. We gather at the palace this morning as usual, but circus preparation is the only thing doing. Most of the regulars are relaxed, and silent. They know it's happening, they have no chance of influencing it, and there's a half-day-holiday mood. 'You think it was like this before you fought the battle of Waterloo?' murmurs McKenna, 'or signed the Treaty of Westphalia?' I'm not really following him. To my irritation I've been dragged back into the circus admin. 'Maybe the moments before the charge of your Light Brigade.'

Prudhomme and Abdelilah have insisted that I sit next to them. The Sultan has commanded I shall arbitrate on any disagreements over the content of the performance. Prudhomme sees me as useful reinforcement of his insistence that the performance shall happen. Abdelilah sees me as a restraining influence on Prudhomme, on behalf of all the unmentioned fears roaming the palace corridors.

I know I can't interfere, and wouldn't even if I could; but I've got to have something concrete to put in the blasted telegram to Tangier, and table-placing will do.

Prudhomme is in a fever of excitement – giddy like a child – like a child going to the circus for the first time. He's so close now. He has made himself an impresario, a *tricolore* genie to satisfy the Sultan's whim. He's going to

313

succeed for France; he can see it clear now. He has endured his last anxious three a.m. Never again will he have to wake alarmed that he only dreamed this opportunity.

He sees danger in every corner; opposition in every open mouth. 'Bonjour, *excellence*', murmurs little Abdelilah, and Prudhomme glares rigid at him, daring him to follow the words with some hint of a problem.

Even in his fever, Prudhomme knows what he's doing. The muscle-movements of bureaucratic procedure are innate after decades. 'As we stand on the threshold of our success, with all prepared for the circus performance tonight, I felt it most important that we have a serious conversation, to ensure that we all feel fully informed.' It sounds like a long conversation, and around the room each man sighs inwardly. 'As we guide our Moroccan friends in their journey of stability and international credibility, it is our own consensus that must remain pre-eminent.' Gods, are his hands actually shaking as he grips the paper? 'However long it takes, we must all feel that our views have been properly represented.' It's not a smile he makes: his teeth are clenched in strain, eyes pleading. 'Now, we are all busy men. We have I think no formal points of agenda...' His tone invites agreement from Abdelilah, but he doesn't even glance at the little Moroccan. 'And thus we have the maximum of flexibility.' Interrupted before he could speak, Abdelilah merely nods busily, and unseen. 'As soon as our discussion is complete we may get back to work.' Around the room, we are becoming optimistic that this might not go on so long. 'The arrangement of this evening is the product of many weeks of careful consideration and professional judgement. All is ready. When there is no further comment, we should waste no more of our time.' More optimistic now. 'His Majesty is waiting with most charming impatience for reassurance.' A hint of a smile at His Majesty's charm.

McKenna murmurs into the moment: 'A word if I may, Mon-sieur', and Prudhomme absolutely jumps. Not American disapproval; not now. 'A word of support.' It surely can't be support; America hasn't spoken once in all these weeks of wrangling. 'Our compliments for your work, Mon-sieur, to get the thing to this point.' Always the easy plurality for the Americans, the assumed unity; but there can be no compliment for Prudhomme, not if it forces him to lose control of the conversation for a heartbeat longer. He is grinning at McKenna like a man surprised in the middle of a heart attack. 'We remain firm believers in the power of the international concert. We want to see Morocco fitting properly into the bigger system, and that means stability and a functioning state. The international concert is the best guarantee of that, and whatever else happens the concert must be preserved.'

The American, like the rest of us, wants to cover his back. As I watch Prudhomme's agony of courtesy, I wonder if McKenna might be deliberately spinning out the platitude.

Prudhomme jumps in in the instant the sentence finishes; clutching the full-stop like a drowning man with a life-buoy. 'Typically a most effective summation, my dear colleague!' Any warmth is overwhelmed by the snapped intensity of the words. 'And a helpful reminder' – he risks taking a breath at last, in the middle of a sentence where there's less chance of interruption – 'of the power of our cohesion as a group!'

Reyes, a little ragged this morning after some seediness of night, sneezes – and Prudhomme gapes at him as if he were the first Prussian turning up at Waterloo.

Reyes pulls out a silk handkerchief, and snorts into it. We all watch; wait.

Eventually he emerges from his handkerchief, and waves a vague apology with it.

Prudhomme has lost control of his breathing. 'I thank...' – gasp – 'er, you. Thank, that is...' – gasp – 'all of you. It really is' – gasp – 'most promising, this collegiality of ours, this...' – gasp – 'consensus. Now if colleagues are sure that there really' – the word hit unnaturally, almost a squeak – 'is no further comment then I ought immediately to go and reassure His Majesty.'

How to describe that 'really' of Prudhomme's?

The suave mendacity of it, all of us entirely aware how hard he has worked to avoid any comment at all. The desperate hope, a man reflecting on his sins as he faces judgement. The delicate glass-bubble fragility of it.

Klug coughs.

Instinctively I look back to Prudhomme. For a moment I wonder if he might actually have had a heart attack.

Klug has been oddly silent. Or shrewdly silent. He can't change it; he's going along with it.

The cough has been neatly injected into the moment when Prudhomme was smiling at the company and drawing breath, and his muscles were preparing to gather his papers and lift himself out of danger.

Klug stands.

Next to me, Prudhomme's whole body is electric with alarm. He's not smiling or breathing now.

Klug makes a little bow, and says: 'Once again Germany offers her compliments to France for this performance, and confirms that all the necessary bureaucracies are in hand to support its success.'

Silence. We wait for the horror of the real sentence.

Klug sits.

Prudhomme gives out a great gasp, head above the waves again.

I wonder what Klug's up to.

◌

In the café on the corner, where the maze of alleys that make up Marrakech market empties onto the great square, the corner where the granite stones have been polished and worn into the ground by centuries of bare feet, morning is at its busiest and hottest. The square does not exist: it is the space between things that exist around it; it is the people that fill the space, and how they fill it.

After the first bustle of morning and as the heat begins to thicken, tomorrow the rhythms of the royal palace will slow. But not today. It is his habit, in this lull, to walk out into the city and to drink a tea with his acquaintances. Tomorrow he may do so again; but not today.

Not to be indiscreet, but everyone's a bit too anxious for that sort of thing today. No conversation: no café.

Or perhaps this particular silence is heard in the mountains and the desert, waiting to reclaim the empty space.

𝕎

The dark woman, sitting on the back of the wagon, observing and absorbing, she too has heard a story of Ali; but its form doesn't really work on the page.

𝕎

So, dear listener: let us slip together through the warm dusk of Marrakech. Be a grain of sand, drifting over the cobbles towards the great square. Be the mind of the Glaoui, seeing all and hearing all and knowing what to think. Be the breeze, fluttering behind the curtain and making a straying girl shiver. Be the tale, spreading from lip to ear through the city. Be the anticipation.

After all of these weeks – and your patience is appreciated – we are but one hour away from the circus performance.

The foreigners are finishing their suppers: performances of European formality to remind themselves who they're supposed to be; flirtatious loungings, to remind themselves who they could be, especially later, after the show, when we're all in party mood. Suits have been brushed; moustaches have been trimmed; extra drinks have been drunk; telegrams have been prepared in outline.

Here is Thomas Somerleigh, his journal entry composing itself in his head as he walks easy through the evening –

This, it turns out, is where I belong. This twilight. Between the heat of the day and the cold of night. Between the crusty formalities of London, and anything too savage or badly plumbed. Walking between the diplomatic quarter and the market alleys. An Englishman abroad; a travelled man among my insular compatriots at home. The son of my parents and my faith and my fields of home, and yet comfortable here. Robert Louis Stevenson – wasn't it? – went off to an island. The journey is the destination, that sort of approach. I shall invest in some good Jermyn Street boots when I'm next in London; I shall pick up one of these Moroccan robe things as a dressing-gown, or perhaps something native by way of a cravat. Bread seller in his usual spot hawking his last loaves; hallo old chap – no, tomorrow morning perhaps – a contented routine among the exotic.

Brahim the poet desperate to meet me, so here I am, in my rightful place in these evening streets. His message sounded very het up – urgent; matter of life and death; public safety – no one else he can speak to. I knew immediately what it would really be about – grim old business, this, with the worthy Sa'id – and I knew I would have to disappoint him. But that's the job, isn't it? And the poor chap's almost certainly right: I'm probably the only person in Marrakech who'll listen to him. Doubt many other foreign diplomats have this kind of relationship with a local. Doubt any Moroccan official would give him a hearing – more likely chuck him in the dungeon to join Sa'id. And so my day will have been diplomatic ritual this morning, and exotic curiosity later tonight, and in the middle this engagement with the real concerns of a real Moroccan. A rummy kind of existence, but distinctive and interesting and I can be it.

As so often, my journey took me across the little square that seems informally to represent the boundary between the palace-diplomatic district and the market sprawl. Some smarter houses, probably successful merchants rather than officials. Couple of cafés for when one wants atmosphere instead of formality. In the twilight: the glowing rectangles of lamp-lit windows; the pools of life and warmth from the cafés; the trees overhead with their leaves black against the sky or ghostly in the light; walking past the gateway to the garden of whatever palace it is, the sultry scent promising the fruit trees within.

The figures and faces of evening: the hooded gowns gliding to and fro, monkish guardians of mysteries; eyes or teeth flashing white out of a shadowed cowl, enthusiasm of courtesy or invitation; a few Europeans at the café tables, faces open and unmysterious, clothing conventional. I was halfway across the square when I had to stop to let a woman pass in front of me: rather taller than the average, head uncovered, pale face, clenching a gown of some sort tight around her. The Belgian dancer woman, and looking even more grumpy and forbidding than ever. One doesn't want to simplify, but surely the point of dancing is to be pleasing to the audience – enticing even. This girl always looks like she wants to punch someone; it made me more curious to see her performance later.

Eva, meanwhile, is walking the alleys with unfamiliar unease. She's had the impression, recently, that she feels at home in these soft suggestive streets – the scents, fabrics, the friendly curiosity, the uncertainties and possibilities in every turn and shadow. But tonight, in an hour or so, she will be obliged to be an Eva she no longer recognizes. Assia asked about supper, and Eva had to remember what her habit was before performance. Tonight she must be that Eva. Assia expects it. Professionalism demands it.

So – a few bits of fruit pushed into her stomach; a failed attempt to seem cheery and assured to Assia, who waves her off as if to marriage or to war – she has hurried out into the Marrakech twilight to find Eva the dancer. She must force herself into that role, like a costume grown too tight. It feels so wrong. She knows this, and it sickens and grieves her as she wanders streets that become less known with each step. You inhabit dance. You become dance. You don't put it on like a mask or a perfume. Where is that Eva? And who is this who hunts her? If she is supposed to be that Eva, then whatever and wherever she is now must be wrong. Marrakech is yet another wayside town, passed in a night, and now she must bid farewell to the brief glimpses of human friendship it offered. Move on.

A square – space, breath. People – an audience? a friendly audience? or just strangers? She passes the Englishman – she has to check twice to remember the unremarkably pleasant face. He's looking rather earnest. And – the clothes, the complexion, the anxious introspective expression, the distinctive combination of bad posture in the shoulders and over-brisk stride – he's looking totally out of place. As he no doubt always is.

And here, alone at a café table, is Giesberts.

Somerleigh again, narrating his evening as he goes –

Brahim, as promised, was waiting at the second café. Not sitting; probably hesitates to when he hasn't got his foreign acquaintance with him. As soon as our eyes met, he turned away and started down one of the alleys that leads towards the heart of the market. Odd. I followed. No doubt all part of his anxiety. Poor chap distressed, seeing spies in every doorway and unfamiliar face. Best to play along:

show respect for him, and also get more out of him. For all his poetical and political flights of fancy, Brahim speaks for the real Morocco; one of the real Moroccos, anyway. The kind of insight that gives weight to a telegram.

A few yards, and another turn down a smaller alley. Real cloak-and-dagger stuff. Obviously one goes carefully, but in all honesty aren't I happier doing this sort of thing in this sort of place, instead of endless stiff-collared protocols in Berlin or Brussels? I'd caught up a little now. He stopped, and pulled aside a curtain, and the light from behind it caught his face: serious; manly; business-like. 'Come', he said. 'Let us do what we must.' He led the way through the doorway.

Hands gripped my shoulders and wrenched my arms back and pushed me through after him.

Eva has only a moment – she knows she has a moment only – to decide if she wants Giesberts to see her.

He looks as she remembers him. He is a study in successful expatriatism – distinctively himself, deliberately aloof from what is alien, and yet adapted comfortably. In a moment he will look round and see her. She sees the practical style and the fit body, natural on the wrought-iron chair. She remembers his body, and hers with his.

Giesberts looks round. She sees his eyes widen and narrow again as he sees her. What was that? she wonders. Surprise? Embarrassment? Admiration? It's important I know what that was.

He half stands. It's a gesture of courtesy – an instinct, but also a deliberate refusal to humble himself more than is required.

To toss her head and stride on would be childish; a surrender of the space and the moment to him. To stay standing and talk would be demeaning; a maid's enforced respect. Eva rests her fingers a moment on the back of an empty chair, and then swirls down into it. An unexpected thrill: in that moment, she was Eva the dancer, fluid and sure. She looks at him – confidence – and then she glances around the square – relaxation – and then she looks at him again – equality.

Her relationship with Giesberts, and the end of her relationship with Giesberts, were matters of her choice. Eva is an adult; Eva is independent.

He considers her. With the familiarity of an old relationship, but none of its intimacy, he says: 'You look well.'

At least it's not bitterness. Better the merchant's appraisal than the lover's reproach.

She feels her own poise in the chair. And then revulsion: this evening more than any other, she has needed that empty compliment; it has warmed and then alarmed her. I am a dancer, she thinks. Tonight at least, I can be a dancer. A dancer's legs are such fragile things.

Giesberts snaps his fingers to summon the waiter, without even checking to see if he's there: he wants to be suave; her presence is making him suave. 'What do you drink?' he asks her.

'No,' she says; 'thank you. I want plenty of time to be ready for the performance tonight. I only stopped to say hallo.' She stands. 'I am happy to see you well.' I too am without bitterness.

Now he has her whole height to admire. 'Fine,' he says; 'so we walk a few steps together.'

Fine. Hard to refuse, anyway. I am mature, I am relaxed. My heart moves with the same assurance my legs do.

'But of course:' he says as he stands; 'tonight you are back to being the dancer again.' He's looking at her again, down at her, as if considering the effect of a new perspective.

Yes, tonight I damn well am the dancer again.

No, this does not have to be a going back.

Eva nods, shrugs; starts to walk on – tentative, testing if he really is coming with her, not wanting to be rude but not wanting to seem to care.

He really is coming with her. He gestures her forwards, validating her first step.

Eva moves well. She knows she moves well.

'So, dancing again!' She shrugs at it. 'Tonight, all shall enjoy your strength and your beauty!'

Something else she remembers now: how I hide a part of myself away, so that even as they stare at my ankles and my hips and my breasts, they shall not see everything.

'I suppose I wanted to take you away from this; to protect you, to purify you.' Yes, I suppose you did. Only, you saw these as positive gestures. 'I suppose I was wrong. You are back to your true nature.' Oh yes. A few more steps in silence, into the garden of whatever palace it is. 'This is what I remember, from when I first looked at you.' He stops, and it obliges her to stop, and to turn to look at his outline in the gloom, and to be looked at. 'This body of yours. This physicality. This passionate reality.'

Lamplight or moonlight is shimmering at the edges of his dark bulk; illuminating teeth, and the eyes that gleam wide and then are squeezed out.

His hand comes up, but does not touch her. Instead, it glides and waves down the length of her torso, as if feeling her aura; as if conjuring her curves.

I am a creature of admirable poise and spirit.

'Well then. Shall we say just one kiss – to prove that we are friends, and free?'

Ah: apparently I am a creature of admirable poise and spirit.

A knife at Somerleigh's neck, his hands tied behind him, handkerchief stuffed in his mouth, journal thoughts tumbling desperate in his head –

Diplomatic protest – Mustn't show it hurts – I know Brahim and he knows me he won't let any harm come to me he's a poet for God's sake – Benefit of the civilizing mission chaps like him learn to behave like humans – Don't hurt me please don't hurt me – Here's real life and no mistake sort of thing you only get in the toughest memoirs – If you'd just let me speak this is how we do things let me speak!

'If only you had understood, Englishman. If only you had listened.'

His hand round my neck – His hand in my hair – His face so close to mine – Beautiful eyes – You see? This is true brotherhood! He knows me – He's heard my sincerity – He likes me – He won't let them hurt me!

'To you we are just scenery, for the play you perform with your European friends. Tonight's show is in Africa. Tomorrow you will be in South America, or India, or Turkey. The same conventions of drama; the same jokes. And always the white man, he has the lead role.'

This serves you nothing – The British Government will take revenge – Why did I ever leave home? Let me speak!

'No one shall hear you. So much suffering in these streets, my friend. So many stories unheard. We have no time for rhetoric.' – He's looking sorry – He's patting my cheek – That's a good sign isn't it? – 'It is the great pretence of your age, is it not? That you govern yourselves, and you govern us, by reason. That your words are clever, and true, and if we are too stupid to understand your clever words you send one of your gunboats or battalions to show us how true they were.'

No! Don't turn away! Come back, dear Brahim, please! – Don't leave me with these unseen arm-wrenching brutes – Put your hand in my hair again, please! – Just let me look into your eyes again, and you'll see –

'My idea was you would be our hostage. I have my seat in the audience for your circus; the seat you very kindly arranged for me. I thought perhaps I could make some demonstration or announcement there. But my colleagues correctly point out it is already too late to save dear Sa'id. So.' – No! Don't come too quickly to that so! We haven't talked enough to conclude anything – 'What is your European phrase? Real politics? Tonight, it is more useful that you die. It is written. Perhaps there will be a violation also; something truly humiliating. You always represent these barbarisms as non-European, so it will be instructive for those who find you to see that Europeans are not immune, if they come here.'

But I'm a nice chap I never wanted to hurt anyone if I'm nice why are you mean to me it's not fair!

'And do not think this is one of your European tragedies. No: tonight, one of the pieces of scenery falls on your head.'

For Eva, it all goes wrong so quickly.

And the thing – a kiss that might be a pleasant transaction between equals becomes an invasion of her throat, her lips forced back against her teeth, and now his teeth tearing at her throat – that's most infuriating – his hands are an admiring possessing stroke of her cheek and then a passionate clutch of her shoulders and then clenching squeezing piercing her arms and pushing her back and down – is that – just don't damage me don't damage me this body is all I have and important to me, men's muscles are such gorgeous flesh why must they use them for violence? – this – a species who can't undo a blouse button without ten minutes' fumbling can overcome a belt buckle and button-fly one-handed in just a few seconds even if you're trying to rip their eyeballs out; the Lord gives them this evolutionary advantage, or perhaps their tailors do – was so – I can tell myself that I want this, this is not a story of my victimhood, much easier and there's a chance I'll be able to wear the dress again; and maybe I'm wrong, maybe this is pleasurable – tediously – But this is not who I am supposed to be! – fucking predictable.

Eva doesn't need Assia's warnings or Olga's traumas or Morocco's narrative tradition to know how this goes.

In the café on the corner, where the maze of alleys that make up Marrakech market empties onto the great square, the corner we're so familiar with, tomorrow morning will reach its busiest and hottest as usual. The square is only the stories we tell in it; the square is, after all, just a framing device.

We know by now that after the first bustle of morning and as the heat begins to thicken, the rhythms of the royal palace slow. We know the habit, in this lull, to walk out into the city and to drink a tea with acquaintances. Tomorrow morning we shall experience it again, as always.

Not to be indiscreet, we may say, but...

A body will have been found in a secluded corner of the garden of one of the smaller palaces. The charm of the setting — fruit scent, old stone, blossom, dew — will add extra poignancy to the brutality of the death. The smashed skull. The savaged throat. The violation. The mutilation. Who had this creature been? What dreams had died with them? What vanity or ambition was punished so harshly? What lessons may we learn?

Two bodies, we will learn, may in fact have been found. A man and a woman, of course. So different: what a mystery. So similar: what a unity. Ah, the stories we may tell of two bodies found together... The anger. The revenge. The betrayal. The despair. The beautiful self-destruction of the impossible. The punishment of the faithless. The price of sin.

Bodies, you say? Well, of course: confining ourselves to one particular garden is good for a tale, but it's hardly logical. The gardens of Marrakech will be fertile with bodies tomorrow, and the dead-end alleys, and the building sites. And don't start on what's been going on outside the walls or we'll never finish; does your tea need refreshing? The fury of the followers of old Sa'id has been unleashed on the complacent city. Those who wanted to suppress old Sa'id and his followers have seized the momentum of his death to finish the job. The slaves have had enough and run amok, or the Jews, or the tribes, or the dark men from beyond the mountains; the people you most fear, you will find that they have seized their opportunity. The Glaoui, of course, is behind it all and has contrived the night to impose his will. Or some foreign schemer, with his own particular tale in mind. The evil spirits conjured by the Sultan in his foolishness are loose. The lions of the circus have escaped their cage and roam the streets of Marrakech, executing a wild poetic justice.

Or perhaps this particular conversation takes place among your acquaintances, with some alternative form of your own inclination.

Tonight, in some deserted bit of ground in Marrakech, an animal is being slaughtered.

In most of the deserted bits of ground in Marrakech, some similar suffering is happening tonight. The judges will interest themselves in so few of the bodies; the birds and street-dogs will deal with the rest. The city cultivates life, and then reabsorbs it.

The animal's struggles are fitful, futile. Sometimes it spasms and the butchers thump it and kick it and adjust their grip. Sometimes it slumps passive, limbs bumping over the earth, still hopeful that by cooperating it will win their kindness. It cannot shout or speak; it mewls and whimpers, and this is how we know that all animals have nightmares.

The animal has collapsed for the last time. Now its trembling is continuous, and a thin whine. It's just waiting. A grip tightens; a knife rises. The last fragments of consciousness: moonlight and shit and fruit trees and hoping it will be quick.

Eva has been slaughtered so many times. She knows this bruising and this anger so sickeningly well, but her reactions are all animal. She is feeling only. Ache in shoulders and back as they sprawl on the ground – Pain of arms pressed down under his hands – Pain where clumsily he knelt on her thigh muscle – Pain when she tries to wriggle to protect her precious ankles and knees from his weight and Slap sharp across her face – Cold of cold earth under neck and thigh and Cold of the naked shock that this is happening – Hot of hell I want to rip your head off and crush it with a rock and Hot of weak wet waking loins on a summer evening – Bitterness because I must have done something wrong for this shit to happen – Hatred because what else can there be in the world when this can happen? – A nauseating treacherous blending of brutality and pleasure, because my body was created precisely for this process, I am to feel joy, biology only confirms what the men have always said, this is my purpose and I must do it right, this being squashed and wrenched and slapped and dug into is my ecstasy, sometimes in the forbidden privacy of my body I have felt these tremors as glorious and can I make them feel the same and I must, give the audience what they want I must and then they leave me alone, you bastard roaring grunting rummaging bully I hate you for you punch and foul my only private beauty, and damn the world it all hurts now. Feeling, too much feeling, and none of it to be trusted any more.

They're writhing, and panting softly, each so focused: he with the fierce dedication he devotes to regulating the machinery for the cold store is working himself into the necessary frenzy, he knows what his triumph is and he will prove himself by attaining it; she's just trying not to get hurt, not to encourage and not to obstruct, knowing that just a bit of real pleasure from her will make this less painful. And then he stops and for one obscene fraction of a second Eva –

Giesberts has heard something – some animal close by in the garden – animals – rustling and scuffling and whining and he's looking and his face in the moonlight is guilt and embarrassment and his grip is slack. One of the many admirable features of Eva's legs is their combination of suppleness and strength, and now she exploits this to drive her knee up into his groin. He rolls and gasps and staggers half upright and the look is cow-stupid and she screams her hatred at him and then the look is wolf-savage and now he really is going to kill her, scrap of woman found dead in a garden and probably abused first it so often happens; but again he hears the other animals and he's looking and she's wriggling away from him and turns back and his blood is still hot enough that he's wondering if he might just but the other animals and socially a bit awkward now and a final glare at her really let him down all her fault and he turns and hurries away. By the time he's reached the gate he'll have rearranged the smart hard-wearing suit, and Luther Giesberts the prosperous merchant will stroll contented across the square re-imagining what has just happened, and when Eva follows she will find him sitting in the same chair with the same poise – easy control and innocence – and the whole encounter can begin again. Panting, frustrated and furious and wanting a mother's hug and wanting to burn a church, Eva lurches upright.

In this cursed night of godless show and restless spirits, a pale gasping wild half-naked witch rising out of the earth with a shriek and a face to destroy mankind will be a hell of a story tomorrow, told timid-reverent and a drink or two later told bold-horny, and no one will ask what we were up to in that garden.

Eva has disturbed something else; somethings. A bark of surprise and growls of alarm and she shrieks her surprise and she shrieks her refusal to be a weaker spirit any longer this night and she wants to be left to prowl this garden alone, safe in her cage until she chooses to be free again, and there's a cursing and a gathering and two creatures scramble out of the earth and go cantering away into the darkness.

Now she sees a body on the ground: a lump of empty flesh the scavengers were feeding on, slumped and already half-absorbed by the soil.

The body gasps a breath in. Then a longer gasp, and longer, hoarse and quavering and hurt and frail. She can't make out what kind of beast it is. It seems to be about to die, and Eva finds that convenient because at the moment she doesn't want a single other living creature in her world.

The beast is oddly hunched, and seems to have scraps of cloth mixed in with the dirt wrapped round it. Now the beast spasms, and wriggles, and suddenly begins to move more freely, and it scuttles a few paces away from her and at last totters upright.

THE JOURNAL, later: At last I managed to wriggle free and the brutes scarpered.

First thing I saw, bizarrely, was the Belgian dancing girl, looking like something the tide had washed up. Looking, indeed, just as wild as when I'd seen her monstering Reyes. Confess I was still hellish shaken – more by Brahim's betrayal, perhaps, than by getting roughed up. But the girl seemed rather upset by whatever she'd been up to, and one has to offer the strong shoulder to lean on.

I badly needed a change of kit. Also – unsettling business – I badly needed to be in my own place with the door locked behind me. When you've been in a scrap – playground and so forth – always a bit of a shock. Form square; circle the wagons. And it became clear that the girl was in more of a state than I realized. So, protocol be damned and priority on these occasions is just get them safe and if Youssef or Sir G. don't like it they can go hang. But what in hell was Brahim thinking? Did he really think he could threaten me into something? Useful lesson, perhaps: have I misjudged his friendship?

Deep breath. The German trader chappie happened to be sitting in the square and, funnily enough, the sight of him helped restore balance a bit. Courteous nod from him as we walked past – and naturally one reciprocates – and I felt that sense of European civility like a fresh breeze. This is how we survive. This is how we will pull Morocco along after us.

Eva has known she will see Giesberts again. Her whole existence has become this certainty. Her mind is focused only on how she can possibly see Giesberts again, what the world will require of her in that moment; all the things that her face must show in that moment, and not show.

She sees Giesberts again. It is so completely what she has been expecting, the universe in that moment achieves such an utter harmony, a flawless lemon swelling in front of her, growing bright and bloating in her gut and bursting – and she vomits in her mouth and stumbles and clutches the passive arm beside her and swallows all the hatred again and stumbles out of the square.

Giesberts saw her. Giesberts saw them.

What has Giesberts really seen? A man escorting a woman. Confirmation that, after all, she wanted what he was offering. This, too, is the harmony of the universe: that Eva must immediately and always be with another man.

'Listen to me.' The Englishman is not listening to her. He's walking automatically, dazed, down the alley away from the horror in the square. She has to grab him by the shoulder and scream it into his face. 'You ridiculous inoffensive pudding man, listen!'

As from far off, the sound comes faintly to him. He looks vaguely interested.

'I've been…' – she can't say it; the words choke her. Instead she can only spit: 'A man. But tonight I have to perform. Tonight I will be a dancer, whatever else the world wants. You touch me, you look at me, you think of me, I rip off your genitals and burn them in front of you.

But I need your help.' She feels the sick rising in her throat with the words.

'Right ho', says the Englishman, rather quietly. 'Sorry. Yes.' She stands waiting – if she must stand waiting a second longer her betrayed cunt will explode across this Marrakech back-street – and glaring. 'My – my place is quite close by. If you don't mind…'

Eva doesn't mind anything anymore. And perhaps life in this obscenity of an evening may yet be possible, and that possibility kindles a moment of self-possession that makes her, just faintly, just for a moment, love herself again. 'Thank you,' she says evenly, 'that will be most satisfactory.'

THE JOURNAL, later (though it's all a bit of a muddle now, isn't it?): No sign of Youssef. Blighter's probably out selling the stuff he's pinched off me, or trying to catch a glimpse of the circus. Or join it, for all I care.

The door has closed behind me, but for some reason I can't settle. Everything rather falling apart.

Probably having the girl with me that does it. Unsettling. You can't relax, can you, with a woman around? And this one is… wild. Unrestrained. Upset and upsetting. Touch of the red in tooth and claw.

Not sure whether it's just her and she's like this all the time, or all women are like this some of the time. No doubt why men are expected to be the steady hand; in the home and in international diplomacy. Not sure I could have this sort of thing around the house on a permanent basis. Wonder if Hortense has her moments. Benefit of protocol, indoors as well as out.

The girl prowls around. A cat that can't settle – and seems to regard me as an interloper. I rather feel I am; the state I'm in. More rattled than I realize, perhaps. Need to sort myself out.

On the rare occasions she's ever met an Englishman, Eva has wondered about their potential as lovers. Has joked about it with Olga. Her doubts have followed the traditional, humorous lines. A breed wholly without passion. A breed raised in isolation, like monks, so that neither temptation nor practical education might give them Spanish ease or German confidence.

'Drink', he says. 'Sort you out, eh?' The idea is so ludicrously inadequate to what she's feeling, what she needs, that it works. This is his diplomatic training, Eva supposes: the power of the utterly fatuous to overcome the unutterably real. In his inadequacy as doctor and as host, he begins to bounce between what she presumes are the names of drinks and reasons why they shouldn't have them, until eventually he is just mumbling to the soda siphon. She wonders how much is his distress at whatever happened in that garden, and how much is distress at her presence. At last she gets a glass of something warming, and gulps at it gratefully.

The Englishman has gulped his own drink. Now she sees him, shaking-handed, pour himself a furtive refill.

The reaction to whatever was done to him in that garden. Such things are not meant to happen to English diplomats. Such reactions are not meant to be seen by women. Under the muddy torn jacket, the shoulders have closed in on themselves.

No, not impressive lovers, nor intriguing. But – empty glass loose in his hand, wandering his home bumping into things and mumbling something about a servant – his total passivity makes him an untroubling, oddly comforting presence. Like a dog; or a piece of old furniture. A vacuum of manhood, in which a woman's character might expand or fluctuate freely. Not natural lovers, but natural husbands perhaps. She wonders how they reach the latter status without ever passing the former. They are the diplomats, of course.

Eva feels the alcohol scorching the inside of her skull. Too much, too quickly, and her mind is wandering down queasy paths. She cannot let go, she must not let go, of the self she still can be tonight. 'Excuse me...' she says. He turns, startled. He had only dreamed a woman here, and now again he must readjust to the reality.

She sees him trying to find a credible way to present the unlikely and the uncomfortable to himself. 'I'm totally lost', she says; 'I think you said you could help.' No man ever tells himself a story of his own impotence and biddability.

'Of course', he says. 'Sort you out in no time. Don't you worry.' The weary muddy shoulders straighten. 'Look – This way...' He wanders off, still clutching his empty glass. She assumes she's supposed to follow.

As she steps through a doorway she bumps into him coming out of it, a bundle of clothes in his arms. He's not offering her one of his suits, is he? She prepares to explain the nature of modern dance. 'That's me sorted', he says. 'I'll get out of your way. Bathroom through there. Use my room here to straighten yourself out. Take your time. I say, I hope it doesn't seem inapp... you know – only option – Need another drink? Probably best not. Don't want anything to eat, do you? Servant's not here – Not sure what I can – Probably out selling my...'

She's losing him again. She manages to get a word in – 'No, thank you; you've given me all I need' – and he smiles in relief and drifts off with his bundle of clothes.

The bathroom is adequate. Eva strips naked, and washes. Bare flesh and cold water: from these elementals she can start again.

His towel wrapped round her – she tells herself the mustiness is comforting – she notices his spartan toiletries. The razor is ancient, its bone handle worn. It is a father's razor, or a grandfather's. A thrifty, inherited manhood.

She feels refreshed. Renewed. Back in his bedroom, she stretches a few times. Reclaims control of herself; reclaims her right to expand and to aspire. Her legs taut, firm in their support however she chooses to glide and to swoop. Her spine twisting almost all the way round, the owl's regard. Her hands as high as she can, reaching for her heaven. She sags to a crouch, bouncing in ankles and knees and hips and shoulders. Hands flat on the floor, she straightens her legs, suppleness becoming strength up the back of her calves and her thighs. She finds she can see under his chest of drawers.

She has laid her clothes neatly across his bed, and now she approaches them as if they might be new. She sponges off the worst of the mud. The tears are not so bad. It's enough to get to the palace, where she'll be able to cast off the costume of reality and damage and start again in her dancer's outfit.

She sees a book on the table by his bed; peers at the chipped gold lettering in the leather.

Standing in the doorway, pulling the dress up and wriggling her arms into it, she says: 'You keep a journal?'

He actually jumps. It looks as though he has been trying to do up his tie while holding onto his glass. The effect of the unexpected voice has consequently been even more catastrophic. He gapes at her, wide-eyed.

Was the leather book such a secret? Was that yet another drink? Is it so atrocious that he hasn't got his jacket on yet? Is her one bare shoulder so disquieting?

Eva wonders if this is what it would be like to be married – to an Englishman, anyway: making of oneself a perpetual shock; having to creep around one's home invisibly, so as to preserve the purity of his cosy bachelor existence. This Englishman may or may not be a virgin; but he's certainly never lived with a woman. It will be a terrible violation for him.

An ugly memory. For a moment Eva has the urge to burn his bookcase and piss on his carpet.

'Oh... no', he says; 'not really. Well – I mean – sort of; yes. Only to... you know.'

'No.'

'Well...' He gives up on both drink and tie, and stands rather dishevelled and lost. 'Just a basic record: what's happened; personal reactions. Useful resource.'

She walks purposefully towards him. 'Pardon me,' she says; 'would you mind...?' He takes a step backwards, collides with a chair and can go no farther. She turns her back on him, and offers her bare spine.

Nothing. Perhaps he has fainted. 'The fastenings are rather difficult. And if I do them up first I'll strain the dress even more.'

He mumbles something. It sounds like agreement, rather than a seizure.

'So, do you record everything? Your deepest feelings?' Eva is wondering about the state of her back: whether too many weeks of Marrakech easy living have weakened its taut musculature.

She can feel his breath against her skin. The bone at the top of her spine is prominent, exposed.

She knows her neck isn't exactly thin – Olga's is like the stem of a flower – but right now it feels very vulnerable. To the executioner's blade; to the strangler's grip; to the rather alcoholic breath of a flustered Englishman.

His fingers have a preliminary attempt at the fastening. It's more like the strangler's grip.

'Well, nothing too sordid. Not... you know, too emotional.'

He runs out of fingers, and retreats.

'Have you seen the emu?'

Unwelcome diversion. 'Oh – I'm... I'm not sure. It's supposed to be quite a character.'

'What do you think of the Sultan's collection? The pianos, and the cameras, and the carriage that was left out in the rain.'

'Well... He's a decent chap really, H.M. And in his way he has quite a scientific interest. Intelligent curiosity.'

'Great men tend to publish their diaries, don't they?'

'Well, you know – not great, obviously – But I wonder whether there might be... some interest – you know, a perspective on an alien culture. Journal of a journey, that sort of thing. Moroccan Musings. Adventures in the Atlas. Desert Diplomat.'

Word-play makes him more confident, and he tries a bolder lunge at the fastening.

'So when you write, you're thinking other people will read it?' Over-bold, it turns out. She re-straightens the dress.

'Well...' Silence. He's thinking, or just summoning up the courage for the final assault on her collar. 'I suppose... yes.'

His fingers move in for the kill.

'And so sometimes you... adjust what you write? For your... diplomacy. So your reader understands what they're supposed to. To avoid too much emotion.'

'Well... Yes, of course.' The fingers fly to safety. He has found that, accidentally, he has succeeded with the fastening.

'Thank you very much – So...' Eva turns, looks up at the Englishman. 'You mean that, in the end, we can't be sure that any of it's really true?'

He gazes down at her. He looks rather lost again; faintly wild. Too much Belgian dancing girl; too much truth.

'Oh', she remembers, 'I found this; under the drawers in your bedroom.' She hands him – a reward for his service – the cuff-link.

☖

THE JOURNAL, later (it doesn't really matter who's telling this bit, does it?):

Brushed down and spruced up, we strode back out into the Marrakech night. The dancing girl needed someone to escort her to her circus performance, and despite the recent kerfuffle it looked like we'd still be there in time. She was calmer now; more composed. Handsome, too, of course; athletic.

Obviously I was still a bit thoughtful after the incident with Brahim and his pals. Hell of a thing. But on with the show, as the dancer was probably saying to herself. The Moroccan evening was casting its usual spell: warmth and spice and murmur and possibility. Bit jumpy around the alley entrances, though.

The girl had stopped chattering now, too. More companionable. Reassured, perhaps, and so less nervy. We felt rather elegant, with our dress-down European styling and easy pace. For a moment I even wondered about offering her my arm. But something in her face hinted that this would be a misjudgement. Too much, of course – wrong; sending the story down a very different alley.

Truth, she wants? It took a deep breath to cross that square again. God, this is the reality, isn't it? The endless unease. Rallying a bit of oomph to overcome the demons lurking in every shadow. I've spent my life anticipating getting duffed up in an alley. Every incident on the edge of the schoolyard. Every sceptical glance on the edge of the meeting.

And so now... I was right – wasn't I? Proved my point? But does that mean I'm now more suited for being in places... with alleys – or less suited? How can one ever feel easy anywhere? Those chaps who spend decades in these dusty places – the likes of Burton, sneaking into Mecca – you'd need the skin of a rhinoceros, or inside you'd be a screaming hysteric. Unless you could kid yourself you were truly at home. That's the trick, isn't it? I fear I'm a foreigner everywhere.

As we were crossing the square I felt the Belgian girl closer to me. For a moment I thought she was going to take my arm. She couldn't know that I was a touch edgy, and she was no doubt feeling our promenade rather congenial. Funnily enough, the thought of her doing it bucked me up somewhat, and I made it across the square in one piece. But she hadn't taken my arm: she'd gripped it, round the bicep, and with each step the grip was fiercer. Perhaps just a different convention where she's from; bit eye-watering. And yet sort of companionable.

Interesting, her remarks about the journal. I wonder if, on occasion, I might have been a little too honest. Some amendment necessary – some tidying of the memories?

Eva has found the journey across Marrakech oddly congenial. Walking with the Englishman is like having an umbrella: some slight protection against the unexpected elements, and a vague sense of rightness – and otherwise unintrusive.

He escorts her confidently into what turns out to be the wrong entrance of the palace. Eva is remembering glimpses of the building from the reception: the austerity of stone; the gorgeousness of marble; the poise of the guards. She shifts her attention to the Englishman, and his confidence as he tries to talk his way in.

He is considerably more assured persuading two impressively-armed Moroccans – scimitars, would those be? – to overlook their strictest duty and let him pass than he is trying to make small-talk with a Belgian woman in his own home. It is a quiet, courteous arrogance. Giesberts would have seen confrontation from the start; would immediately have been trying to prove his force and importance. The Englishman – it takes her a moment to understand – is absolutely certain of his rightness. He knows he must be, purely because he is who he is. And so instead of the resistance that the Germans find everywhere, the Englishman only finds an occasional unfortunate who needs the way of the world politely pointing out. The imposition of will becomes remedial education in international protocol.

He wanders casually between languages – as well as helping him round linguistic obstacles, it makes him seem more persuasive and impressive – and this is a surprise. He's picked up some practical Arabic. He also – more remarkable still – has passable French.

His charm – the hypnotic power of English mumbling – persuades one of the guards to bustle off for advice or reinforcements. The other guard turns to stone in front of them, and the two foreigners are left to wait.

Silently, Eva begs the guard to hurry up. Otherwise she will have to talk to the Englishman. With the Englishman, she will have to be pleasant or she will have to be sincere. Neither will be easy to stomach.

The moments pass. The guard gazes sightless through her.

'I say,' says the Englishman, 'are you... toddling along all right now? Back on the old horse, eh? After... before.'

She can make sense of neither the words nor the emotions.

She shrugs, and feels Assia looking out of her. 'It is inevitable', she says.

Bad Eva: not pleasant; not simple. He frowns; tries to produce a question and doesn't quite succeed.

Eventually she says: 'There was a man I spent the night with.' She sees his alarm. This is not how fairy-stories are supposed to begin. It's how they often end, of course, but even then we don't go into the details; not with the English, anyway. 'Another Belgian. He had been in Africa; the Belgian colonies – the rubber plantations. At a certain moment I asked him about his work – hinted at how brave he must have been, how impressive. Always we have to...

to inflate the men, yes?' For a moment she stares at the Englishman, feels a grim satisfaction at his bewilderment. 'Never do I forget his face, as he prepared to answer.'

She sees: the face, as she has often seen it; the shabby details of the room; the flickers of light from outside against the window, the possibility of interruption or rescue. She feels: the fatness of his hand; his stubble; the blanket under her naked back; her unease.

'His face... Somehow I had asked the right question – I felt so pleased – and it was a triumph to him to be able to answer this question. But also I had opened a door to something. This story – it would be... inflicted on me; it would be a punishment, an... ordeal. He took a great breath – of pleasure, but also it was preparation for the ordeal: he was the executioner getting ready his whip or his axe. Then: "It is a hell", he said. Never do I forget the phrase; he was trying to impress me. "The things we must do to survive and to succeed... You people here at home, you cannot imagine." And because I could not imagine, he told me. Leaning over me, on that stinking mattress, he sang me his dark lullaby. The constant danger he was under. How every moment was a fight, and his hand bit harder on my shoulder because apparently now was also a fight. The difficulties of getting anything done in Congo, the demands from Brussels for greater success. The challenge of securing the respect of the natives. "If they are not to frighten you, they must fear you."'

She is not seeing the Englishman now; the performance flows. 'He was already rather drunk; emotional. And he kept on drinking. And sweating, as if he was still in Africa.' She feels his clutch, his half-excitement against her hip; she sees how his face glistened. 'He got angry again: how the natives were always up to their tricks, they were obstructive, they were stupid, they were dirty and thus always catching disease, they tried to use witchcraft to interfere with the work or to harm the managers, they poisoned their bodies so that when white men coupled with them they would be infected. I could see – I could feel, in his grip – how furious it still made him, that such people would not recognize his efficiency, his rightness. He was furious as he described the endless obligations necessary to secure the profits that people like me were apparently demanding. Did I know what it was like to whip a man until the skin slid from his back? Such a question… Did I know the pain of ordering a dozen hands hacked off so that the other hands would work at least twice as hard? Could I imagine him climbing a hill of bodies to make a speech, and could I imagine his emotions when that month his district had the best results, and was I aware that when I paid a centime less for a child's balloon this was his triumph? And this big brave horrifying man, his face collapsed in tears – in sobs – at the terrible things that… that I had made him see and do. "Do you understand?" he shouted at me. "Do you understand?" And I nodded desperately and assured him that I understood. And he shouted – he screamed – "No!" No, I did not understand; no I could not understand. He slapped me. He slapped me because I did not understand. He slapped me harder because I could not understand. He roared – like a… like a wounded beast he roared – and with a big swing of the back of his hand he struck my face again.' Her eyes are closed, her hand pressed to the cheek again. 'And then he fu–'

She opens her eyes to the audience, wary of the effect of her violence. 'What word will help you understand this? He… made love to me. With – great force; so I did not walk for a day and the next night I could only do a simple dance.' She shrugs. 'And: I did not say no to him, so…'

She considers the Englishman's paralyzed face. 'Pardon me. Better always if we dance in silence. If we answer your question with only "yes".'

The first guard emerges from the gloom of the entrance chamber, bringing a palace official. Eva remembers from

342

the reception that the more senior the person, the more simple the costume; remembers wondering what the Sultan wears. This man is in the traditional wrapping, and it's almost all white.

There are elaborate greetings between him and the Englishman, the latter extremely deferential without in any way losing the assurance that he more or less owns the place. They exchange courtesies in very formal French. Eva finds herself presented, as if she were some exotic gift brought as an offering to the host. Just as her spirit is starting to rebel at the fatuousness of it all, she realizes that she has somehow adopted her companion's comfortable *politesse*, that she is bowing, that she is murmuring eyes-lowered oriental courtesies that she can only have picked up from a provincial theatre show.

'But most certainly', says the official, his voice like the hundred-year-old French general she was once introduced to after a performance somewhere; 'Monsieur Somerleigh is appointed by His Majesty to arbitrate in all matters pertaining to the composition of tonight's performance.' Still French so the foreigners know what's being said, simple enough for the guards to understand. 'He goes anywhere he wishes with the woman.' The message is repeated in Arabic.

With another bow, and one of the guards as escort, they are welcomed into the building.

The Englishman – Somerleigh, the official said? she recalls it from some previous introduction; but now she also recalls seeing it written somewhere in his house, and the letters and sounds don't go together at all – is obviously pleased with himself. But he has only succeeded in talking himself into the wrong part of the palace complex, while she has only ever seen one chamber of it. The guard, meanwhile, has only the vaguest idea of who the two foreigners are, and keeps peeking furtively at them as if he's not even sure they're real. It can't be too long before the performance is supposed to start; to Eva, their journey through the endless succession of cool beautiful mysterious passages and chambers is more like a fairy-tale, or a dream.

She is Cleopatra in her palace, seeking the asp and dancing the swaying seductive fatal waltz with it. She is a high priestess in some Grecian temple, whirled by the spirits she has roused. She is a pagan warrior, unleashed in the ruins of Rome. Her audience see the palace around her because she has conjured it as she moves.

Now she has conjured a courtyard, small and plain and gloomy. There are formalities in the stonework around the doorways. There are centuries of wear in the undulating flagstones. But it seems less grand; less visited. She glances between the two men. The Englishman is gazing around, with a tourist's benign curiosity; occasionally he has thrown out an observation on architecture or culture unrelated to wherever they are – authority to distract from ignorance; knowledge in lieu of wisdom. He re-tells the story of the Sultan's mad collection; Eva thinks of the emu. The guard hurries beside them, struggling with his costume and weapon and the effort to keep up with the bustling diplomat and the long-legged dancer; alarmed at their trespassing and awed by whatever order the official gave him.

So who is leading the way?

Again Eva must conclude that she is: her spirit has offered the men this hidden courtyard.

'What's that, then?'

The Englishman has stopped suddenly, and points to one side of the courtyard. It is the least ornate, but the most imposing. Two fat square stone pillars support a fat square stone lintel, around a wooden door. Torches flare and rasp on either side, hinting at the fat fibres of the door timbers, the big iron studs that hold it together, the outlines of sentries. In this building of exquisite craftsmanship and refinement, the architect left this one example of raw materials in their simplest form; just to show where it all came from.

'Prison', says the escort.

A brute word to match the door. The Englishman double-checks the word in Arabic and then French.

And then, at the same moment, we say 'Where the old man is?'

This was when I had my wheeze. Close beside me, the Belgian girl was clearly distressed. She'd no doubt been told that poor old Sa'id was due for the chop during tonight's performance; can only imagine how she felt about that. And it had been preying on my mind too, of course. Now, actually seeing the entrance to this grim place...

'I must see him now, please.' Silence. Everyone shocked. 'All matters pertaining to the composition of tonight's performance.' The exact phrase used by the senior official, repeated in French and then an inspiration of correct Arabic.

It has the power of magic, or miracle. The guard is babbling something to the sentries and then the vast timber door swings open.

Bluff called. In we go.

We have dropped out of the world now. Lightning flash and stage-light trick and everything is reversed. Eva's dream is turned dark and grotesque and she does not know where she leads them. We are stumbling through a delirium of stone and cold, shadow and echo, and hurt animal moaning.

She can feel the Englishman's fear. In his heavier harder breathing. In the trembling rigidity of his arm when she clutches it. Screaming out of his silence. This breath-wavering unease is how he walks through the world.

Another corridor, another well of darkness dropping away in front of us. Step by step, the suggestion of cell doors – simple iron grilles. Behind each door... anything is possible. The mind fills each cell with horrors: our eyes tremble with their movements and torments; our ears whisper with their agonies.

At last we have stopped. Another iron grille door. Another pit of night behind it. Another version of man's malice and pain.

Eva is convinced and I am convinced that in a moment the door will open and we will be flung in. And we will never stop falling. Each hears the other's anguished breathing, clings to it as the last hint of life.

'We take him now. We escort him to the circus.' Silence. There is no one here; anywhere. 'All matters pertaining to the composition of tonight's performance.' The exact phrase again, a last desperate attempt at the magic spell.

No arm is seen opening the cell door in the darkness, no human shall have to take responsibility; yet open it is.

A gust of wind passing; a rustling through straw. The old man is only the suggestion of a body, stumbling out of the night of the cell into the evening of the corridor. He breathes an endless shallow gasp. But what lungs does he strain to fill, what flesh does he bear any more?

I didn't like to think what he might have gone through. He stumbled into me and I barely felt it; for the first fifty paces I was supporting him and he was just a sack of bones, flapping and rattling against my side.

Eva has not met the old man before, and she cannot really see him now. But she has imagined his confinement, and his tortures – and his eventual death in front of her on the stage. When in the gloom she cannot make out an eye, or a foot, she assumes it is not there. A freak of lantern-light and she glimpses a shoulder, but a moment later it has gone. She begins to understand that their reckless quest was too late: the old man is dead meat slumped in the cell, just like the bodies she saw after the desert massacre, and now she and the Englishman are trapped with death in this labyrinth because their justification for coming in here was also their justification for getting out again, and the figure between them is a mirage only, flickering and fading and leading them mad.

The old ghost becomes the guarantee of escape from the catacombs. After fifty yards, an arm round his brittle shoulders and desperate invocations in his ear begging him to come back to life and to show the way out, he begins to support himself; he walks more normally; he begins to breathe more steadily.

In the courtyard again: blinking in the relative light; seeking a dependable reality. A familiar face: 'Why, but it is dear Monsieur Somerleigh!' The voice has always been other-worldly, its strength coming from somewhere far away. Claw-hands clutching shoulders, testing the real. Eyes gazing into eyes: wonder; confirmation. 'A most interesting development, this.' Has the old man always known that this is how his story would run? 'Are you my escort to execution, Monsieur Somerleigh? So much more reassuring, when the foreign powers show their approval for a proceeding. I am honoured. And yet...'

The eyes – and there are surely two of them, black stars – consider Eva. One skeleton arm reaches up in curiosity and grips her shoulder. Squeezes. Feels her. The palm rests against her muscle; draws its warmth. The hand runs down her arm, tracing its contours and firmness. Eva feels her arm more distinctly; shivers in the sensation of being so known.

A thin smile. 'Please excuse me, Mademoiselle. I am a man trying to discover if he is alive. And also... I am a man. As we walked, I was convinced that you were an angel of paradise, that my Lord had clasped me to Him with no pain, and I was glad.'

'I... I am sorry to disappoint. This is not heaven after all.'

'Ah, but now I have seen you, perhaps this is how it will be.'

'Look, I'm sorry to butt in, but we've told the guard that we're escorting you to the performance. We ought to look like we mean it.'

And so at last out of the lost courtyard. 'Perhaps you are my dark angel after all, Monsieur Somerleigh? So mysterious, you English: watching the rest of the world from out of your sea, and deciding the fate of nations. So forbidding. They say England is very cold, no?' Still the guard shuffles and clatters alongside.

Eva's enchantment has weakened. She can no longer conjure new and infinite palace chambers. A walkway opens on one side. Through pillars, they see the courtyard of the performance. The guard has successfully escorted them all the way here. Duty done, he hurries back to his post, consigning his strange visions to their proper realm.

But the image is faulty; incomplete. Perhaps it is after all another mirage, flickering between circus bustle and empty stonework, colours and not colours, familiar faces and absences.

One hundred finely-carved wooden chairs have been arranged in rows for the audience. Perhaps a half are occupied. We recognize some of the diplomatic corps. If we have been paying attention, we recognize some of the Moroccan dignitaries. Vast banners of golden silk and crimson silk, any one of them enough to buy the circus for a year, hang against the sandstone walls and ripple in unseen breezes.

We are used to seeing the circus in Tuscan fields, Provençal town squares, Flanders wool marts, Saxon great halls, Polish forest clearings. We don't know what it's supposed to look like in a Moroccan palace. It could look like this.

Two palace servants are sweeping the empty performance area, supervised by someone we're trying to recognize but can't. In one corner of the courtyard a group of local musicians – deluxe versions of traditional costume and exquisitely-decorated instruments – are practising the *Marseillaise*: a goat-skin thumping to stir the heart of a desert Napoleon; a wandering ululation to haunt his exile.

Eva watches it as through a window, or from the audience. This is not yet real and she doesn't know if she wants it to be real: she can't be sure what this reality means for the old man, or for her. 'They say I am to be executed on the stage', he says; 'during the circus performance. Is it known precisely when... and how?' A glance to Eva: 'One likes to prepare oneself, no?'

Eva nods.

A darker face looms in front of them, smiling eyes in the night. 'I know your fortune', she says; 'I tell you, yes I do.' She sways and settles in front of each of them: 'I tell you, yes I do. I tell you, yes I do.'

No, she doesn't: for rather different reasons, each of the three pulls back uncomfortably from their fortune.

At last Eva has recognized a face: this dark woman. From the lodging room, that first night in Marrakech; another orphan, adopted by the circus or occupying it. Who better than she to tell improbable futures?

Then a squeak of unrestrained happiness and a hug that threatens to crush Eva's ribs and rip away the weakened dress: Olga. Already in costume, a diamond glittering in the dusty evening; she has proved too compact, too implausibly tough, to be altered by Marrakech.

Perhaps this really is the circus. Perhaps she really will dance tonight.

'You're here!' Olga whispers with desperate joy. She stretches up and kisses Eva on the lips. 'Now. Now.'

Eva knows how she feels. You get used to the lost comrades – gone haughtily to better things; reported dead in their bed that morning; just vanished and you're all struggling to fill the unexpected gap in the programme – but you cling sentimentally to those who haven't yet betrayed you, you pray that you might be able to betray them first.

Eva still isn't getting her hopes up about this evening.

Jan the Pierrot will not perform; will never perform again. Someone saw him outside the palace, preaching against the circus for its multiple sins and sacrileges, scuffling with the palace guards. Shevzod is here, but he's mumbling about his heart. 'Honey pastries non-stop for a month,' whispers Olga, awed and cross; 'he's just melted in the heat.' Johanna is here, but it's always fifty-fifty whether she and her horses feel like performing. Salomon has apparently been seen a few times, but his appearances have been brief and unconfirmed and accompanied by thefts of money or meat. No one else has been going near his lions – not with the ramshackle state the cage was in – let alone wanted to try to do anything with them.

And none of it matters, because there is still no Maestro. Now we come to think of it, we can't remember seeing him since… Has he visited the circus since it arrived in Marrakech? Someone visited him; early on. We've heard stories about him; so obviously someone's seen him. But when did anyone from the circus last see him?

There was talk, of course: his excesses; his despairs. That sort of story's only going one way. Didn't someone tell us what it led to?

On the other side of the courtyard, a passageway has been allocated to the circus for its preparations, its entrances and exits. Straw covers the marble flagstones. Still the image of horses, tugging at their tethers and shivering their manes and whinnying discontentedly under the elegant vaulting – vaulting almost high enough for the giraffe – is fantastical. Perhaps tomorrow, when the image is just a dream again, a few strands of horse-hair will still be trapped unseen under an iron door-stud, where one of the animals was scratching itself.

On a table at one side of the passageway, in dignified solitude, is the Maestro's top hat.

The Maestro decides what we perform. The Maestro commands our going on and our coming off. The Maestro introduces and interprets us to the audience. Without the Maestro, we are merely a random collection of diverse and oddly-dressed individuals doing peculiar things, without coordination or meaning. Even a variety act needs a narrative.

So there's going to be a delay, then. And –

I really don't feel like squeezing into my seat yet. After what happened with… Not in the mood for unnecessary restriction. Catch my breath first. And –

Eva isn't ready. She still can't believe in this courtyard, the circus, her dance. And –

The old man is naturally happy not to reach the time and the place for as long as possible. Fate may be inevitable, but surely there's no need to rush. So: instinctive backward steps; perhaps three figures were seen at the edge of the courtyard, but no longer; the image of the circus is glimpsed and then it has vanished, or we have.

Once again Eva is conjuring new halls and corridors, age-worn stones and untouchable details of carving, shadows and drifting figures.

There is no guard now. No one to restrict or guide or narrate the journey. No structure or purpose to this digression.

'It's very kind of you… to escort us.'

'Not at all, Cher Monsieur Somerleigh: you escort me. Were it not for you, I would not be allowed to exist in these magnificent chambers. For you, the Sultan of Morocco is host and ally and customer, and you see him regularly. For the people of Morocco he is an idea, unseen like all ideas; he exists only in our dreams and our stories.' A vast marble hall, its extremities lost in shadows and echoes. 'Unless I am executed tonight in front of him. In that moment I shall see him seeing me, and he shall see me bleeding; and thus we shall know each other real at last.'

'I hear he has a crazy collection,' Eva says, 'of all kinds of different and ridiculous things.'

'Indeed, Ma-demoiselle,' – the title is pronounced with rich care, emphatic and possessive – 'I too have heard that.'

'You believe it?'

'Of course we believe it, Mademoiselle. Otherwise you would not have heard it.'

'But why, do you think? Buying all those unnecessary European trinkets?'

'Because, Mademoiselle, he believes that this way he makes the Europeans happy.' But what shall we choose to believe today? 'Whatever the reality of His Majesty's collection, and whatever the reason for it, I perceive it makes Europeans happy to believe the story. Eh, Monsieur Somerleigh?'

'Well... I have actually seen one or two things. My own eyes, you know?'

'You have seen? My dear boy, you are a visionary beyond even my own reputation. I think that Mademoiselle here, she dreams of seeing the emu, does she not?'

Eva has dreamed of seeing the emu, and now her dream leads them onward into the palace, into quarters never seen by foreign eyes, beyond the imagination of Moroccan hearts. Marble stairs soar upwards, footsteps far and faint, optimism and exaltation and faith; sandstone stairs drop downwards, footsteps clumsy and scratching, narrowing simple brutal confined animal reality. Surely the palace extends far beyond the walls of Marrakech, and always another vast chamber blurring at its margins into night, another corridor that stretches farther than first thought, another secret and another possibility. The Royal Palace of Marrakech is a fantasy of foreign exoticisms and of private intimacies, of shadows threatening and shadows intriguing, of voices seditious and voices seductive. A hall of sandstone, taller than ten men, guarded by pillars of sandstone. A mighty door of iron. A hall of marble, taller than twenty men, guarded by pillars of marble. A door of copper, smaller. A hall of purple granite, taller than men could climb or see, guarded by pillars of purple granite. A door of gold one must bend to pass through. An unexpected draught. Dreams. Doubts. Whispers.

The last door opens. The door opens, the veil is lifted, the dress falls and for once the dream does not end. A small chamber, old timber pillars, hints of fading murals on the walls, age-worn stones underfoot. And in its shadows there are hints of unimaginable treasures, jewels from the deepest places in the earth, fabrics that take more than one lifetime to weave, gold beyond counting. In the centre of the room is a brass cage, and in the cage is the emu. The emu is dead.

Whispers. Doubts. Dreams but now they seem sour and less certain. An unexpected draught, and a shiver – of exposure, of vulnerability. And so back through the palace, the chambers we dreamed now blurring and collapsing around us.

Eva thinks: the emu was alive once; now it has been stuffed.

Get a grip, Somerleigh. I was remembering some of the Sultan's other bits and bobs that I'd seen; after all, the emu is just another of the mechanical toys. Peculiar instinct, these artificial versions of real life.

'I think, Chère Mademoiselle, that perhaps the real emu is somewhere else.'

Reality wakes sudden: the courtyard of performance; the audience almost full; two armed guards and an official voice. 'Who is this? This is the man for execution, yes?'

A last desperation; a last defying of reality. 'No!'

'Your pardon, Monsieur Somerleigh; but we naturally assume... I think this is the old preacher, no?'

Eva says: 'He's the clown.'

No one understands this. It's a serious conversation: the eyes turn away from the woman to look for something more reliable. But each of the others can only repeat, in his different bewilderment: 'The clown?'

'He's the clown', Eva says again. 'The pierrot. Every circus has one. Our old one disappeared. This is his replacement.'

The woman insists on speaking. It would be more comfortable, more comprehensible, if she did not.

'That's right', I said; 'the clown. Everyone knows you've got to have a clown. As important as the giraffe.'

'Naturally, Monsieur Somerleigh, your guidance is the most trusted...'

'Gentlemen, I'm just your guest here, and I really don't want to seem to impose on such a distinctly Moroccan occasion. But I think His Majesty made me responsible for all matters pertaining to the performance precisely to be able to avoid these little misunderstandings. Simple fact is the circus must have a clown. And this chap's the only one available.'

'But surely this filthy old wretch...'

'Is the clown. Laughable get-up, isn't it? Look, we'd better get a wiggle on. Everyone's waiting out there.'

'My dear young people', Sa'id says in farewell, 'this was a narrative trick worthy of Ali himself! I thank you.'

'Oh yes!' I say, and 'Yes, people keep talking about him,' says Eva. 'I do so want to hear him once.'

'But my dear young people...' Sa'id is sincerely surprised. 'Surely you know that Ali does not exist? To invoke Ali is but to give weight to a tale – better than "a friend of a friend" or "I hear in the market". Ali is a... a figure of speech.'

It was only as I took my seat, I think, that the excitements of the evening really caught up with me. The nasty business in the park. The encounter with the extraordinary Belgian girl. Busting old Sa'id out of clink –

and of course I still didn't know if that was going to come off. Perhaps in Morocco the clown always gets executed; tricky business, humour. Anyway, as I sat I seemed to feel all the oomph go out of me.

Perhaps that's why it took me a bit longer to cotton on to who was sitting next to me. Shouldn't have been a surprise, of course, since I'd got him the ticket as my guest. But there he was, anyway. I was fair startled, and can you blame me?

An eye-opener for him too, of course. And he got another surprise later when old Sa'id wandered onto the stage to do his bit.

Brahim stared straight ahead, his voice a murmur. 'Truly the Lord of all fates is miraculous: I see two dead men returned to life.'

'It's what's possible, if we work together instead of trying to kill each other.'

'Oh, my dear friend; how ridiculous you are.' His tone, I confess, almost hurt me more than his setting his thugs on me. 'As a believer, I commend your humane instinct towards that dear old man. But I fear it will only make you weaker in your contests with France and Germany. And for us? Ten men will die of torture tonight, and a hundred from disease; tomorrow a thousand in the inevitable unrest, and the day after ten thousand, when France forces her rule on us.'

As ever, I was adrift in his melodramatic style. Unsettled by what his logic might mean, if he was typical, for British efforts here. Unsure, as ever, about where I might fit into any of it.

Brahim leaned closer to me, and the murmur was lower. 'Tell me instead the stories of those you did not save.' He patted my arm. 'I wonder: do you think you are the hero of this tale?'

Do you see it?

The circus performance is really happening at last.

Over the sandstone wall, outside the palace, there are faint screams. The final strand of fibre holding the cage shut has snapped, and the lions are wandering the alleys of Marrakech, hungry and curious and uncomprehending: frenzy and colours and flesh. There is so much anger and fear loose in the city now: the Europeans have decreed death; the old man's followers are avenging death; unleashed, nature is death. The last to cling to humane restraint is the first to die.

We do not hear the screams. We've been waiting so long for the performance.

A strange man says things that do not quite make sense, and we laugh. He looks ridiculously dishevelled; at one point he stumbles. We laugh. There is a zebra, and an acrobat. Did you get your fortune told? Maybe later. Horses, after all. A strongman is introduced, and he introduces his two young assistants, and they do relatively impressive feats of lifting; can you imagine what he might be capable of? Theatrical clattering panic from somewhere out of sight and a lion trots into the middle of the performance area, blood-muzzled. It roars, and we applaud, and it trots away into the city again. More novelties and peculiarities, energy and escape, and we are enjoying ourselves. When we tell our families about this extraordinary night, perhaps we will emphasize the giraffe.

The diplomatic telegrams may or may not emphasize the giraffe, but they will certainly give polite prominence to Herr Klug of the German Embassy. It is no longer clear whose the circus really is – let it politely be described as the Sultan's. It remains, of course, ludicrous to think that this rather fanciful episode will mean anything against the growth of French influence in the country – let Herr Klug be said to have tried to prove a point, at least. Nevertheless,

Herr Klug's been closely involved in making this remarkable night happen: he's paid for something, hasn't he? And if it will never be entirely clear whose the original idea for the circus was, his energy has certainly been instrumental; lot of get-up-and-go about Herr Klug. Perhaps it really will be the German century. And a closer regard will have noticed him paying diligent attention to some of the trivial administrative details for this evening. Herr Klug deserves his seat of relative honour, and his dry correct little speech.

What is there that may safely be recorded about Monsieur Prudhomme, of the French Embassy?

His success, perhaps – should professional jealousy allow. Back when it was merely a bitter mouthful, his sense of duty and calculation resolved him to swallow the circus. Now it has grown inside him, swelled in his heart and in his mind. The circus has become his energy, and he has acted for it and spoken for it. The circus will seem different things to different people – and to different diplomatic telegrams – but among them it will be a distinctly French affair. And it has cemented the relationship with His Majesty. By making himself one with the Sultan's desire, this French diplomat of the second rank has made his nation essential in Morocco.

The circus has become something personal, too. It has suckled at his diligence and eventually his passion. It has been roused and guided by his many admirable qualities. Once it was 'Klug's wretched circus', spat out and dismissed as he walked past his wife and into his study at the end of the day. It has become 'My little circus', murmured affectionately as he sits beside her on the *chaise longue* – and Madame has recalled the young diplomat she married, his energies and eagernesses and little touches of elegance.

Here he is, then; and so here is the circus. A smash of cymbals to get our attention, a thumping of drums, and His

Majesty the Sultan walks out into the courtyard, white robes shining like moonlight. Not a confident or dominating presence, but he's done this sort of thing before and he knows what he's supposed to do. Beside him and a courteous half-step behind is Hector Prudhomme; then a retinue of guards, because royalty is theatre.

For that moment, Prudhomme rules the universe. He appears as he should: the traditional diplomatic uniform immaculate, the head high, oiled, shining. Everything he has worked for is happening; the mirage is real around him. Everyone knows this is he and his; across the desert, his Ambassador in Tangiers knows; far imagined Paris shall know. Younger officials there shall admire him; older officials shall approve him.

Prudhomme can see, first of all, the Sultan immediately in front of him. He could reach out and touch the royal shoulder and adjust its direction. He could whisper in the royal ear. France has the ruler of Morocco exactly where she wants him. Then he can see the audience: that blur of pink faces – oh, and brown – only reflects his luminousness. No other performer tonight shall enjoy greater regard, greater fulfilment. In his head he has prepared the description of this moment for the telegram a hundred times. He shall recount it – perhaps a cigarette, perhaps even his collar undone – on the *chaise longue* to Madame.

His Majesty's traditional robes restrict his legs. But Hector Prudhomme, envoy of the French Republic to the Royal Court of Morocco, glides across the performance space. As they approach the central block of seats, reserved for the Court and its officials only, one chair in the middle of the front row uniquely larger, golden and empty, Prudhomme offers an empty elegant gesture to show the Sultan to his place of honour, pretends to murmur something to him.

And then:

The shock; the slap in the face; the spit in the eye; the turd in the new municipal water-pipe; the gunboat in the bay. Prudhomme's glory sours and shrivels and drops from the tree into the gutter.

A figure stands and steps forward, from the chair next to His Majesty's, to crush the slimy former glory under its boot: Klug.

How is Klug not among the diplomats in the block of seats to the right of the Court? How is he not one of the crowd there, waiting for Prudhomme to take the only unoccupied chair in the diplomatic block, in the middle of its front row, reserved for the representative of France? Prudhomme will finally understand much later tonight when – Madame long gone to bed alone, her eager curiosity about the evening knocked aside – he is peering through the relevant document for the third or fourth time. The seating arrangements make no reference to the German, nor any other foreign diplomat, in the area reserved for the Sultan and his officials. But there is naturally a prominent place beside His Majesty for the Court Treasurer Extraordinary, Comptroller of Supply for Alien Entertainments in the State Administration. Berlin has bought herself a little victory after all.

Prudhomme finds himself – betrayed, humiliated, small – adrift in the performance area, instinctively avoiding discourtesy or challenge but desperate to find a place and a role, now that His Majesty has sat and Klug has begun the few words of introduction that had been France's concession to him. A sudden inspiration, and Prudhomme performs it vividly, eyes bright and finger raised: he shall go to check that all is ready for His Majesty's performance.

(There ensues an uncomfortable contest of wills, because both Klug and Prudhomme know that the man who sits last is the most prominent – automatically the one who commands whatever happens next. Prudhomme continues to lurk in the shadows of the performers' area off-stage, wondering why the straw under his boot feels soggy. Klug continues to speak, regretting that the German traditions do not lend themselves to such elaborations. The effect for everybody else in the courtyard is frankly tedious; history does not record who won.)

Do you see it yet? The clown, the horses, the relatively strong-boys, the acrobat? Do you see a giraffe?

Of course not. You can't see it.

The news has filtered through now. We know it. We hear it. We guess it. The Maestro is never coming. The Maestro is no more. He cannot be found. He has been found. He has been seen through a keyhole. He has been smelt. Somewhere in Marrakech, in the warren of possibilities, he is slumped dead. The pitiful – or at least doubtful – origins, that first awe at a Punch & Judy show, the early street hustles, the gathering of freaks and lost souls, the creation of a life beyond imagination: it has led to this fairy-tale decay, covered in rich fabrics and pastry crumbs and dust. Every step and every performance was conjured by the power of his words; this one more night he could not cajole into being. Famous last words will become available.

On the table, in the performers' area to the side of the expectant and increasingly restless courtyard: an empty top hat.

Hector Prudhomme gazes at the top hat. He glares at the figures around him in the gloom, stunned and silent and immobile, fading into an unlikely gathering of oddly-dressed regular people. To the empty hat again.

With the exercise of all his skills he has conjured a circus; it is dead on this table. It seems to crumple and pale, like the body somewhere out in the city. If he lifts it, he knows there will be nothing surprising underneath. Perhaps his hand will swipe through empty air; perhaps this whole wretched city will flicker and vanish.

The top hat. Empty.

It is pathetic. It is ridiculous. It is elegance soiled. It is class decayed. It is culture degraded. It is pretension exploded. It is a foreign totem, now foolish. It is everything artificial about performance. It is everything absurd about diplomacy. It is trapped. It is dead. It is nothing.

Somewhere in the night, little Abdelilah's story has reached its climax. Something has ripped through the white cloak, through the starched European shirt-front he has been experimenting with, and it has opened his chest.

Prudhomme gazes at the top hat. Shouts somewhere: his confusion, his betrayal, his anger. Screams somewhere: all the malicious sneering jealous voices in his head, and at last he can bear them no longer and he screams back. Running feet, alarm, a warning: a lion is attacking someone, just round the corner. The voices rise around him; the voices fill him. All is chaos now. He can still hear the German mumbling – he has not given these weeks of his life and all his diplomatic skill just to invite the Sultan to a German speech – or perhaps it is merely the echo of Klug's speech – an echo that hangs under the elegant palace arches and Prudhomme will hear in the small hours of all his nights. It is shameful, it is unfair, it is unendurable.

Do you see it at last? The circus comes to life!

At the very climax of our anticipation – murmuring rising to excitement and even to anger – look at the Sultan there, is he even awake? – a growing sense of some great energy outside the walls, boiling this courtyard like a cauldron – the yelling of a thousand voices – surely this builds to something; it must build to something – we know it, because we know how stories work – only the Sultan sits silent and steady, sure of the power of this magic – just when our hearts will burst with the despair of a mirage – just when there can be no greater tumult, comes a greater tumult: screams, and the roar of a lion –

roars – echoing around us, surrounding us – can there be more lions? what a stupendous effect! –

And a figure leaps into the arena!

How we cheer! We hadn't realized there was so much energy within us, needing release. And this wild figure speaks for us – he lives our energy – he is something stifled exploding out, a cruel restraint finally broken. He is a thin dark man who does not know how to move and cannot stop himself, a whirling spider of a man. Let us be free! It is surely the true euphoria of being in this country that we may be ourselves unchecked. We have fiddled too long with these postures of encouragement and sponsorship; let us order as we need and take what we want. A circus can happen, however many old men we have to kill! Part of the market quarter is ablaze now, and the flames flash in his face. The blood of wild deaths is smeared across his pale skin. It is Hector Prudhomme at last, top-hatted and triumphant.

☖

What else do you see?

Somewhere – somewhere nearby, surely; surely you should be able to see – there is Eva.

Eva has shrugged off whatever was left of the costume in which we last saw her. It has slipped down, from those shoulders we have only imagined. What shall we say, in our cafés, of what she wears now? A first flourishing, of those arms we have heard of but never felt. A flexing of the thighs we have but wondered at. The dancer's breaths: deliberate, focused, summoning her potential, defining her difference from us. Eva is suppleness, and then poise. The last moment of stillness – the world breathless, the world unborn – in this nothing, anything is possible – the ecstasy of anticipating the ecstasy – and –

Eva is free. Dance is narrative, and now at last we understand that she is drawing on all of this: recalling it, reviving it, realizing everything as if for the first time. A journey from ocean through wilderness and civilization to madness. The untaught wonder of a boy in the desert. The possibility of imagined cities and the reality of cages. The discipline of palace guard and soup ration. The brazenness of a savaged body. The texture of lemon rind and sandstone wall and adolescent skin. The rhythm of drums and devotions. The glide of silk. The honesty of women alone. A liberty that only she can know.

The places and people that surround her as she dances exist only because she conjures them, for as long as she conjures them. All of this world, its fibres and its sap, is being absorbed up through her legs as they rest a moment on the sand; all of it flows and flowers from her outstretched arms. She imagines these walls, these unfamiliar musical instruments, these furtive desert breezes – and she exists in them. A palace, a prison, a prince; fear and freedom. She is feeding on this atmosphere: it fills her; it lifts her; it turns her, turning slowly at first, bashful, tempted and tempting, then faster – freer – abandoned to the dance. Her exquisite control of her limbs, their strength and their swoop, now turns and floods back into her. Her arms begin to lift away as she whirls, her feet need the support of the sand less and less, she is looser, lighter, she feels the goat-skin drums thumping in her chest and the breeze blowing through her, Africa is cinnamon and stars and at last she is away and gone, up from the page and flying quite out of narrative.

You do not see this. You are not here; you are not her. Nor am I.

◉

Peters finished his coffee. He first licked his lips with discreet precision, and then dabbed them firmly with a napkin. He set off through morning Mogador, his eyes now accustomed to overlook its squalor and to dwell a discreet moment on its little joys. A coincidence of colour between gown and sky, a gust of cinnamon from a doorway, the diligence of an old man bent to some fanciful bit of carving.

Not too accustomed: a dog had deposited some squalor in the middle of the alley, and he stopped, circumnavigated it, and proceeded on his way.

The wind was off the sea, and from the west it brought freshness.

In the office, he unlocked the drawer and removed Somerleigh's report, and placed it in the middle of his desk; not touching anything. He had read it the previous afternoon but, as was his habit, delayed composing his regular onward telegram until a new day. Let things digest.

'Let things digest', he called after Hamid, who was off as bidden to crank up the telegraph machine; 'that's the ticket.'

HMAMBASSADOR TANGIER FROM PETERS MOGADOR CALM IN THE SOUTH STOP CONSISTENT YOUR INSTRUCTIONS BRITISH INTERMEDIATION ENSURES USUAL FRANCOGERMAN MANOEUVRES MARRAKECH SETTLED WITHIN STRUCTURES OF DIPLOMATIC CONCERT AND WITHOUT DISTURBANCE TO FRENCH LOCAL PREDOMINANCE AND DIGNITY STOP COASTAL STORMS LESS SEVERE THAN FEARED THUS TEA RESUMED FORMER PRICE IN MARKET STOP

☾

Author's Note:

This tale was conjured during one Essaouira winter (Eva and her generation knew the town as Mogador), to keep the author's brain warm.

It does not claim any insight on what it was or is like to be Moroccan. And yet Chinua Achebe was right, and

Africa can never be merely backdrop. The tale is driven by some beliefs about European colonialism in the early 20th century, and by some sense of the reality of European colonialism in the early 21st, and of what it is like to be a semi-conscious agent of it. It is coloured by the extraordinary hospitality of Morocco, by the vividness of life there. It is a tale shaped, like so many, by the story-telling tradition of the vast Jamaa el-Fna square in Marrakech.

The Conference of the European Great Powers in Algeciras, on the southern tip of Spain looking across to Morocco, took place between January and April 1906. Germany had provoked the conference, notionally in support of greater Moroccan independence from the existing and agreed French influence, in order to claim a more prominent position in European affairs. But German diplomatic incompetence, and lack of co-ordination between the impetuous Kaiser and his officials, led them to overplay their hand and be out-manoeuvred. The French were unhelpfully stubborn, and the default position of the British – uneasy at Germany's mischief – was to support France. The Moroccan delegation entered the conference expecting a reinforcement of their independence; three months later they emerged having signed away management of their national security and finances to France. (Contemporary Moroccan perspectives on the conference are now hard to find: one analysis by a merchant is a model of moderation and good sense and restrained frustration, and now tragic in how totally that point of view was ignored.) In the traditional narrative, the 'Moroccan Crisis' of 1905 and the 1906 Conference were significant steps along the path towards the First World War less than a decade later: the French and British perceived further proof that Germany was unreliable and belligerent; Germany perceived further proof that the traditional diplomatic arrangements were intended to isolate and disadvantage her.

Whether or not there were lions loose in the alleys of Marrakech in the spring of 1906, there was certainly a serial killer. Hadj Mohammed Mesfewi is reckoned to have drugged and decapitated dozens of young women of the city before the family of one of his victims identified him. He was sentenced to crucifixion, but the international diplomats protested that this was sacrilegious; instead he was walled up alive – at the edge of the Jamaa el-Fna.

The arrival of a circus on the Moroccan coast, and the commissioning of a performance for the Sultan, is told by British writer Walter Harris. A long-time resident of Morocco, Harris was a rich source for its current affairs and culture – his account so colourful and self-serving as to be highly suspect, along with so much of the European representation of the country.

Sultan Abd-al-Aziz's collection of curiosities is legendary – and perhaps a little mythical, mediated as it is through the amused and patronising accounts of European visitors. Apparently a genuinely pleasant chap who enjoyed games of bicycle polo with the foreign diplomats, he spent his reign trying to balance necessary conformity to European pressure with efforts to protect Morocco's sovereignty. As such, his support for the Algeciras conference backfired disastrously, and his credibility with his people never recovered. He was overthrown in 1908 by his brother, the erstwhile Caliph of Marrakech – himself renowned as a collector of mechanical toys. Having thus come to power by exploiting anti-European sentiment, Sultan Abd-al-Hafid found himself increasingly powerless to resist it. Individual attacks on Europeans were met with indiscriminate French bombardment and localized occupation. In the face of popular unrest, in 1912 the Sultan was forced to sign away his country's independence entirely and then to abdicate. Morocco would remain a French protectorate until 1956.

The Glaoui hang over the events described in this book, just as they did over the lives of three generations of Moroccans. The family emerged from relative obscurity among the tribes of the Atlas and, a few mis-steps and misfortunes aside, made themselves useful and then indispensable to successive Moroccan rulers – including the French, who during the First World War were obliged effectively to sub-contract rule of all southern Morocco to them. Their intimate knowledge of everything that went on in Marrakech and beyond was proverbial. Before his final miscalculation, amid the chaos of nationalism and the collapse of the protectorate, Thami El-Glaoui enjoyed decades of untouchable influence and spectacular wealth: a man who displayed his defeated rivals' heads outside his gate and who represented his country at the coronation of Queen Elizabeth II; a man who emerged from endless tribal conspiracies and unspeakable desert brutalities, and frequently hosted Winston Churchill on his private golf course. Cynical, cruel and endlessly mischievous the family may have been, but any account must respectfully acknowledge the deftness and endurance. After all, the lord of Glaoui may well be reading it.

Ⓤ

Ali holds his audience.

He has carried them on a long journey, through the desert.

His mouth is so dry, his tongue a sandy scrap of flesh baked in the sun; but he saved a few drops of sap to give it life at the last. He does not have to raise his voice at all now, so absorbed are the faces around him, frozen like characters waiting to be commanded, eyes wide and not daring to blink lest the mirage in front of them vanish. The joints of his crossed legs are screaming, but he imagines himself free of them; he will hobble away into the gloom, like the old man he became and will become. Still the audience gape. Ali has seduced them with fantasies, and soothed them with the certainty that every word is true. The storyteller's audience are his to inflame and his to sedate; his to conjure, his to command; his to wake, in the very moment that –

He knows not to try to hold them for a moment too long.

By the tale we tell ourselves who we are. By the tale we tell ourselves why we are. By the tale we pick the fragments of life nearest us and arrange them, just so, and assert that thus there is meaning. By the tale we place two facts in close adjacency, or two people, and assert that there may thus be a relationship between them.

By the tale, we stride out into a landscape that is already well-populated, and we plant a flag and stand four-square and declare: this is mine and this is I; recognize me in this, or defy me.

Life is a desert, and when the darkness falls we huddle closer around the fire, and we pretend – for just one more night – that we understand each other, that we are something together, that together we may defy the wild beasts that scavenge nearer. By the tale we keep ourselves warm.

Ali lets the last word drift off his lips and float away into the night over the square, with the charcoal smoke and the breeze. He lets his hands fall into his lap, lowers his eyes, and waits.

POSSIBLE REFLECTIONS FOR BOOK GROUPS

1. What does the Sultan's emu represent?

2. Who is the hero of this tale?

3. Do women make good colonialists?

4. Is there a link between men's attitude to women, colonialism and story-telling?

5. What's the significance of the different characters' versions of tales told by Ali the story-teller?

6. Like the diverse café interpretations of the new preacher, different characters seem to have different impressions of the emu and of the Sultan's collection. What do they tell us – and what's yours?

7. When Eva is journeying from Mogador towards Marrakech through the desert, she passes through a town. To what extent does this town exist?

8. Nigerian novelist Chinua Achebe suggested that for western writers, 'Africa is not like anywhere else they know... there are no real people in the Dark Continent, only forces operating', and that 'no man can understand another whose language he does not speak'. What does this mean for our writing and our reading?

Shakespeare & Sherlock

'So we rode again into Scotland, Sherlock Holmes and I; only this time we came at the head of an army.'

The greatest detective and the most notorious crimes in all literature: what happens when Sherlock Holmes and Dr John Watson find themselves players in the extraordinary dramas previously told by William Shakespeare? How will they survive, and what new truths will they uncover, amid the wild mysticism of Macbeth's Scotland or the fevered conspiracies of Helsingør?

'Was this an end to the blood and to the chaos?'
Holmes gazed at me. 'An end?' he said, and his voice was deathly. 'My dear Watson: it has not yet begun.'

The Gentleman Adventurer

A new hero. A new series of historical entertainments.

In 1968, *Le Figaro* reported the discovery of a dossier of papers in a concealed compartment in a trunk, 'the property of a lady'; they proved to be the memoirs of the 'renowned traveller, adventurer and libertine' Harry Delamere, in the years before the First World War. Made public at last after 50 years, his exploits are now being published in a series of thrillers.

Death and the Dreadnought
Poison in Paris
Bolsheviks at the Ballet

'Ye Gods', said Winston Churchill, 'Harry Delamere... It must be worse than we feared.'

The Comptrollerate-General

Immersive historical novels exploring what was really going on in the shadows during the periods of greatest crisis in British history, and showing how one remarkable organization has survived centuries of upheaval to maintain stability - for better or for worse. The discovery of a trove of documents under Whitehall, some now published for the first time, has transformed our understanding of the moments when the world turned, and cast new light on the reputation of the Comptrollerate-General for Scrutiny and Survey.

Traitor's Field (1648-51)
Treason's Spring (1792)
Treason's Tide (1805)
The Spider of Sarajevo (1914)

'A rare clever treat of a novel.' – *The Times*

'Beautifully written, wonderfully clever, this is a triumph.' – *Daily Telegraph*

'A learned, beautifully-written, elegant thriller.' – *The Times*

'Bernard Cornwell meets Ken Follett in a Southwark pub and someone gets coshed. That is to say, great, intelligent fun.' – *Time Out*

Elbow Publishing is a small independent group of creative people coming together to produce lovely books. Visit us online to explore the rest of our catalogue.

R. J. Wilton was advisor to the Prime Minister of Kosovo in the years leading up to the country's independence and head of an international human rights mission in Albania. He co-founded The Ideas Partnership, a charity working to support the education and empowerment of marginalized communities in the Balkans. A prize-winning historical novelist, he also writes on culture, history and international intervention in the region, and translates Albanian literature into English.